James Burks

Bird & Squirrel

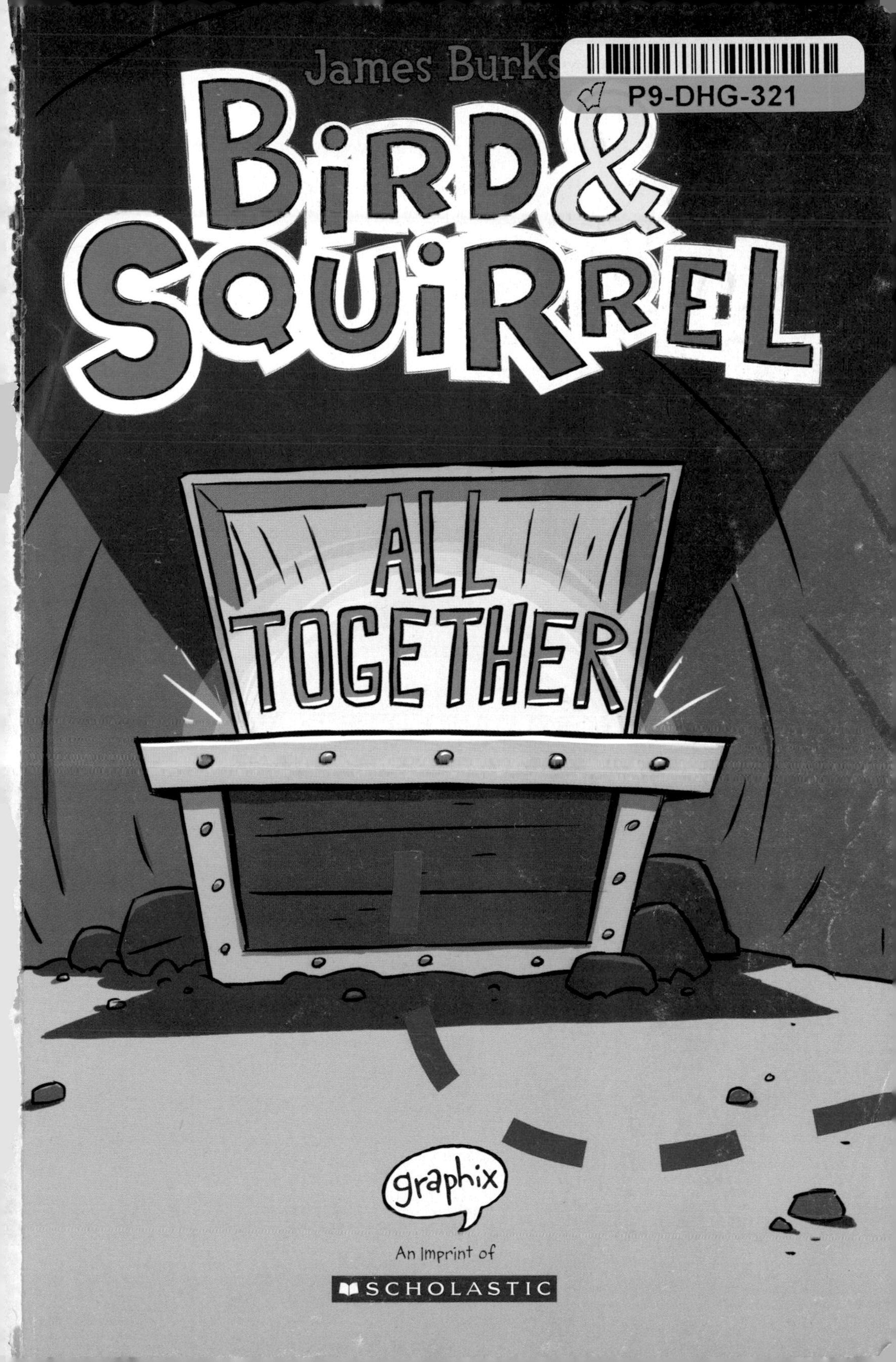

ALL TOGETHER

graphix

An Imprint of

SCHOLASTIC

For Ken Min - A true friend
and amazing person, thank you!

Library of Congress Control Number: 2021948717

ISBN 978-1-338-25236-1 (hardcover)
ISBN 978-1-338-25233-0 (paperback)

10 9 8 7 6 5 4 3 2 1 22 23 24 25 26

Printed in China 62

First edition, October 2022
Edited by Adam Rau and Jonah Newman
Book design by Steve Ponzo
Creative Director: Phil Falco
Publisher: David Saylor

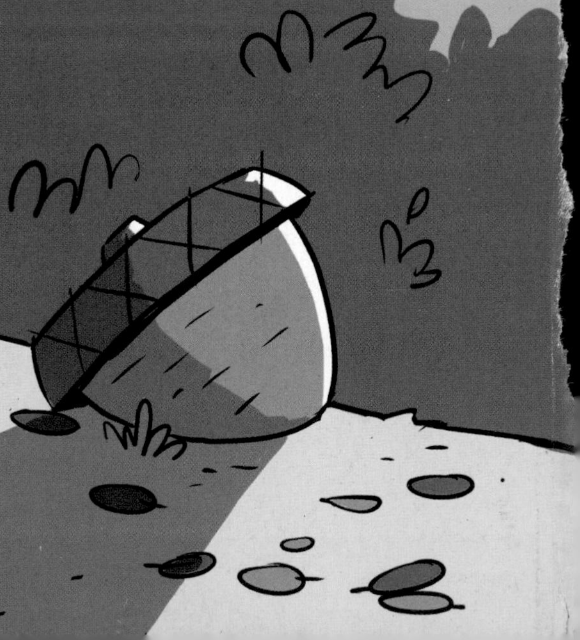

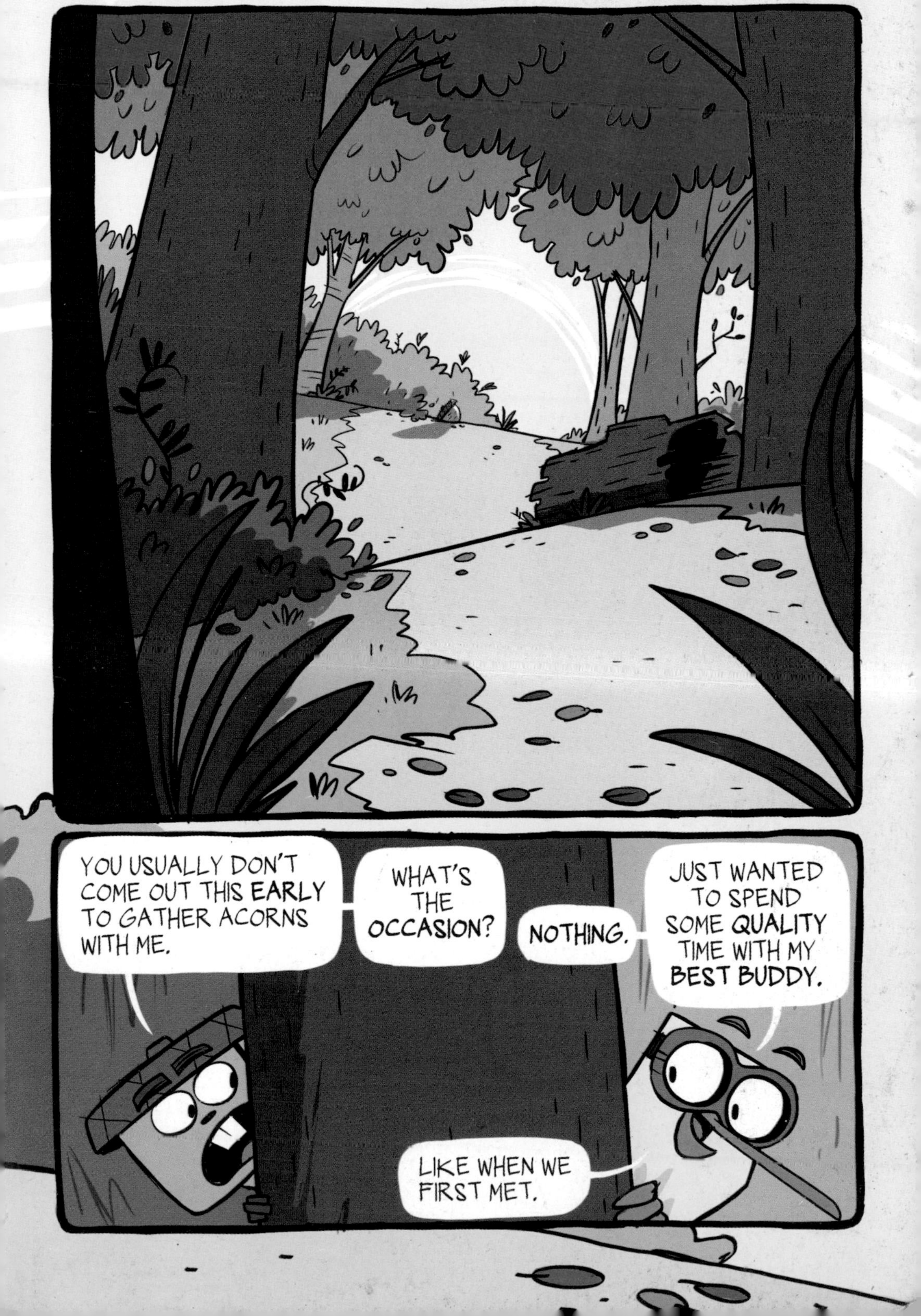
YOU USUALLY DON'T COME OUT THIS EARLY TO GATHER ACORNS WITH ME.
WHAT'S THE OCCASION?
NOTHING.
JUST WANTED TO SPEND SOME QUALITY TIME WITH MY BEST BUDDY.
LIKE WHEN WE FIRST MET.

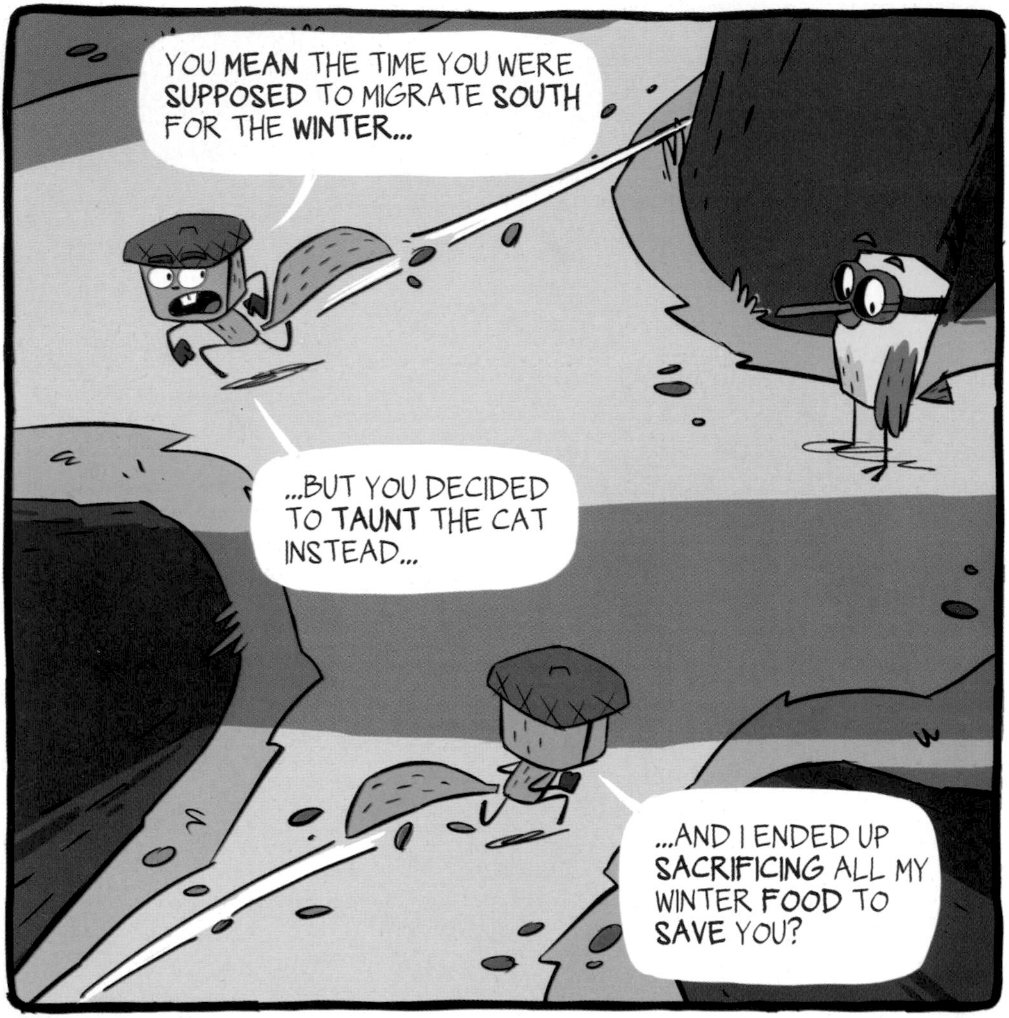
YOU MEAN THE TIME YOU WERE SUPPOSED TO MIGRATE SOUTH FOR THE WINTER...
...BUT YOU DECIDED TO TAUNT THE CAT INSTEAD...
...AND I ENDED UP SACRIFICING ALL MY WINTER FOOD TO SAVE YOU?

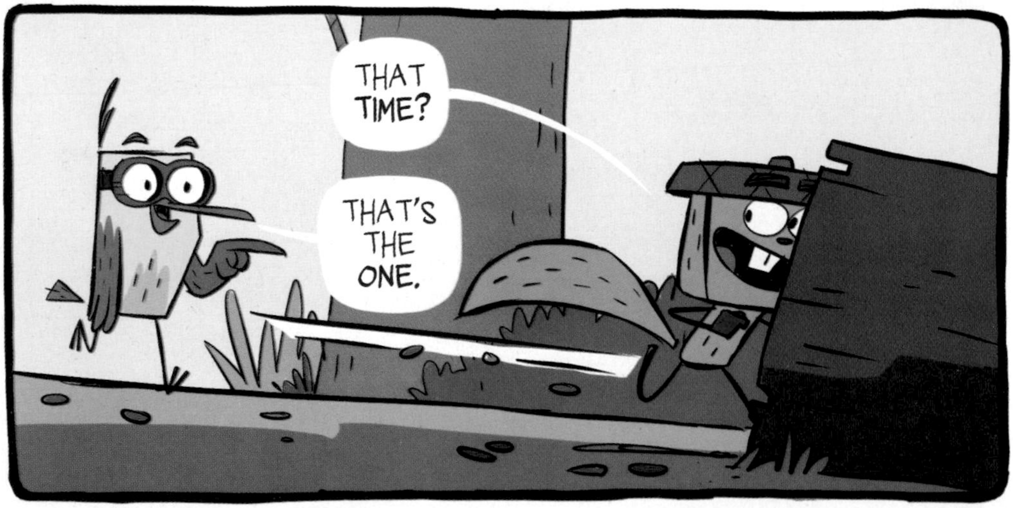
THAT TIME?
THAT'S THE ONE.

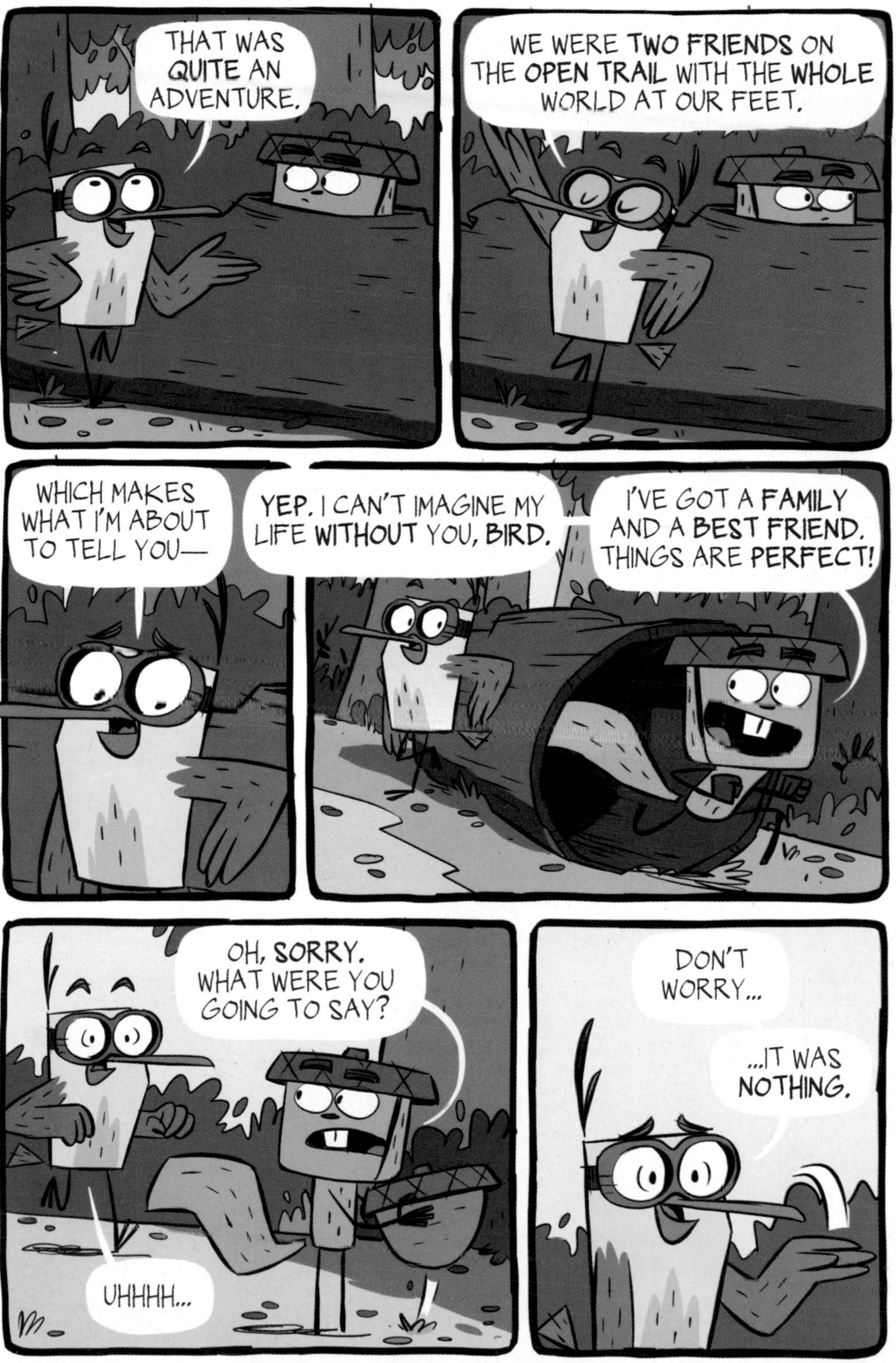

THAT WAS QUITE AN ADVENTURE.
WE WERE TWO FRIENDS ON THE OPEN TRAIL WITH THE WHOLE WORLD AT OUR FEET.
WHICH MAKES WHAT I'M ABOUT TO TELL YOU—
YEP. I CAN'T IMAGINE MY LIFE WITHOUT YOU, BIRD.
I'VE GOT A FAMILY AND A BEST FRIEND. THINGS ARE PERFECT!
OH, SORRY. WHAT WERE YOU GOING TO SAY?
UHHHH...
DON'T WORRY...
...IT WAS NOTHING.

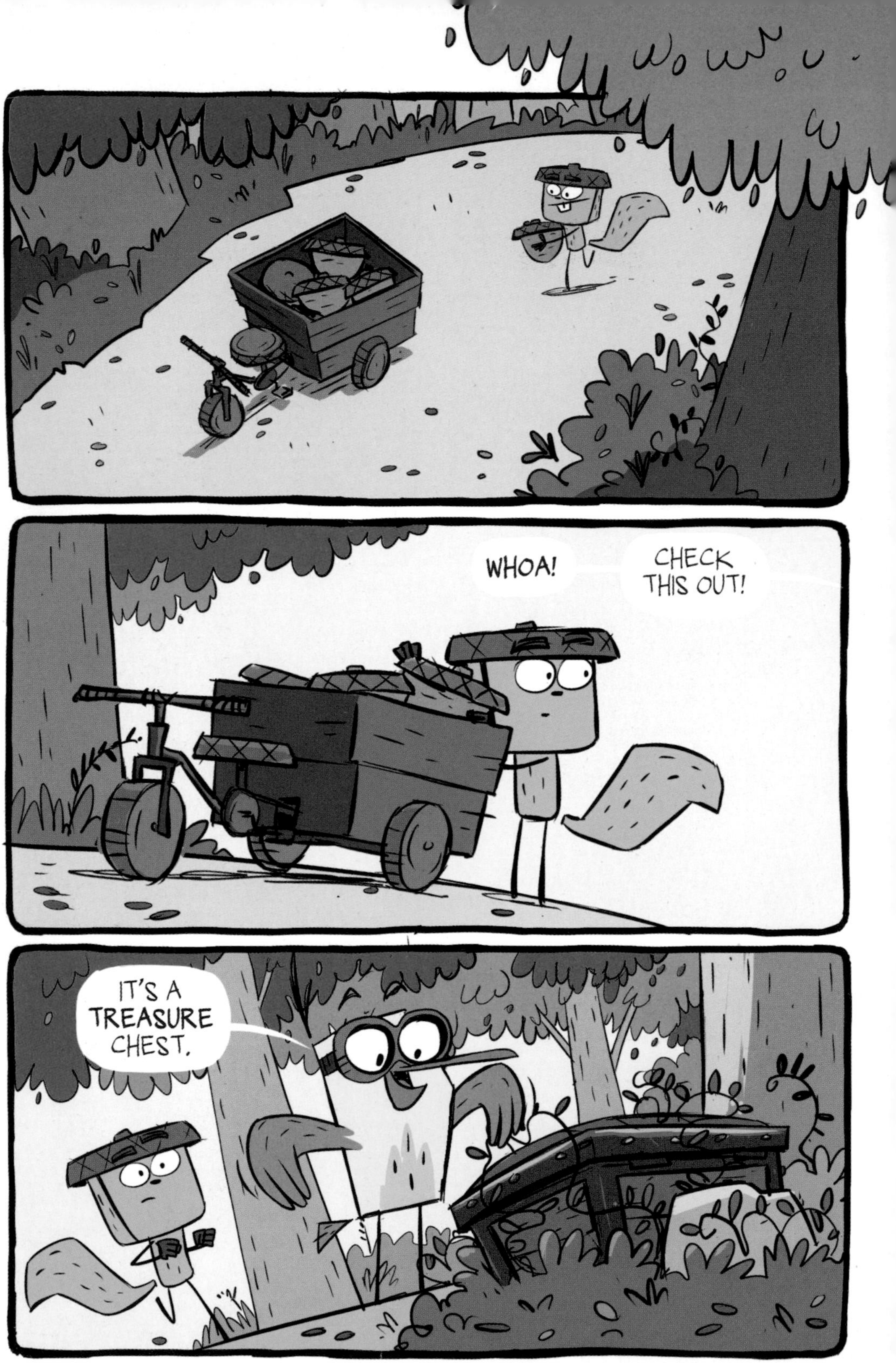
WHOA!
CHECK THIS OUT!
IT'S A TREASURE CHEST.

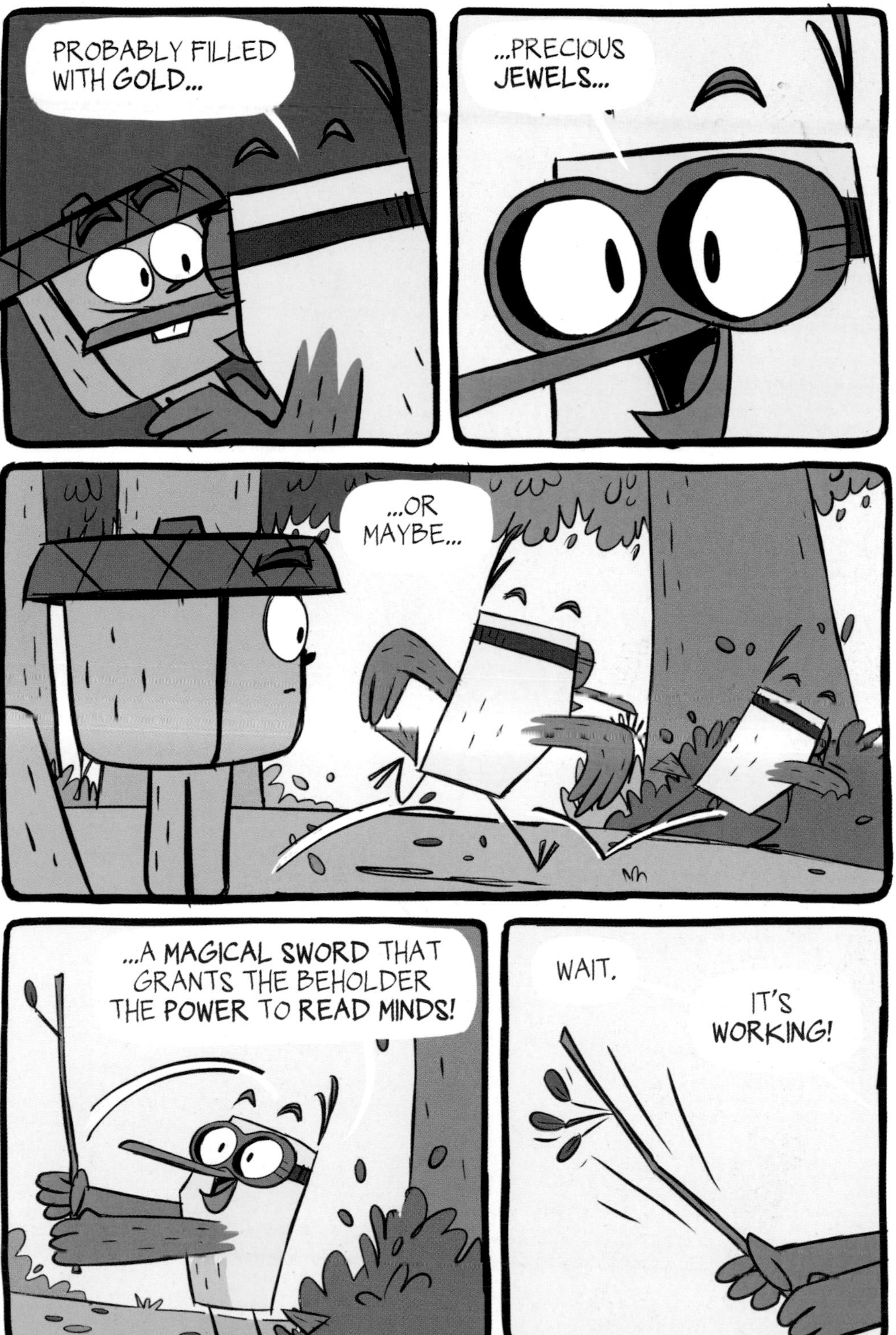
PROBABLY FILLED WITH GOLD...
...PRECIOUS JEWELS...
...OR MAYBE...
...A MAGICAL SWORD THAT GRANTS THE BEHOLDER THE POWER TO READ MINDS!
WAIT.
IT'S WORKING!

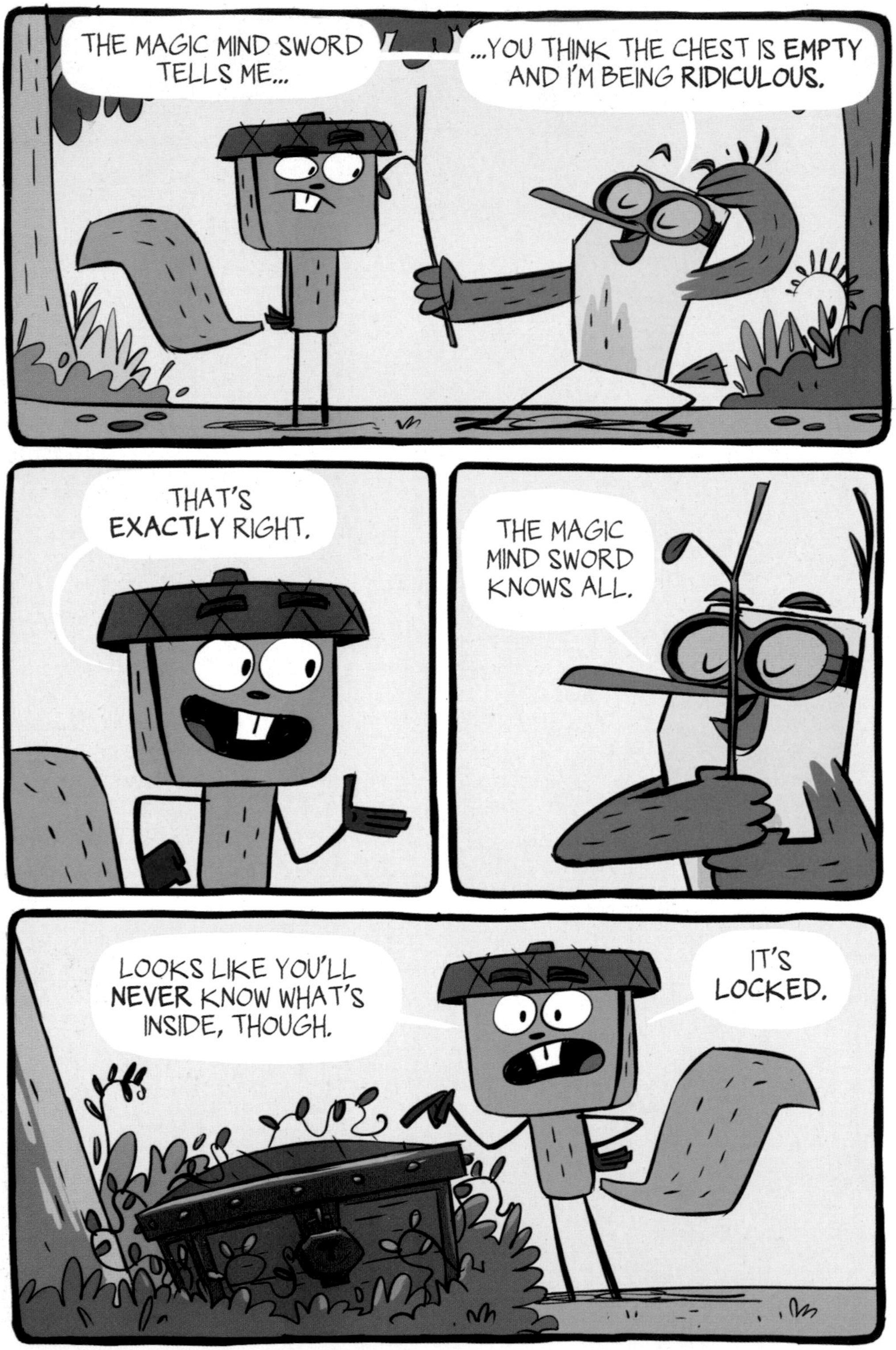
THE MAGIC MIND SWORD TELLS ME...
...YOU THINK THE CHEST IS EMPTY AND I'M BEING RIDICULOUS.
THAT'S EXACTLY RIGHT.
THE MAGIC MIND SWORD KNOWS ALL.
LOOKS LIKE YOU'LL NEVER KNOW WHAT'S INSIDE, THOUGH.
IT'S LOCKED.

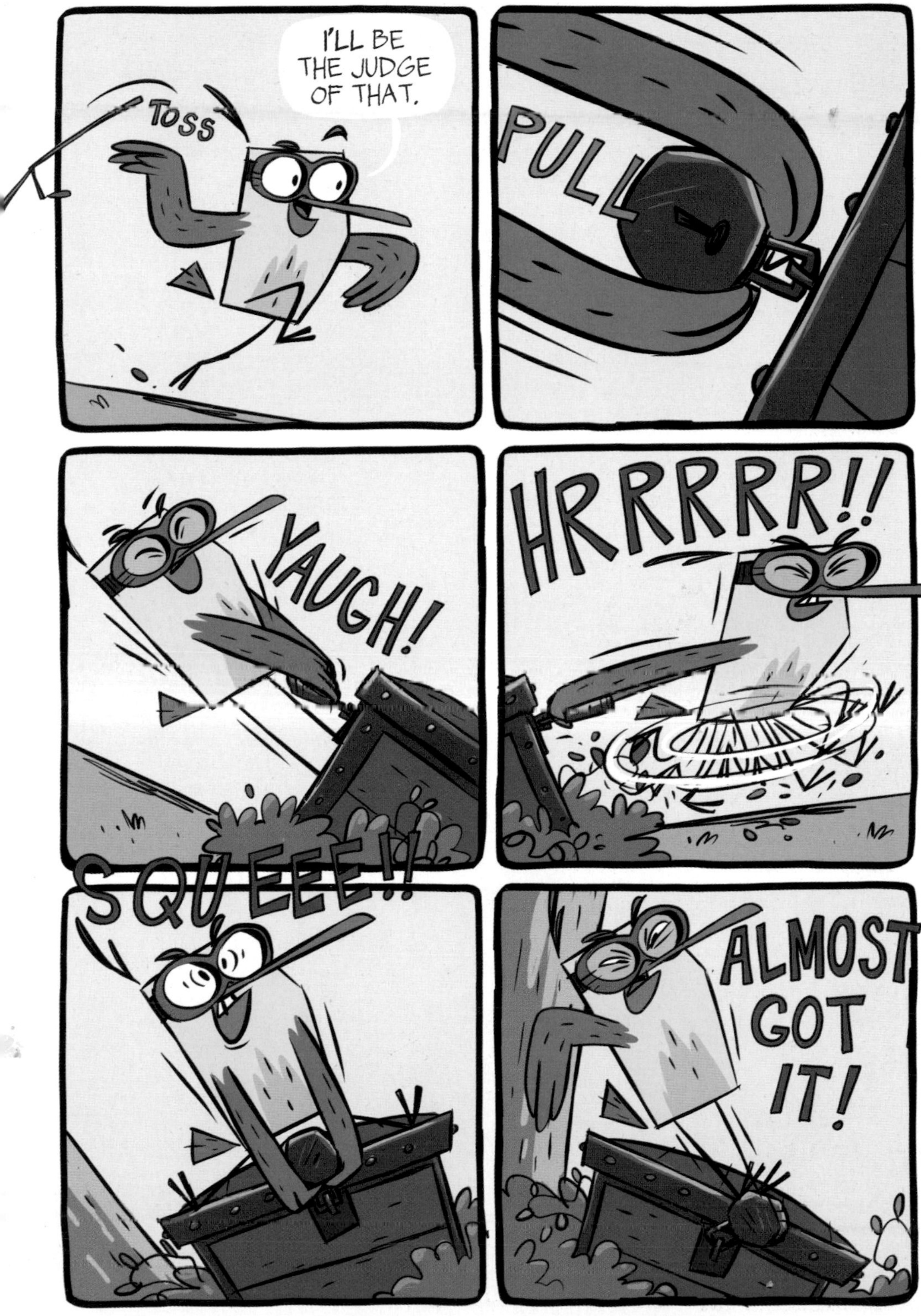
TOSS
I'LL BE THE JUDGE OF THAT.
PULL
YAUGH!
HRRRRR!!
SQUEEE!!
ALMOST GOT IT!

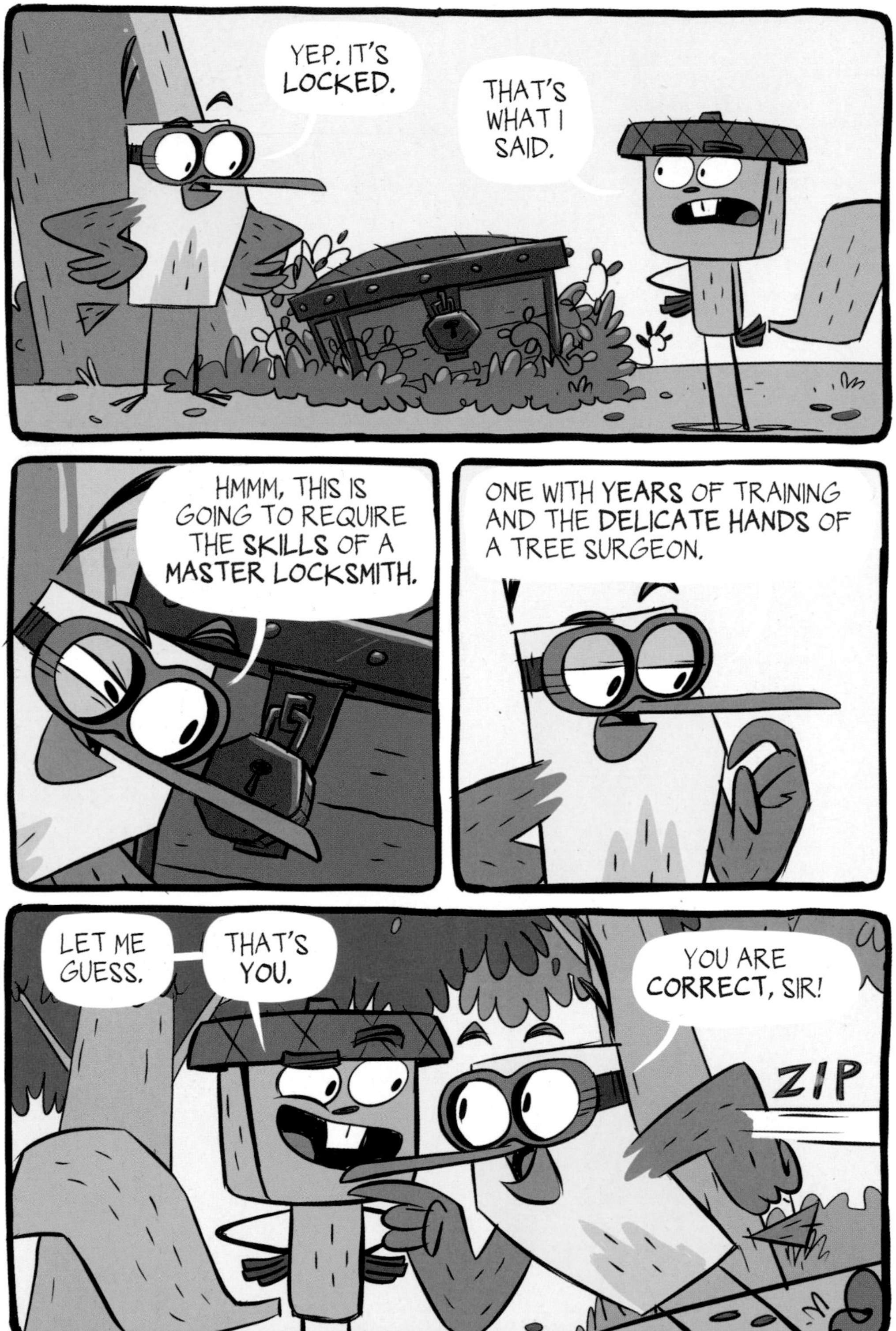
YEP. IT'S LOCKED.
THAT'S WHAT I SAID.
HMMM, THIS IS GOING TO REQUIRE THE SKILLS OF A MASTER LOCKSMITH.
ONE WITH YEARS OF TRAINING AND THE DELICATE HANDS OF A TREE SURGEON.
LET ME GUESS.
THAT'S YOU.
YOU ARE CORRECT, SIR!
ZIP

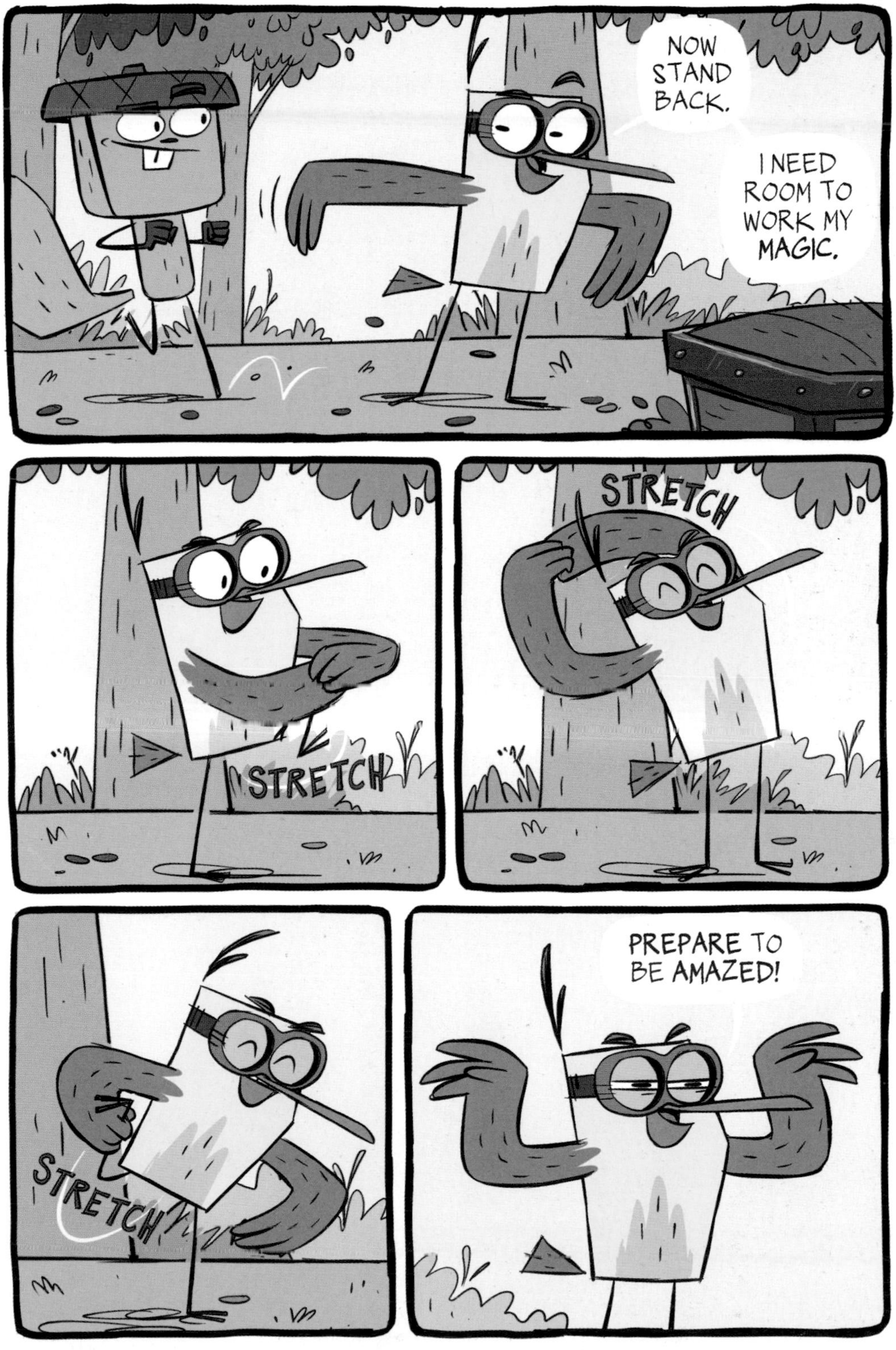
NOW STAND BACK.
I NEED ROOM TO WORK MY MAGIC.
STRETCH
STRETCH
STRETCH
PREPARE TO BE AMAZED!

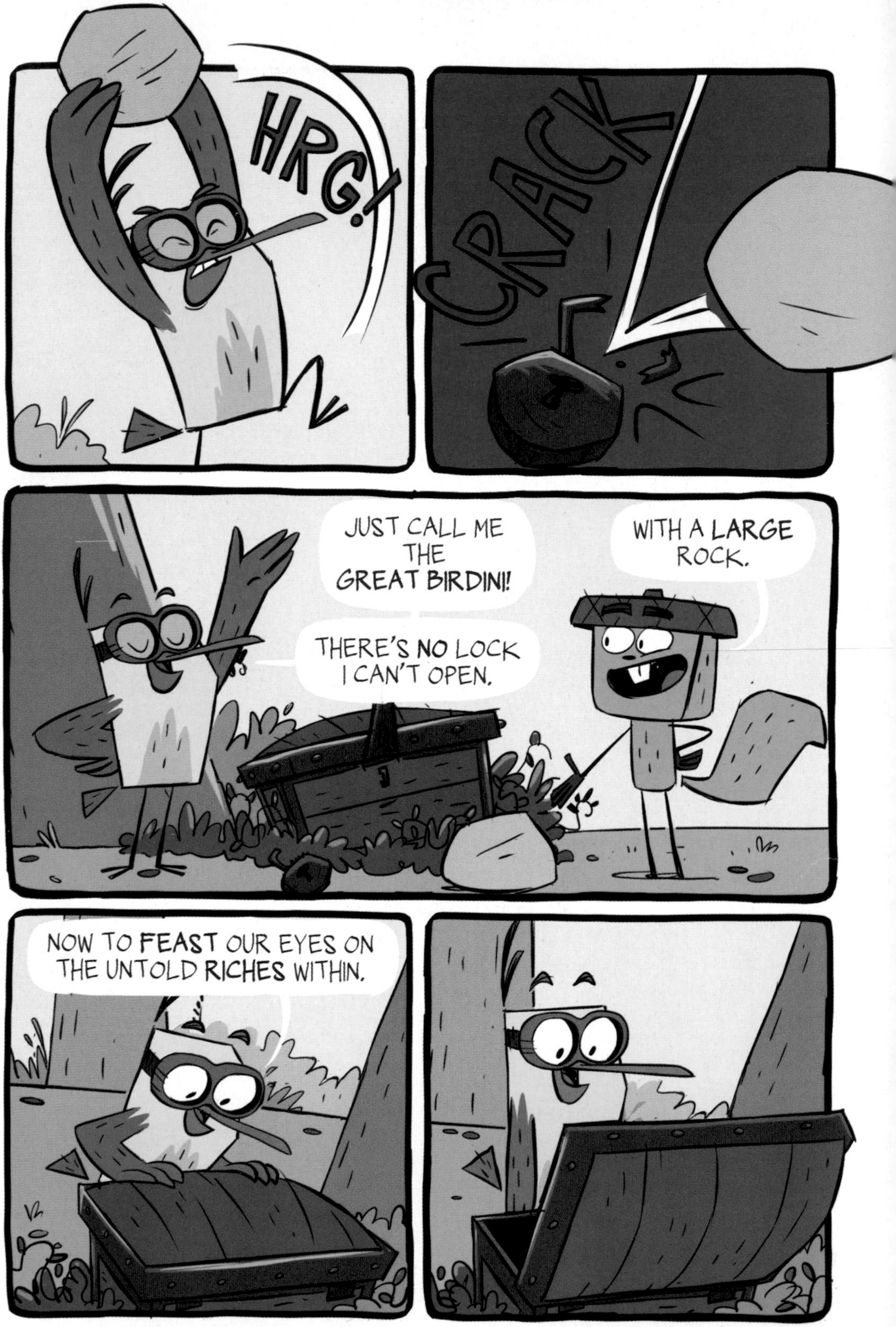
HRG!
CRACK
JUST CALL ME THE GREAT BIRDINI!
THERE'S NO LOCK I CAN'T OPEN.
WITH A LARGE ROCK.
NOW TO FEAST OUR EYES ON THE UNTOLD RICHES WITHIN.

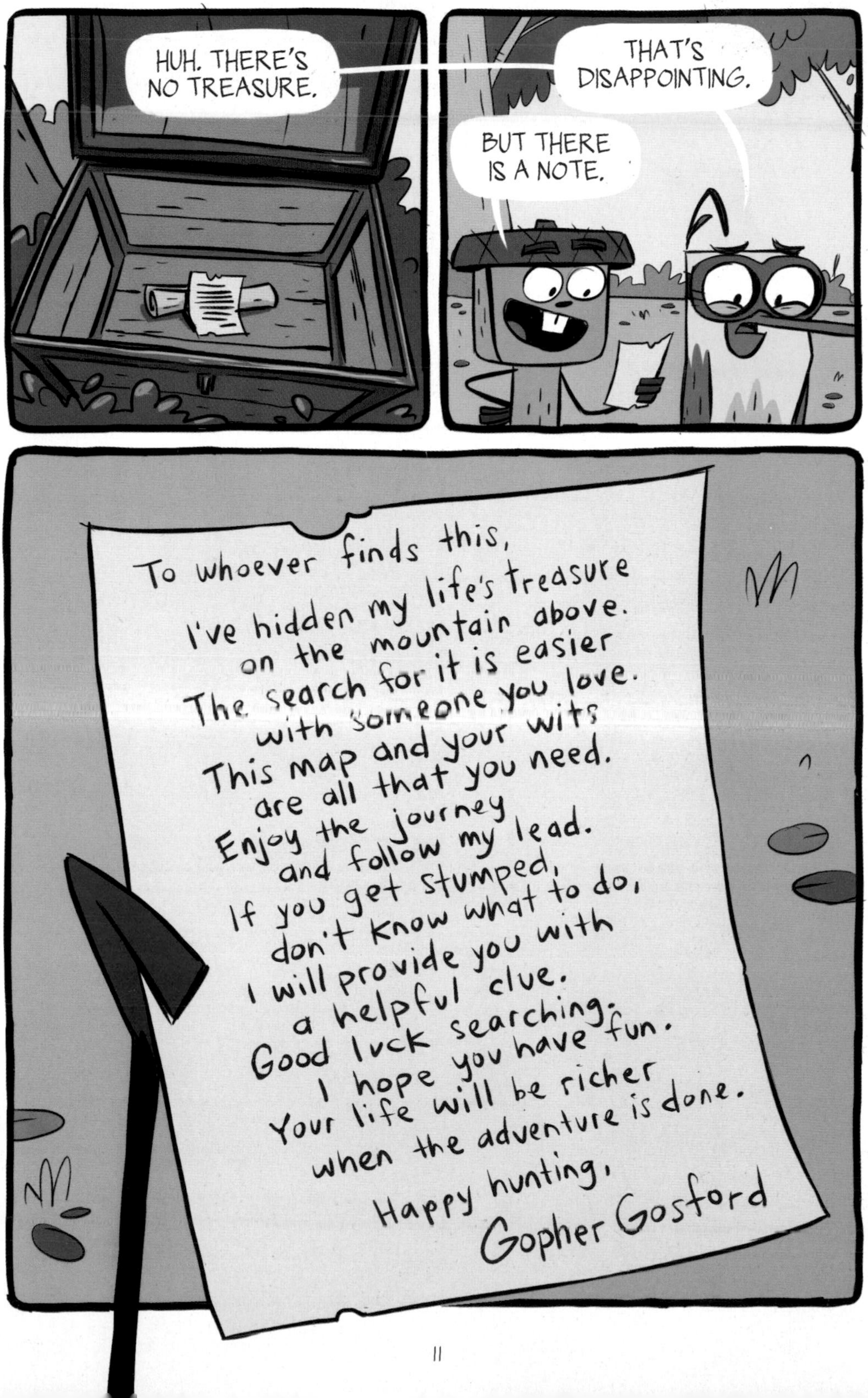
HUH. THERE'S NO TREASURE.
THAT'S DISAPPOINTING.
BUT THERE IS A NOTE.
To whoever finds this,
I've hidden my life's treasure
on the mountain above.
The search for it is easier
with someone you love.
This map and your wits
are all that you need.
Enjoy the journey
and follow my lead.
If you get stumped,
don't know what to do,
I will provide you with
a helpful clue.
Good luck searching.
I hope you have fun.
Your life will be richer
when the adventure is done.
Happy hunting,
Gopher Gosford

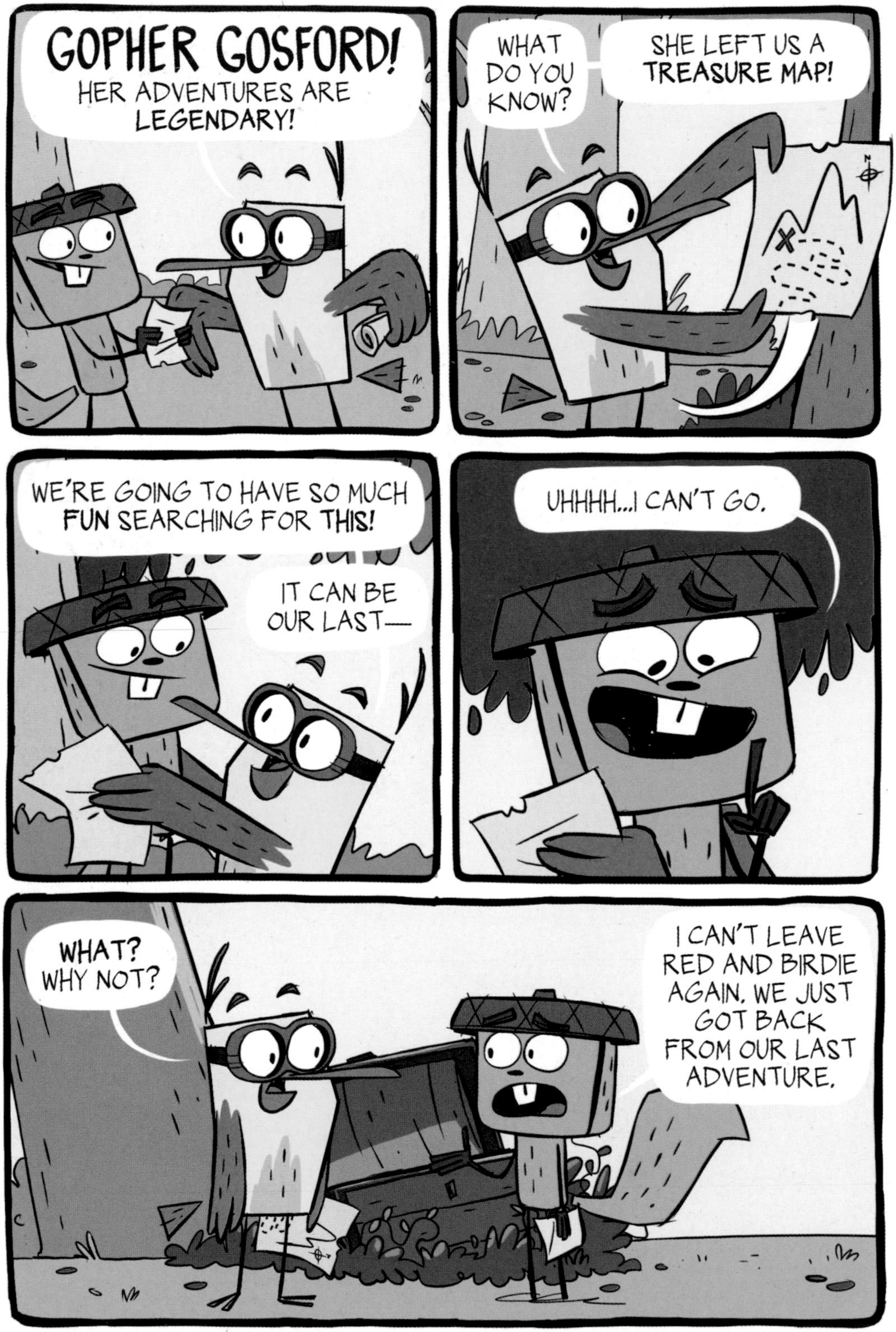
GOPHER GOSFORD! HER ADVENTURES ARE LEGENDARY!
WHAT DO YOU KNOW?
SHE LEFT US A TREASURE MAP!
WE'RE GOING TO HAVE SO MUCH FUN SEARCHING FOR THIS!
IT CAN BE OUR LAST—
UHHHH...I CAN'T GO.
WHAT? WHY NOT?
I CAN'T LEAVE RED AND BIRDIE AGAIN. WE JUST GOT BACK FROM OUR LAST ADVENTURE.

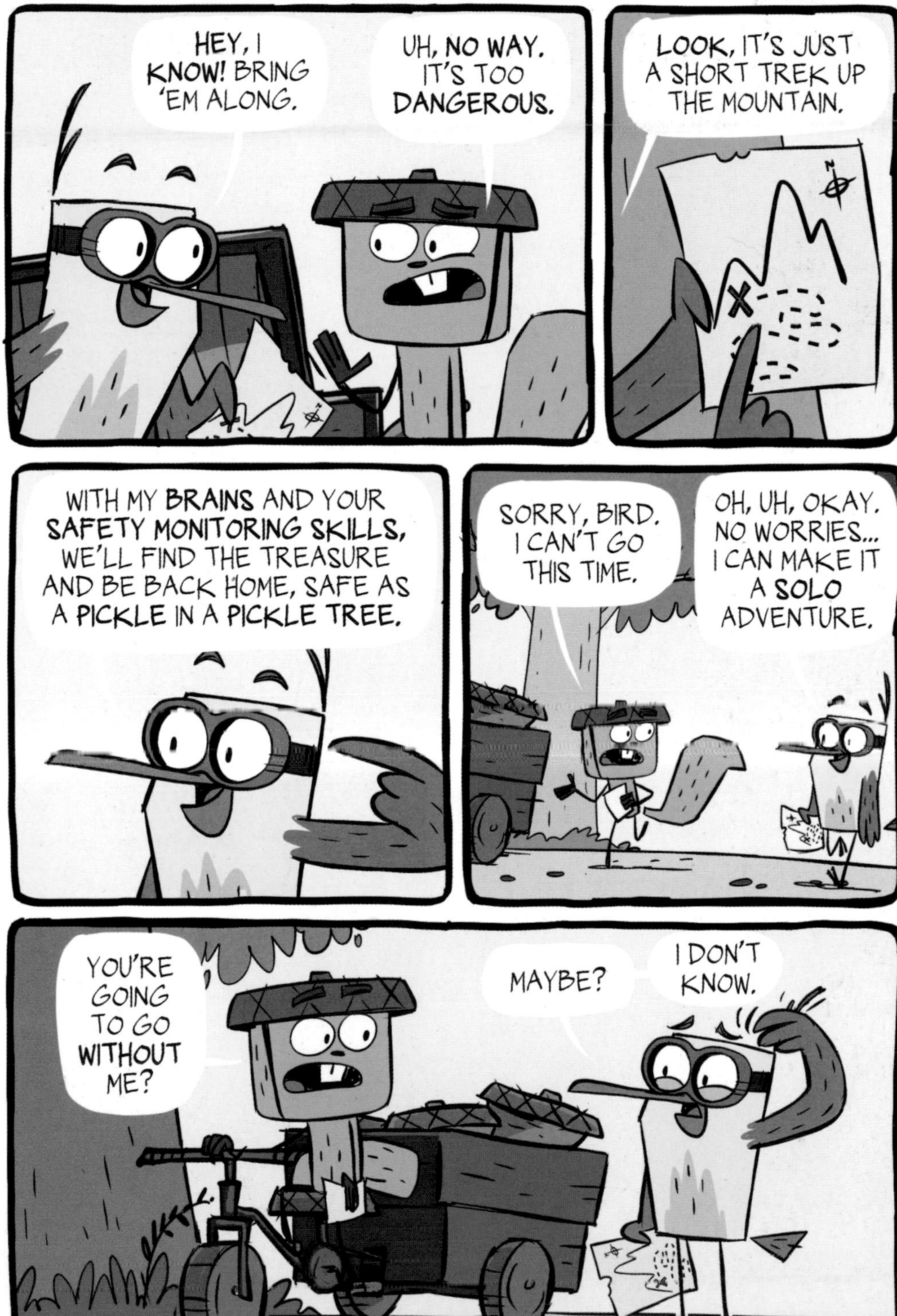
HEY, I KNOW! BRING 'EM ALONG.
UH, NO WAY. IT'S TOO DANGEROUS.
LOOK, IT'S JUST A SHORT TREK UP THE MOUNTAIN.
WITH MY BRAINS AND YOUR SAFETY MONITORING SKILLS, WE'LL FIND THE TREASURE AND BE BACK HOME, SAFE AS A PICKLE IN A PICKLE TREE.
SORRY, BIRD. I CAN'T GO THIS TIME.
OH, UH, OKAY. NO WORRIES... I CAN MAKE IT A SOLO ADVENTURE.
YOU'RE GOING TO GO WITHOUT ME?
MAYBE?
I DON'T KNOW.

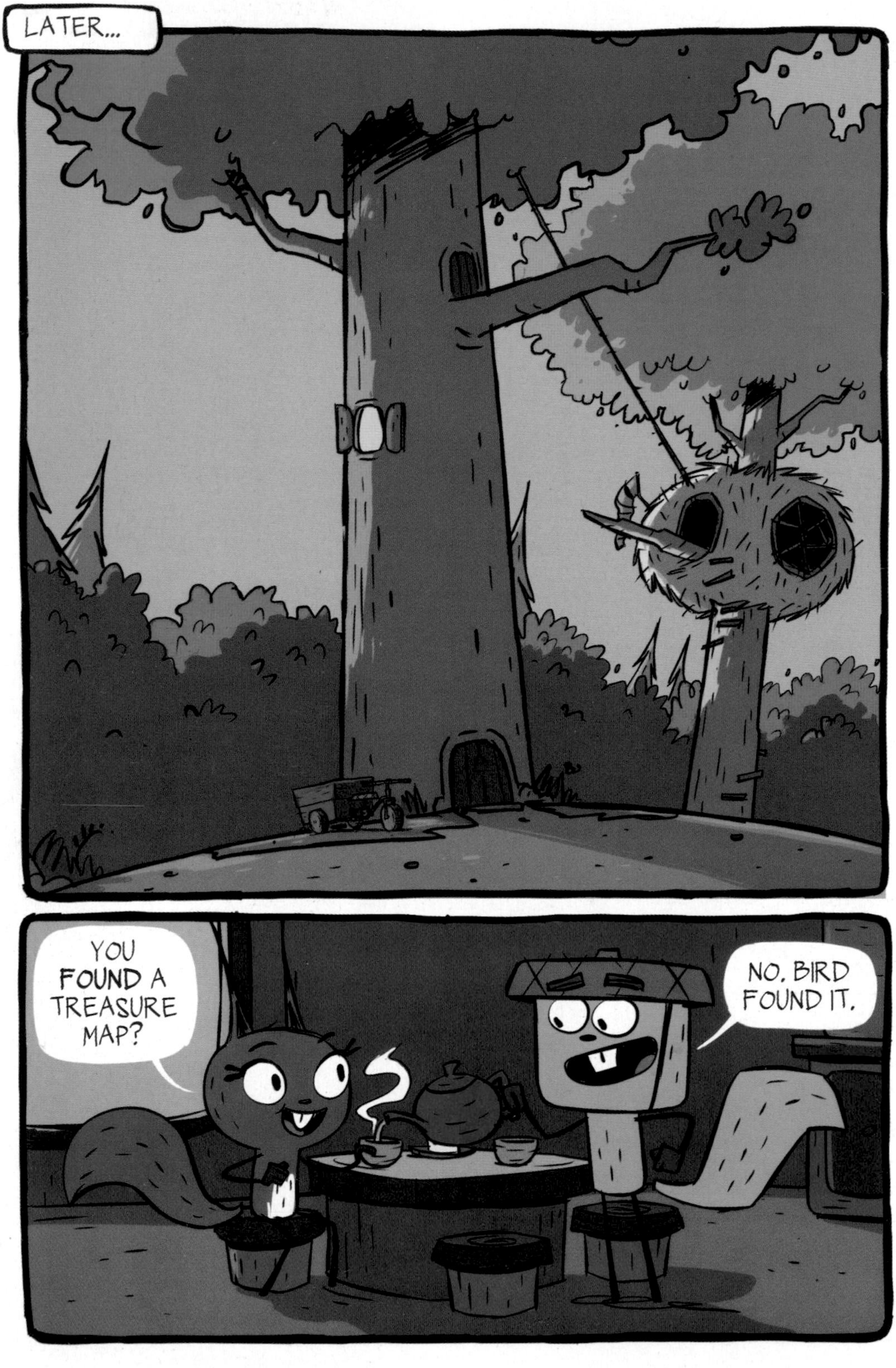
LATER...
YOU FOUND A TREASURE MAP?
NO. BIRD FOUND IT.

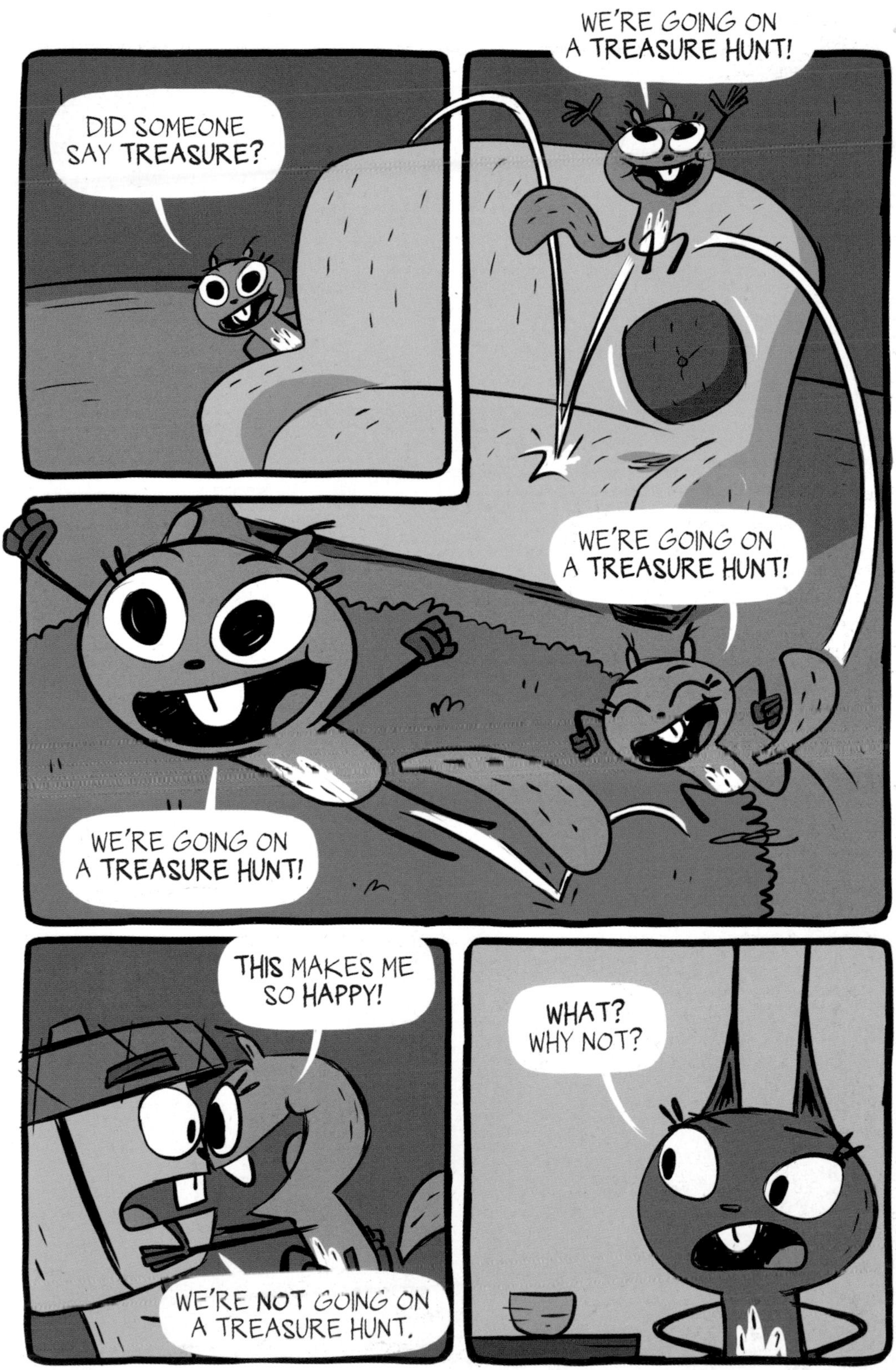
DID SOMEONE SAY TREASURE?
WE'RE GOING ON A TREASURE HUNT!
WE'RE GOING ON A TREASURE HUNT!
WE'RE GOING ON A TREASURE HUNT!
THIS MAKES ME SO HAPPY!
WE'RE NOT GOING ON A TREASURE HUNT.
WHAT? WHY NOT?

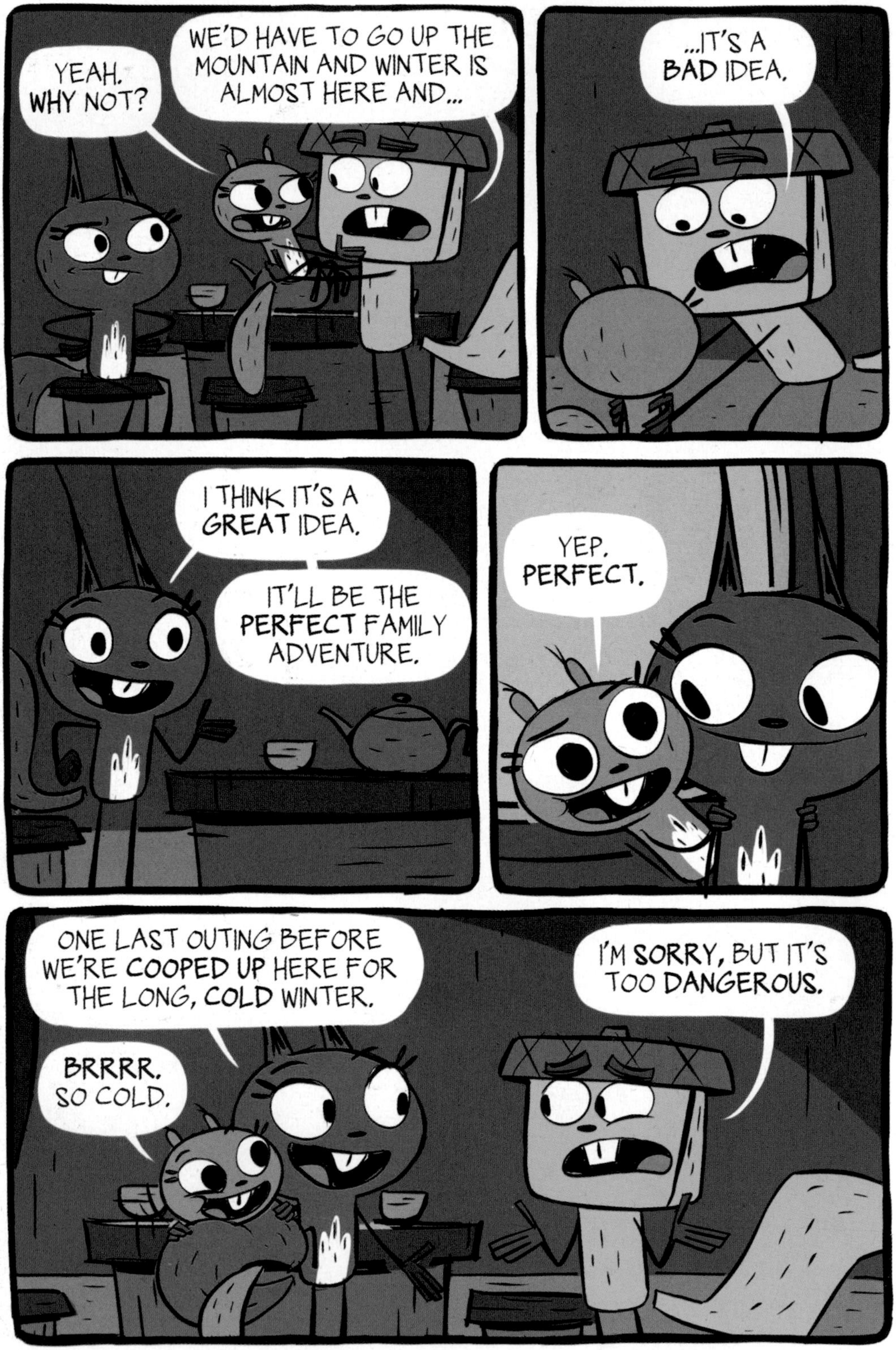
YEAH. WHY NOT?
WE'D HAVE TO GO UP THE MOUNTAIN AND WINTER IS ALMOST HERE AND...
...IT'S A BAD IDEA.
I THINK IT'S A GREAT IDEA.
IT'LL BE THE PERFECT FAMILY ADVENTURE.
YEP. PERFECT.
ONE LAST OUTING BEFORE WE'RE COOPED UP HERE FOR THE LONG, COLD WINTER.
BRRRR. SO COLD.
I'M SORRY, BUT IT'S TOO DANGEROUS.

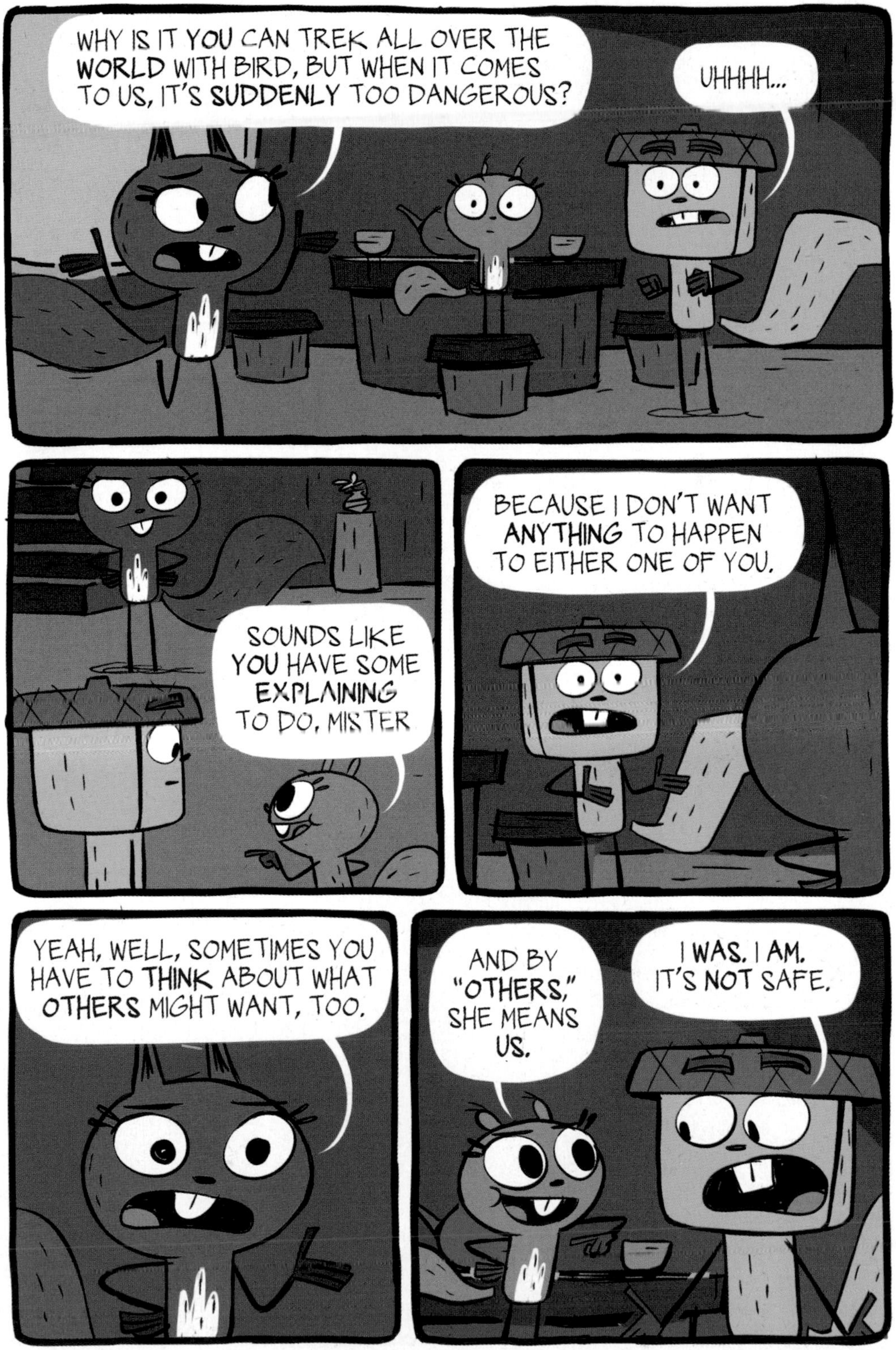
WHY IS IT YOU CAN TREK ALL OVER THE WORLD WITH BIRD, BUT WHEN IT COMES TO US, IT'S SUDDENLY TOO DANGEROUS?
UHHHH...
SOUNDS LIKE YOU HAVE SOME EXPLAINING TO DO, MISTER.
BECAUSE I DON'T WANT ANYTHING TO HAPPEN TO EITHER ONE OF YOU.
YEAH, WELL, SOMETIMES YOU HAVE TO THINK ABOUT WHAT OTHERS MIGHT WANT, TOO.
AND BY "OTHERS," SHE MEANS US.
I WAS. I AM. IT'S NOT SAFE.

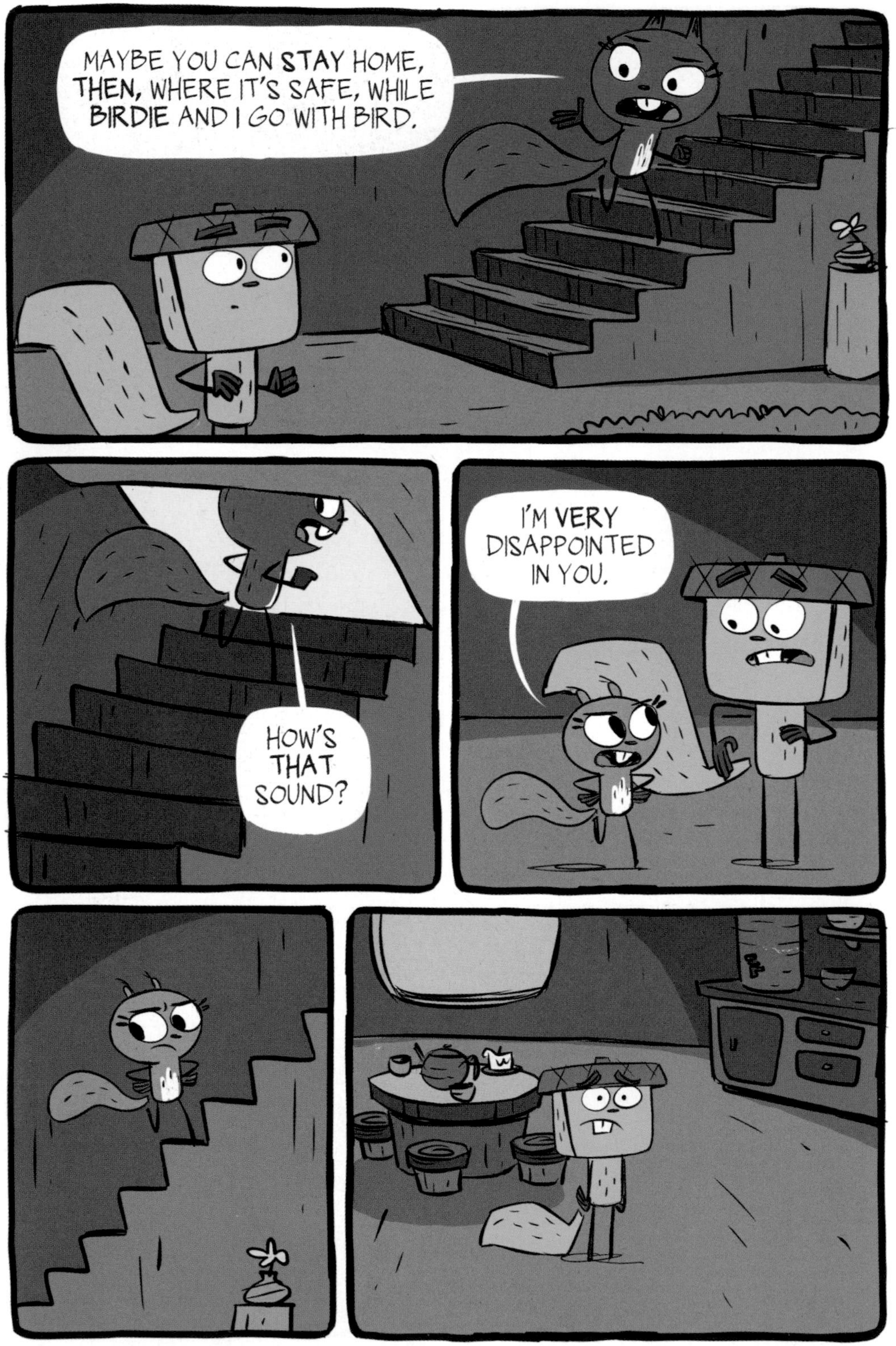
MAYBE YOU CAN STAY HOME, THEN, WHERE IT'S SAFE, WHILE BIRDIE AND I GO WITH BIRD.
HOW'S THAT SOUND?
I'M VERY DISAPPOINTED IN YOU.

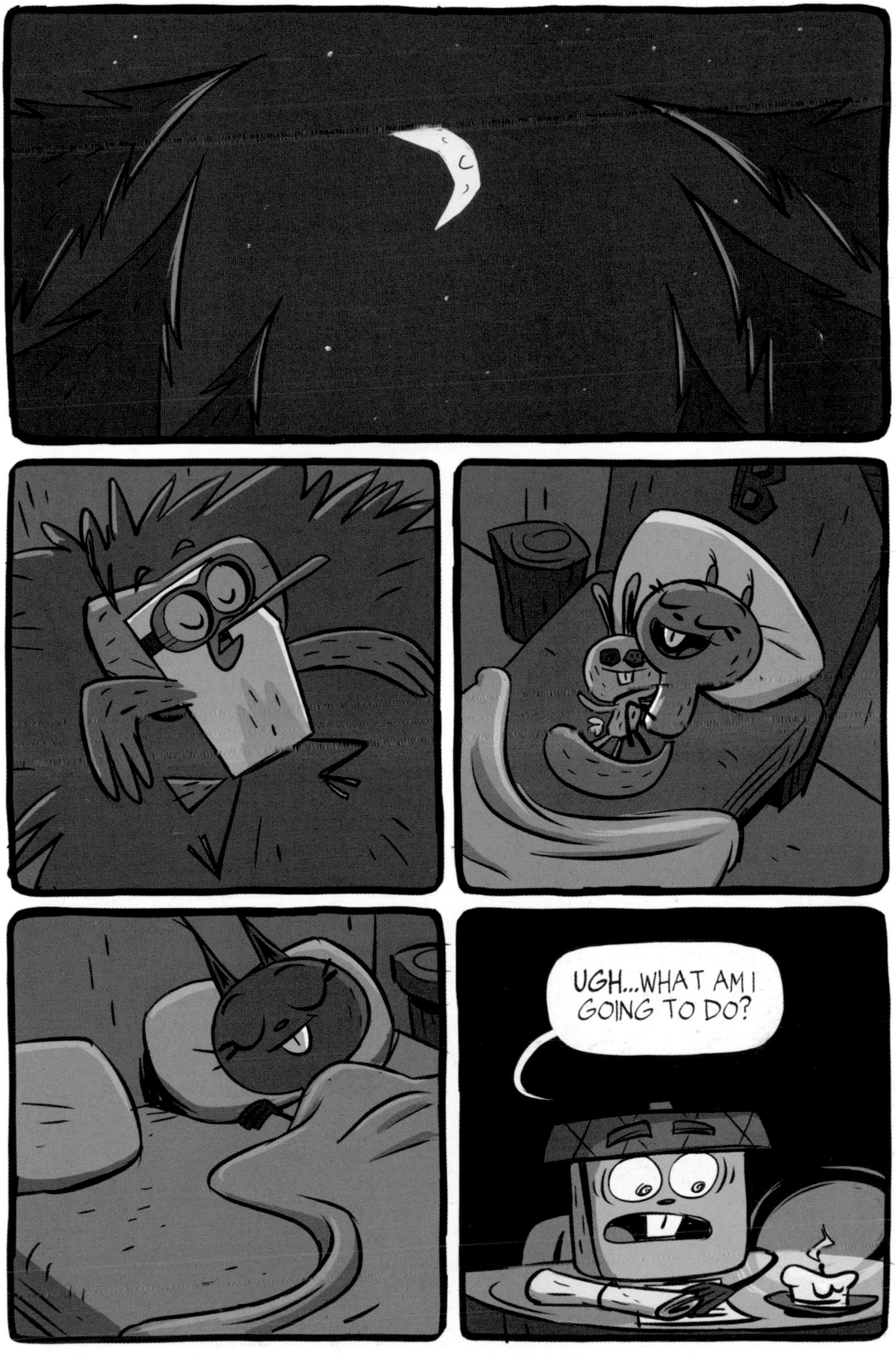
UGH...WHAT AM I GOING TO DO?

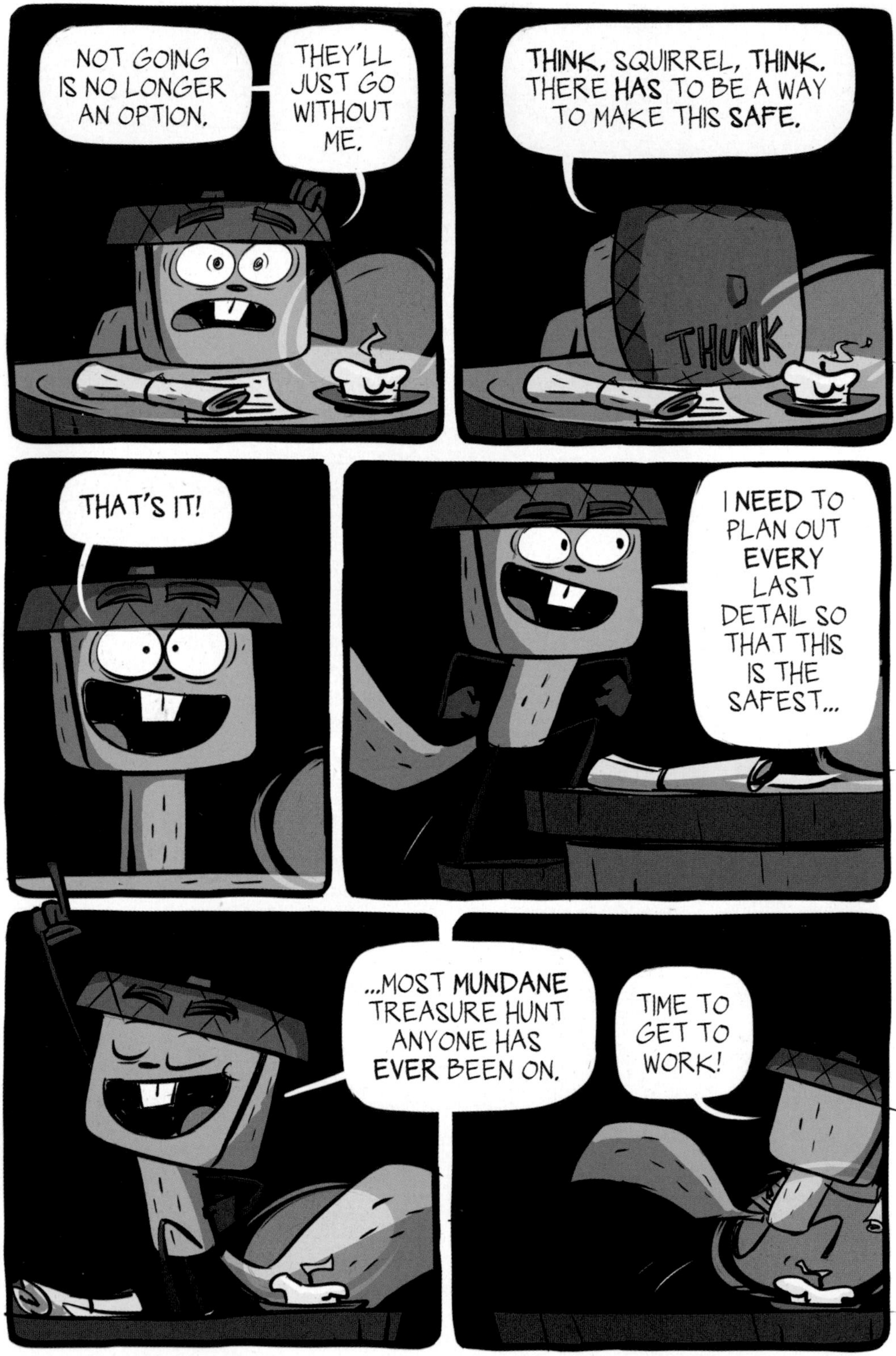
NOT GOING IS NO LONGER AN OPTION.
THEY'LL JUST GO WITHOUT ME.
THINK, SQUIRREL, THINK. THERE HAS TO BE A WAY TO MAKE THIS SAFE.
THUNK
THAT'S IT!
I NEED TO PLAN OUT EVERY LAST DETAIL SO THAT THIS IS THE SAFEST...
...MOST MUNDANE TREASURE HUNT ANYONE HAS EVER BEEN ON.
TIME TO GET TO WORK!

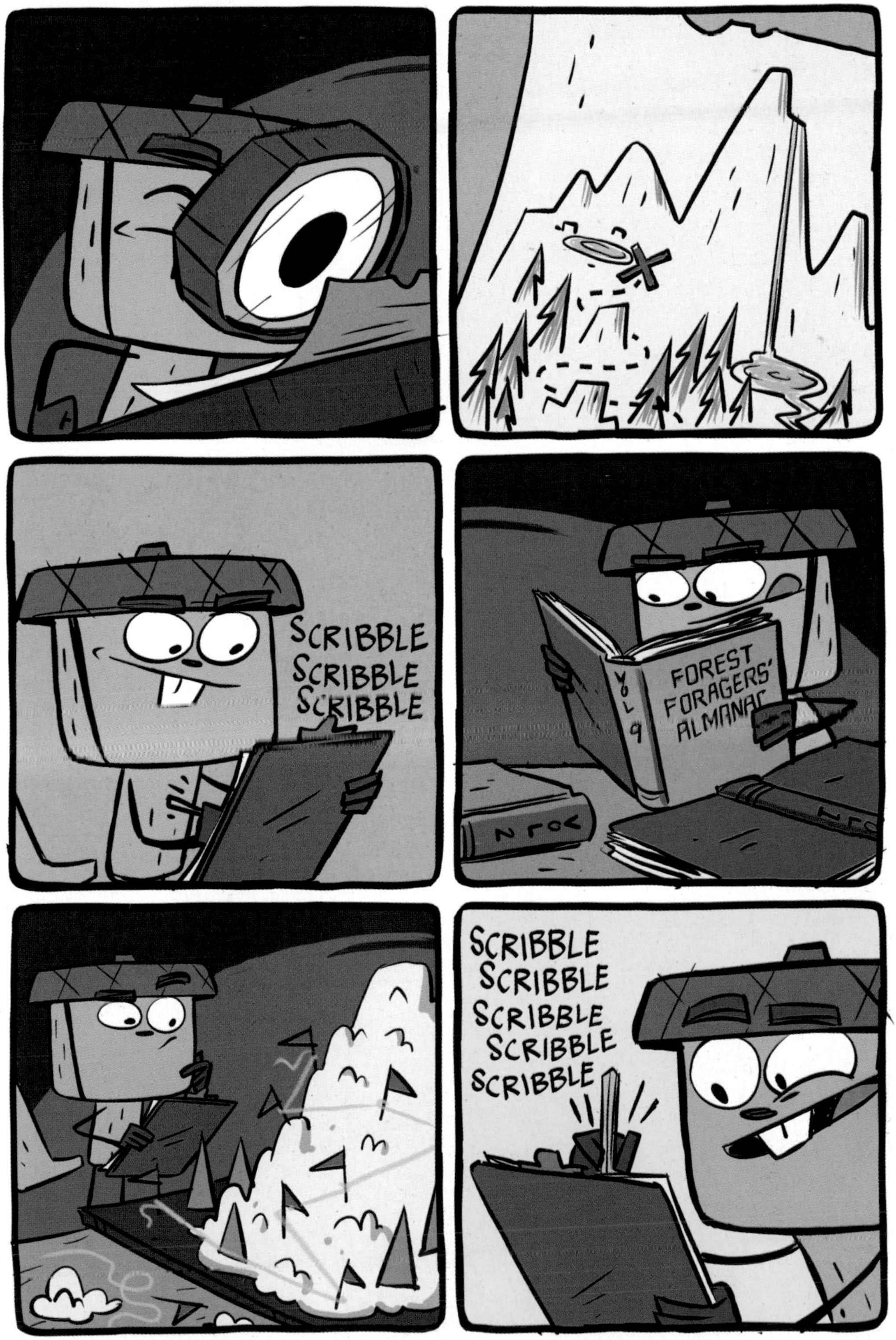
SCRIBBLE
SCRIBBLE
SCRIBBLE
FOREST FORAGERS' ALMANAC
VOL 9
SCRIBBLE
SCRIBBLE
SCRIBBLE
SCRIBBLE
SCRIBBLE

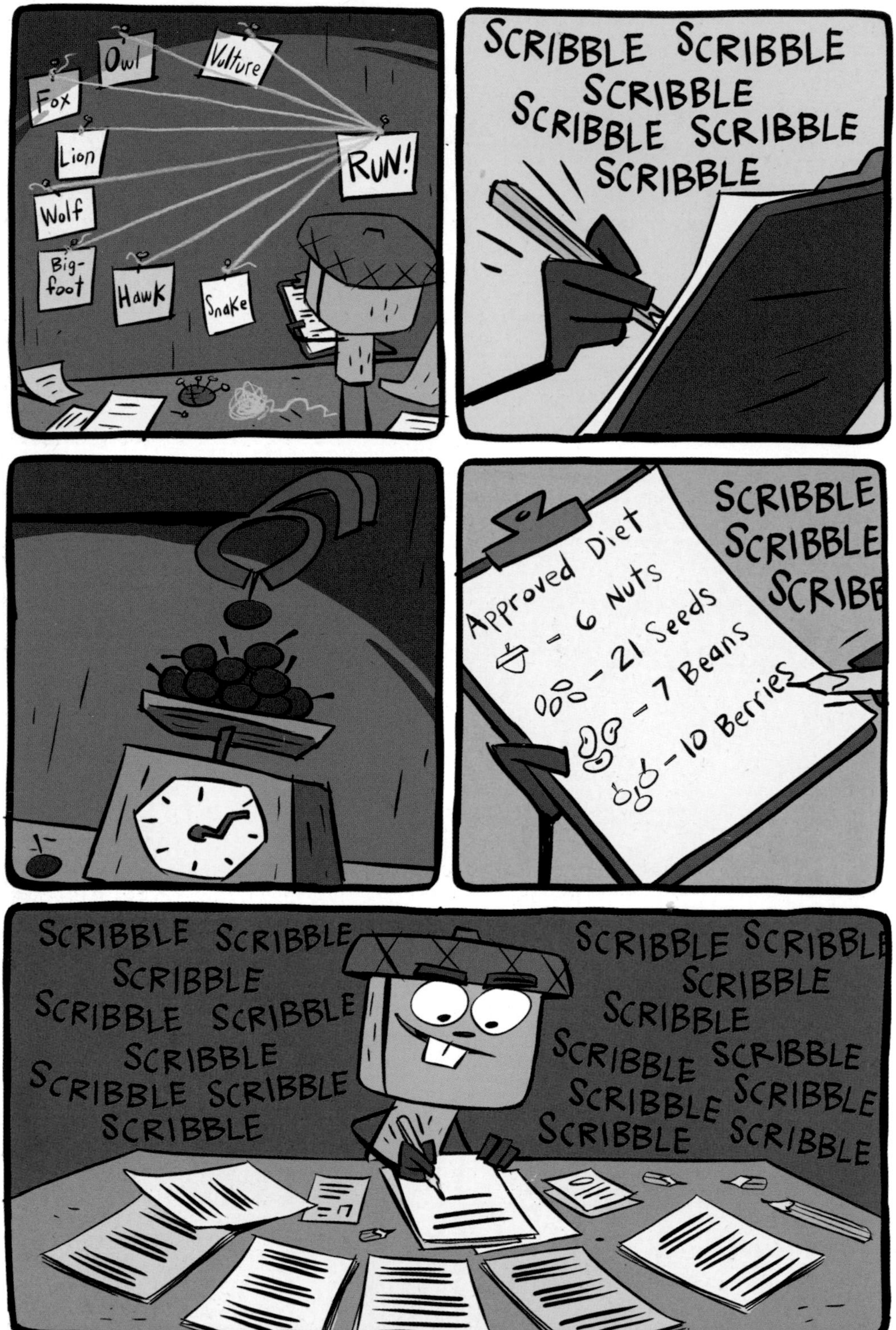
Owl
Vulture
Fox
Lion
RUN!
Wolf
Big-foot
Hawk
Snake
SCRIBBLE SCRIBBLE
SCRIBBLE
SCRIBBLE SCRIBBLE
SCRIBBLE
Approved Diet
- 6 Nuts
- 21 Seeds
- 7 Beans
- 10 Berries
SCRIBBLE
SCRIBBLE
SCRIB
SCRIBBLE SCRIBBLE
SCRIBBLE
SCRIBBLE SCRIBBLE
SCRIBBLE
SCRIBBLE SCRIBBLE
SCRIBBLE
SCRIBBLE SCRIBBLE
SCRIBBLE
SCRIBBLE
SCRIBBLE SCRIBBLE
SCRIBBLE SCRIBBLE
SCRIBBLE SCRIBBLE

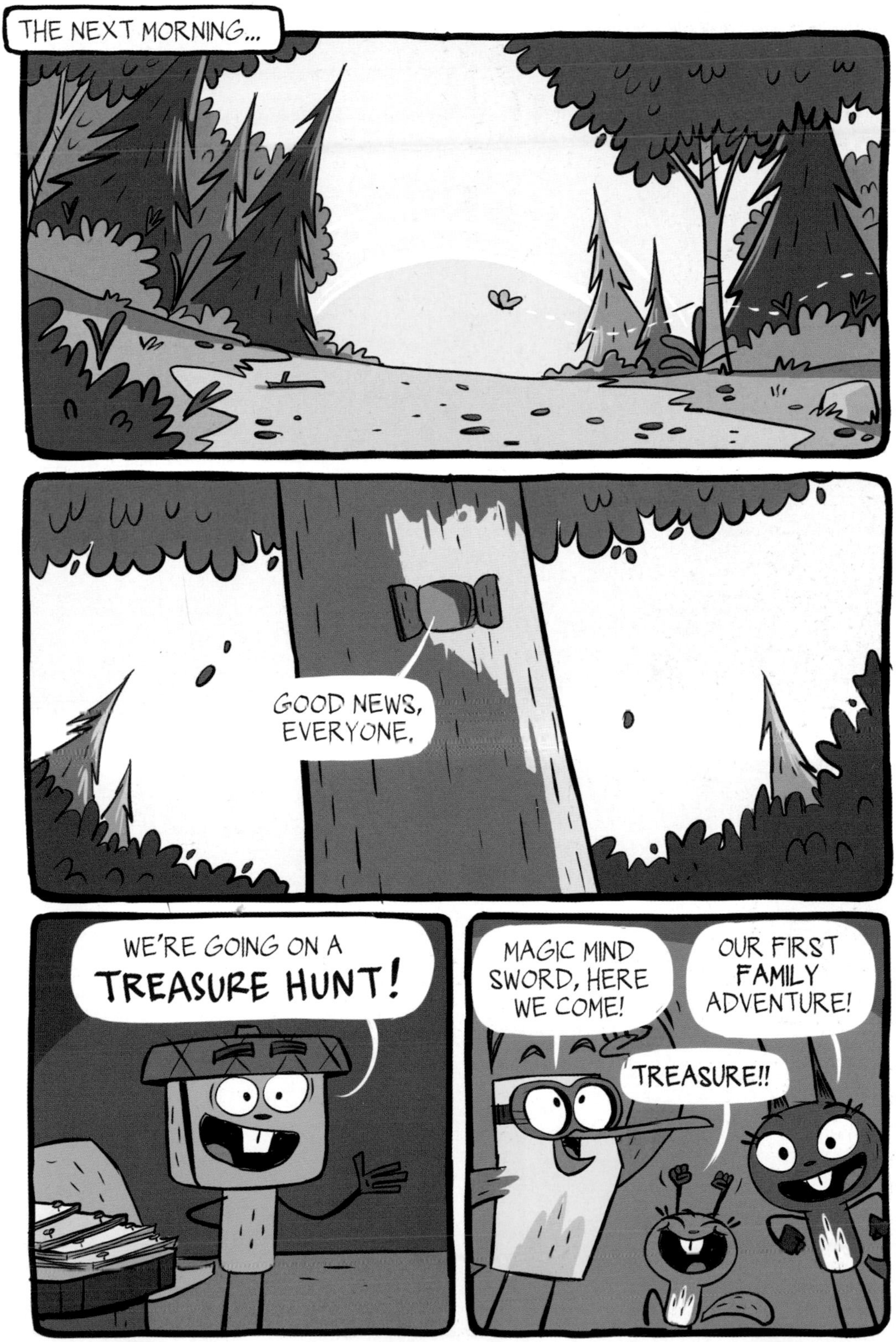
THE NEXT MORNING...
GOOD NEWS, EVERYONE.
WE'RE GOING ON A TREASURE HUNT!
MAGIC MIND SWORD, HERE WE COME!
OUR FIRST FAMILY ADVENTURE!
TREASURE!!

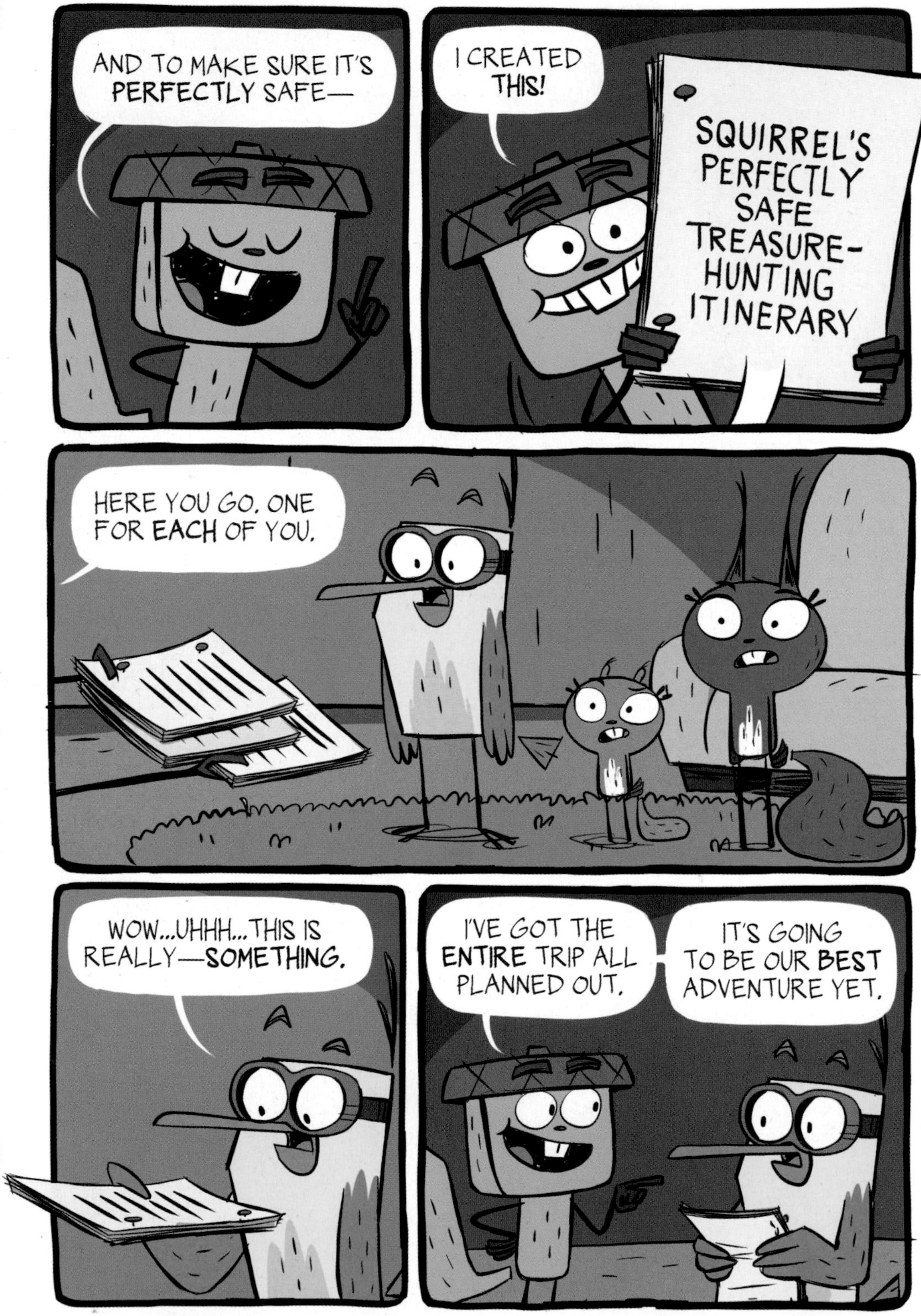
AND TO MAKE SURE IT'S PERFECTLY SAFE—
I CREATED THIS!
SQUIRREL'S PERFECTLY SAFE TREASURE-HUNTING ITINERARY
HERE YOU GO. ONE FOR EACH OF YOU.
WOW...UHHH...THIS IS REALLY—SOMETHING.
I'VE GOT THE ENTIRE TRIP ALL PLANNED OUT.
IT'S GOING TO BE OUR BEST ADVENTURE YET.

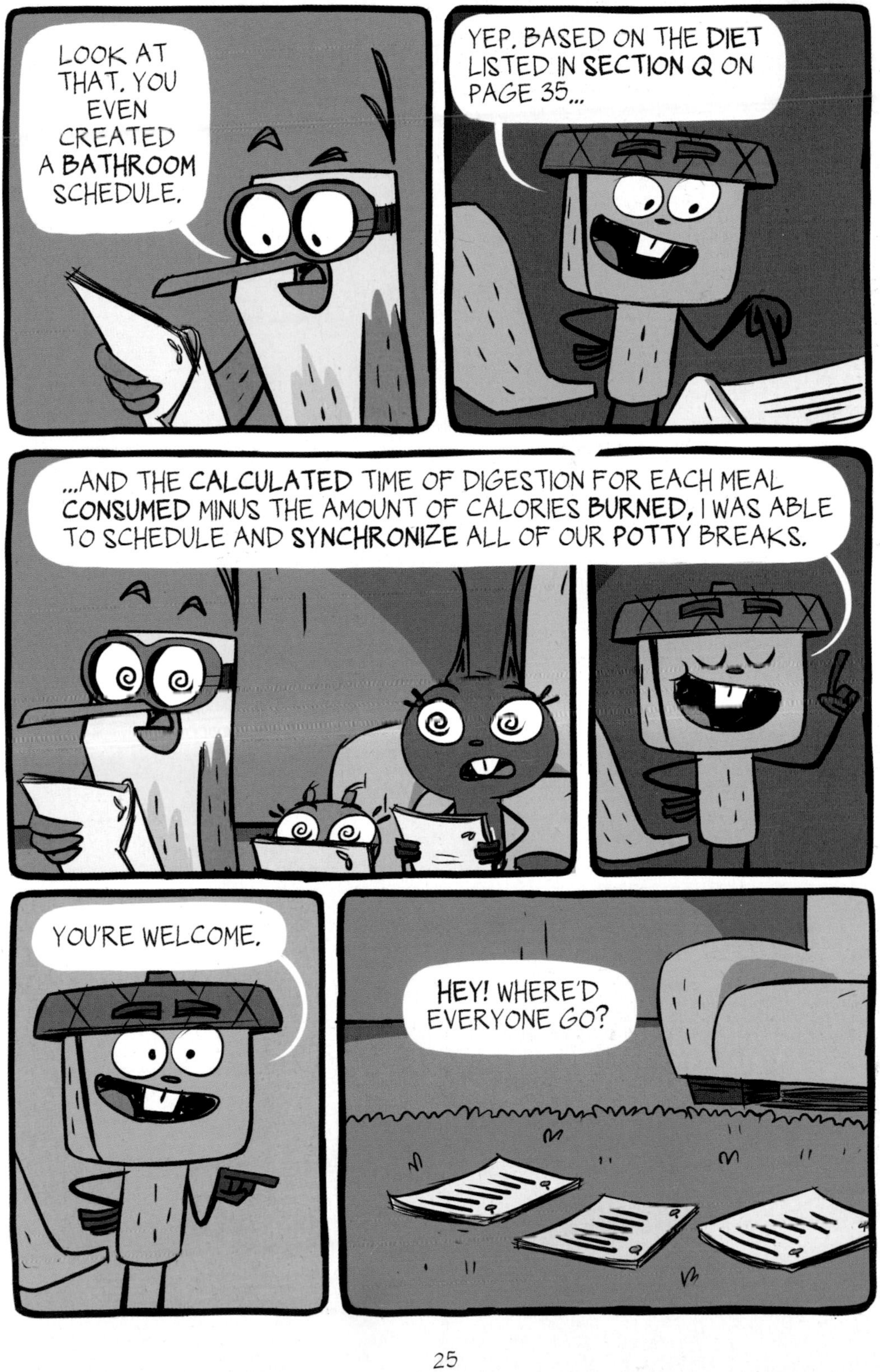
LOOK AT THAT. YOU EVEN CREATED A BATHROOM SCHEDULE.
YEP. BASED ON THE DIET LISTED IN SECTION Q ON PAGE 35...
...AND THE CALCULATED TIME OF DIGESTION FOR EACH MEAL CONSUMED MINUS THE AMOUNT OF CALORIES BURNED, I WAS ABLE TO SCHEDULE AND SYNCHRONIZE ALL OF OUR POTTY BREAKS.
YOU'RE WELCOME.
HEY! WHERE'D EVERYONE GO?

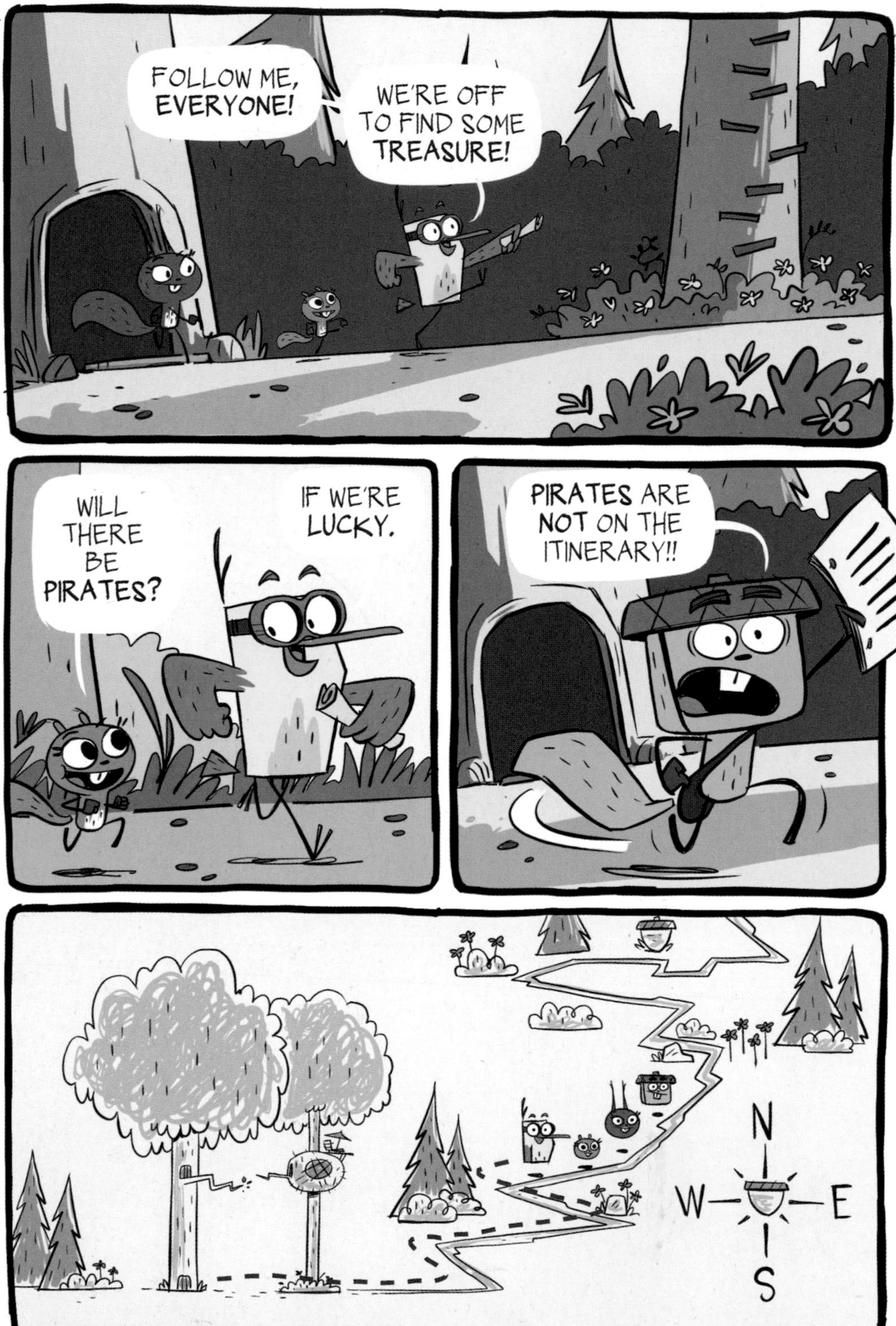
FOLLOW ME, EVERYONE!
WE'RE OFF TO FIND SOME TREASURE!
WILL THERE BE PIRATES?
IF WE'RE LUCKY.
PIRATES ARE NOT ON THE ITINERARY!!
N
W
E
S

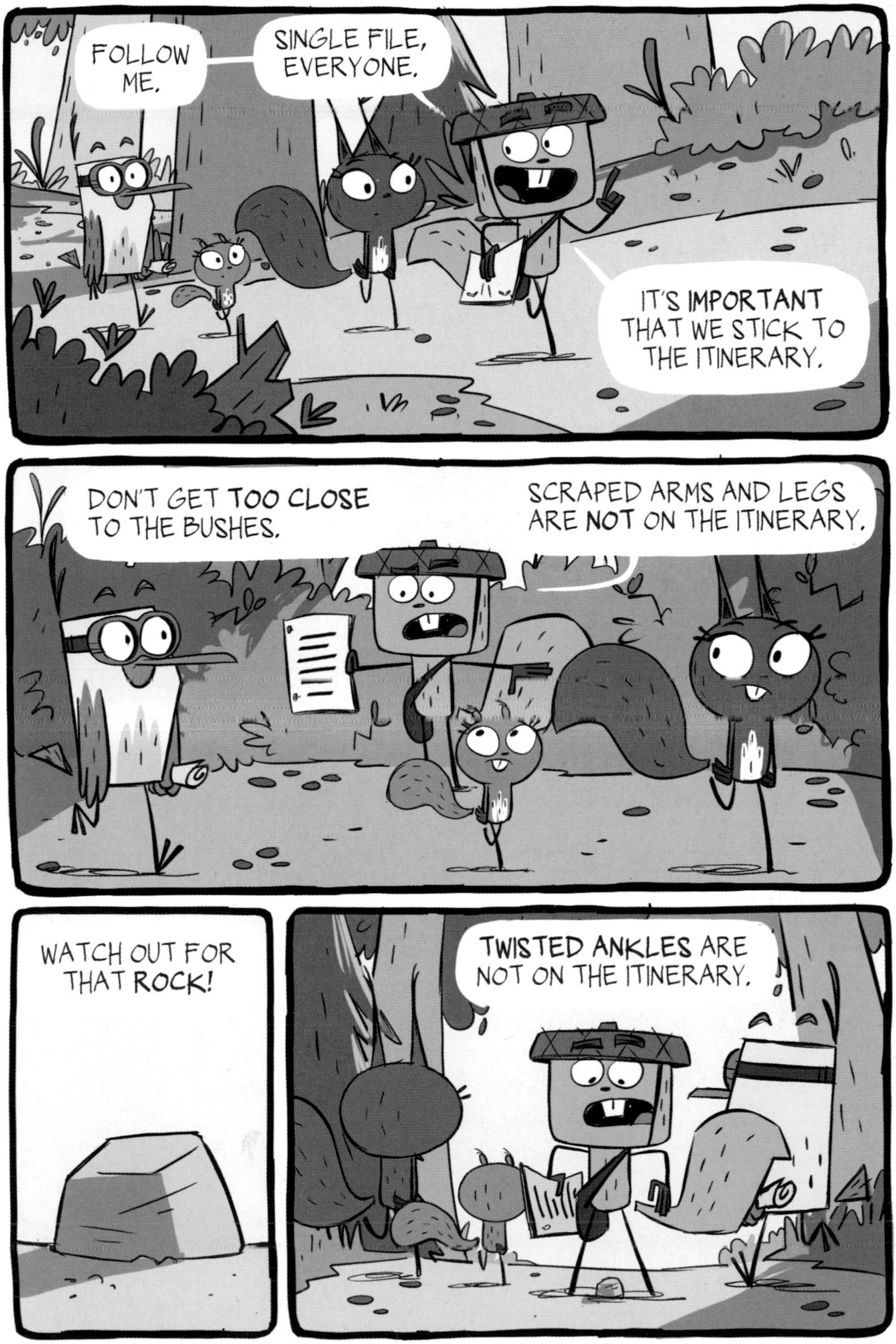
FOLLOW ME.
SINGLE FILE, EVERYONE.
IT'S IMPORTANT THAT WE STICK TO THE ITINERARY.
DON'T GET TOO CLOSE TO THE BUSHES.
SCRAPED ARMS AND LEGS ARE NOT ON THE ITINERARY.
WATCH OUT FOR THAT ROCK!
TWISTED ANKLES ARE NOT ON THE ITINERARY.

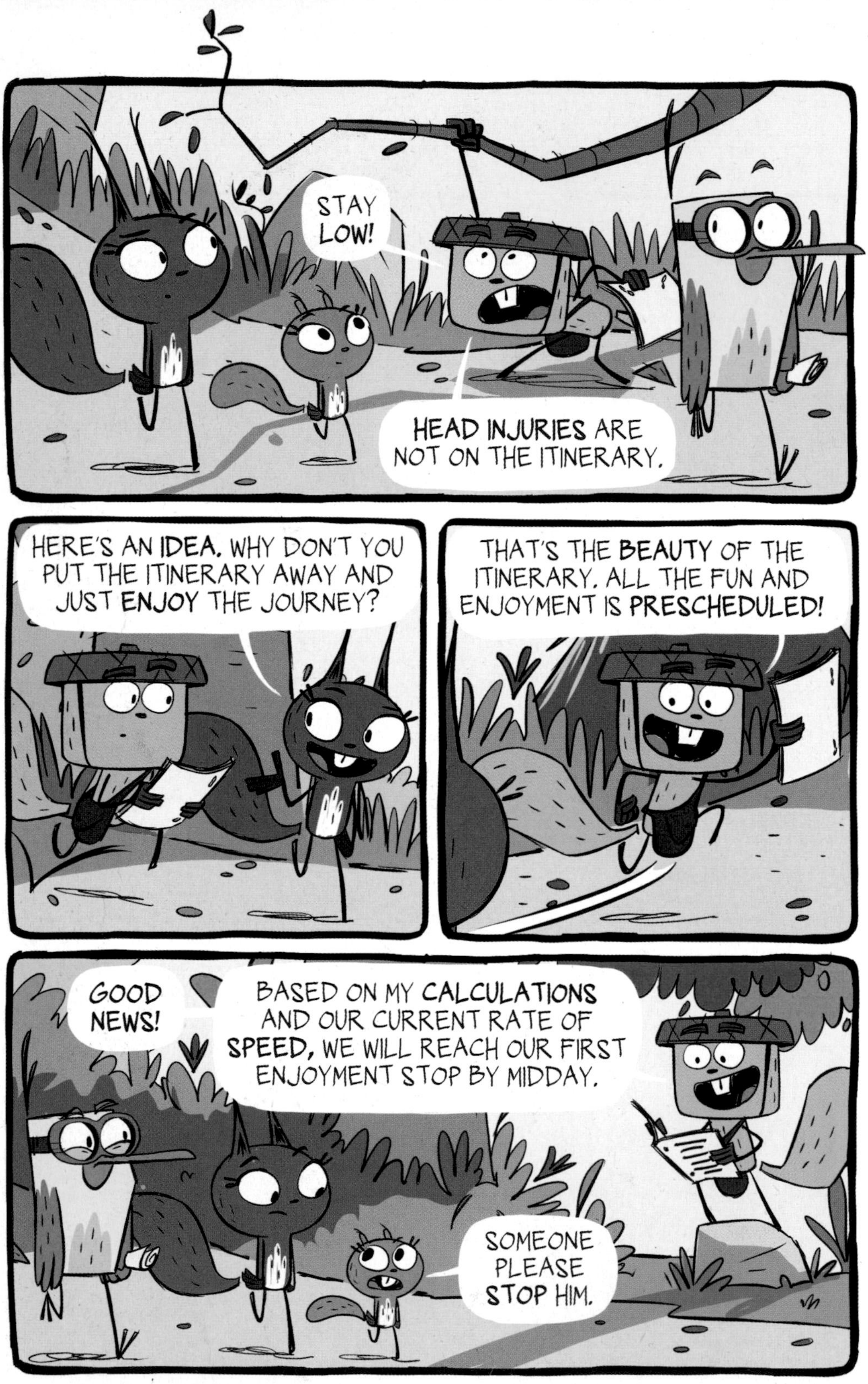
STAY LOW!
HEAD INJURIES ARE NOT ON THE ITINERARY.
HERE'S AN IDEA. WHY DON'T YOU PUT THE ITINERARY AWAY AND JUST ENJOY THE JOURNEY?
THAT'S THE BEAUTY OF THE ITINERARY. ALL THE FUN AND ENJOYMENT IS PRESCHEDULED!
GOOD NEWS!
BASED ON MY CALCULATIONS AND OUR CURRENT RATE OF SPEED, WE WILL REACH OUR FIRST ENJOYMENT STOP BY MIDDAY.
SOMEONE PLEASE STOP HIM.

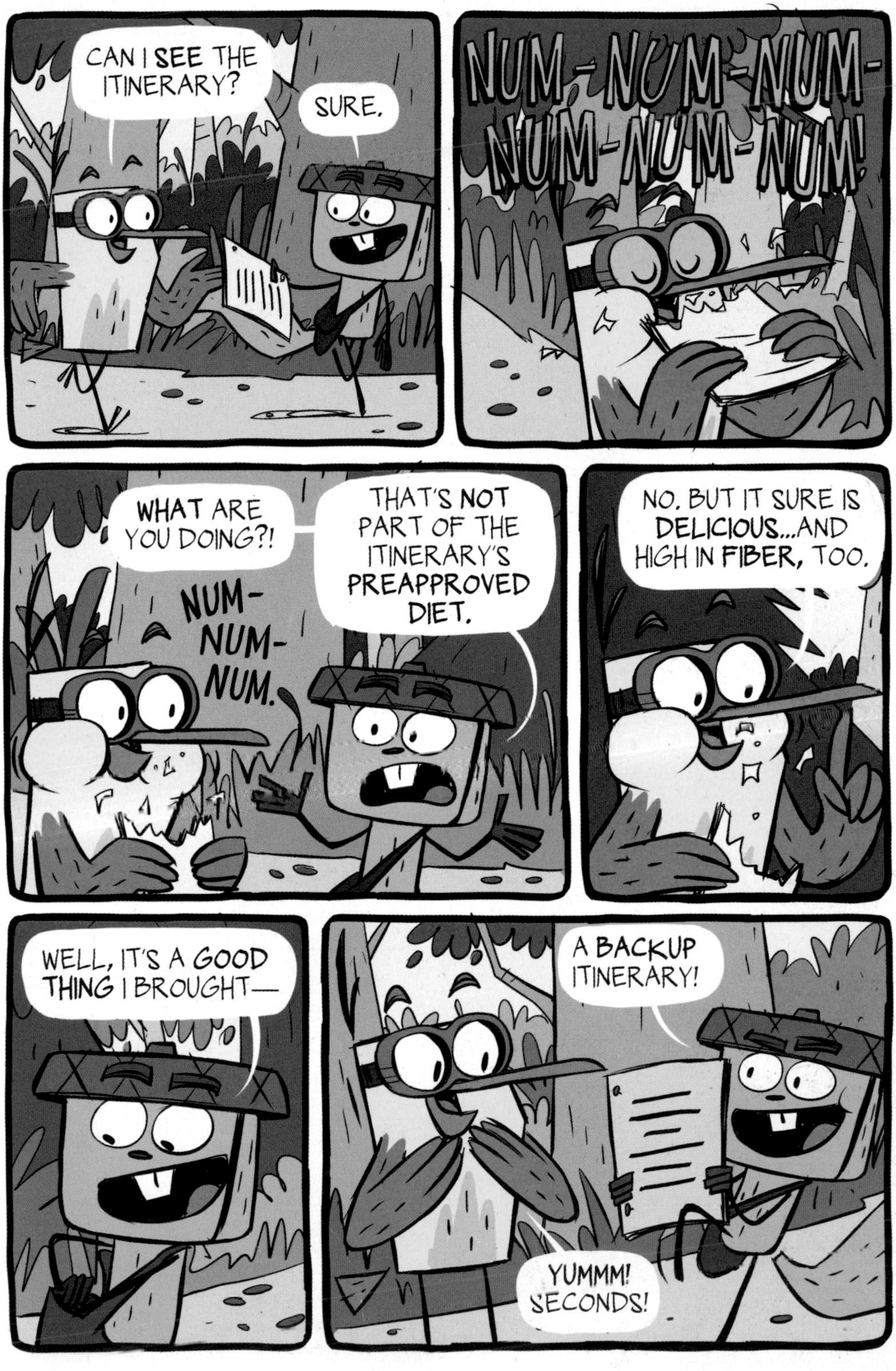
CAN I SEE THE ITINERARY?
SURE.
NUM-NUM-NUM-NUM-NUM-NUM!
WHAT ARE YOU DOING?!
NUM-NUM-NUM.
THAT'S NOT PART OF THE ITINERARY'S PREAPPROVED DIET.
NO. BUT IT SURE IS DELICIOUS...AND HIGH IN FIBER, TOO.
WELL, IT'S A GOOD THING I BROUGHT—
A BACKUP ITINERARY!
YUMMM! SECONDS!

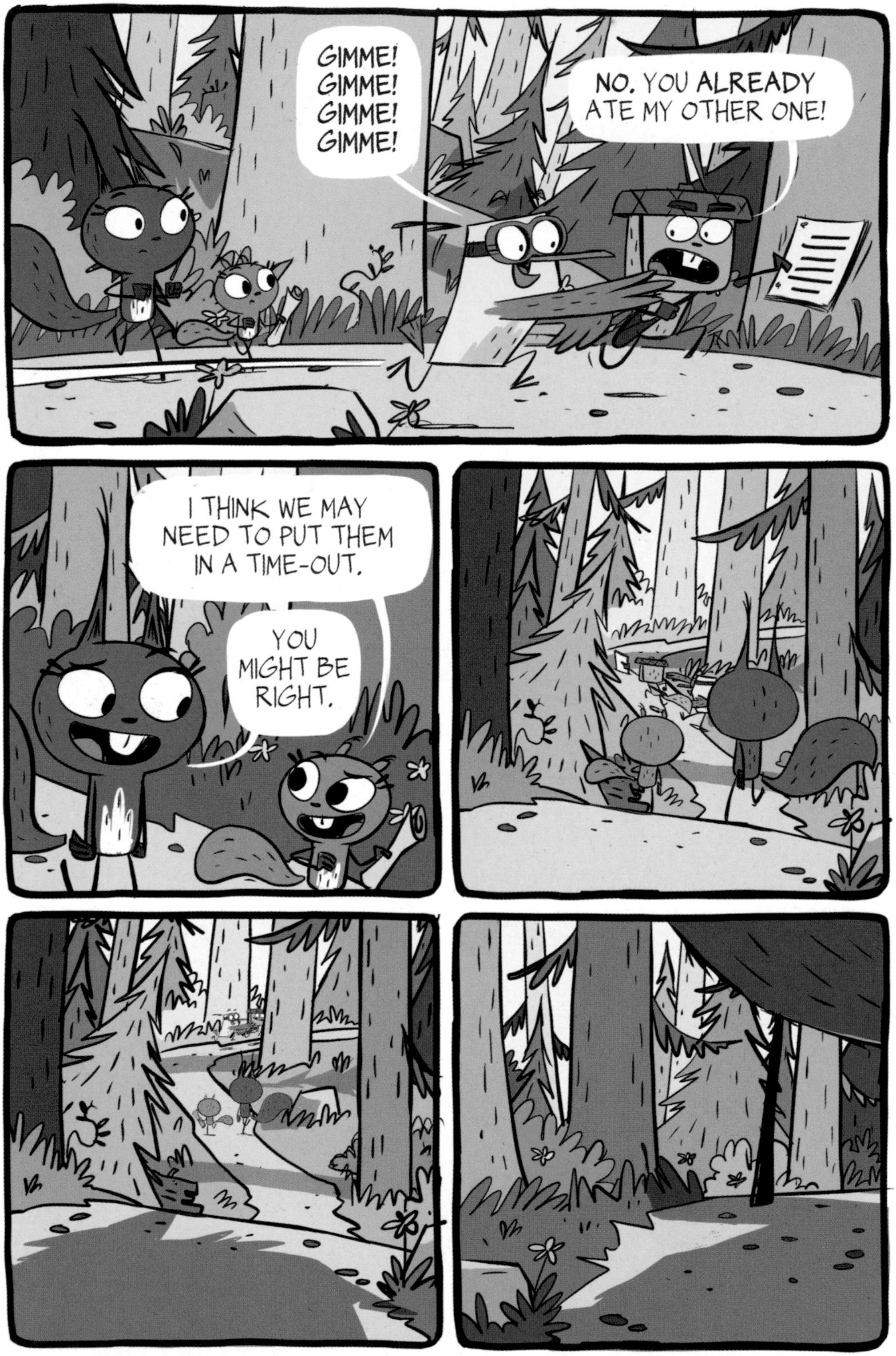
GIMME! GIMME! GIMME! GIMME!
NO. YOU ALREADY ATE MY OTHER ONE!
I THINK WE MAY NEED TO PUT THEM IN A TIME-OUT.
YOU MIGHT BE RIGHT.

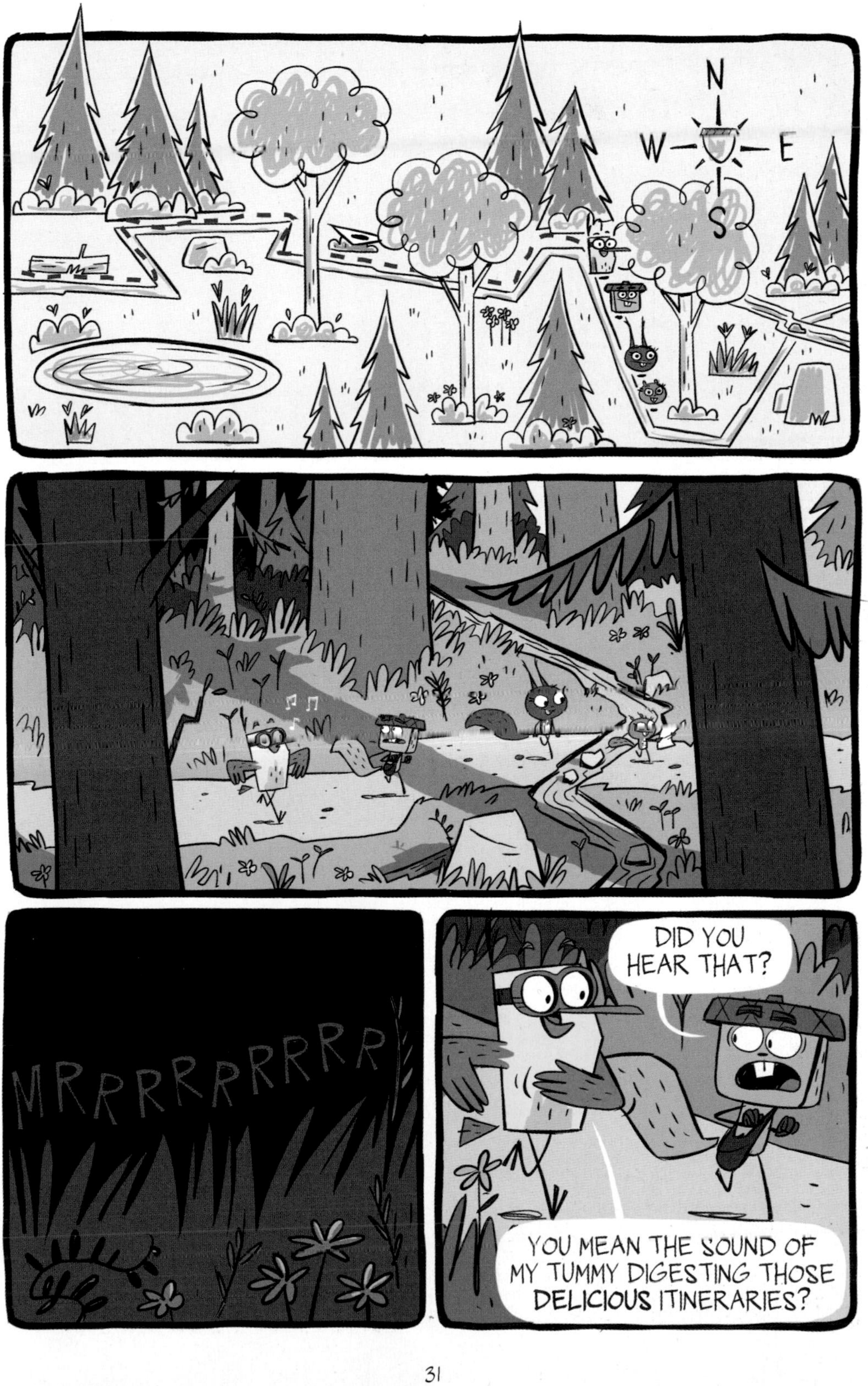
N
W
E
S
MRRRRRRRRRR
DID YOU HEAR THAT?
YOU MEAN THE SOUND OF MY TUMMY DIGESTING THOSE **DELICIOUS** ITINERARIES?

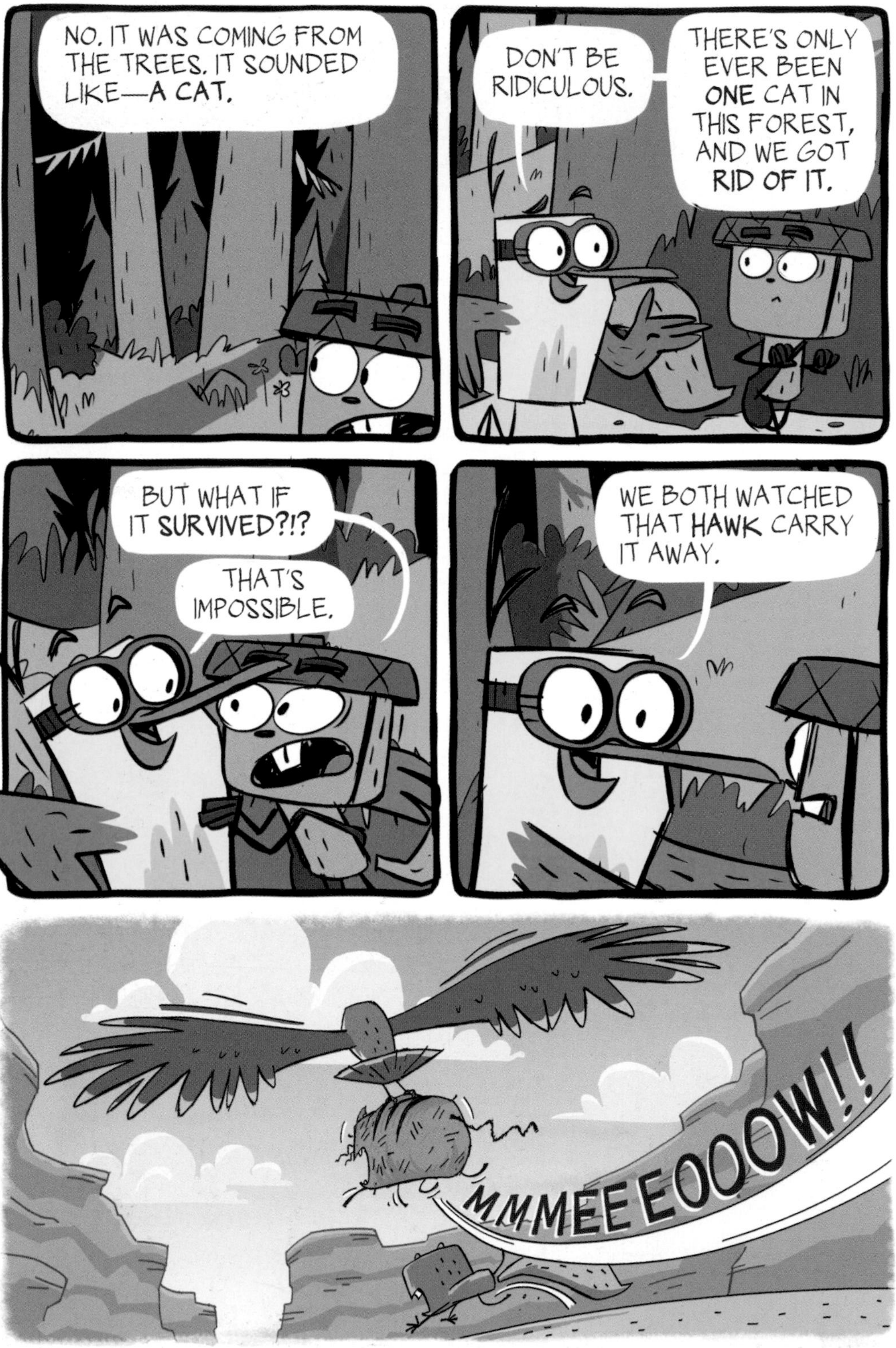
NO. IT WAS COMING FROM THE TREES. IT SOUNDED LIKE—A CAT.
DON'T BE RIDICULOUS.
THERE'S ONLY EVER BEEN ONE CAT IN THIS FOREST, AND WE GOT RID OF IT.
BUT WHAT IF IT SURVIVED?!?
THAT'S IMPOSSIBLE.
WE BOTH WATCHED THAT HAWK CARRY IT AWAY.
MMMEEEOOOOW!!

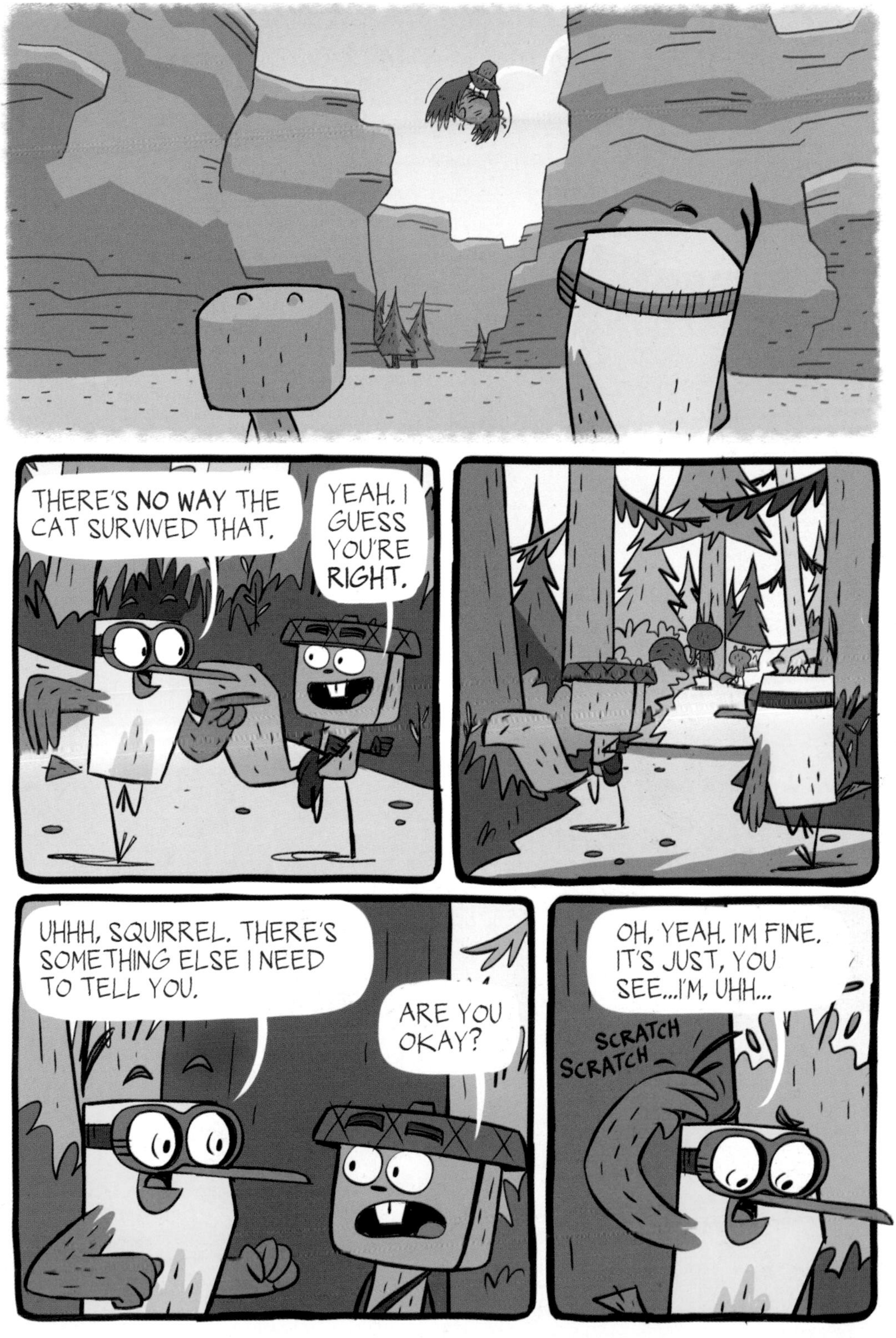
THERE'S NO WAY THE CAT SURVIVED THAT.
YEAH, I GUESS YOU'RE RIGHT.
UHHH, SQUIRREL. THERE'S SOMETHING ELSE I NEED TO TELL YOU.
ARE YOU OKAY?
OH, YEAH. I'M FINE. IT'S JUST, YOU SEE...I'M, UHH...
SCRATCH SCRATCH

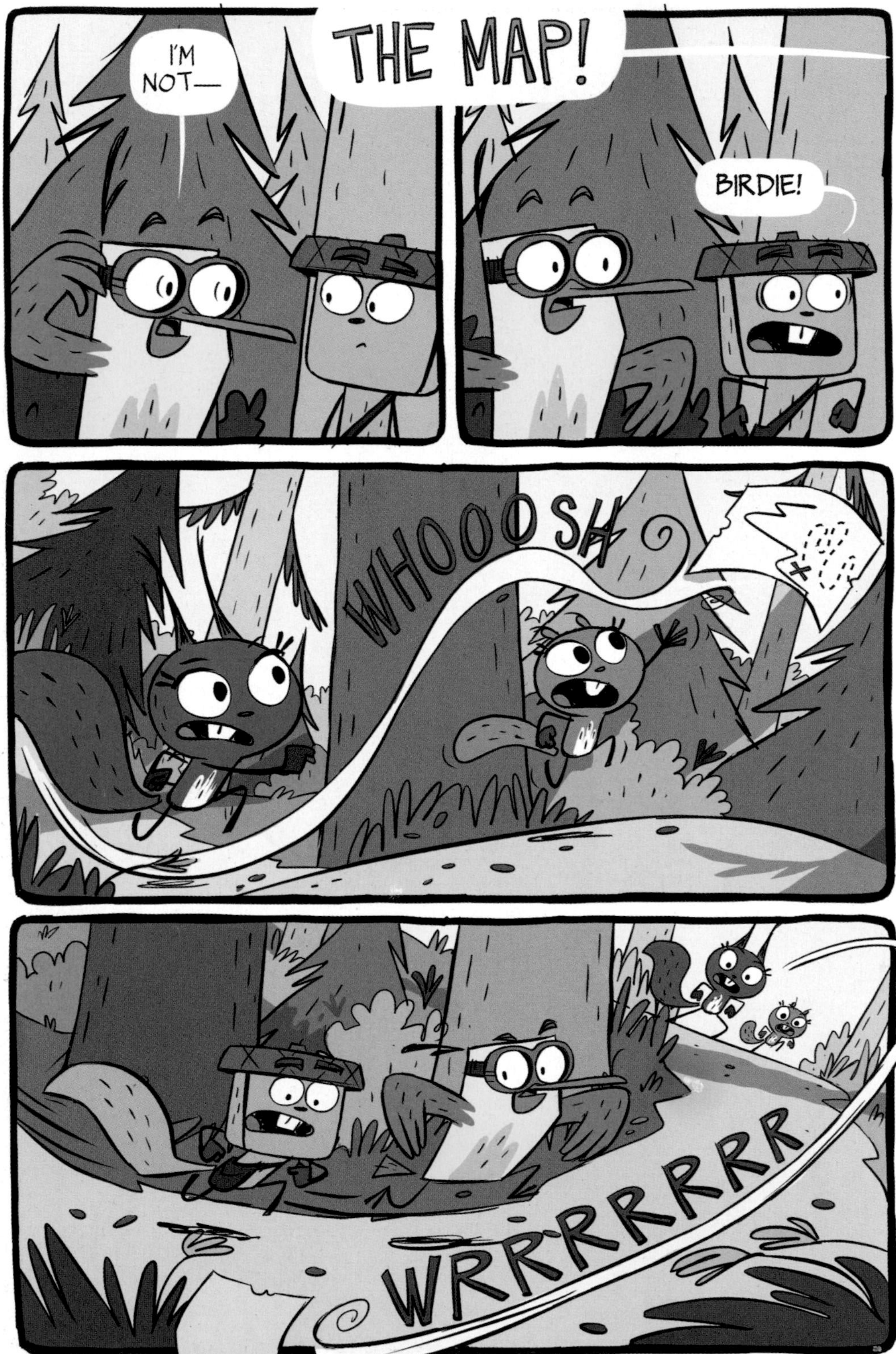

I'M NOT—
THE MAP!
BIRDIE!
WHOOOOSH
WRRRRRRRR

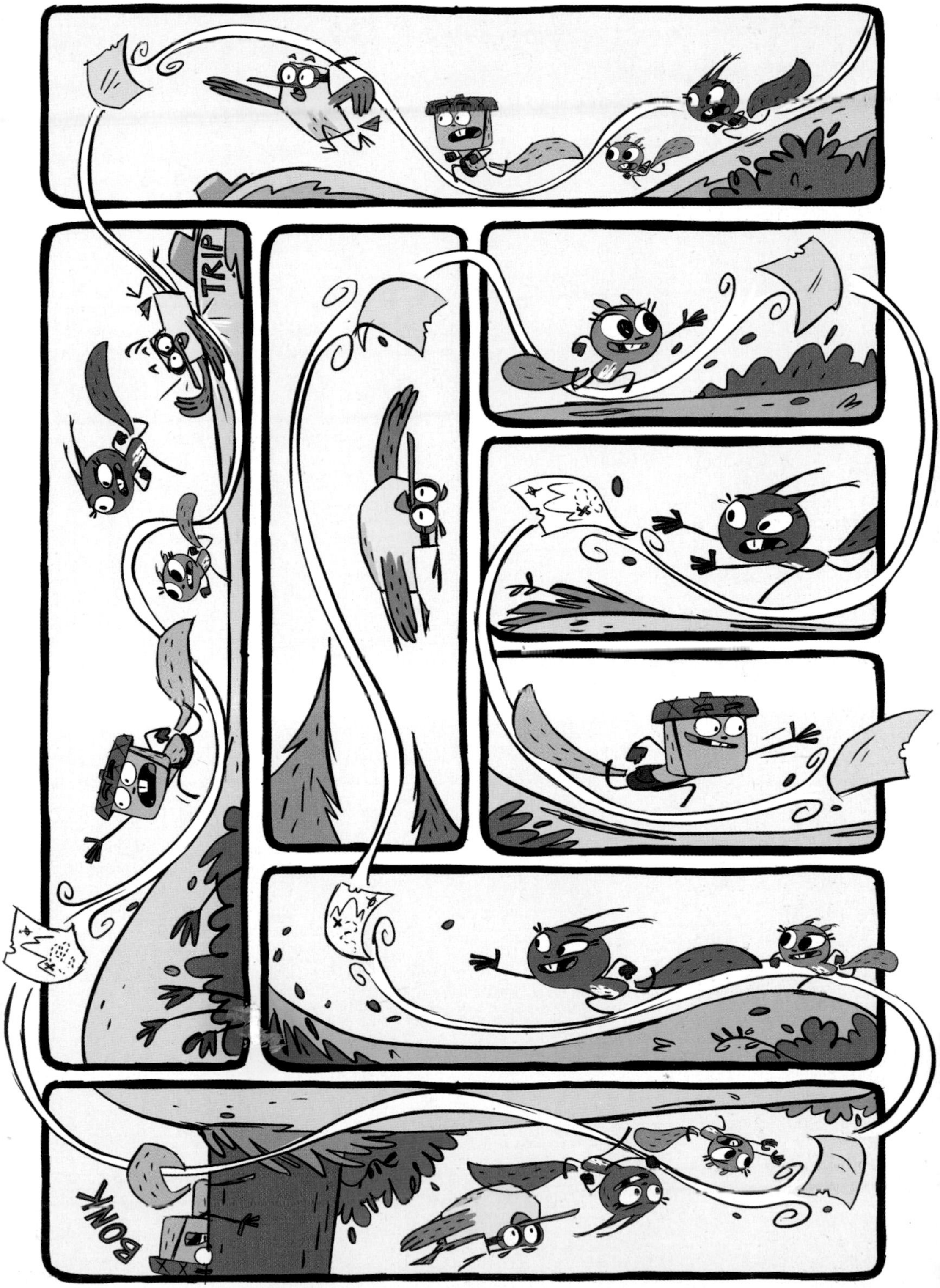

TRIP
BONK

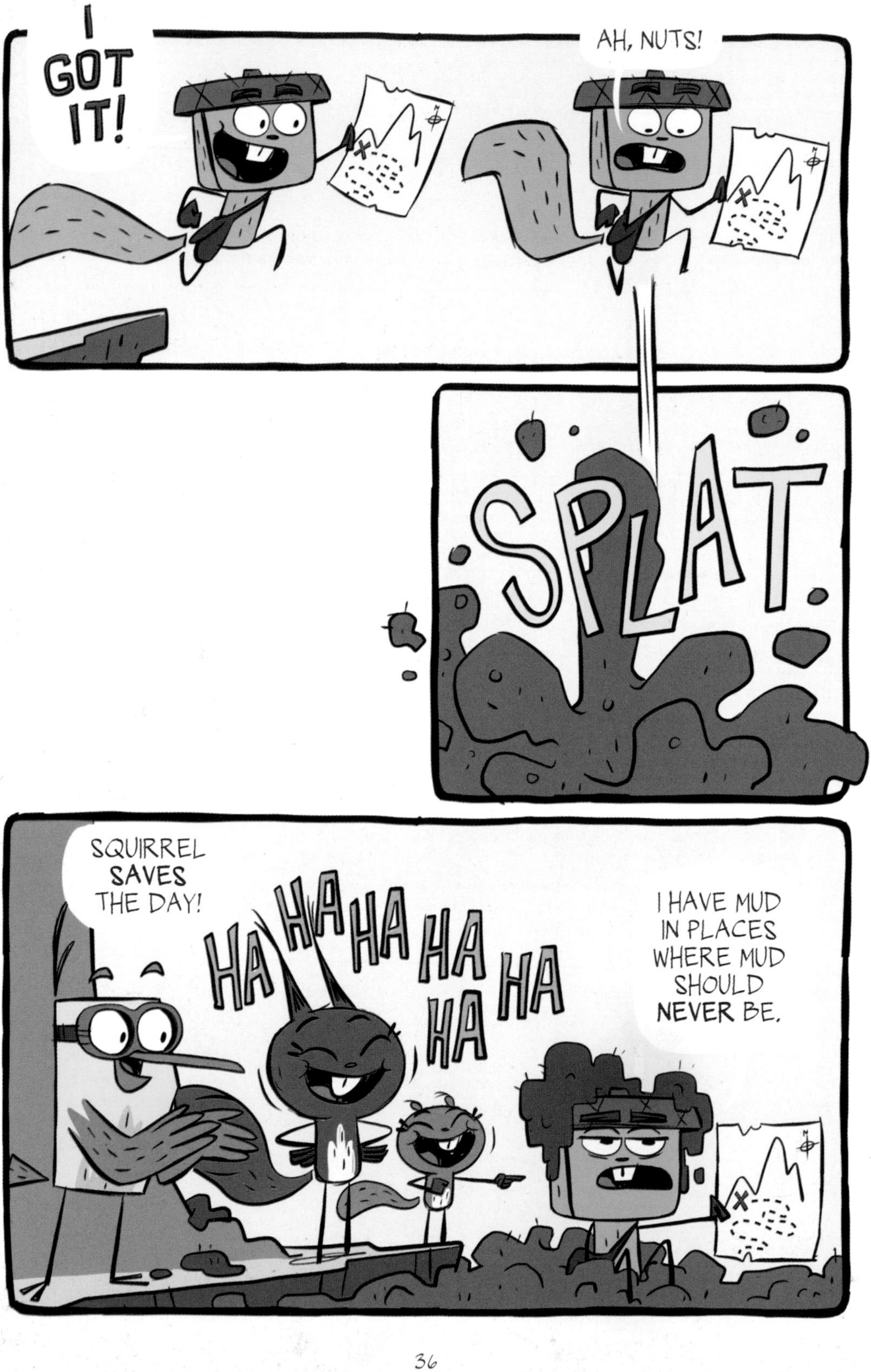
I GOT IT!
AH, NUTS!
SPLAT
SQUIRREL SAVES THE DAY!
HA HA HA HA HA HA HA HA
I HAVE MUD IN PLACES WHERE MUD SHOULD NEVER BE.

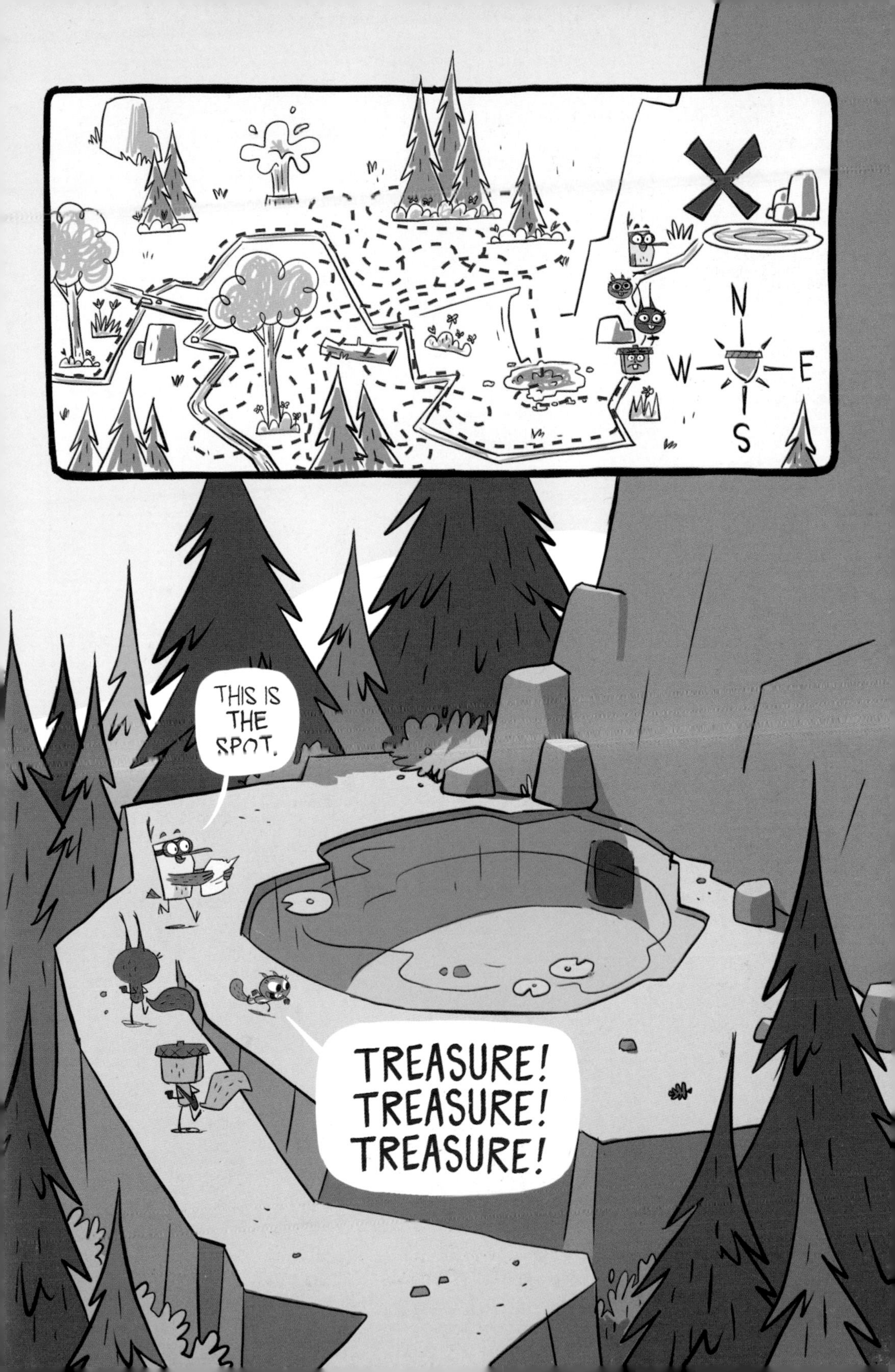
N
W
E
S
THIS IS THE SPOT.
TREASURE! TREASURE! TREASURE!

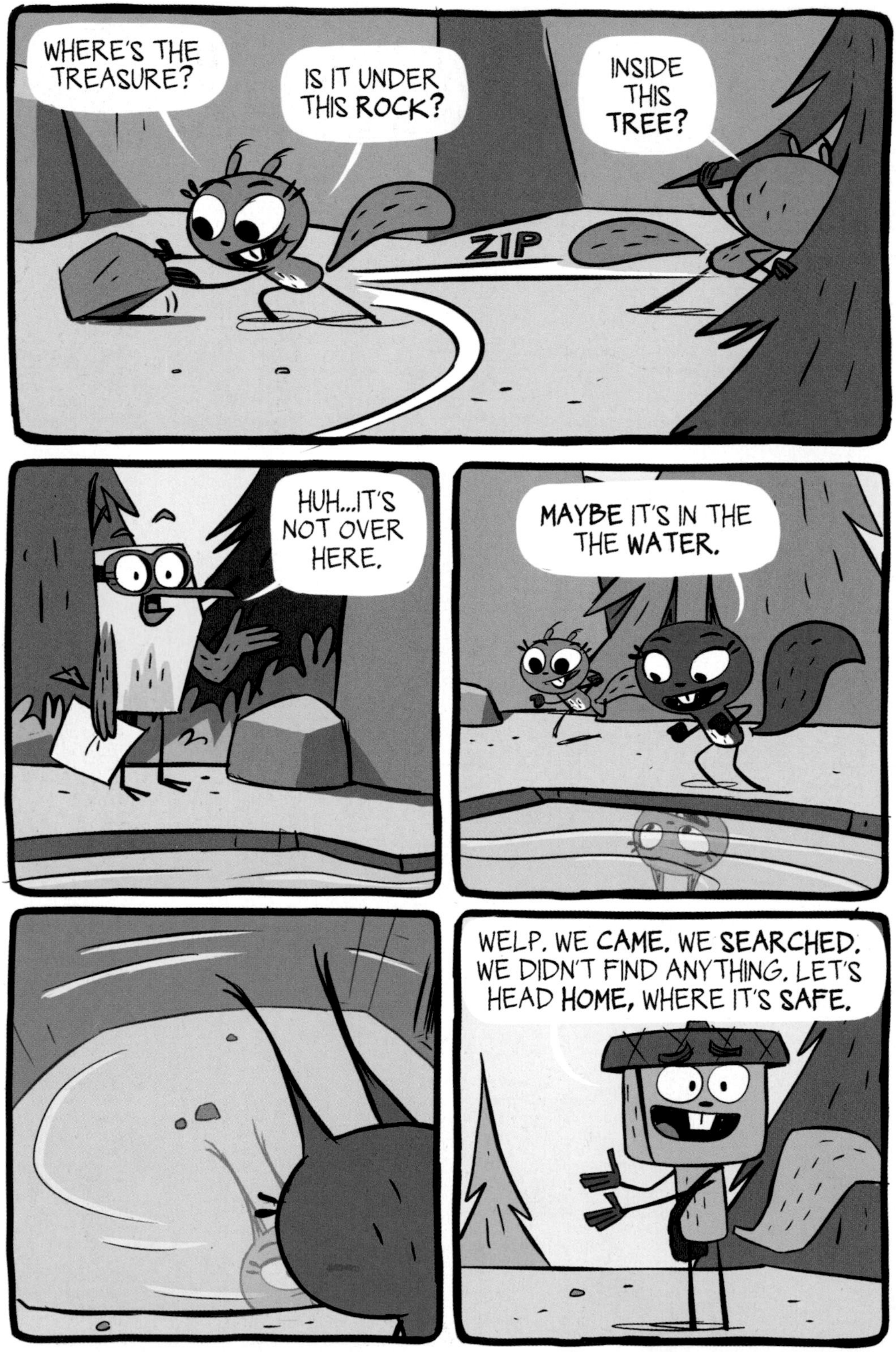
WHERE'S THE TREASURE?
IS IT UNDER THIS ROCK?
INSIDE THIS TREE?
ZIP
HUH...IT'S NOT OVER HERE.
MAYBE IT'S IN THE THE WATER.
WELP. WE CAME. WE SEARCHED. WE DIDN'T FIND ANYTHING. LET'S HEAD HOME, WHERE IT'S SAFE.

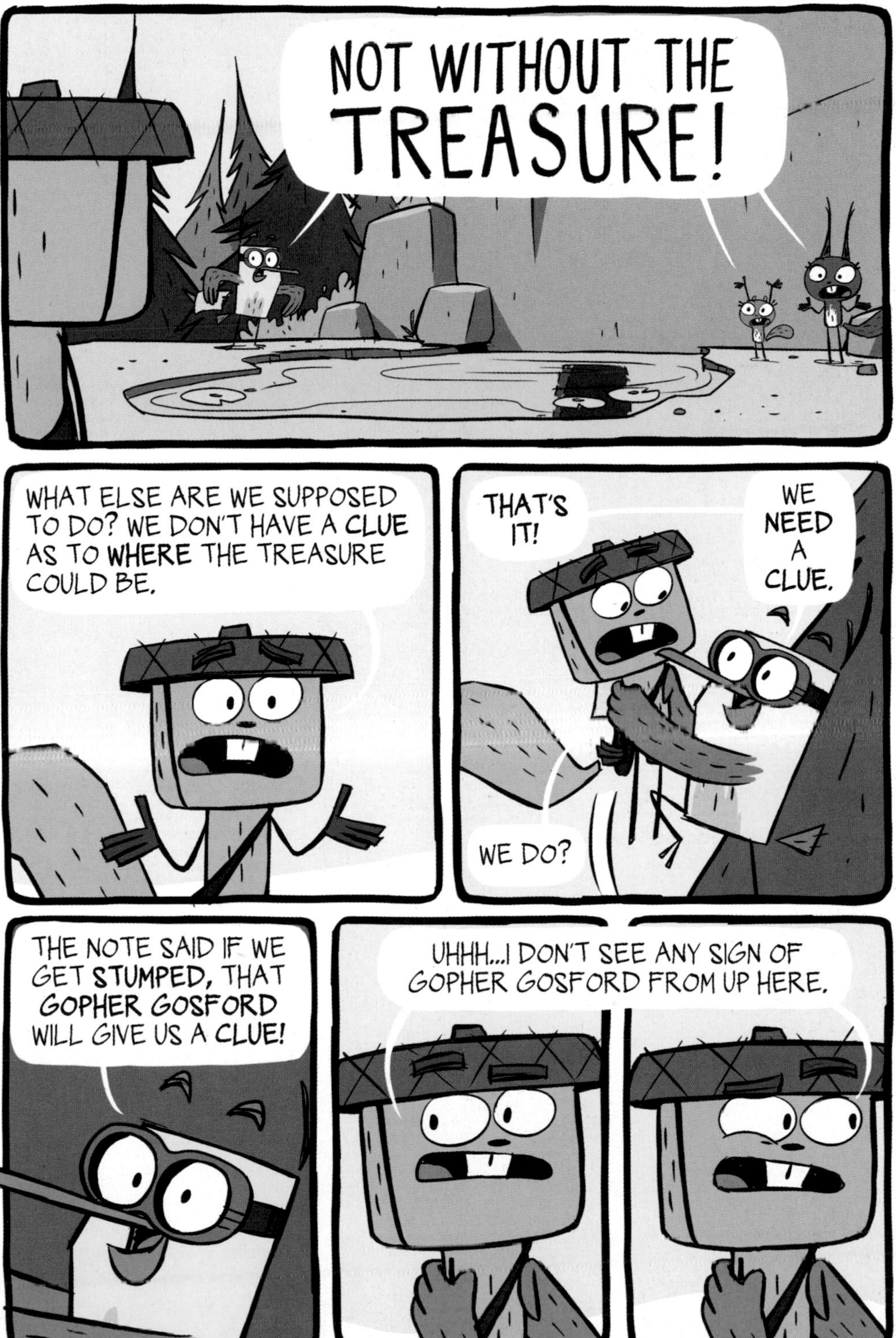
NOT WITHOUT THE TREASURE!
WHAT ELSE ARE WE SUPPOSED TO DO? WE DON'T HAVE A **CLUE** AS TO **WHERE** THE TREASURE COULD BE.
THAT'S IT!
WE **NEED** A **CLUE.**
WE DO?
THE NOTE SAID IF WE GET **STUMPED,** THAT **GOPHER GOSFORD** WILL GIVE US A **CLUE!**
UHHH...I DON'T SEE ANY SIGN OF GOPHER GOSFORD FROM UP HERE.

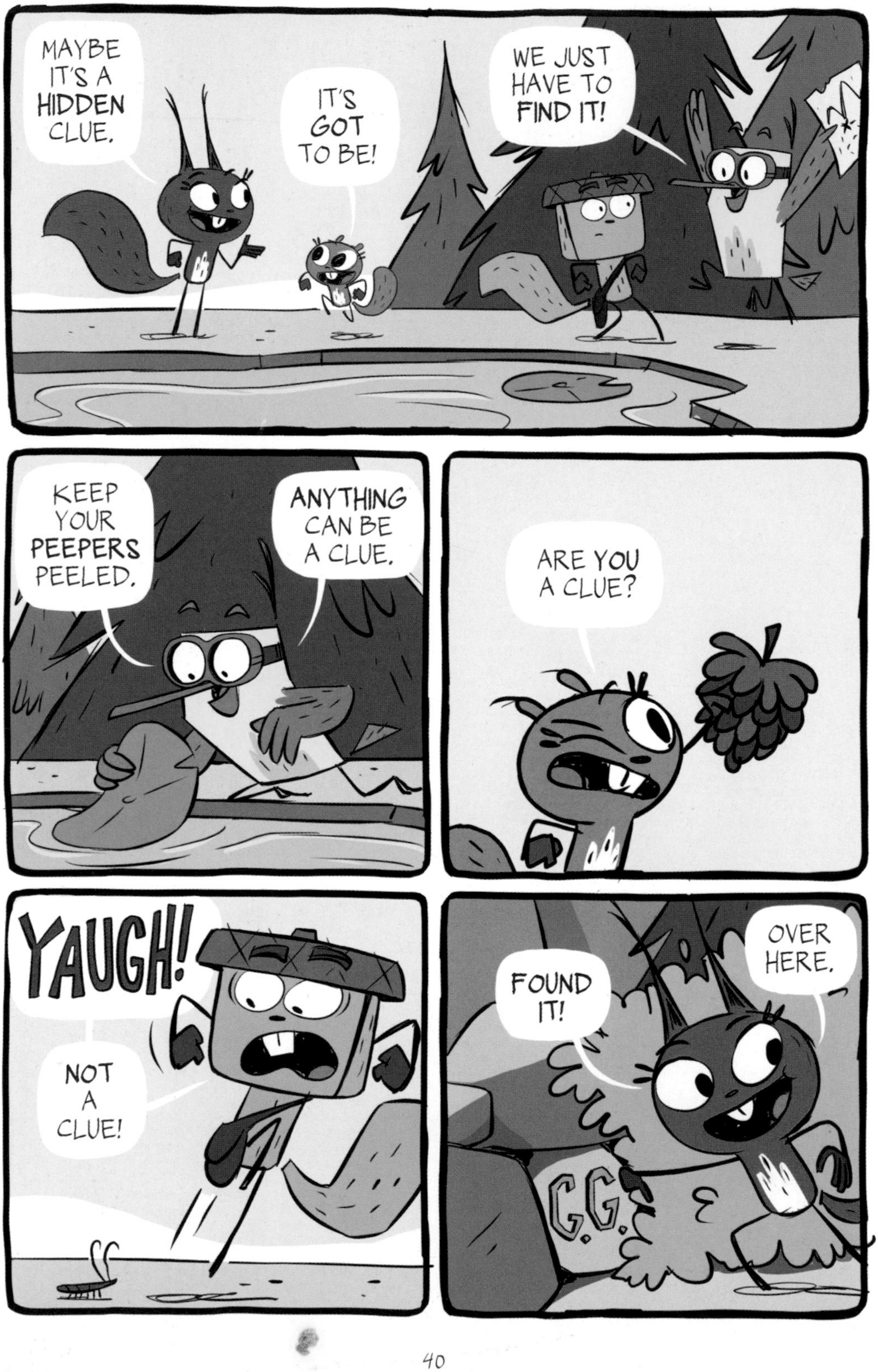
MAYBE IT'S A HIDDEN CLUE.
IT'S GOT TO BE!
WE JUST HAVE TO FIND IT!
KEEP YOUR PEEPERS PEELED.
ANYTHING CAN BE A CLUE.
ARE YOU A CLUE?
YAUGH!
NOT A CLUE!
OVER HERE.
FOUND IT!
G.G.

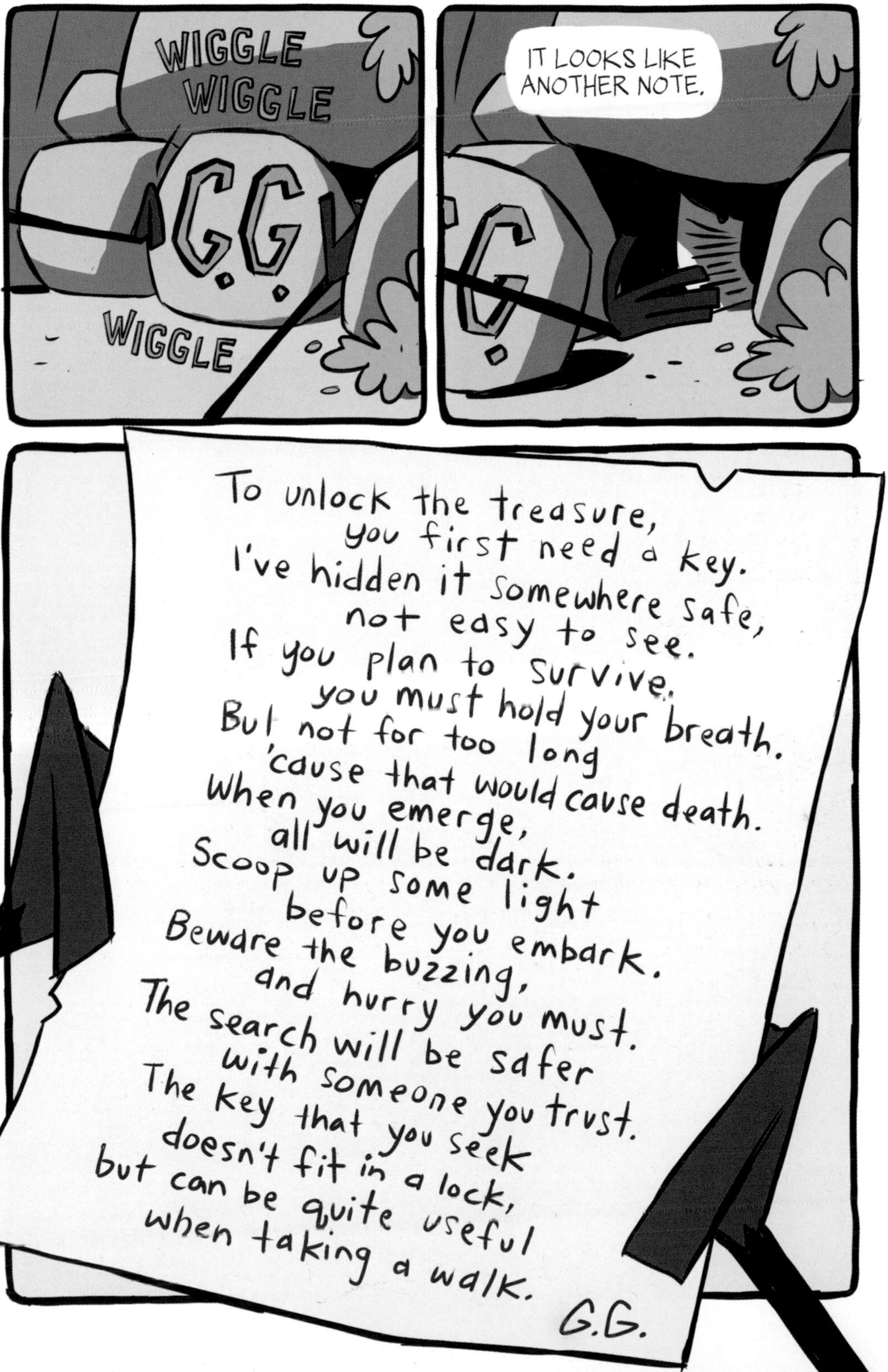
WIGGLE
WIGGLE
G.G.
WIGGLE
IT LOOKS LIKE ANOTHER NOTE.
G.G.
To unlock the treasure,
you first need a key.
I've hidden it somewhere safe,
not easy to see.
If you plan to survive,
you must hold your breath.
But not for too long
'cause that would cause death.
When you emerge,
all will be dark.
Scoop up some light
before you embark.
Beware the buzzing,
and hurry you must.
The search will be safer
with someone you trust.
The key that you seek
doesn't fit in a lock,
but can be quite useful
when taking a walk.
G.G.

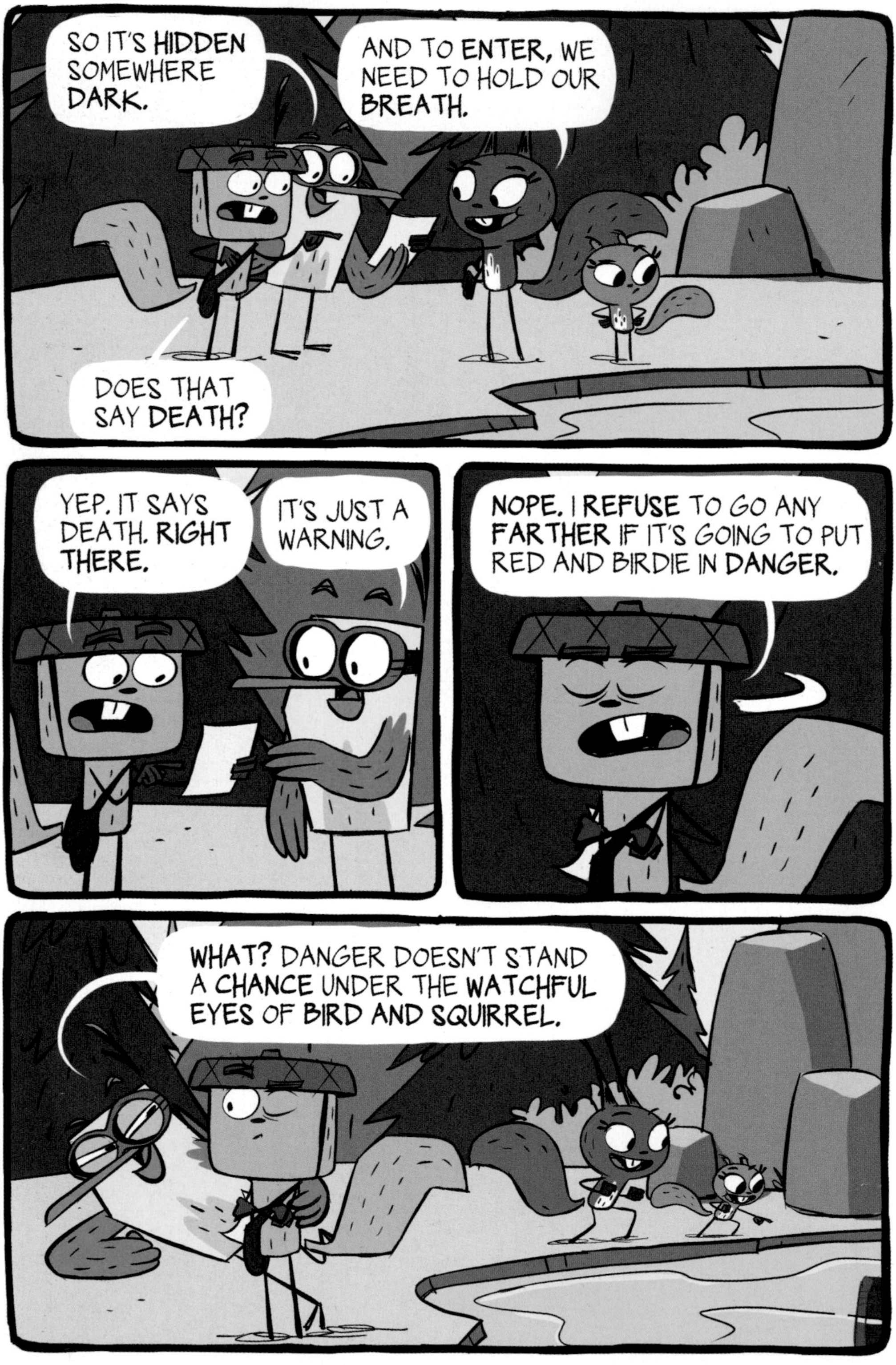
SO IT'S HIDDEN SOMEWHERE DARK.
AND TO ENTER, WE NEED TO HOLD OUR BREATH.
DOES THAT SAY DEATH?
YEP. IT SAYS DEATH. RIGHT THERE.
IT'S JUST A WARNING.
NOPE. I REFUSE TO GO ANY FARTHER IF IT'S GOING TO PUT RED AND BIRDIE IN DANGER.
WHAT? DANGER DOESN'T STAND A CHANCE UNDER THE WATCHFUL EYES OF BIRD AND SQUIRREL.

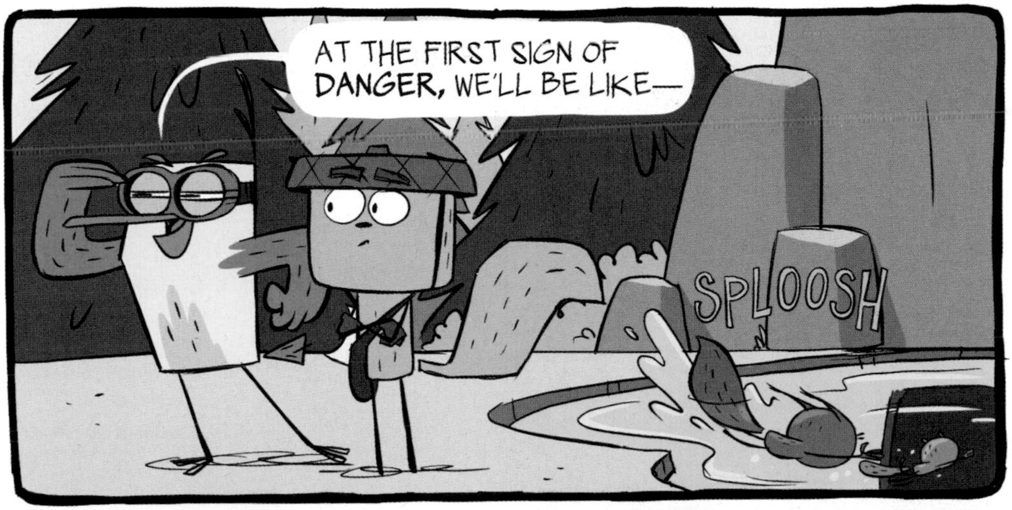
AT THE FIRST SIGN OF
DANGER, WE'LL BE LIKE—
SPLOOSH

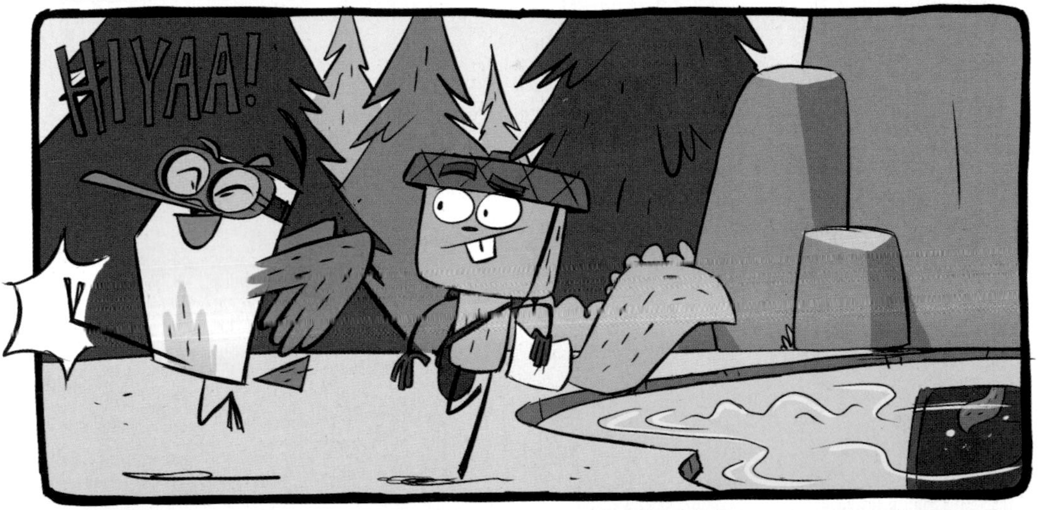
HIYAA!

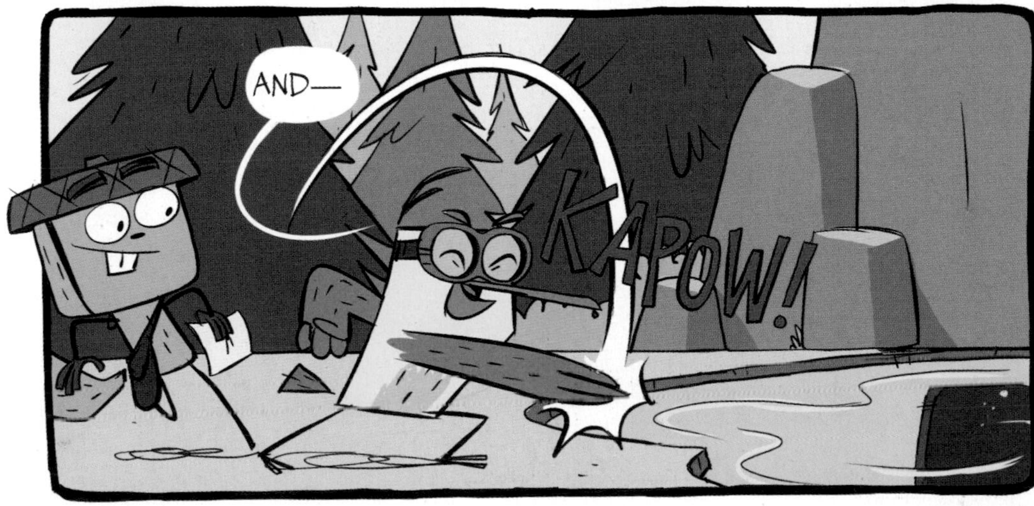
AND—
KAPOW!

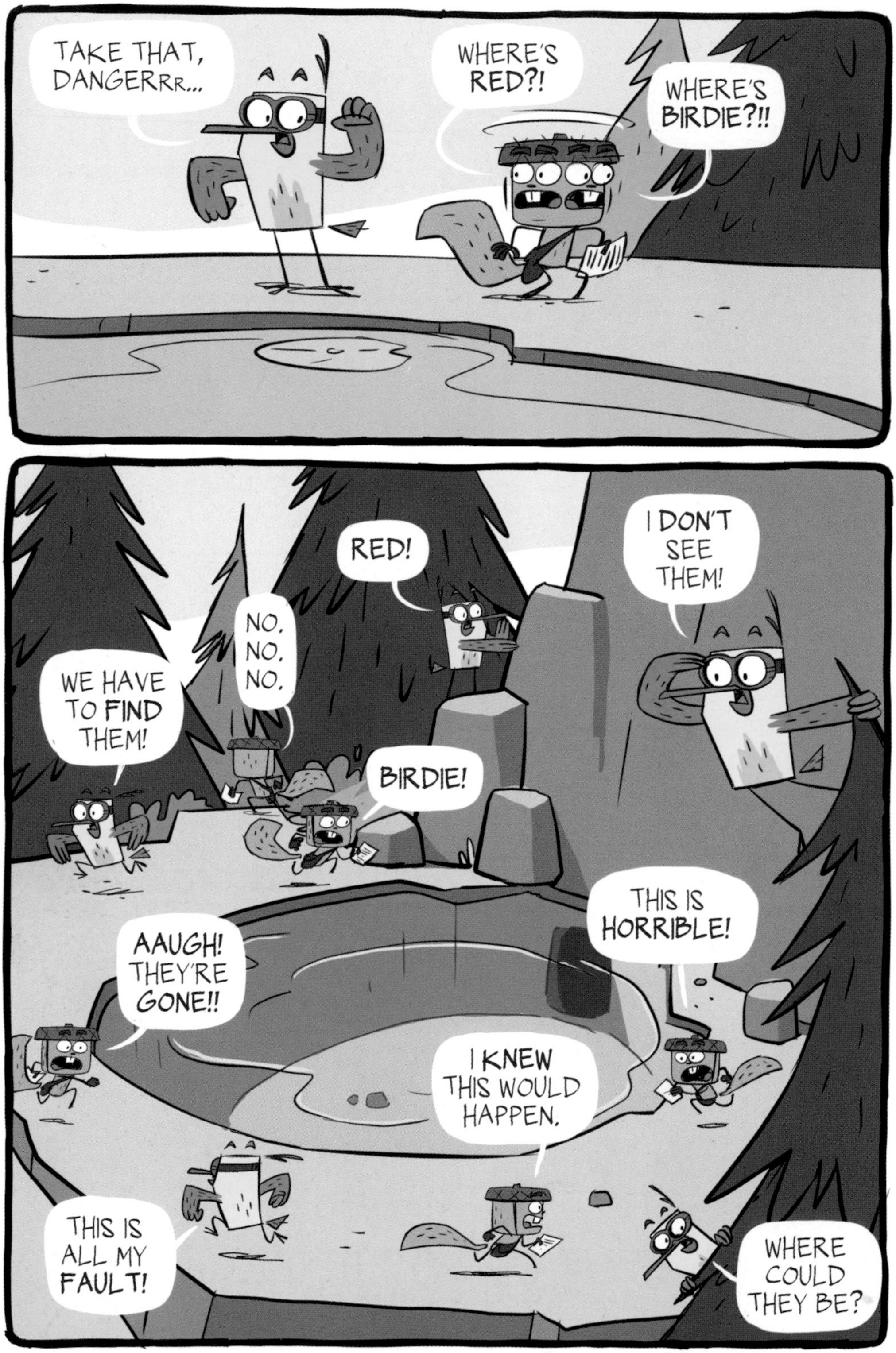
TAKE THAT, DANGERRR...
WHERE'S RED?!
WHERE'S BIRDIE?!!
RED!
I DON'T SEE THEM!
NO. NO. NO.
WE HAVE TO FIND THEM!
BIRDIE!
THIS IS HORRIBLE!
AAUGH! THEY'RE GONE!!
I KNEW THIS WOULD HAPPEN.
THIS IS ALL MY FAULT!
WHERE COULD THEY BE?

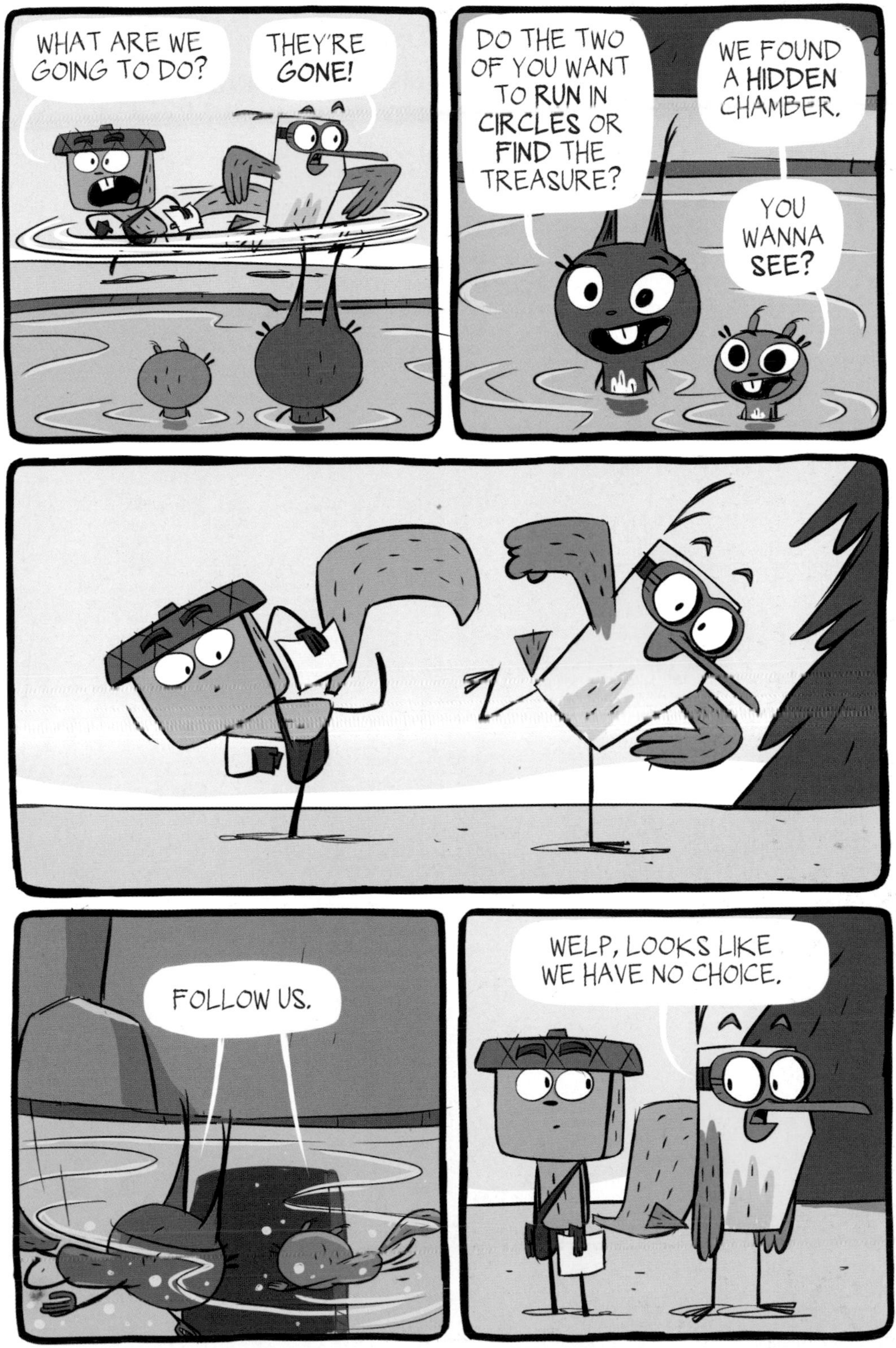
WHAT ARE WE GOING TO DO?
THEY'RE GONE!
DO THE TWO OF YOU WANT TO RUN IN CIRCLES OR FIND THE TREASURE?
WE FOUND A HIDDEN CHAMBER.
YOU WANNA SEE?
FOLLOW US.
WELP, LOOKS LIKE WE HAVE NO CHOICE.

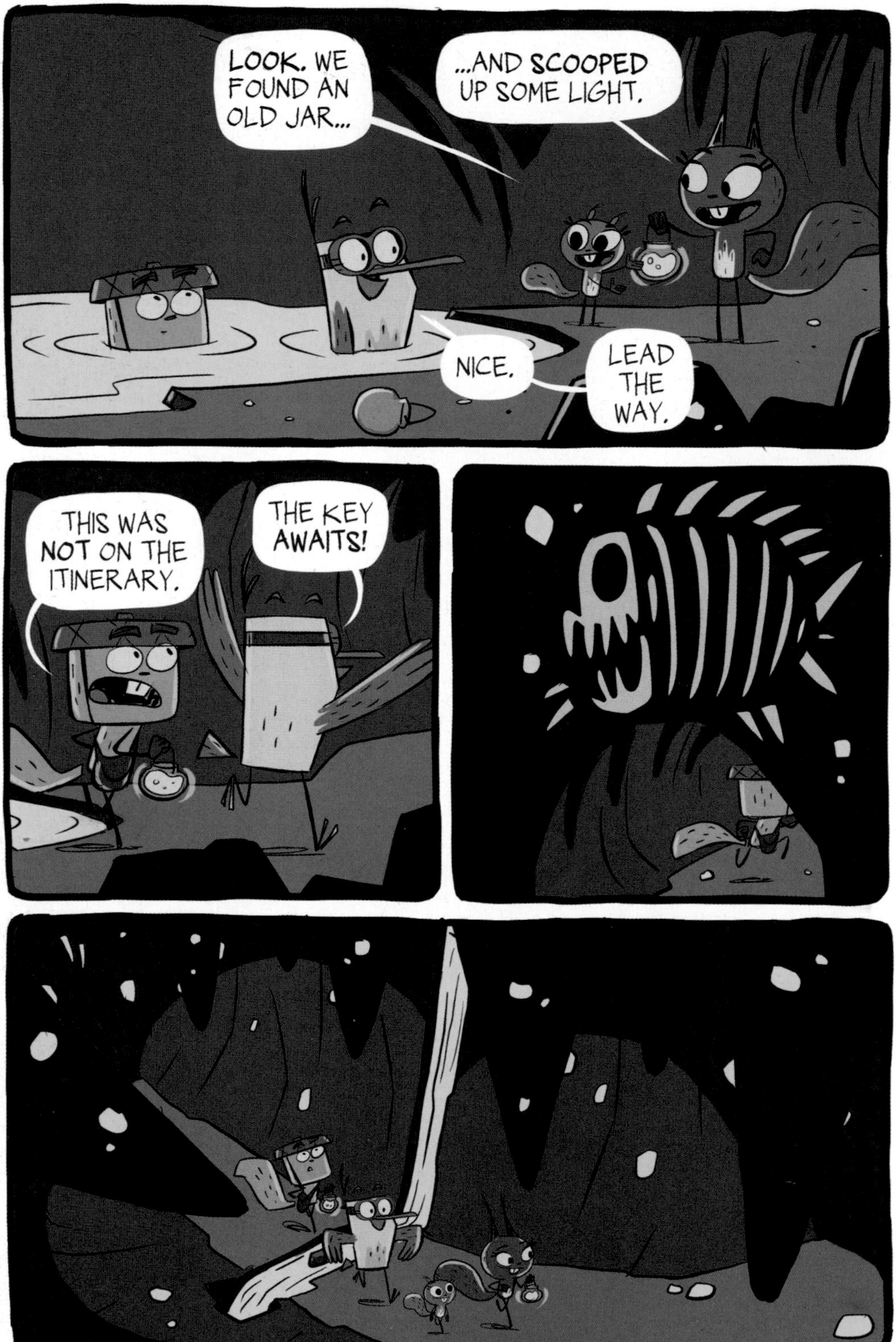
LOOK. WE FOUND AN OLD JAR...
...AND SCOOPED UP SOME LIGHT.
NICE.
LEAD THE WAY.
THIS WAS NOT ON THE ITINERARY.
THE KEY AWAITS!

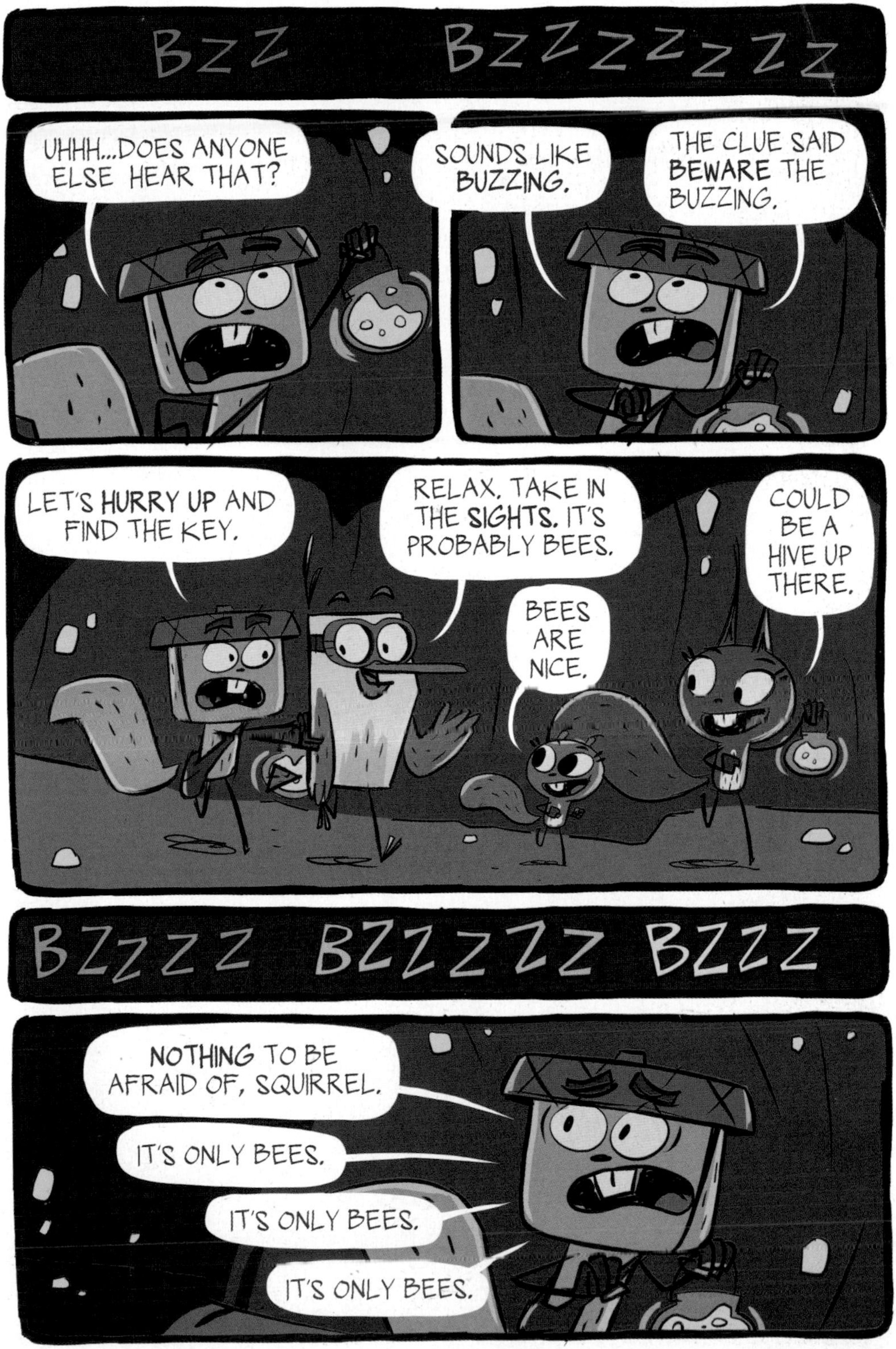
BZZ BZZZZZZZZ
UHHH...DOES ANYONE ELSE HEAR THAT?
SOUNDS LIKE BUZZING.
THE CLUE SAID BEWARE THE BUZZING.
LET'S HURRY UP AND FIND THE KEY.
RELAX. TAKE IN THE SIGHTS. IT'S PROBABLY BEES.
COULD BE A HIVE UP THERE.
BEES ARE NICE.
BZZZZ BZZZZZ BZZZ
NOTHING TO BE AFRAID OF, SQUIRREL.
IT'S ONLY BEES.
IT'S ONLY BEES.
IT'S ONLY BEES.

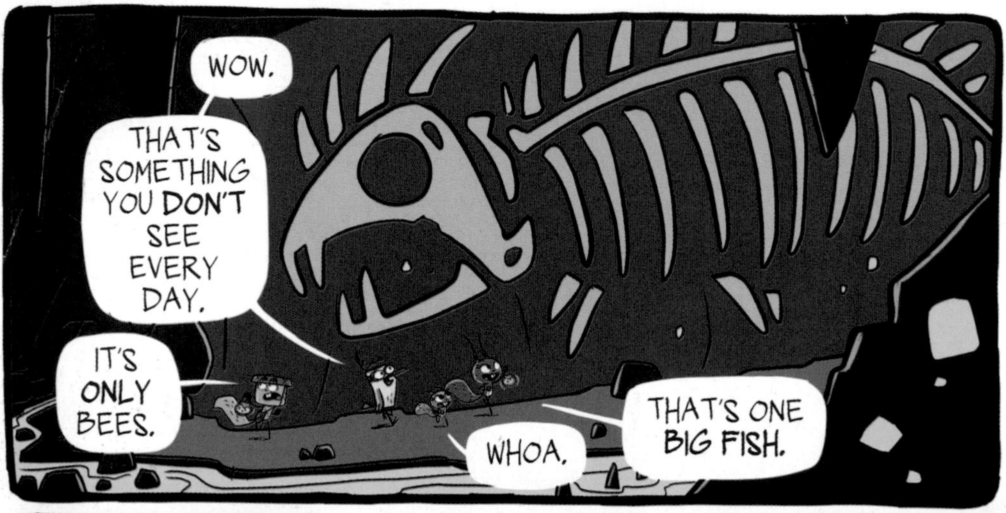
WOW.
THAT'S SOMETHING YOU DON'T SEE EVERY DAY.
IT'S ONLY BEES.
WHOA.
THAT'S ONE BIG FISH.

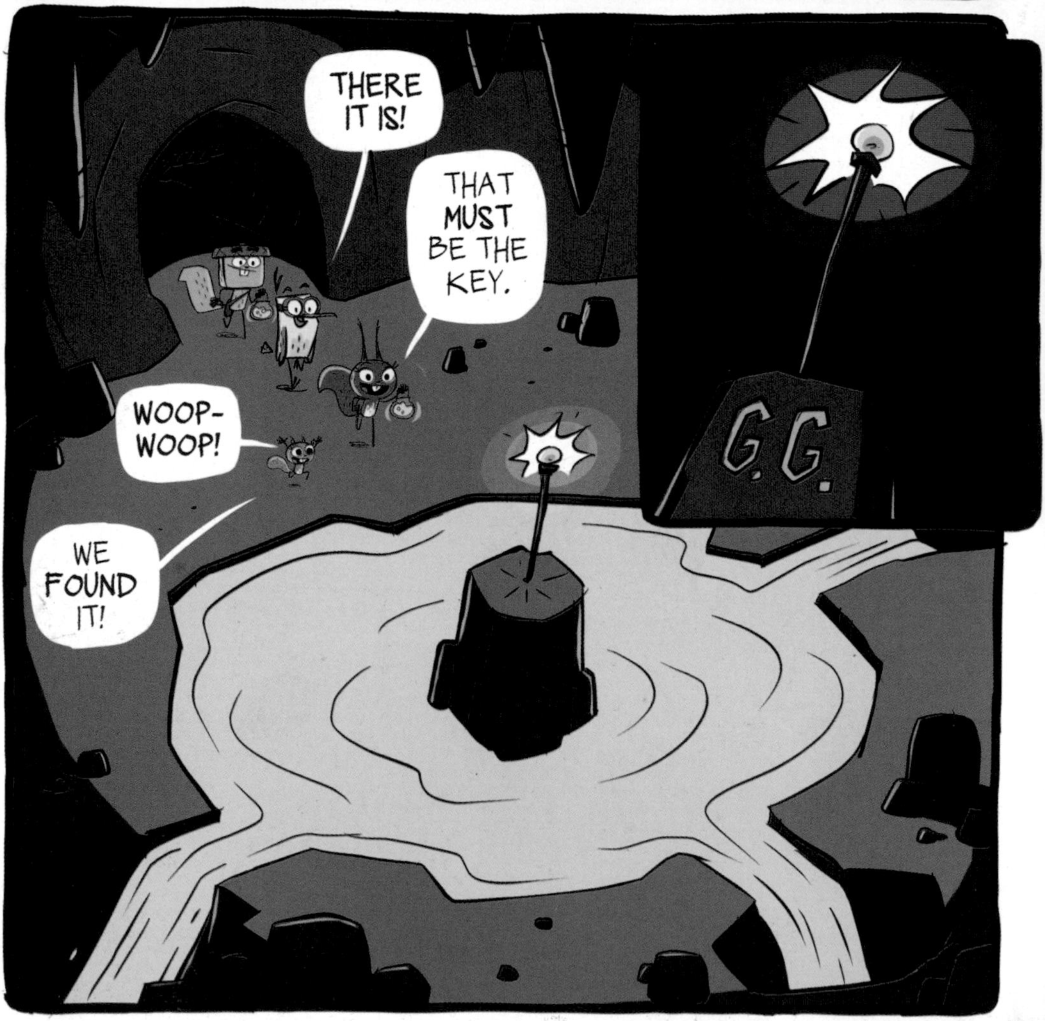
THERE IT IS!
THAT MUST BE THE KEY.
WOOP-WOOP!
WE FOUND IT!
G.G.

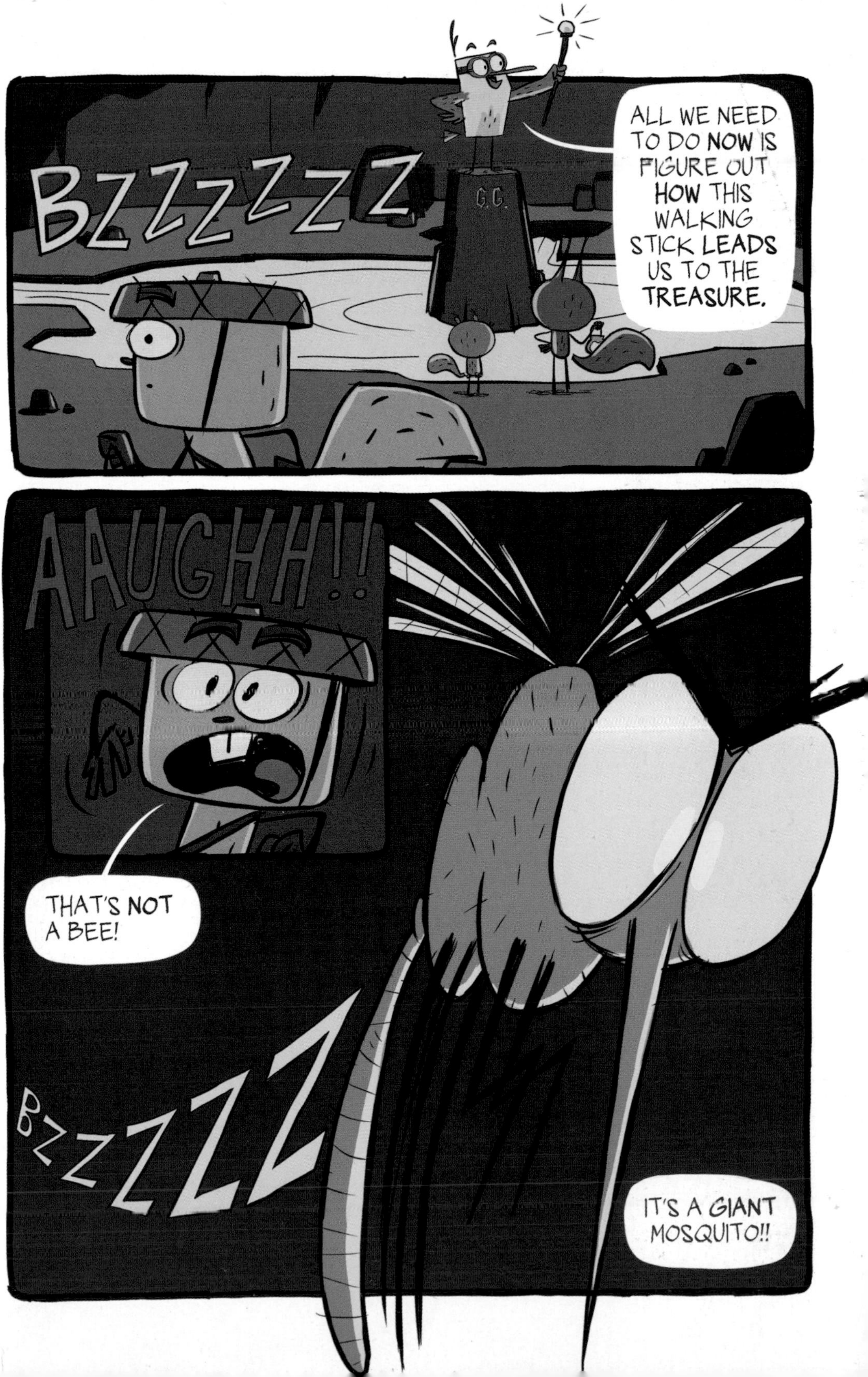
ALL WE NEED TO DO NOW IS FIGURE OUT HOW THIS WALKING STICK LEADS US TO THE TREASURE.
BZZZZZZ
G.C.
AAUGHH!!
THAT'S NOT A BEE!
BZZZZZ
IT'S A GIANT MOSQUITO!!

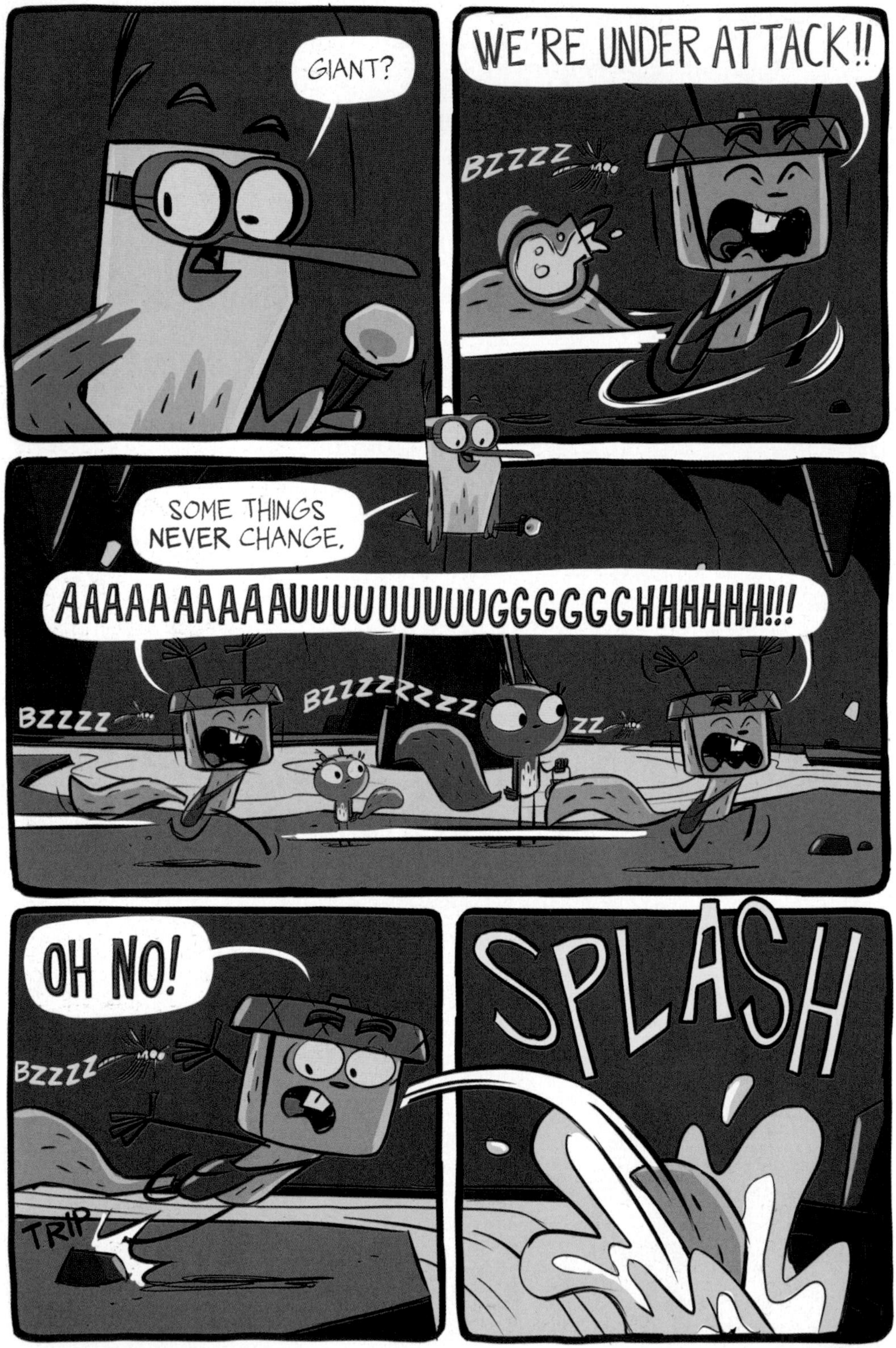
GIANT?
WE'RE UNDER ATTACK!!
BZZZZ
SOME THINGS NEVER CHANGE.
AAAAAAAAAAUUUUUUUUUGGGGGHHHHHH!!!
BZZZZ
BZZZZZZZZ
ZZ
OH NO!
BZZZZ
TRIP
SPLASH

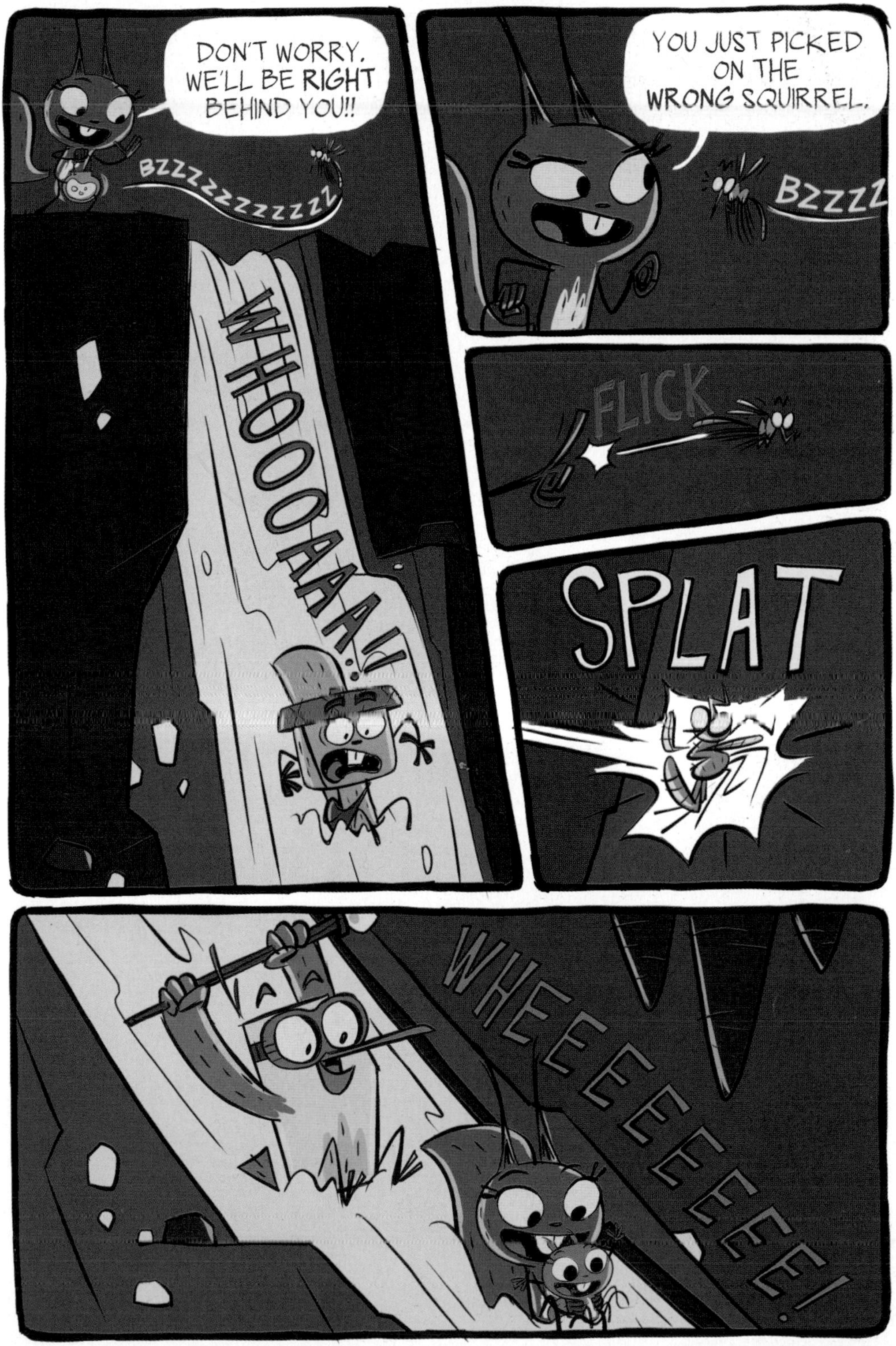
DON'T WORRY. WE'LL BE RIGHT BEHIND YOU!!
BZZZZZZZZZZZZ
WHOOOAAAA!
YOU JUST PICKED ON THE WRONG SQUIRREL.
BZZZZ
FLICK
SPLAT
WHEEEEEEEE!

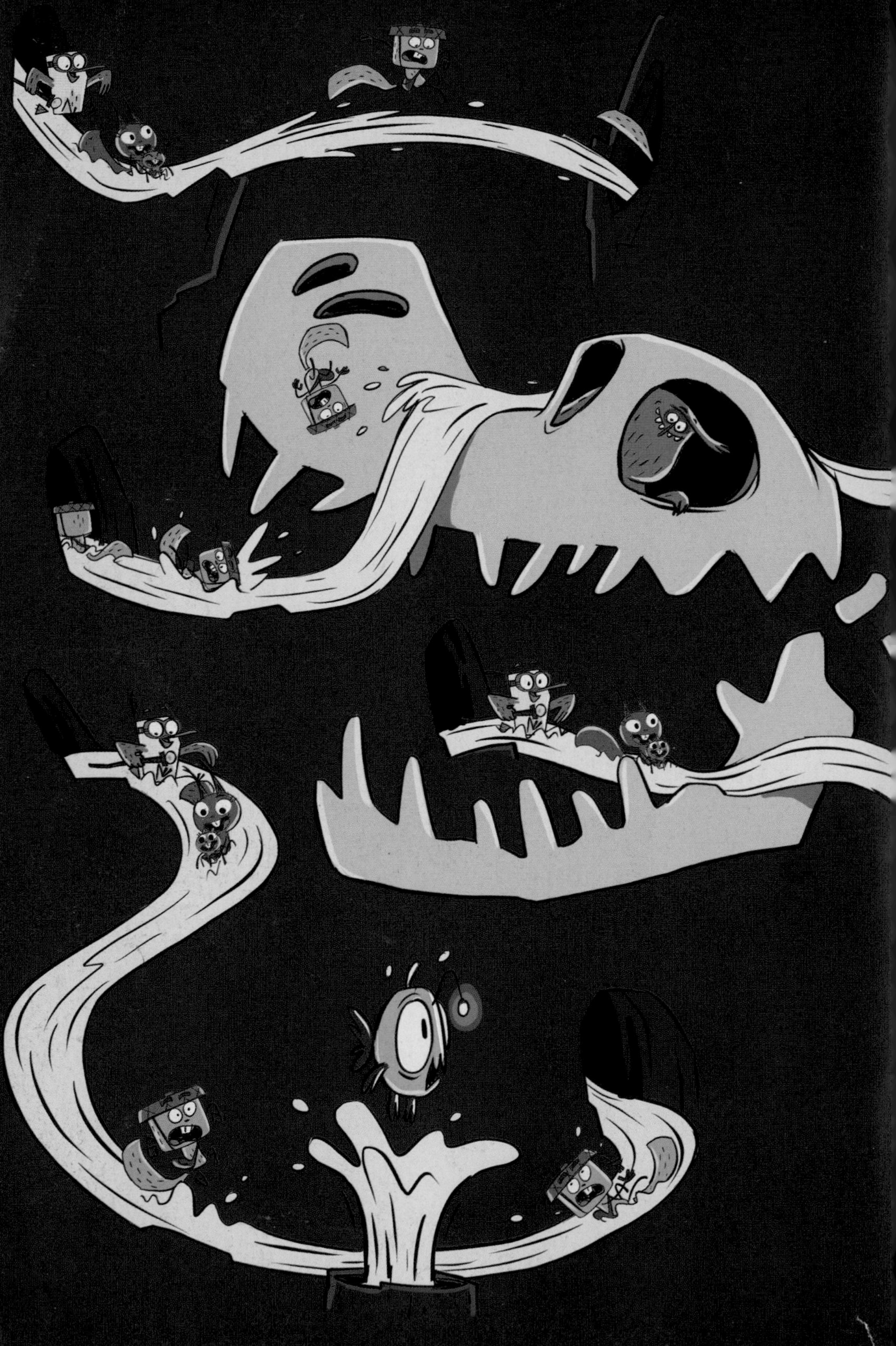

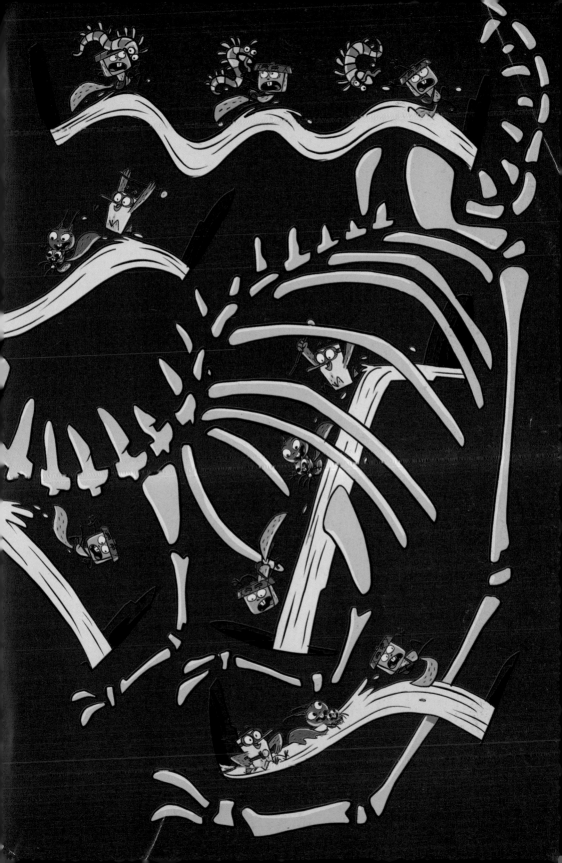

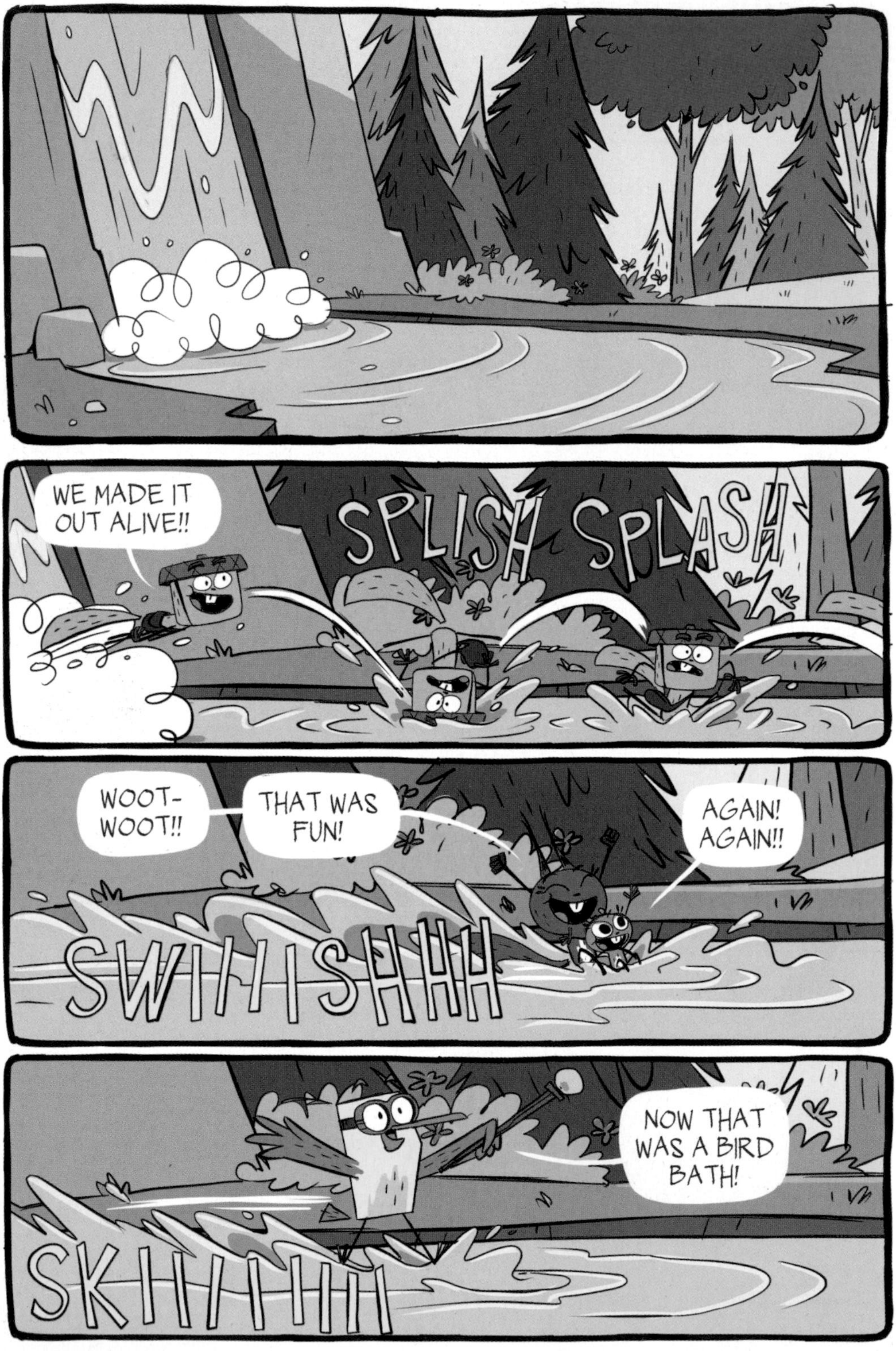
WE MADE IT OUT ALIVE!!
SPLISH SPLASH
WOOT-WOOT!!
THAT WAS FUN!
AGAIN! AGAIN!!
SWIIIISHHH
NOW THAT WAS A BIRD BATH!
SKIIIIIIII

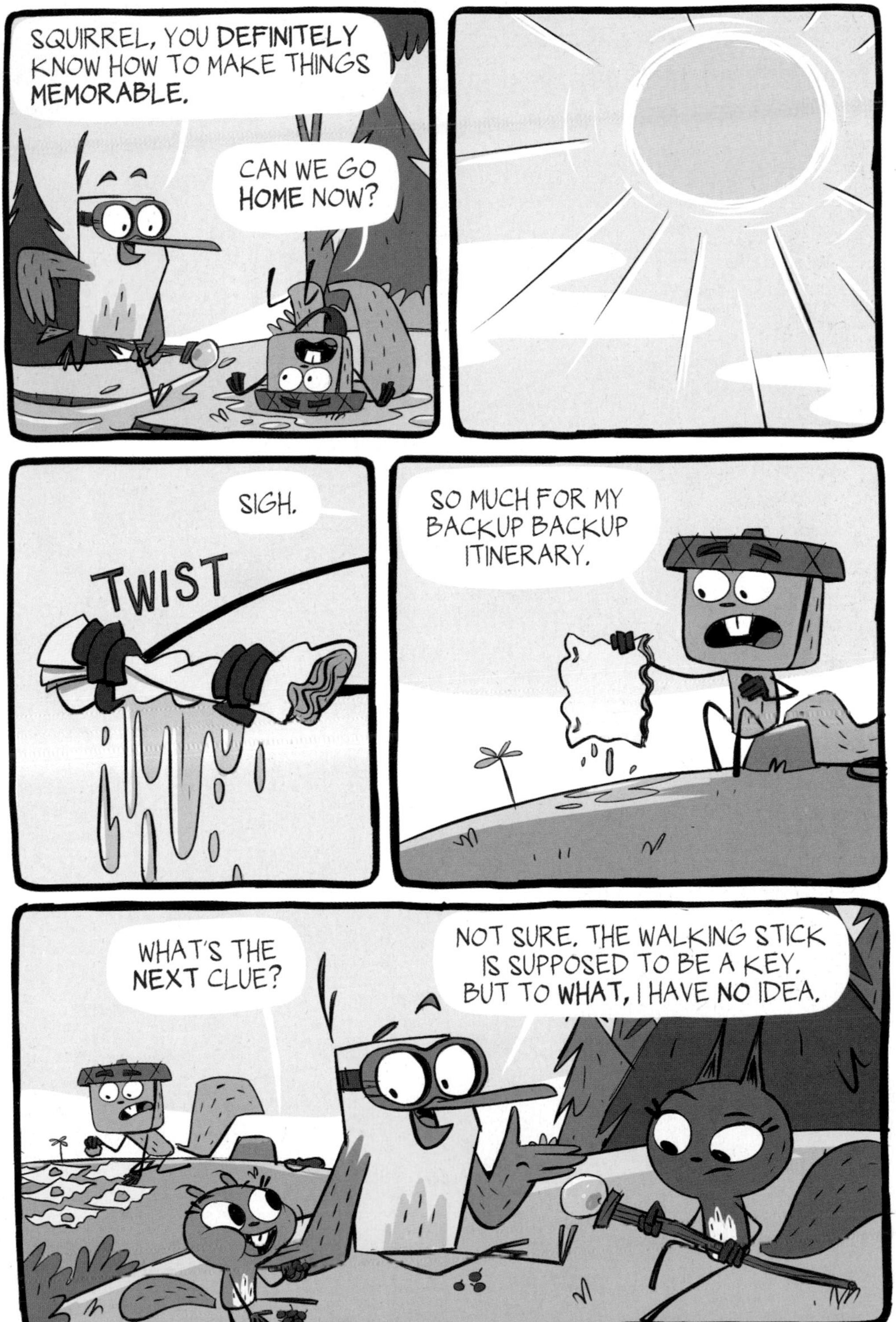
SQUIRREL, YOU DEFINITELY KNOW HOW TO MAKE THINGS MEMORABLE.
CAN WE GO HOME NOW?
SIGH.
TWIST
SO MUCH FOR MY BACKUP BACKUP ITINERARY.
WHAT'S THE NEXT CLUE?
NOT SURE. THE WALKING STICK IS SUPPOSED TO BE A KEY. BUT TO WHAT, I HAVE NO IDEA.

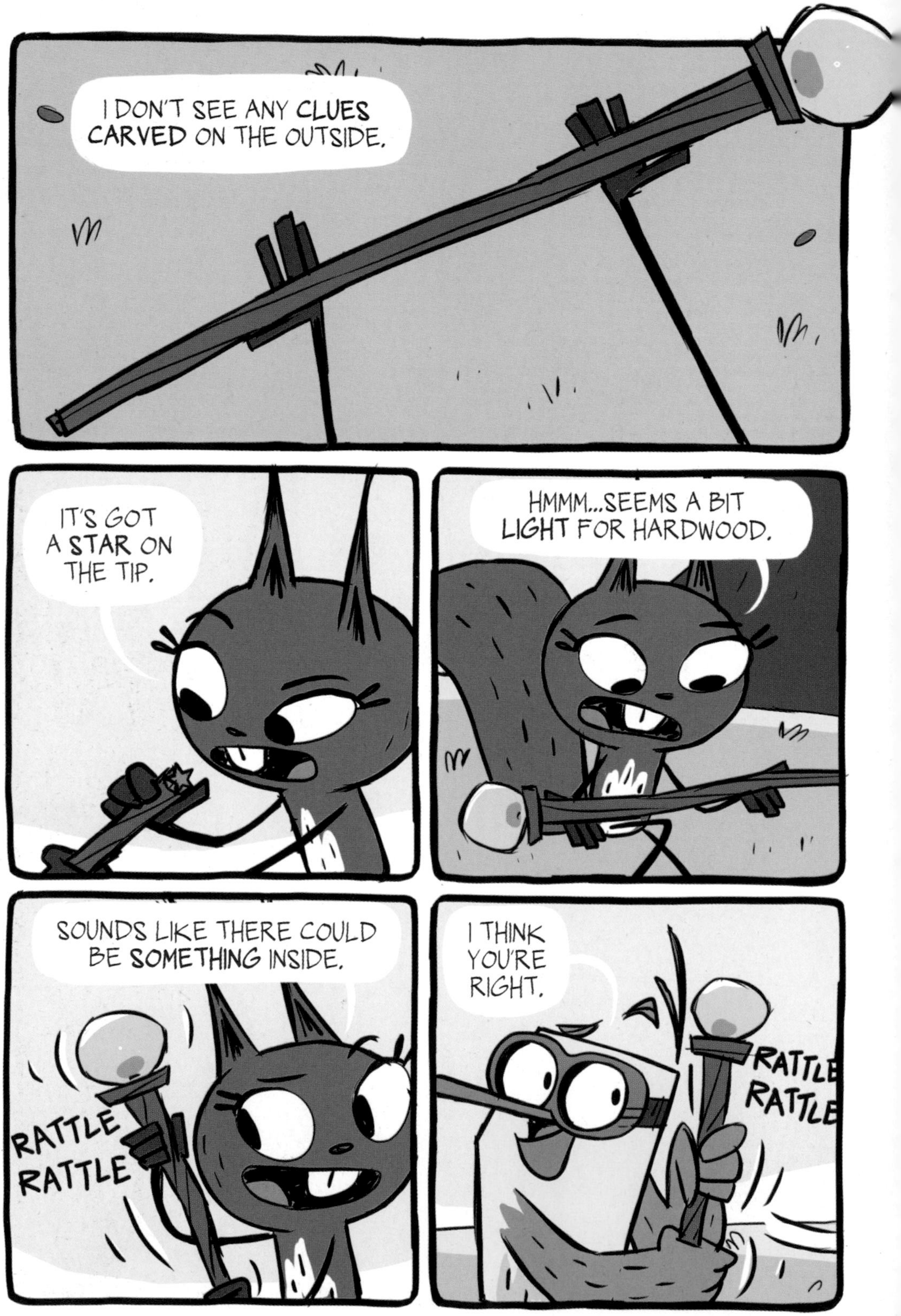
I DON'T SEE ANY CLUES CARVED ON THE OUTSIDE.
IT'S GOT A STAR ON THE TIP.
HMMM...SEEMS A BIT LIGHT FOR HARDWOOD.
SOUNDS LIKE THERE COULD BE SOMETHING INSIDE.
RATTLE RATTLE
I THINK YOU'RE RIGHT.
RATTLE RATTLE

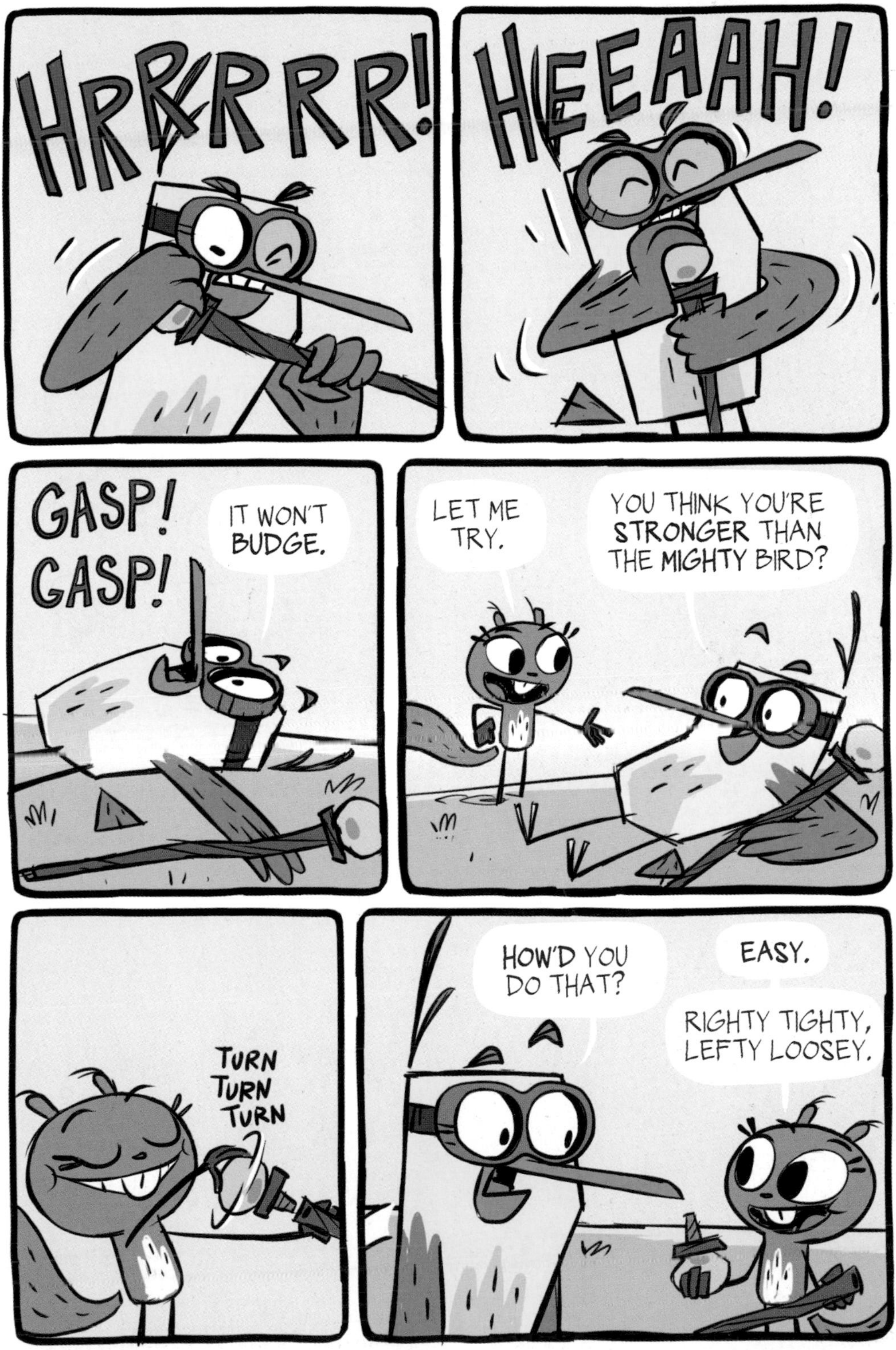
HRRRRRR!
HEEAAH!
GASP! GASP!
IT WON'T BUDGE.
LET ME TRY.
YOU THINK YOU'RE STRONGER THAN THE MIGHTY BIRD?
TURN TURN TURN
HOW'D YOU DO THAT?
EASY.
RIGHTY TIGHTY, LEFTY LOOSEY.

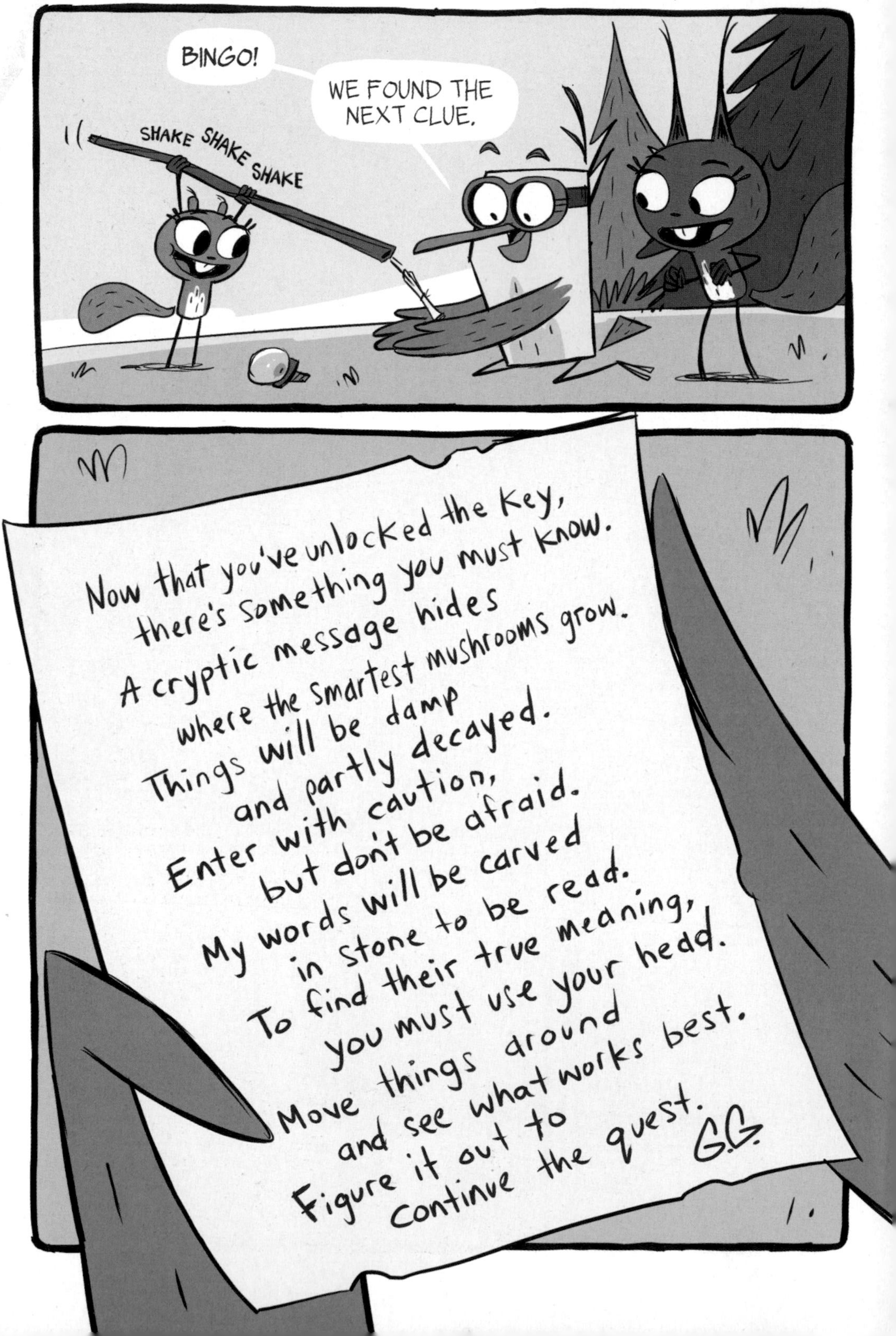

BINGO!
WE FOUND THE NEXT CLUE.
SHAKE SHAKE SHAKE
Now that you've unlocked the key,
there's something you must know.
A cryptic message hides
where the smartest mushrooms grow.
Things will be damp
and partly decayed.
Enter with caution,
but don't be afraid.
My words will be carved
in stone to be read.
To find their true meaning,
you must use your head.
Move things around
and see what works best.
Figure it out to
continue the quest.
G.G.

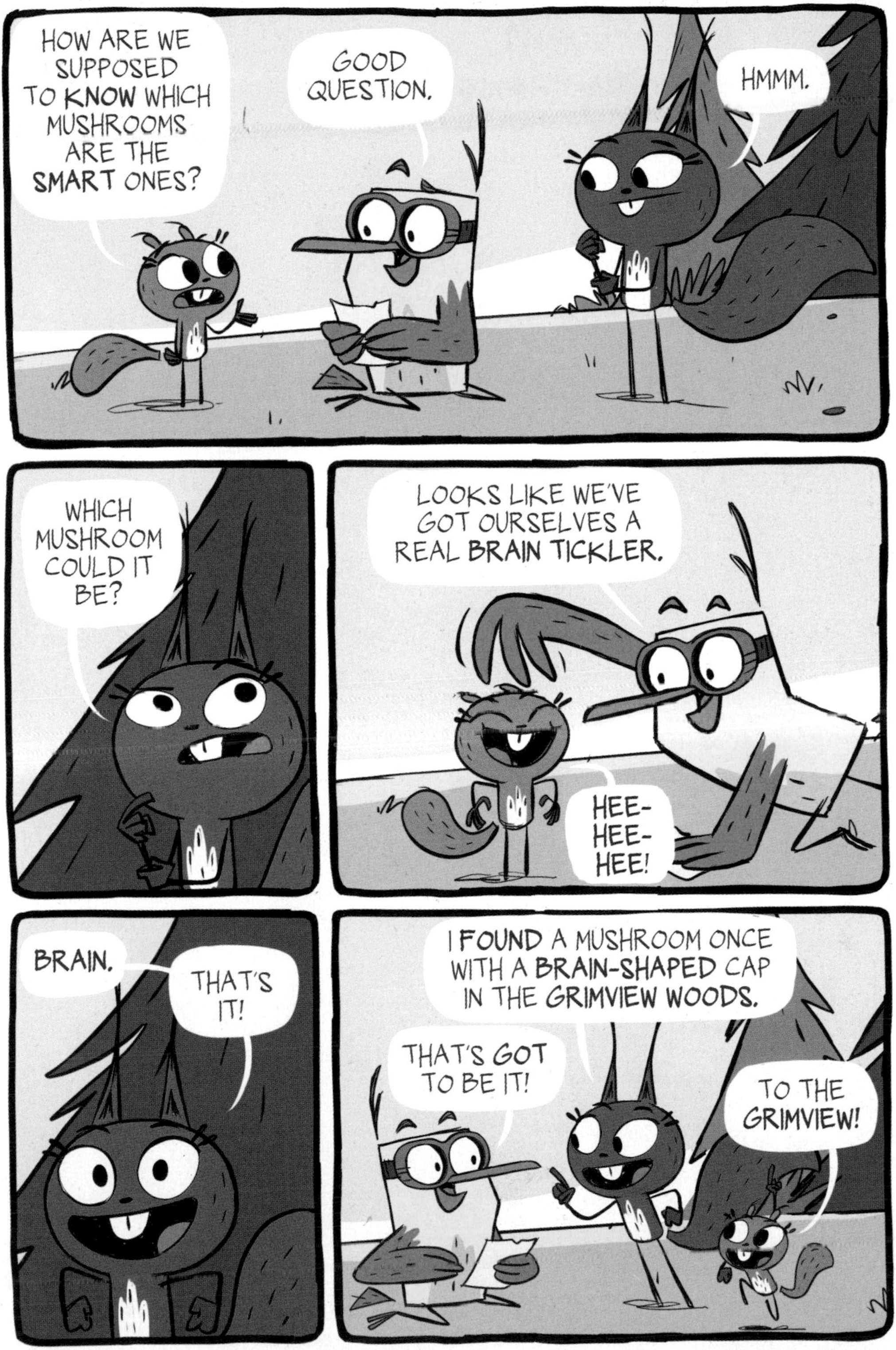

HOW ARE WE SUPPOSED TO KNOW WHICH MUSHROOMS ARE THE SMART ONES?
GOOD QUESTION.
HMMM.
WHICH MUSHROOM COULD IT BE?
LOOKS LIKE WE'VE GOT OURSELVES A REAL BRAIN TICKLER.
HEE-HEE-HEE!
BRAIN.
THAT'S IT!
I FOUND A MUSHROOM ONCE WITH A BRAIN-SHAPED CAP IN THE GRIMVIEW WOODS.
THAT'S GOT TO BE IT!
TO THE GRIMVIEW!

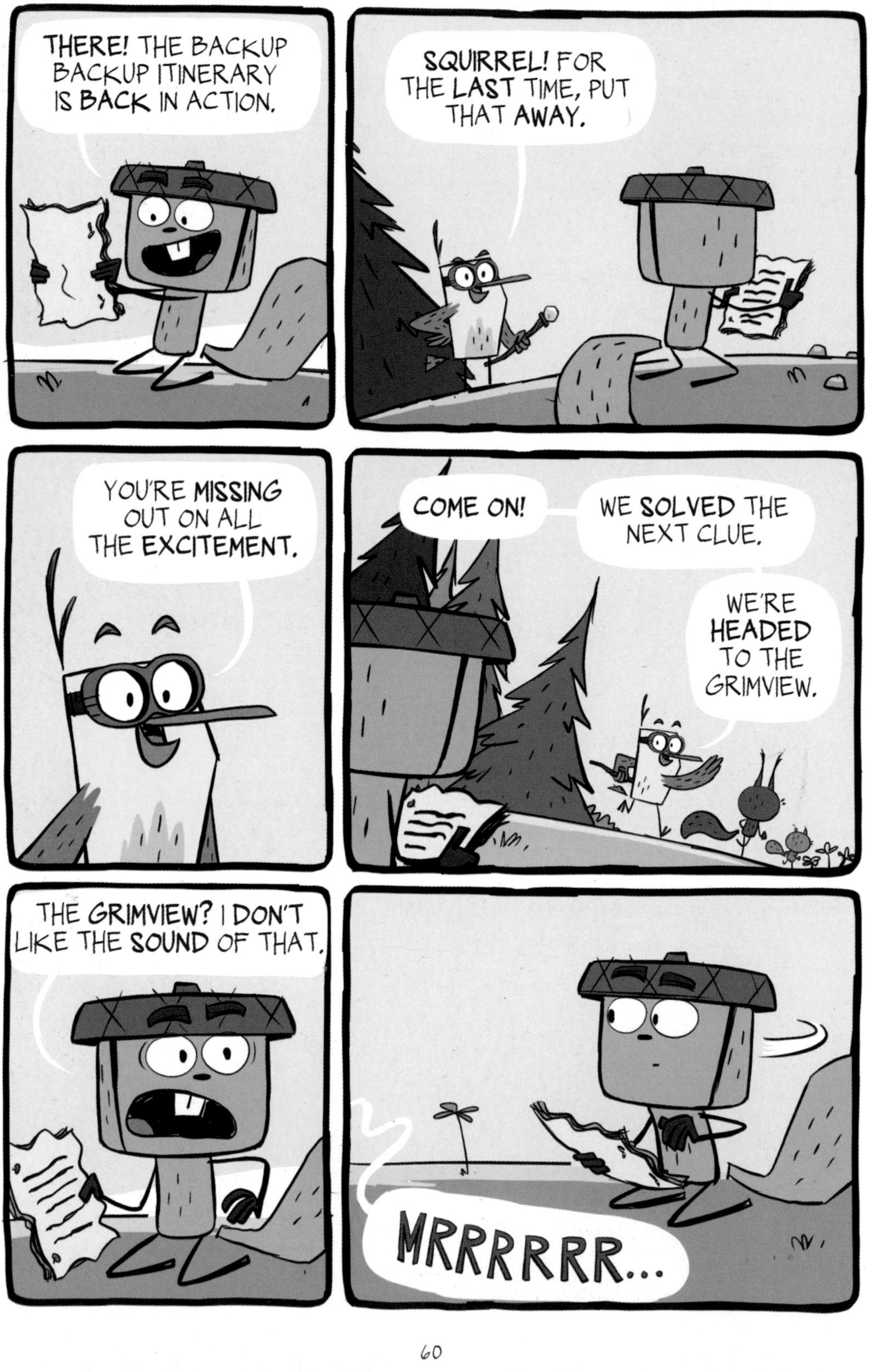
THERE! THE BACKUP BACKUP ITINERARY IS BACK IN ACTION.
SQUIRREL! FOR THE LAST TIME, PUT THAT AWAY.
YOU'RE MISSING OUT ON ALL THE EXCITEMENT.
COME ON!
WE SOLVED THE NEXT CLUE.
WE'RE HEADED TO THE GRIMVIEW.
THE GRIMVIEW? I DON'T LIKE THE SOUND OF THAT.
MRRRRRR...

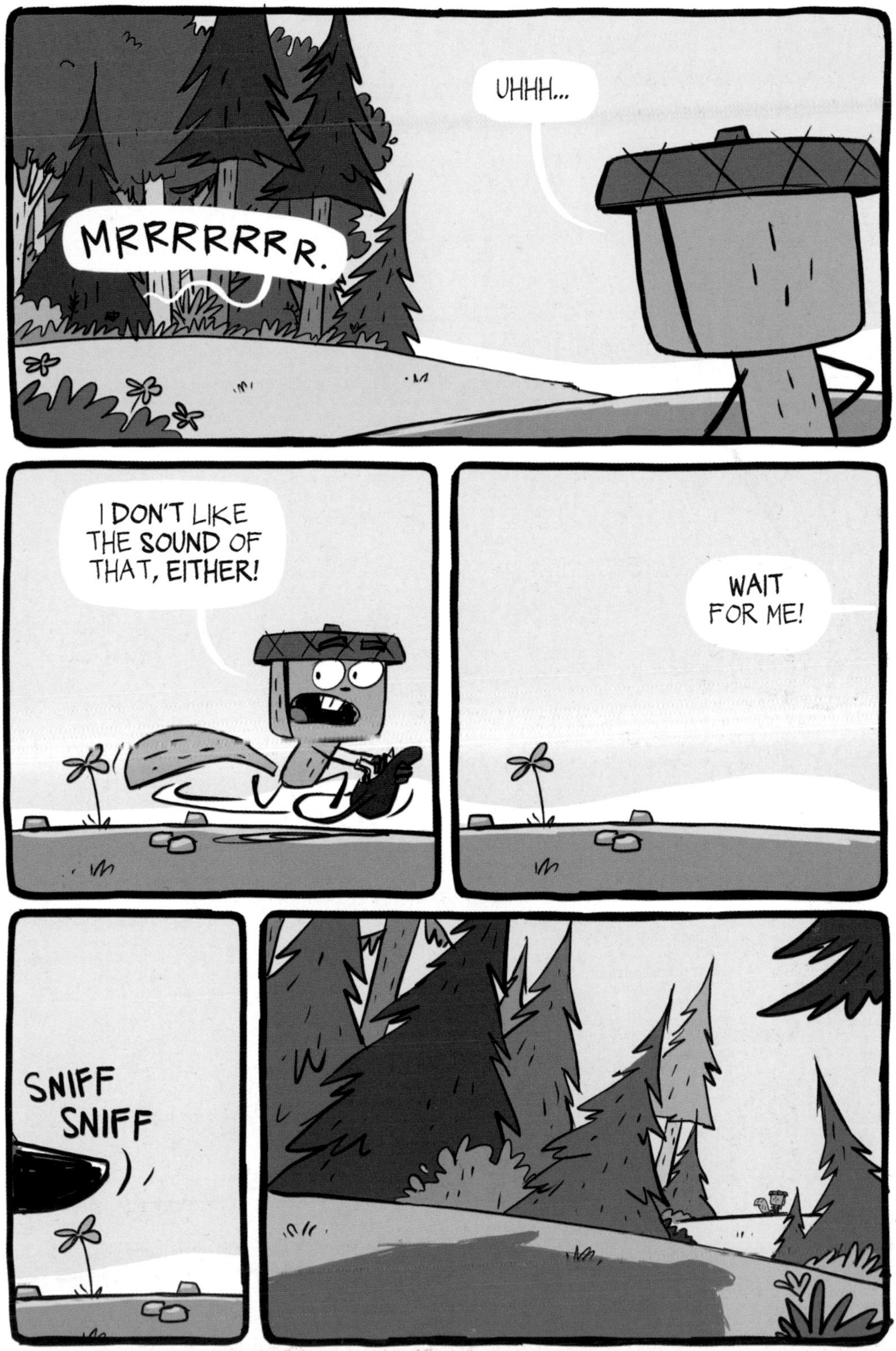
MRRRRRRR.
UHHH...
I DON'T LIKE THE SOUND OF THAT, EITHER!
WAIT FOR ME!
SNIFF SNIFF

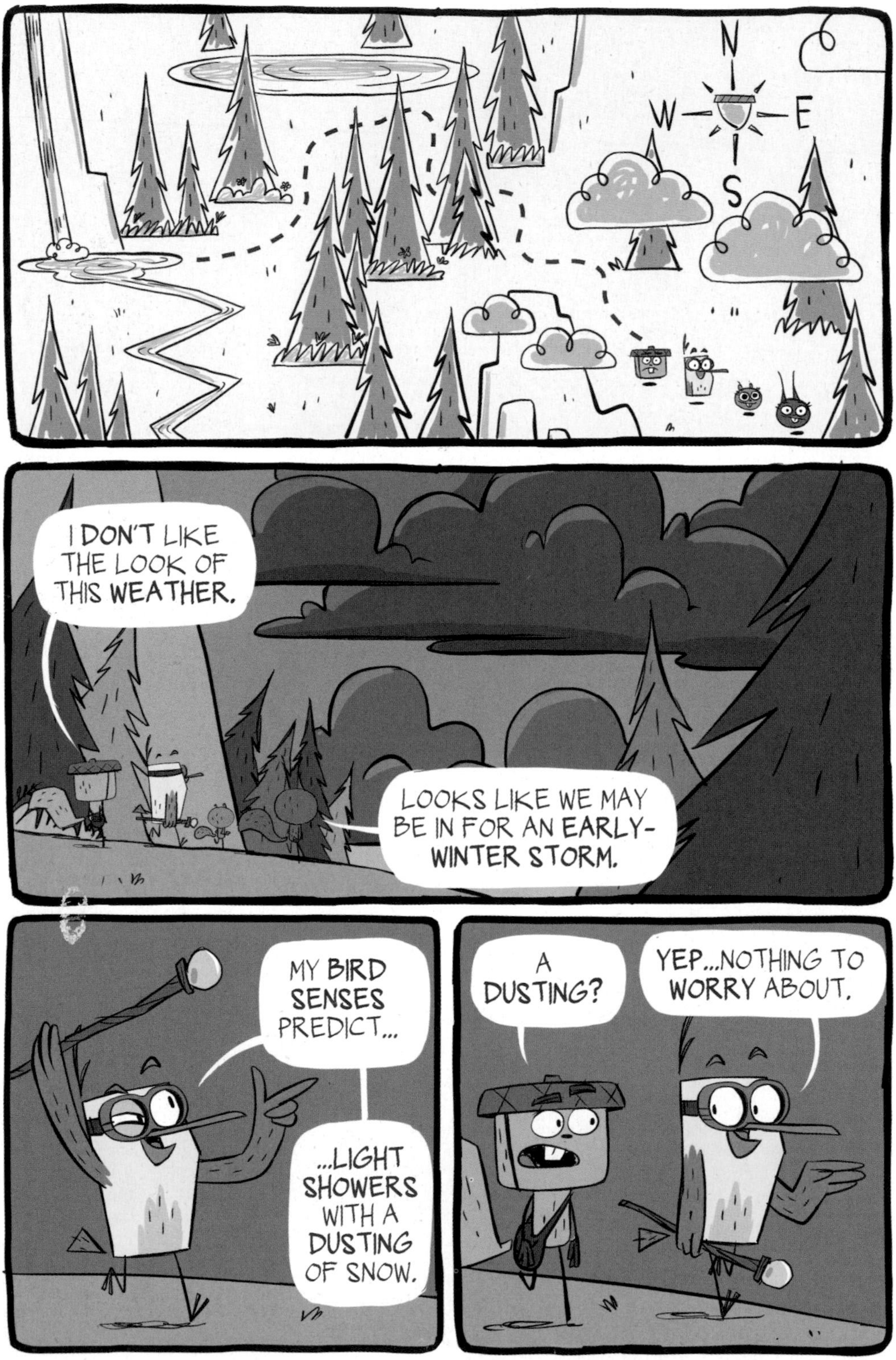
N
W
E
S
I DON'T LIKE THE LOOK OF THIS WEATHER.
LOOKS LIKE WE MAY BE IN FOR AN EARLY-WINTER STORM.
MY BIRD SENSES PREDICT...
...LIGHT SHOWERS WITH A DUSTING OF SNOW.
A DUSTING?
YEP...NOTHING TO WORRY ABOUT.

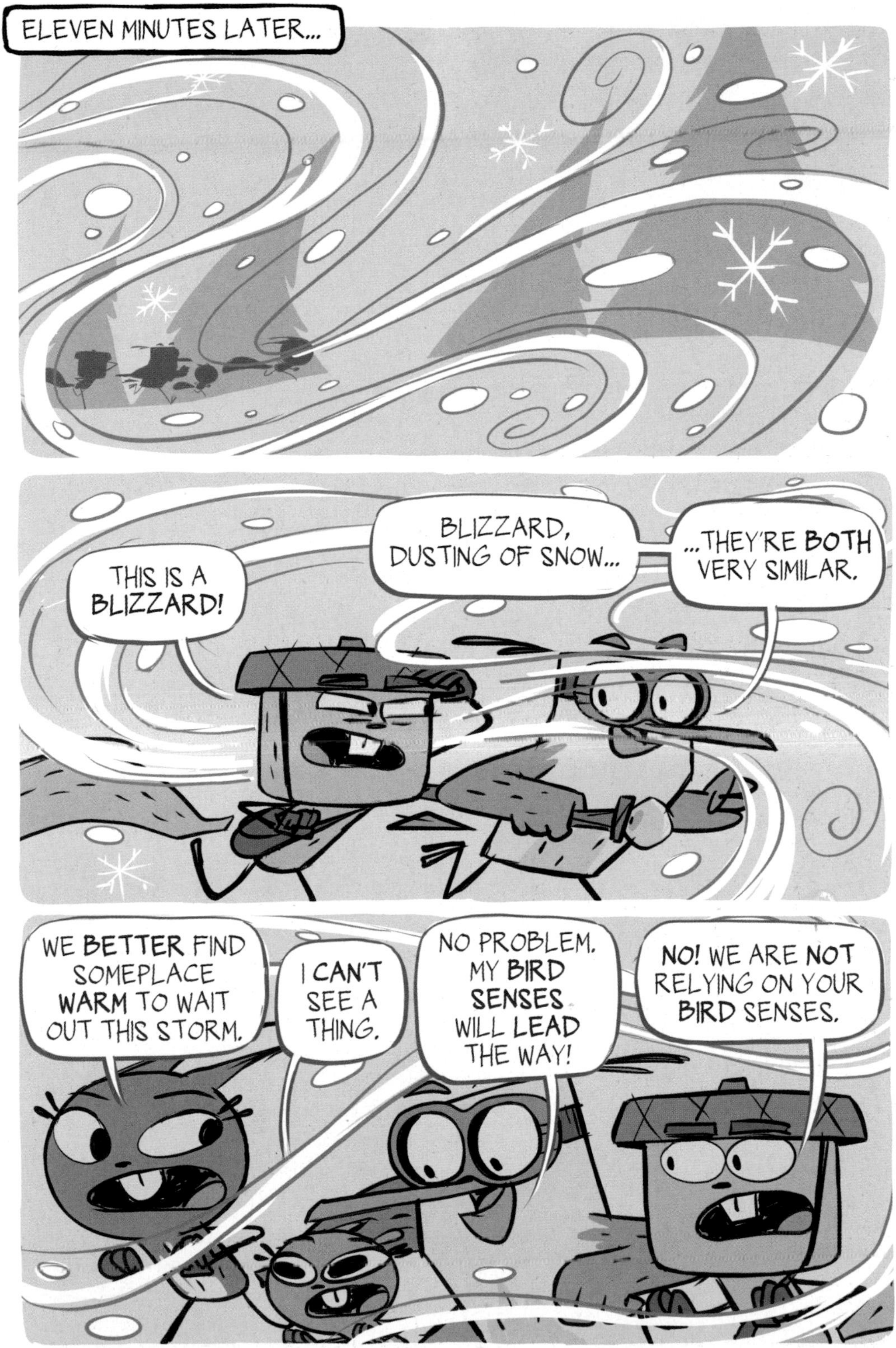
ELEVEN MINUTES LATER...
THIS IS A BLIZZARD!
BLIZZARD, DUSTING OF SNOW...
...THEY'RE BOTH VERY SIMILAR.
WE BETTER FIND SOMEPLACE WARM TO WAIT OUT THIS STORM.
I CAN'T SEE A THING.
NO PROBLEM. MY BIRD SENSES WILL LEAD THE WAY!
NO! WE ARE NOT RELYING ON YOUR BIRD SENSES.

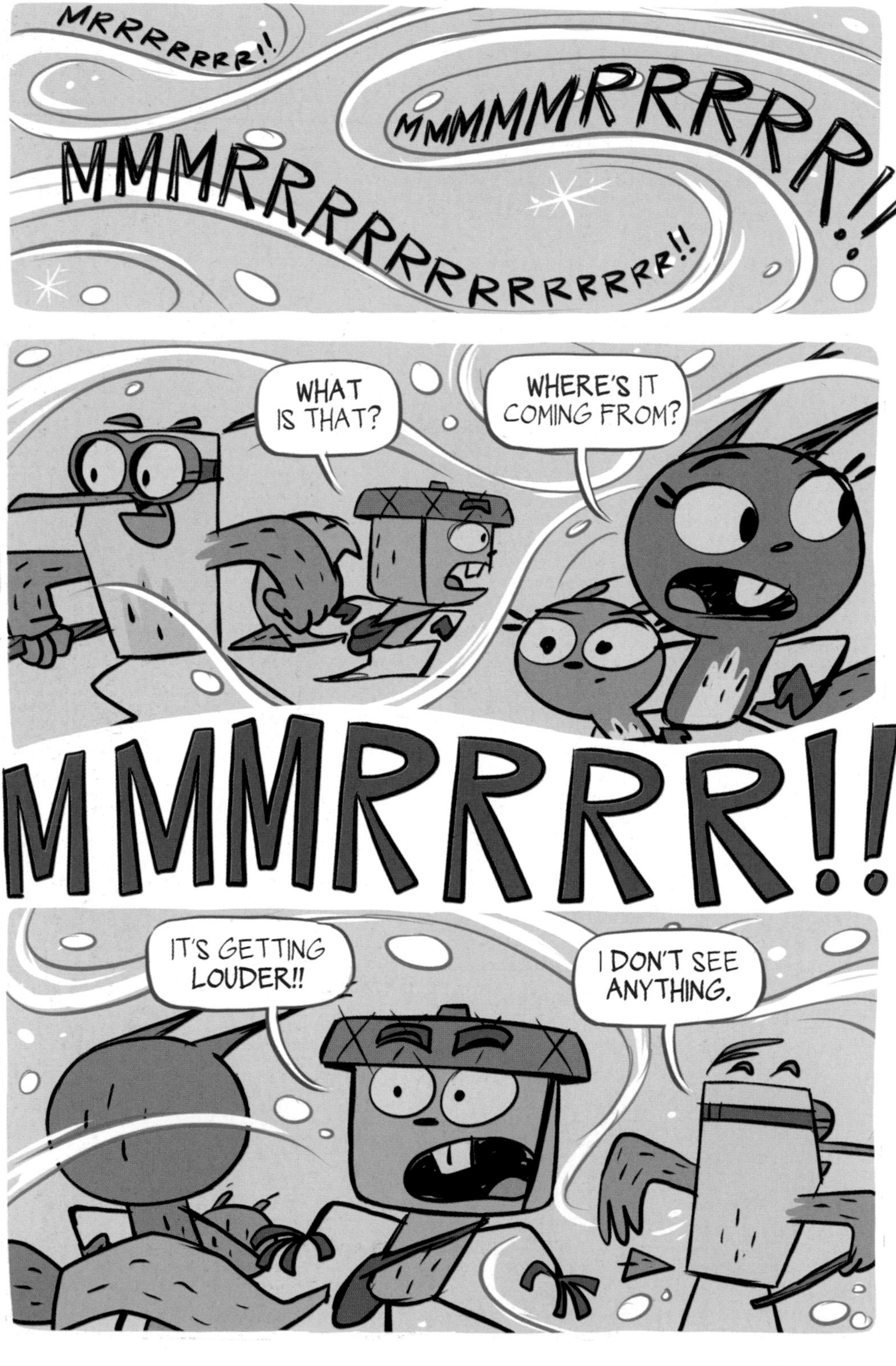
MRRRRRRRR!!
MMMMMRRRRRR!!
MMMRRRRRRRRRRRRRRR!!
WHAT IS THAT?
WHERE'S IT COMING FROM?
MMMRRRRR!!
IT'S GETTING LOUDER!!
I DON'T SEE ANYTHING.

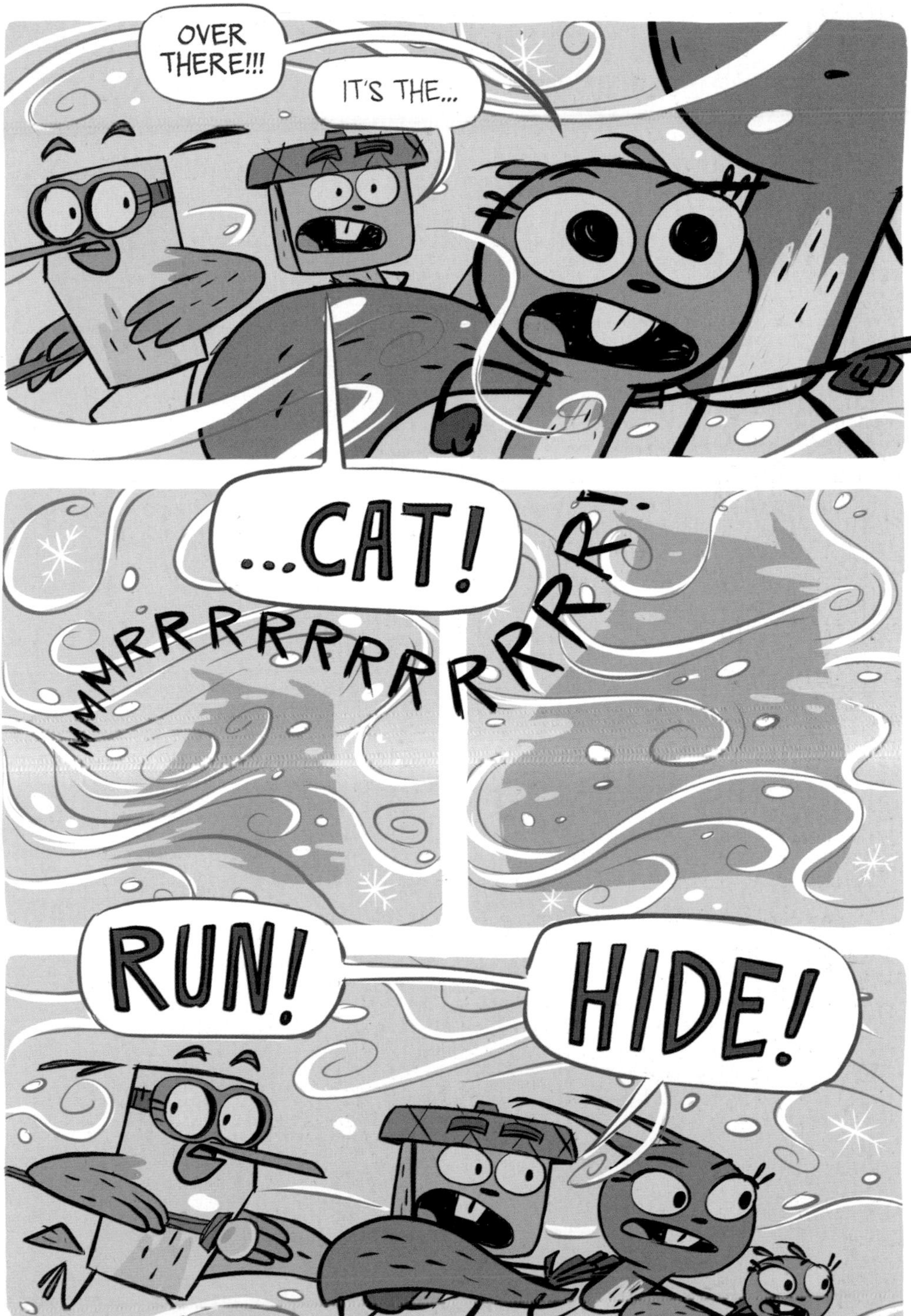
OVER THERE!!!
IT'S THE...
...CAT!
MMMRRRRRRRRRRRRR!
RUN!
HIDE!

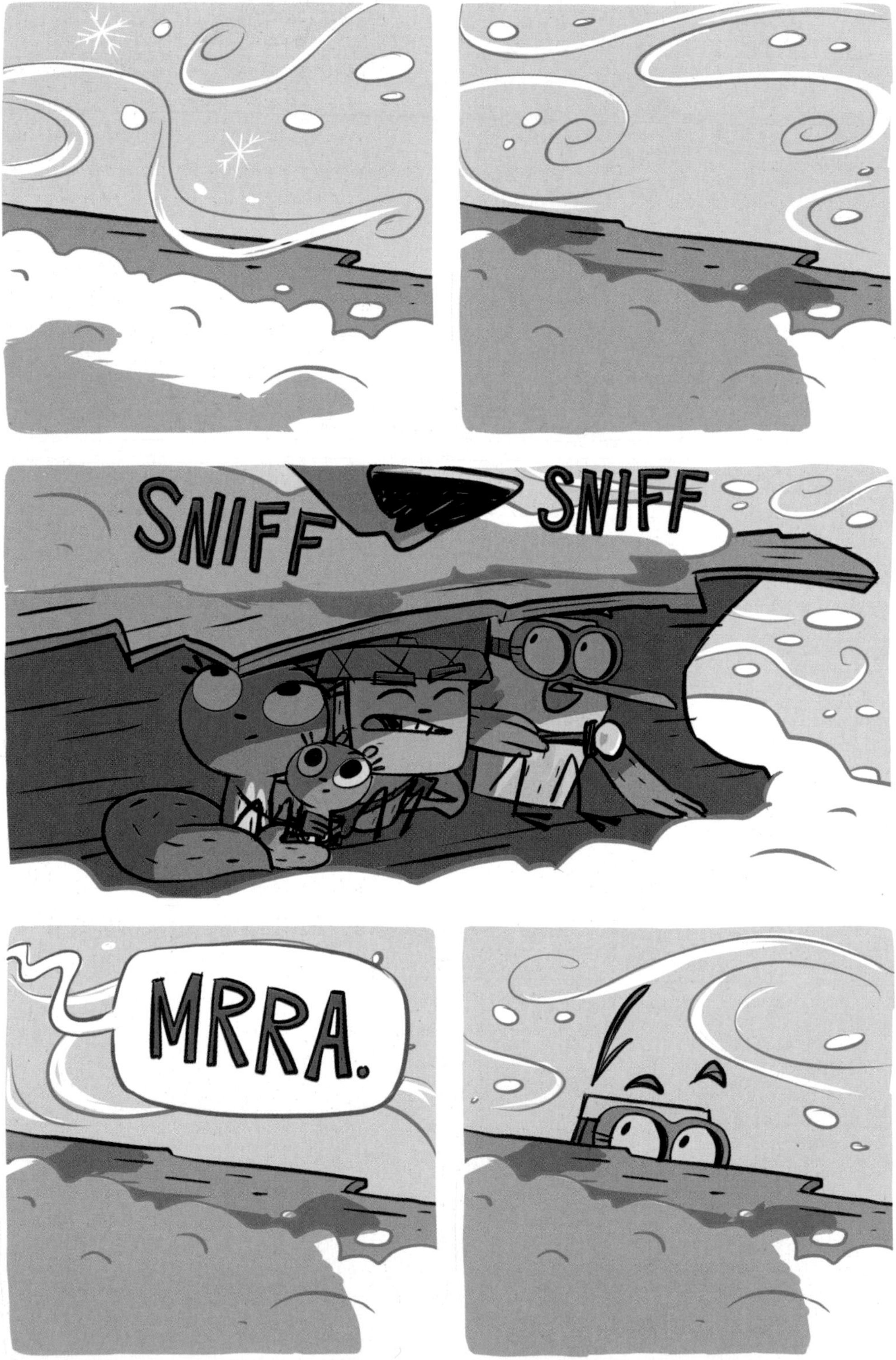
SNIFF
SNIFF
MRRA.

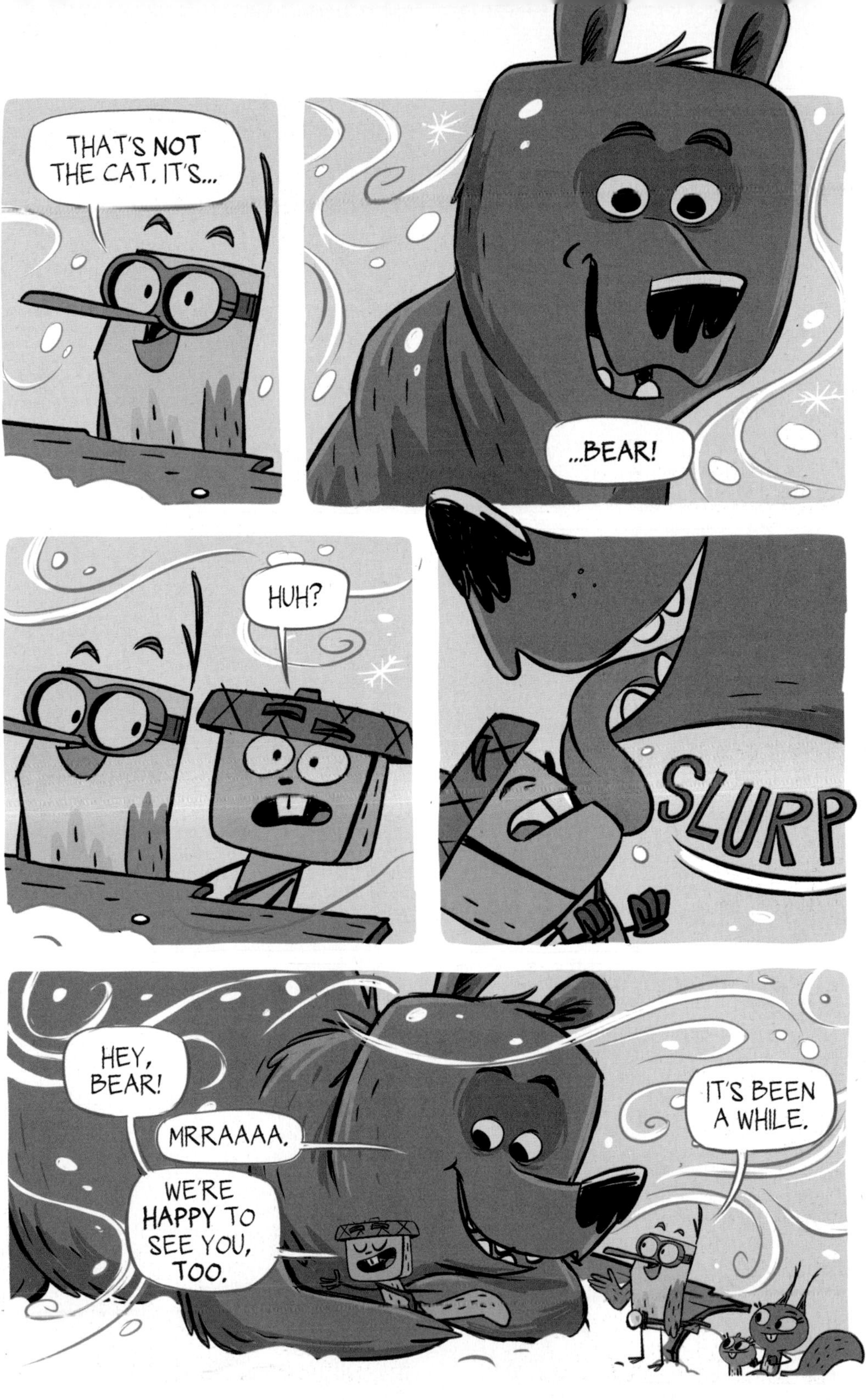
THAT'S NOT THE CAT. IT'S...
...BEAR!
HUH?
SLURP
HEY, BEAR!
MRRAAAA.
WE'RE HAPPY TO SEE YOU, TOO.
IT'S BEEN A WHILE.

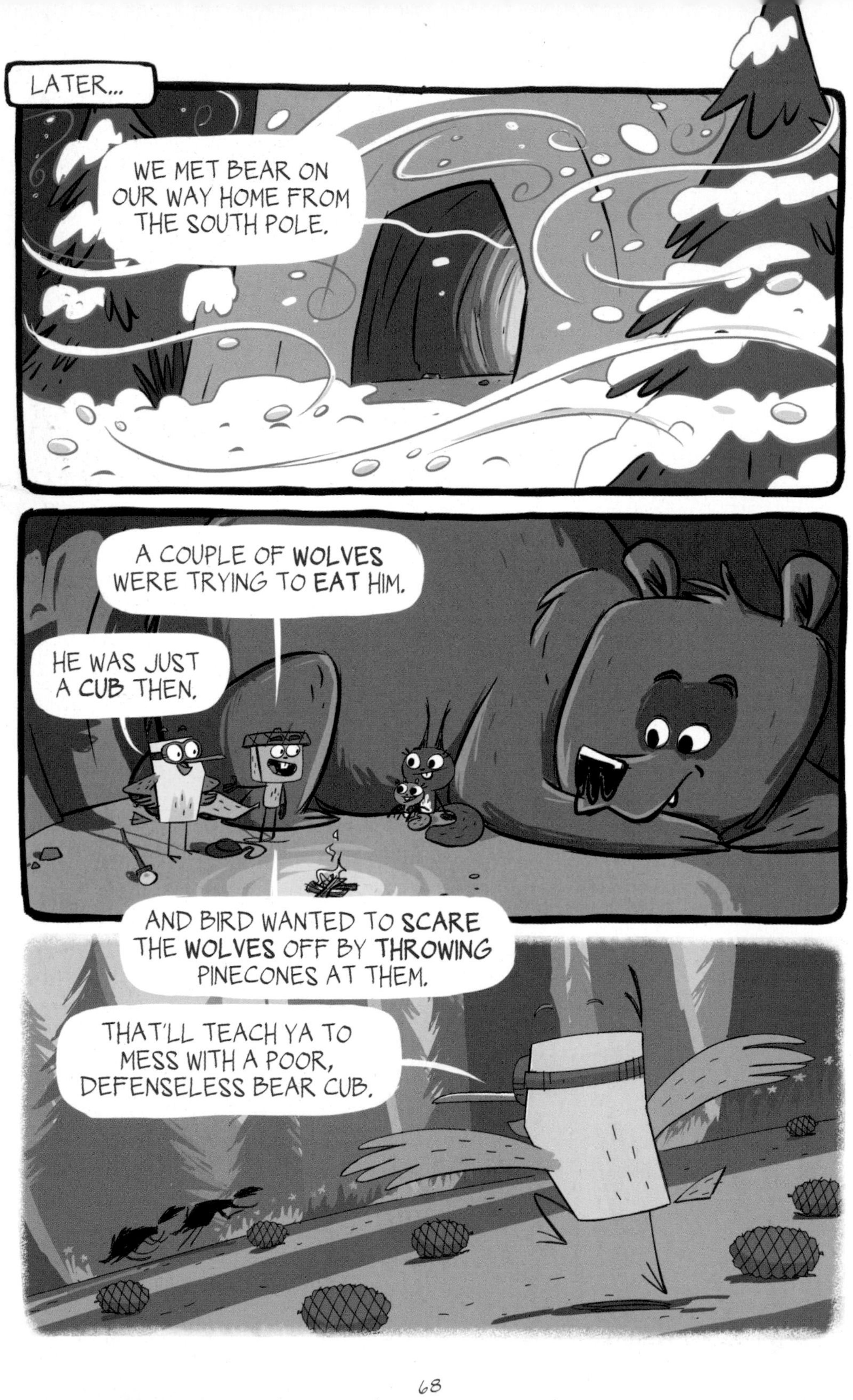
LATER...
WE MET BEAR ON OUR WAY HOME FROM THE SOUTH POLE.
A COUPLE OF WOLVES WERE TRYING TO EAT HIM.
HE WAS JUST A CUB THEN.
AND BIRD WANTED TO SCARE THE WOLVES OFF BY THROWING PINECONES AT THEM.
THAT'LL TEACH YA TO MESS WITH A POOR, DEFENSELESS BEAR CUB.

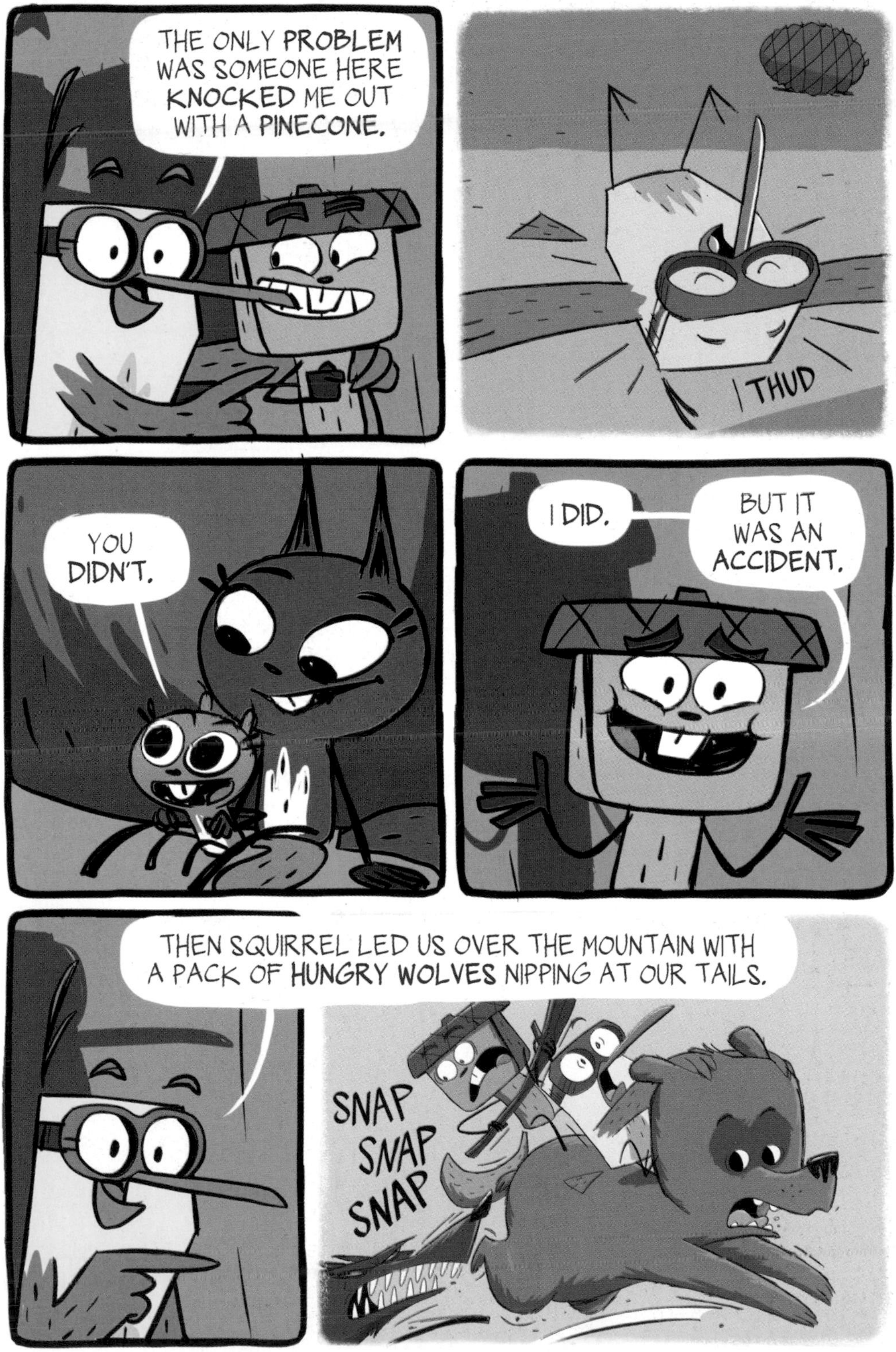
THE ONLY PROBLEM WAS SOMEONE HERE KNOCKED ME OUT WITH A PINECONE.
THUD
YOU DIDN'T.
I DID.
BUT IT WAS AN ACCIDENT.
THEN SQUIRREL LED US OVER THE MOUNTAIN WITH A PACK OF HUNGRY WOLVES NIPPING AT OUR TAILS.
SNAP
SNAP
SNAP
SNAP

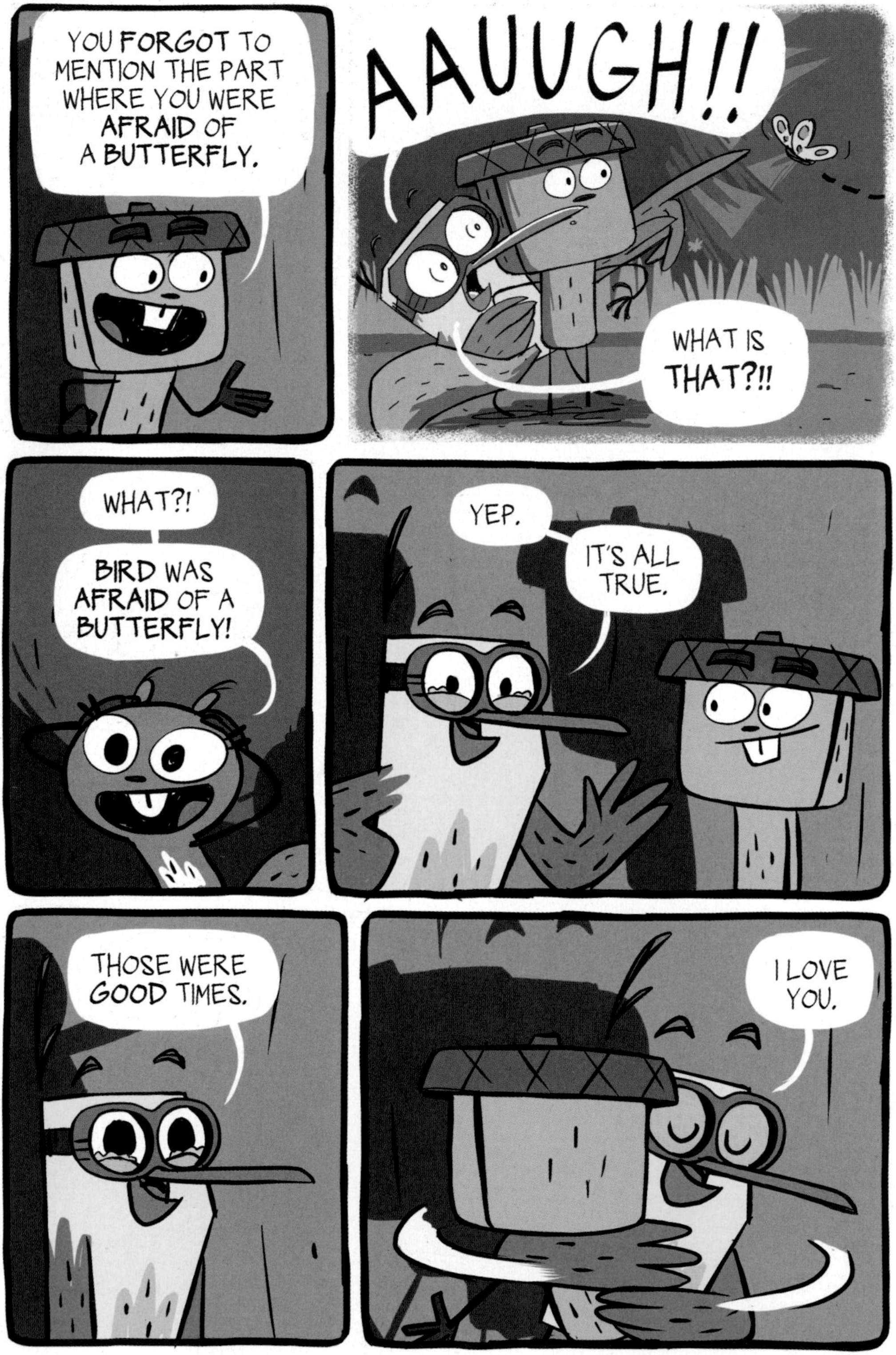
YOU FORGOT TO MENTION THE PART WHERE YOU WERE AFRAID OF A BUTTERFLY.
AAUUGH!!
WHAT IS THAT?!!
WHAT?!
BIRD WAS AFRAID OF A BUTTERFLY!
YEP.
IT'S ALL TRUE.
THOSE WERE GOOD TIMES.
I LOVE YOU.

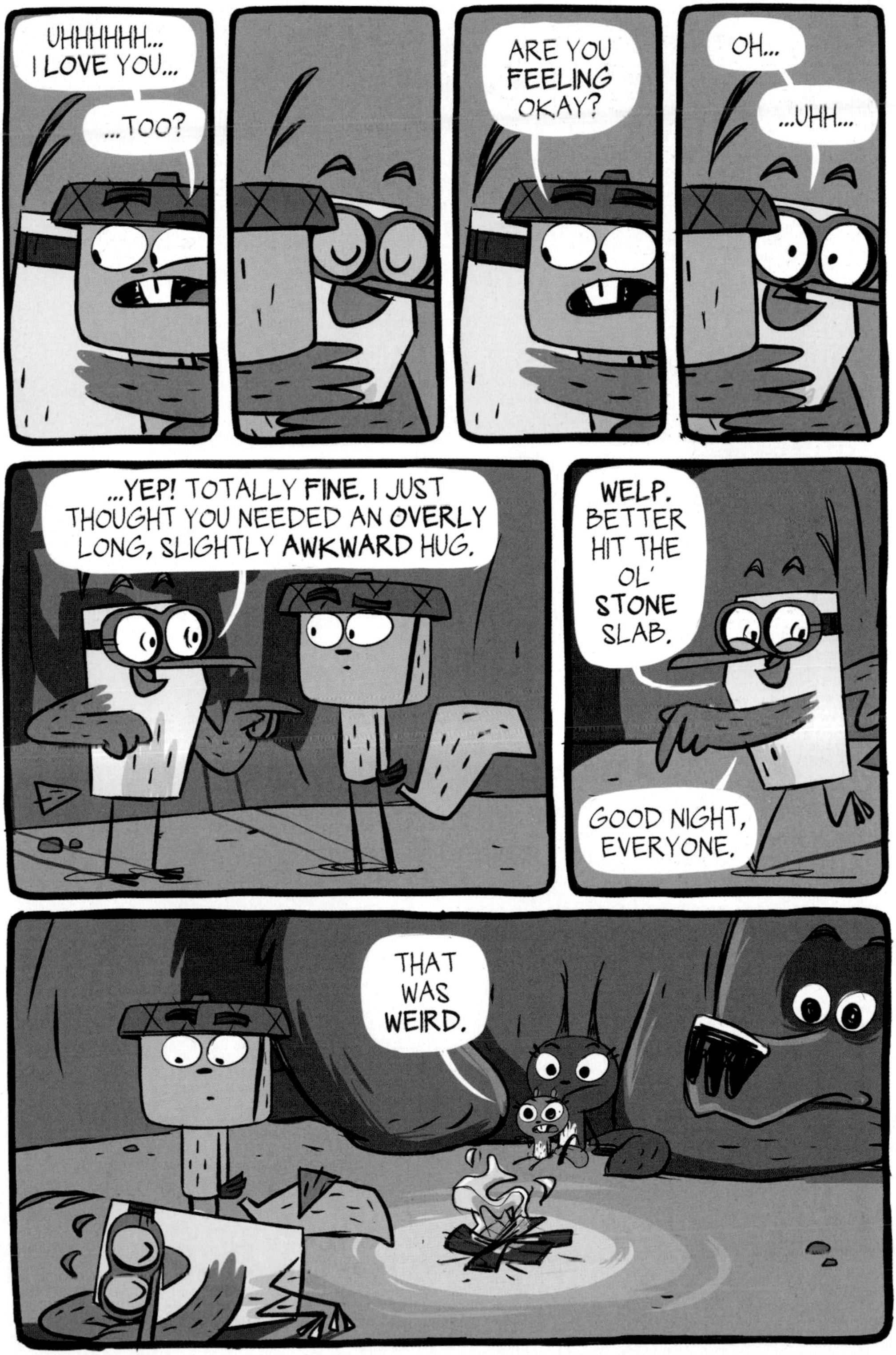
UHHHHHH... I LOVE YOU...
...TOO?
ARE YOU FEELING OKAY?
OH...
...UHH...
...YEP! TOTALLY FINE. I JUST THOUGHT YOU NEEDED AN OVERLY LONG, SLIGHTLY AWKWARD HUG.
WELP. BETTER HIT THE OL' STONE SLAB.
GOOD NIGHT, EVERYONE.
THAT WAS WEIRD.

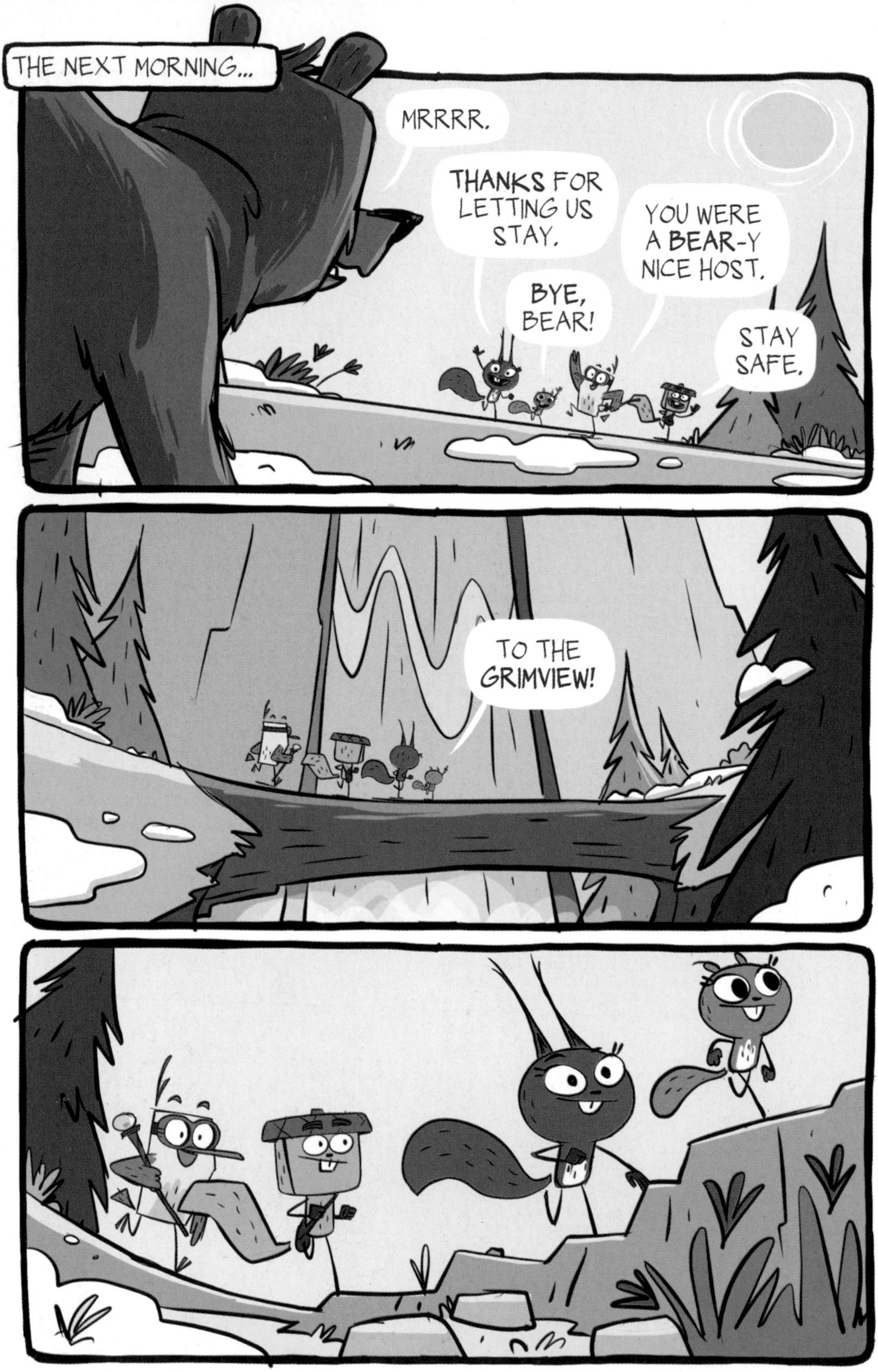
THE NEXT MORNING...
MRRRR.
THANKS FOR LETTING US STAY.
BYE, BEAR!
YOU WERE A BEAR-Y NICE HOST.
STAY SAFE.
TO THE GRIMVIEW!

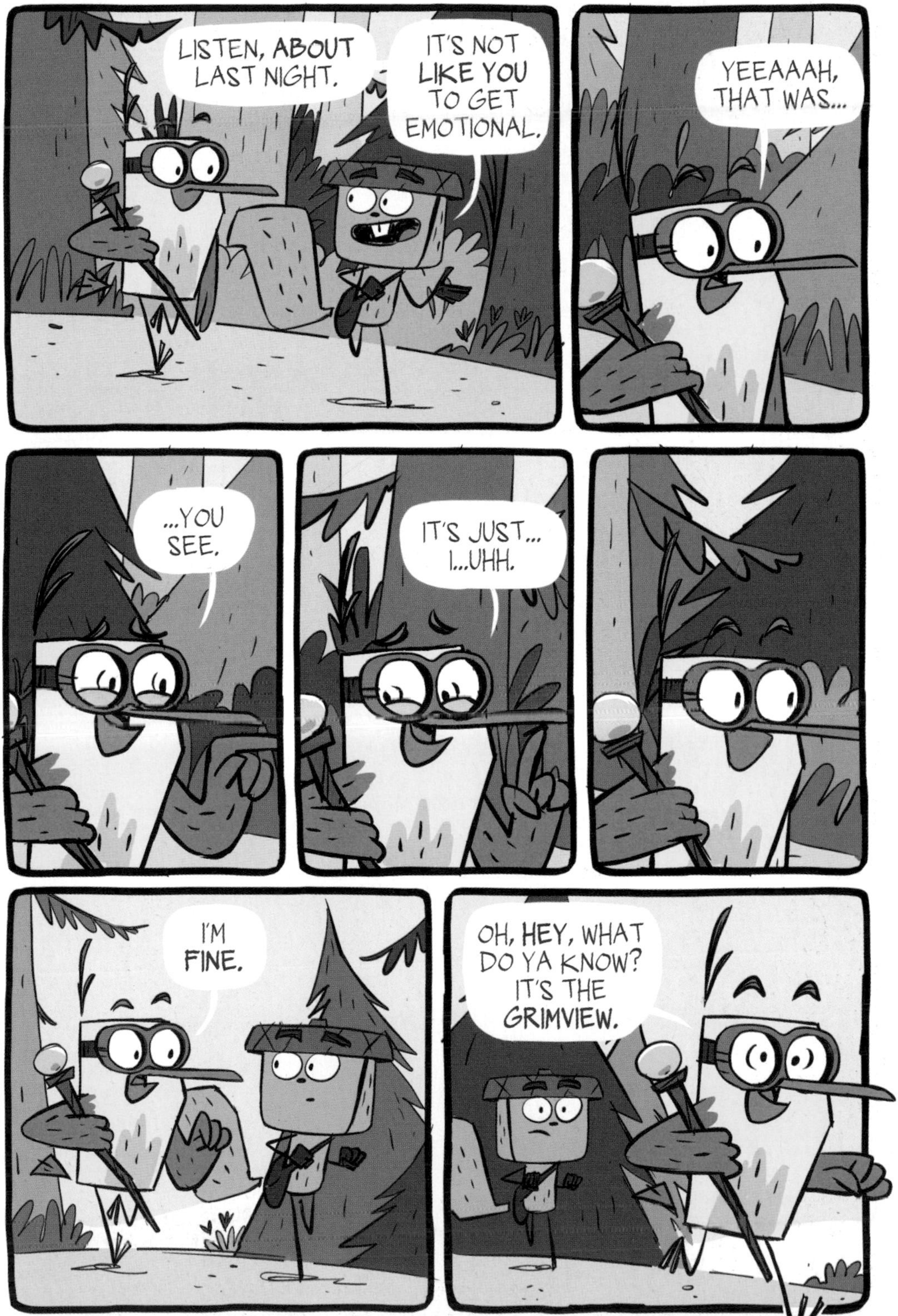
LISTEN, ABOUT LAST NIGHT.
IT'S NOT LIKE YOU TO GET EMOTIONAL.
YEEAAAH, THAT WAS...
...YOU SEE.
IT'S JUST... I...UHH.
I'M FINE.
OH, HEY, WHAT DO YA KNOW? IT'S THE GRIMVIEW.

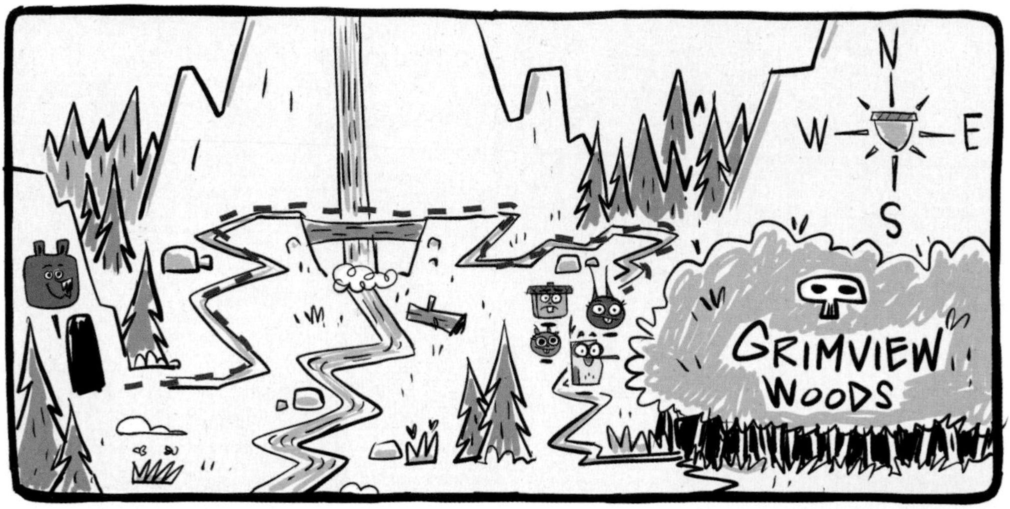
N
W
E
S
GRIMVIEW WOODS

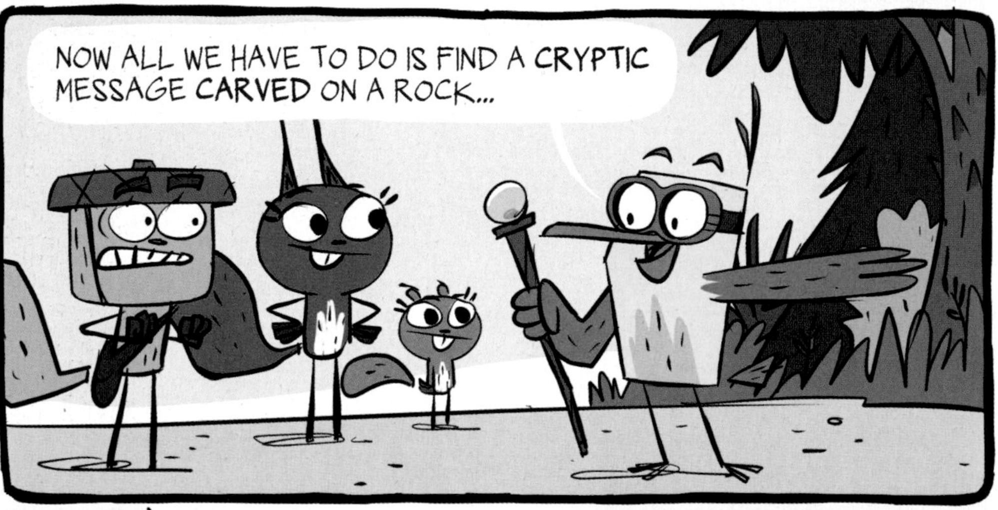
NOW ALL WE HAVE TO DO IS FIND A CRYPTIC MESSAGE CARVED ON A ROCK...

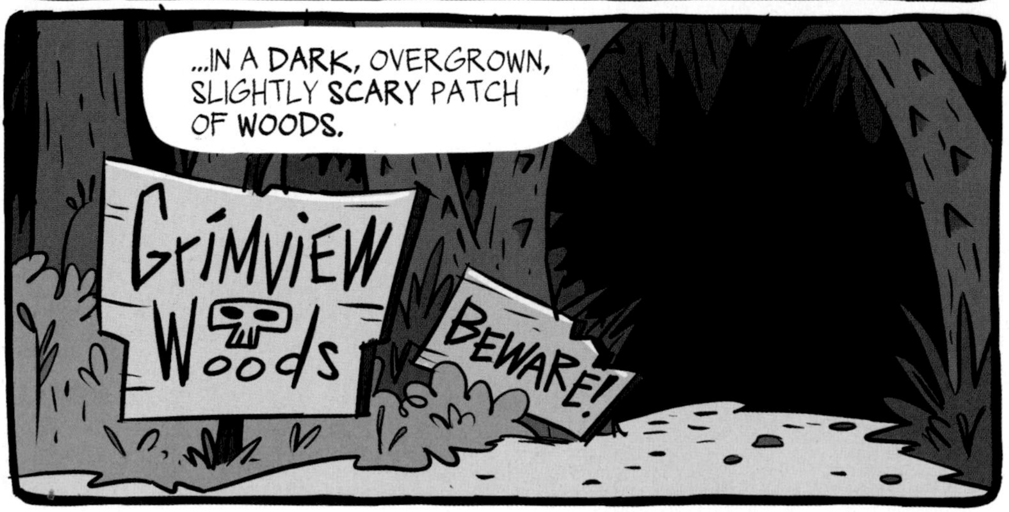
...IN A DARK, OVERGROWN, SLIGHTLY SCARY PATCH OF WOODS.
GrimviEW Woods
BEWARE!

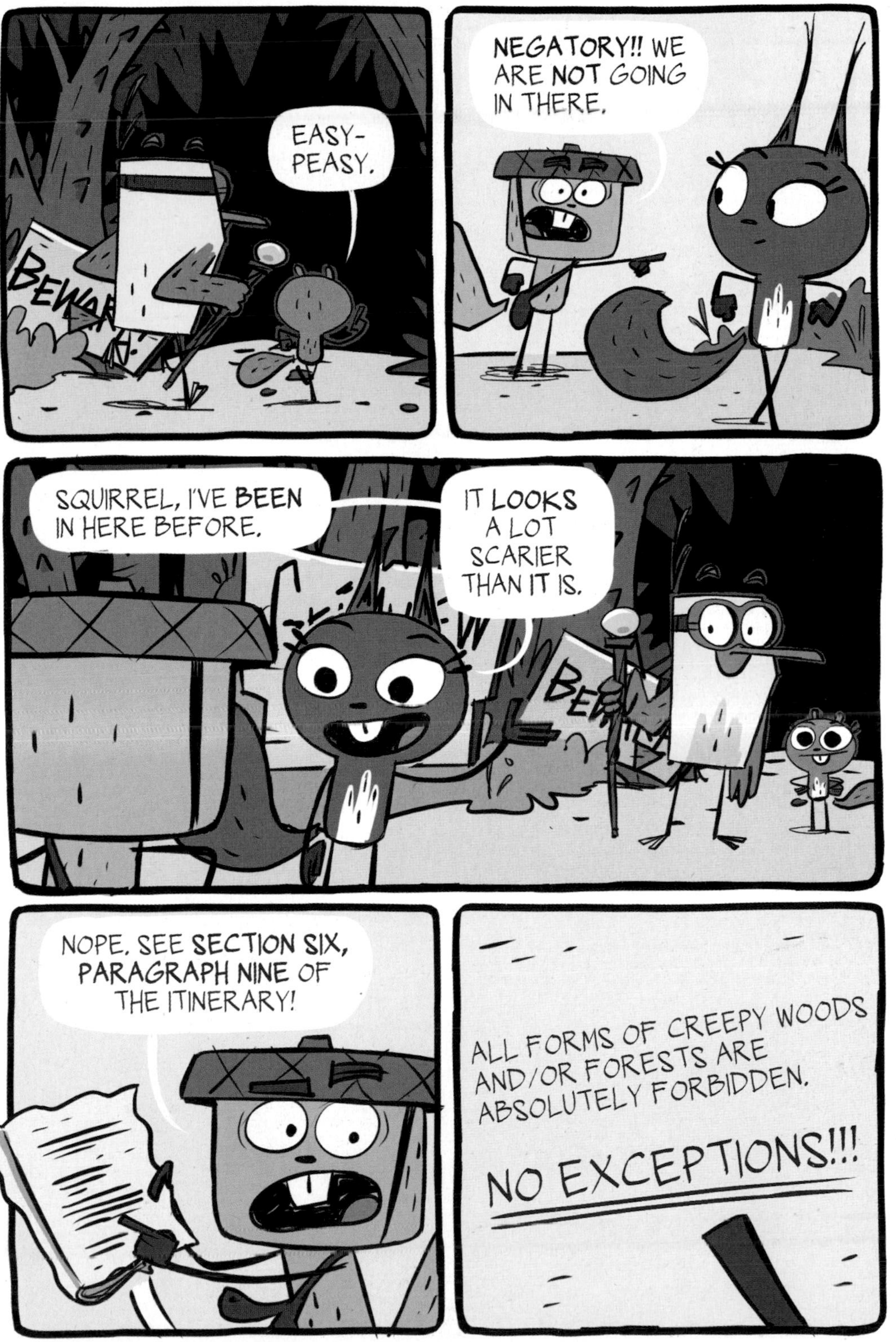

EASY-PEASY.
BEWAR
NEGATORY!! WE ARE NOT GOING IN THERE.
SQUIRREL, I'VE BEEN IN HERE BEFORE.
IT LOOKS A LOT SCARIER THAN IT IS.
NOPE. SEE SECTION SIX, PARAGRAPH NINE OF THE ITINERARY!
ALL FORMS OF CREEPY WOODS AND/OR FORESTS ARE ABSOLUTELY FORBIDDEN.
NO EXCEPTIONS!!!

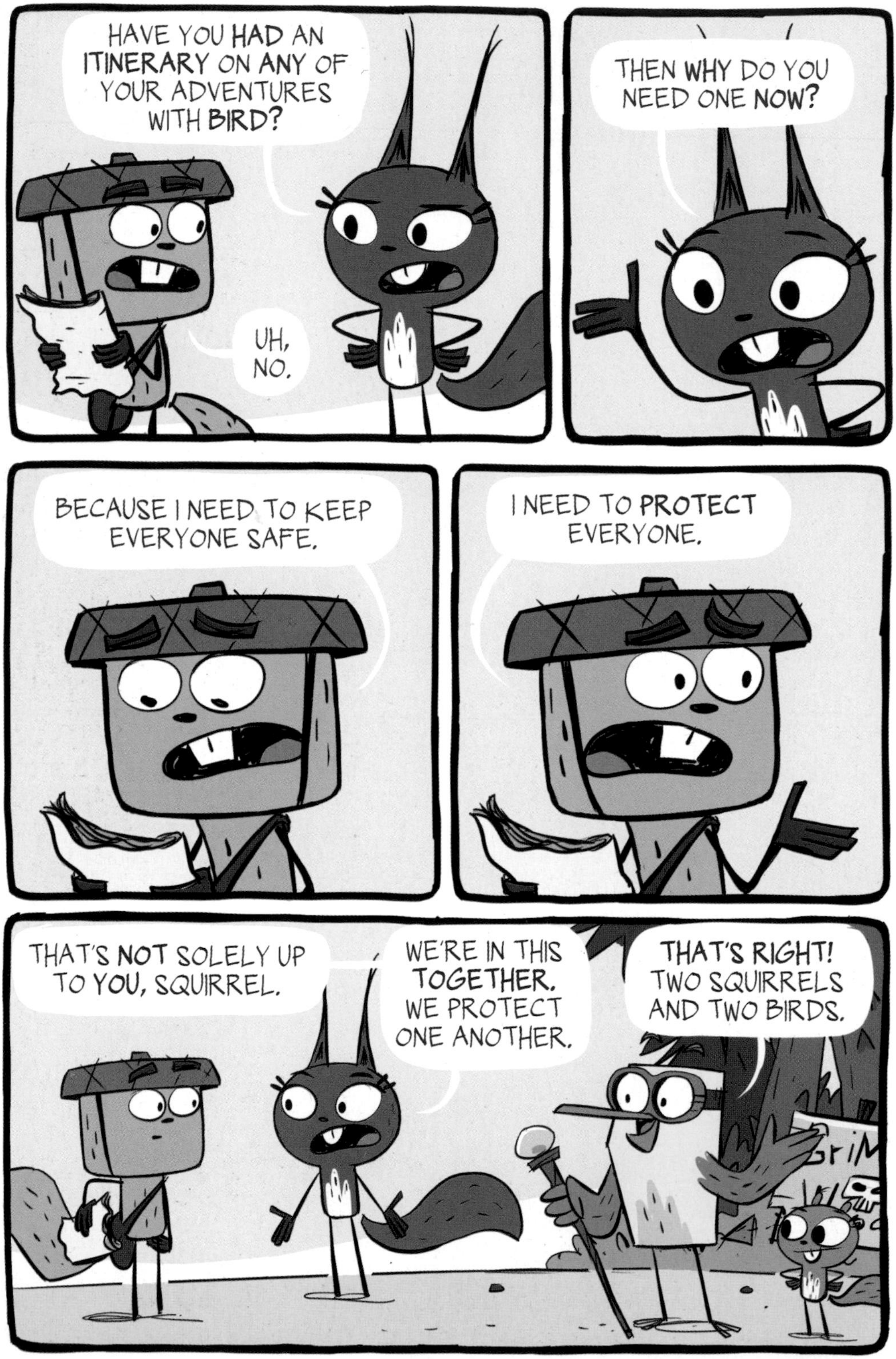
HAVE YOU HAD AN ITINERARY ON ANY OF YOUR ADVENTURES WITH BIRD?
UH, NO.
THEN WHY DO YOU NEED ONE NOW?
BECAUSE I NEED TO KEEP EVERYONE SAFE.
I NEED TO PROTECT EVERYONE.
THAT'S NOT SOLELY UP TO YOU, SQUIRREL.
WE'RE IN THIS TOGETHER. WE PROTECT ONE ANOTHER.
THAT'S RIGHT! TWO SQUIRRELS AND TWO BIRDS.

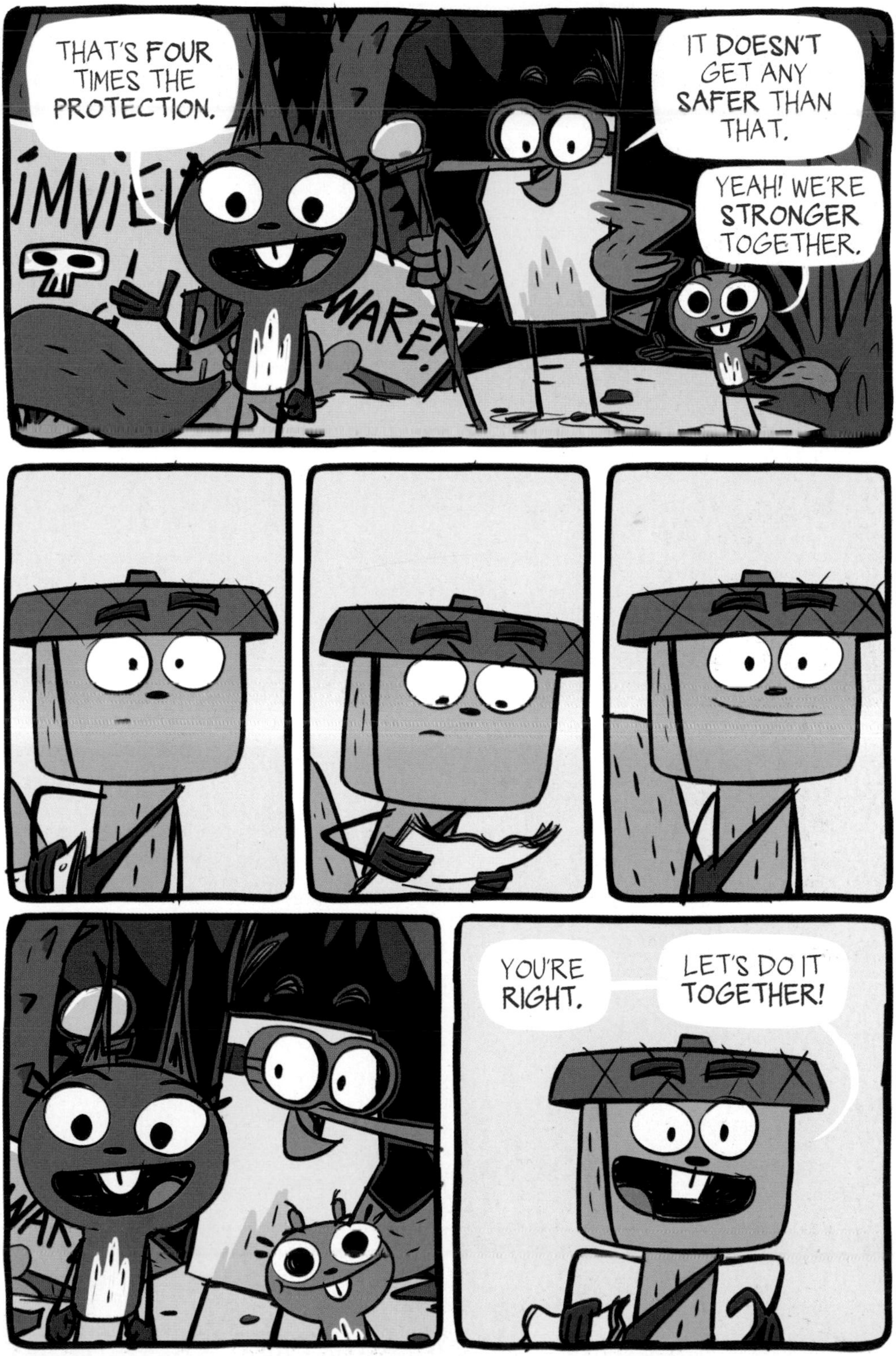
THAT'S FOUR TIMES THE PROTECTION.
IT DOESN'T GET ANY SAFER THAN THAT.
YEAH! WE'RE STRONGER TOGETHER.
YOU'RE RIGHT.
LET'S DO IT TOGETHER!

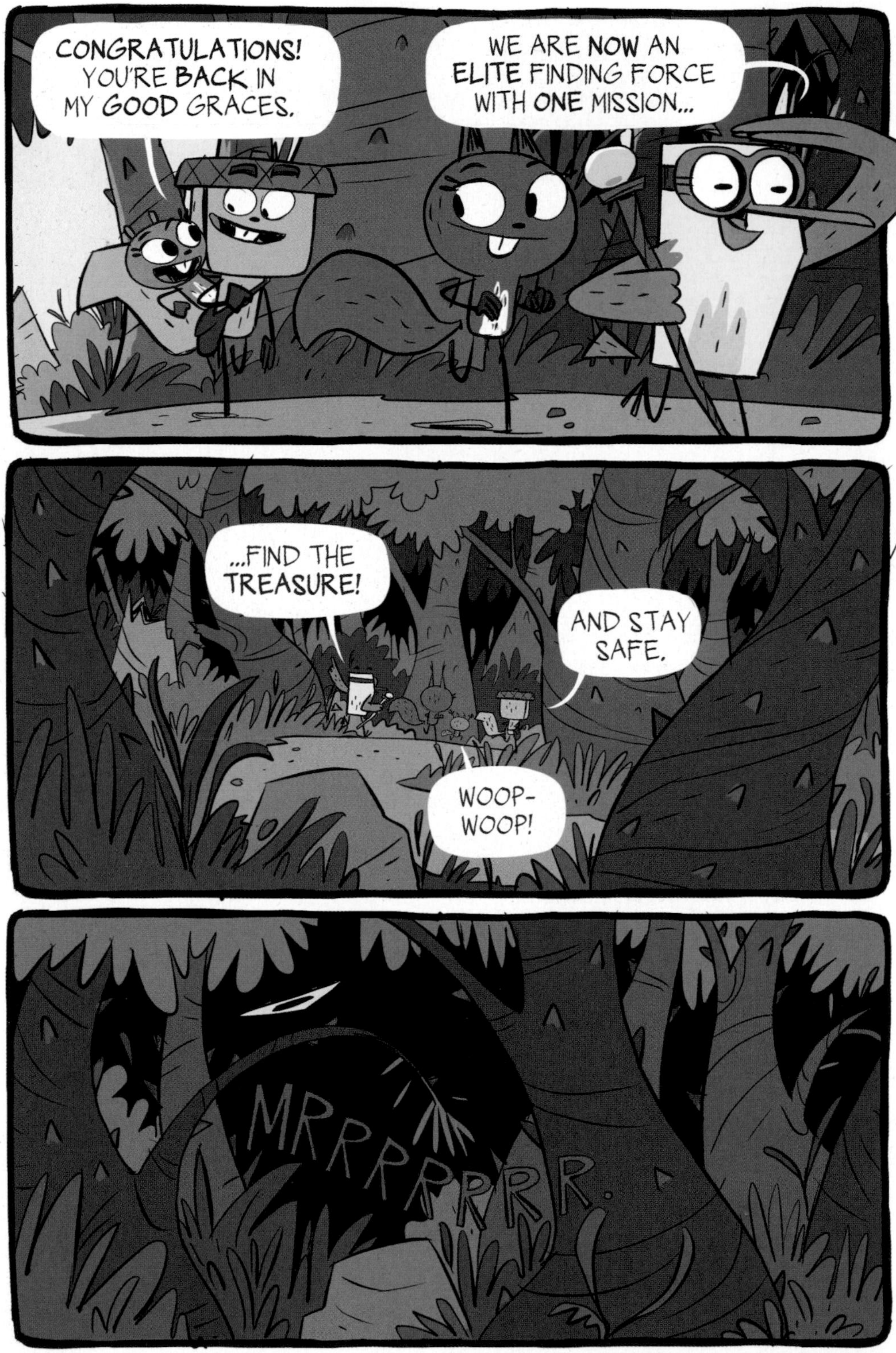
CONGRATULATIONS! YOU'RE BACK IN MY GOOD GRACES.
WE ARE NOW AN ELITE FINDING FORCE WITH ONE MISSION...
...FIND THE TREASURE!
AND STAY SAFE.
WOOP-WOOP!
MRRRRRRR.

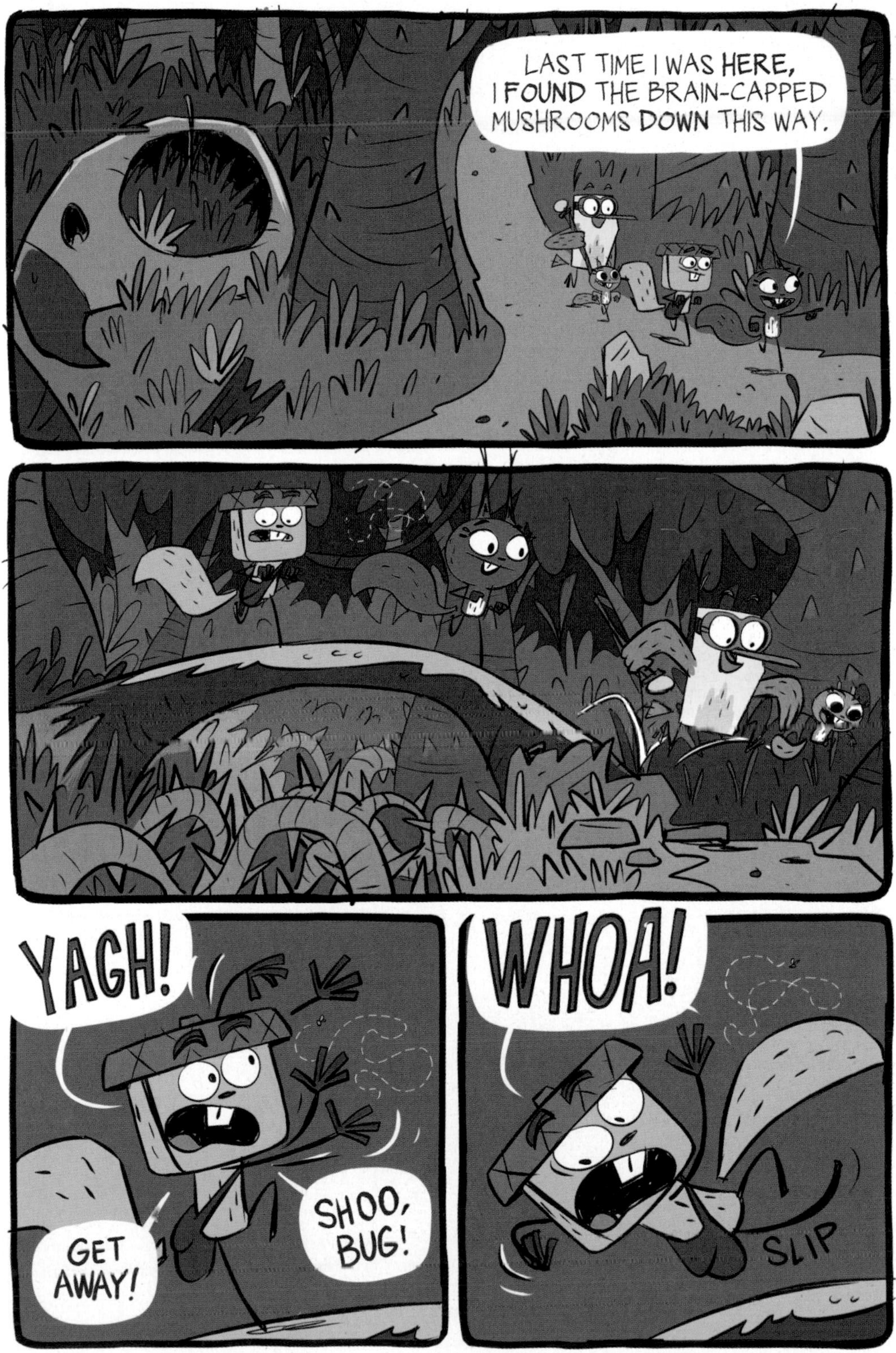
LAST TIME I WAS HERE, I FOUND THE BRAIN-CAPPED MUSHROOMS DOWN THIS WAY.
YAGH!
GET AWAY!
SHOO, BUG!
WHOA!
SLIP

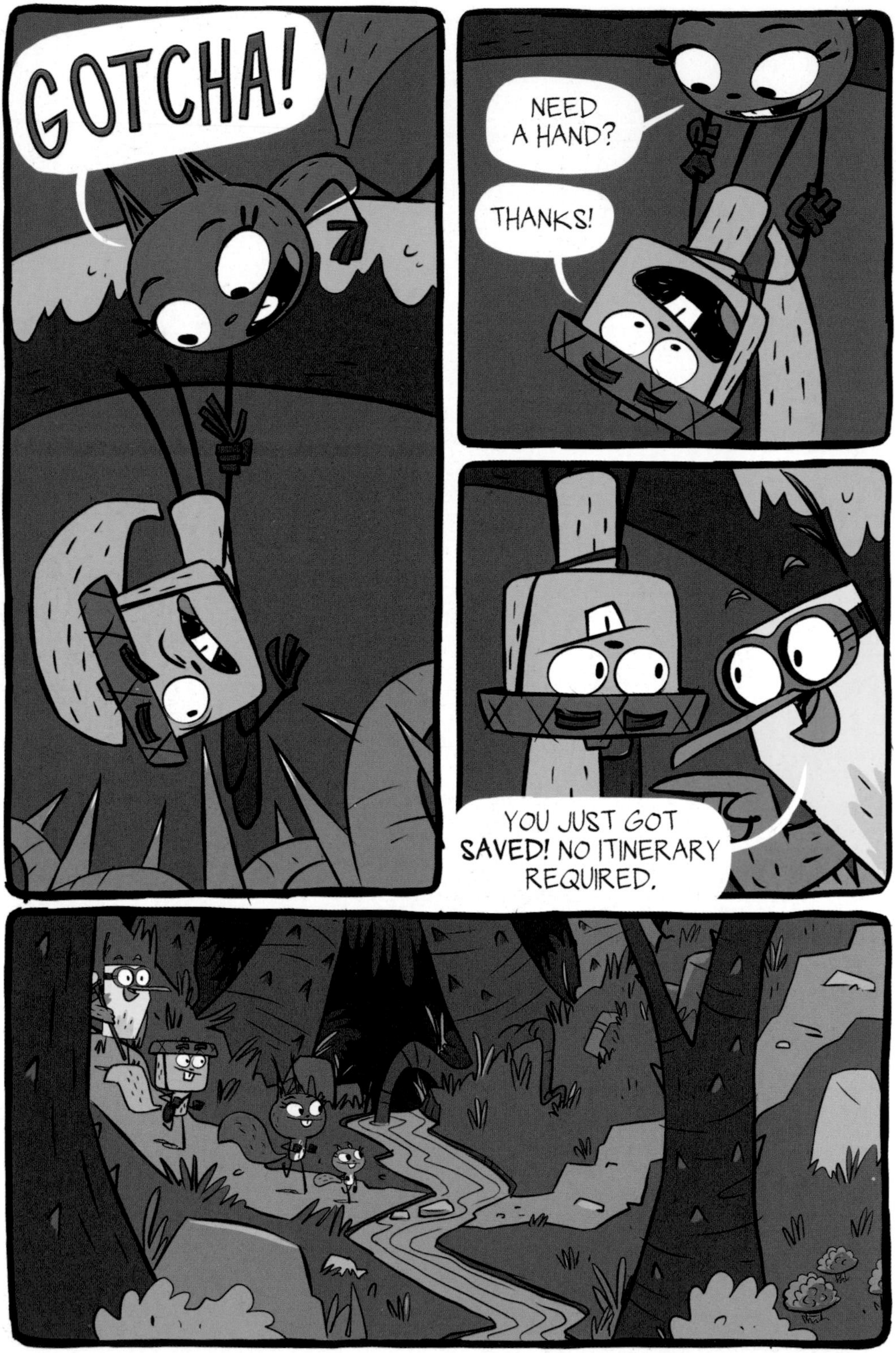
GOTCHA!
NEED A HAND?
THANKS!
YOU JUST GOT SAVED! NO ITINERARY REQUIRED.

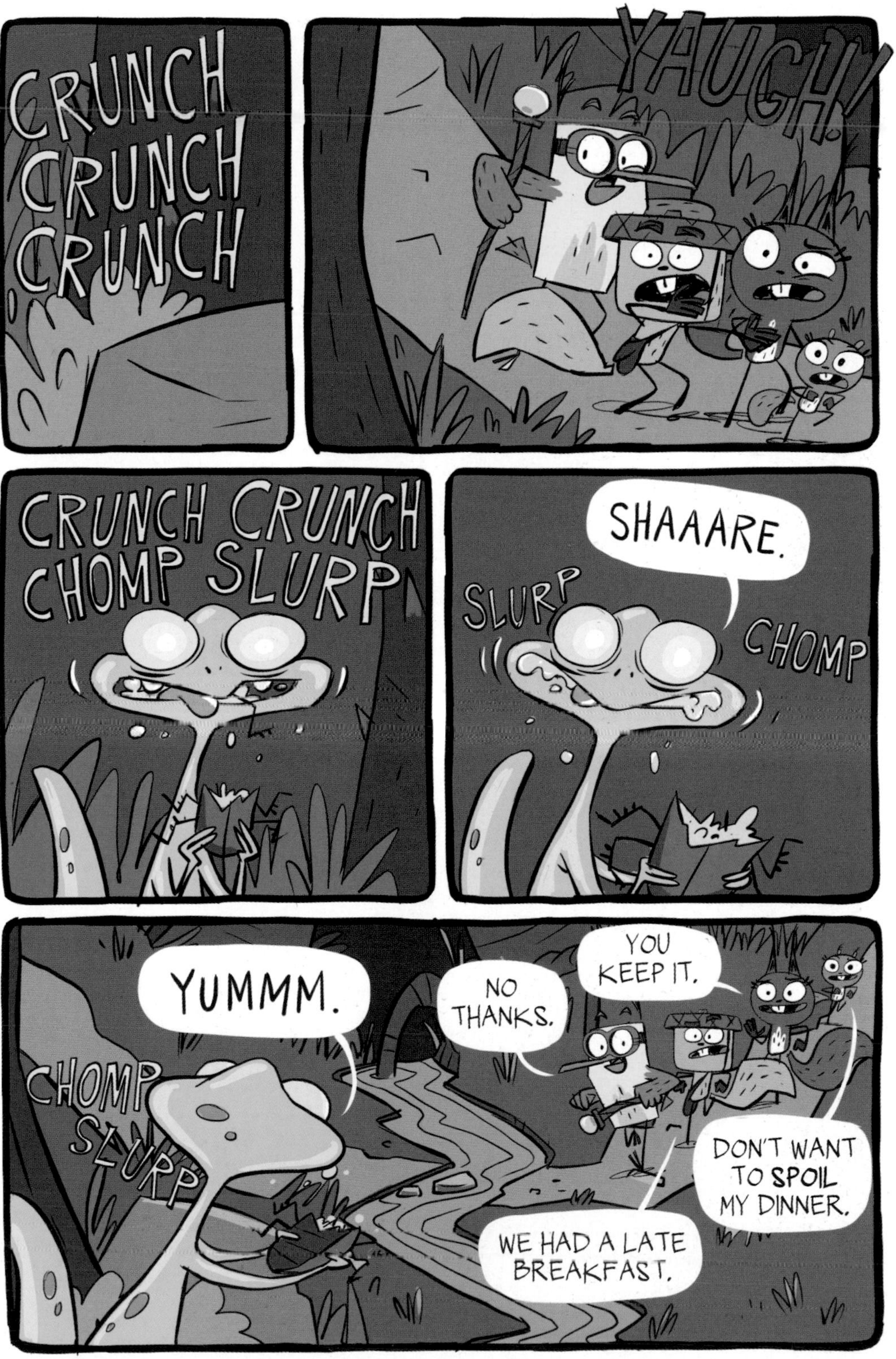
CRUNCH
CRUNCH
CRUNCH
YAUGH!
CRUNCH CRUNCH
CHOMP SLURP
SHAAARE.
SLURP
CHOMP
YUMMM.
CHOMP
SLURP
NO THANKS.
YOU KEEP IT.
DON'T WANT TO SPOIL MY DINNER.
WE HAD A LATE BREAKFAST.

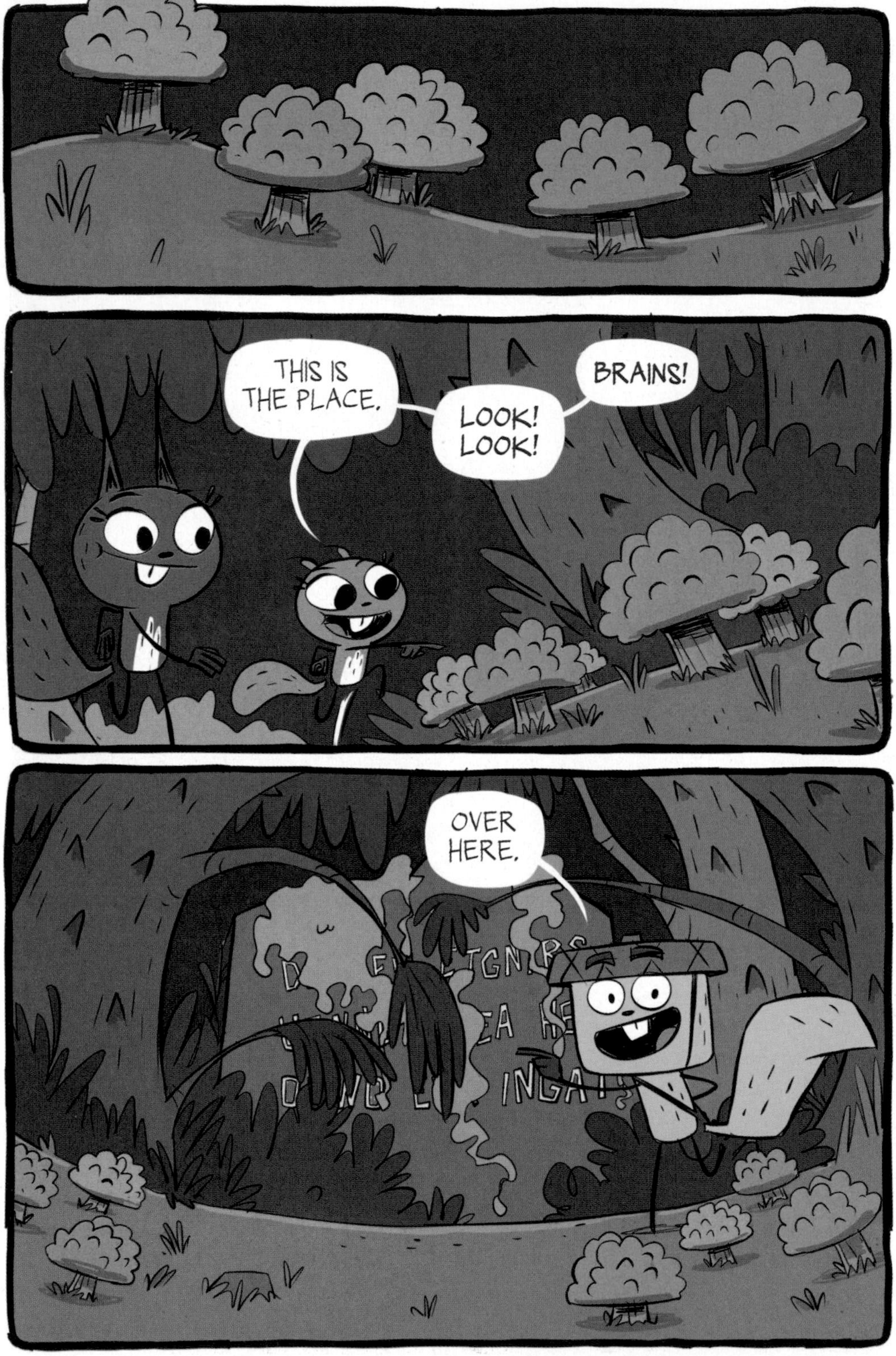
THIS IS THE PLACE.
LOOK! LOOK!
BRAINS!
OVER HERE.

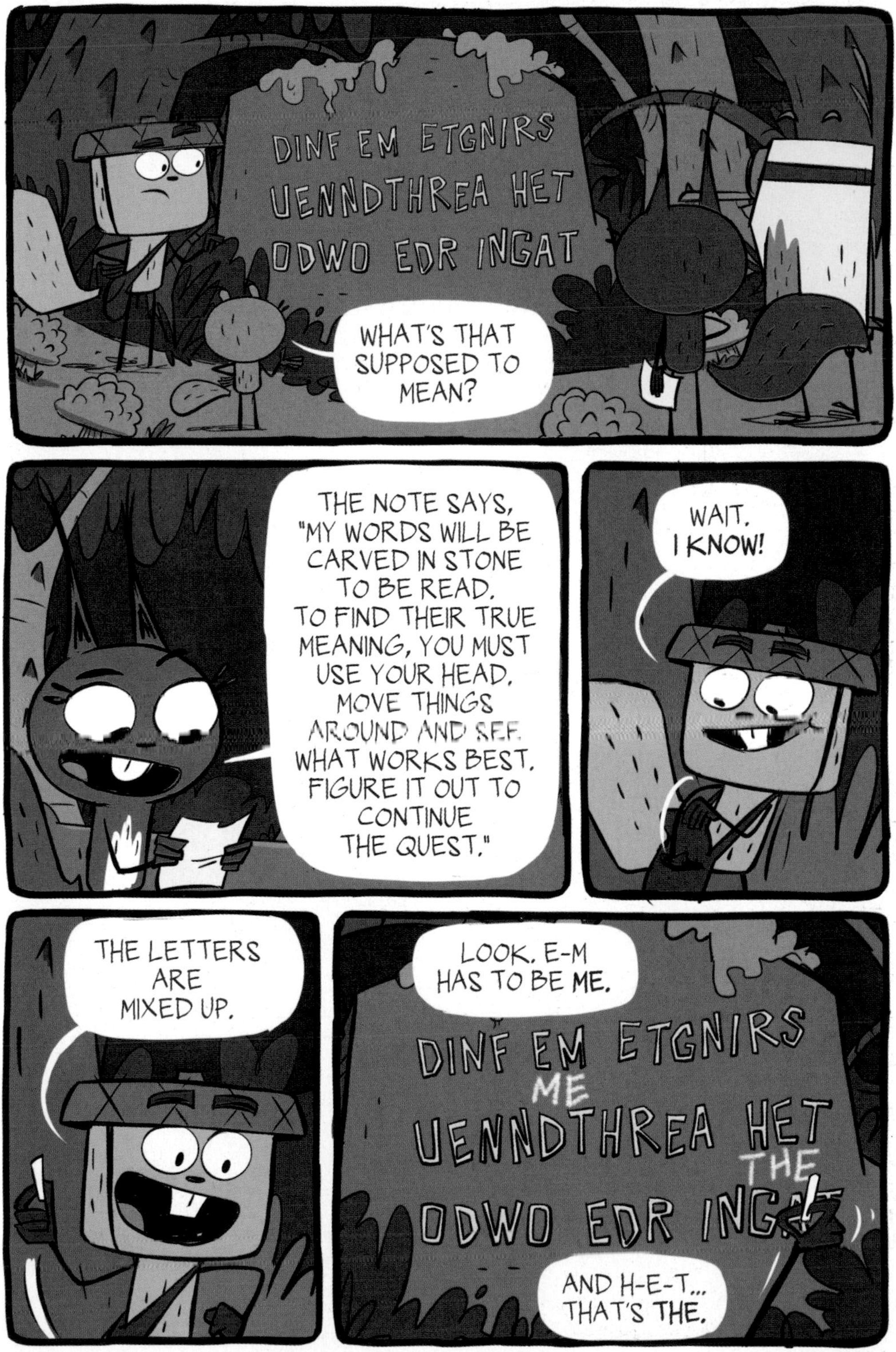
DINF EM ETGNIRS
UENNDTHREA HET
ODWO EDR INGAT
WHAT'S THAT SUPPOSED TO MEAN?
THE NOTE SAYS, "MY WORDS WILL BE CARVED IN STONE TO BE READ. TO FIND THEIR TRUE MEANING, YOU MUST USE YOUR HEAD. MOVE THINGS AROUND AND SEE WHAT WORKS BEST. FIGURE IT OUT TO CONTINUE THE QUEST."
WAIT. I KNOW!
THE LETTERS ARE MIXED UP.
LOOK. E-M HAS TO BE ME.
DINF EM ETGNIRS
ME
UENNDTHREA HET
THE
ODWO EDR INGAT
AND H-E-T... THAT'S THE.

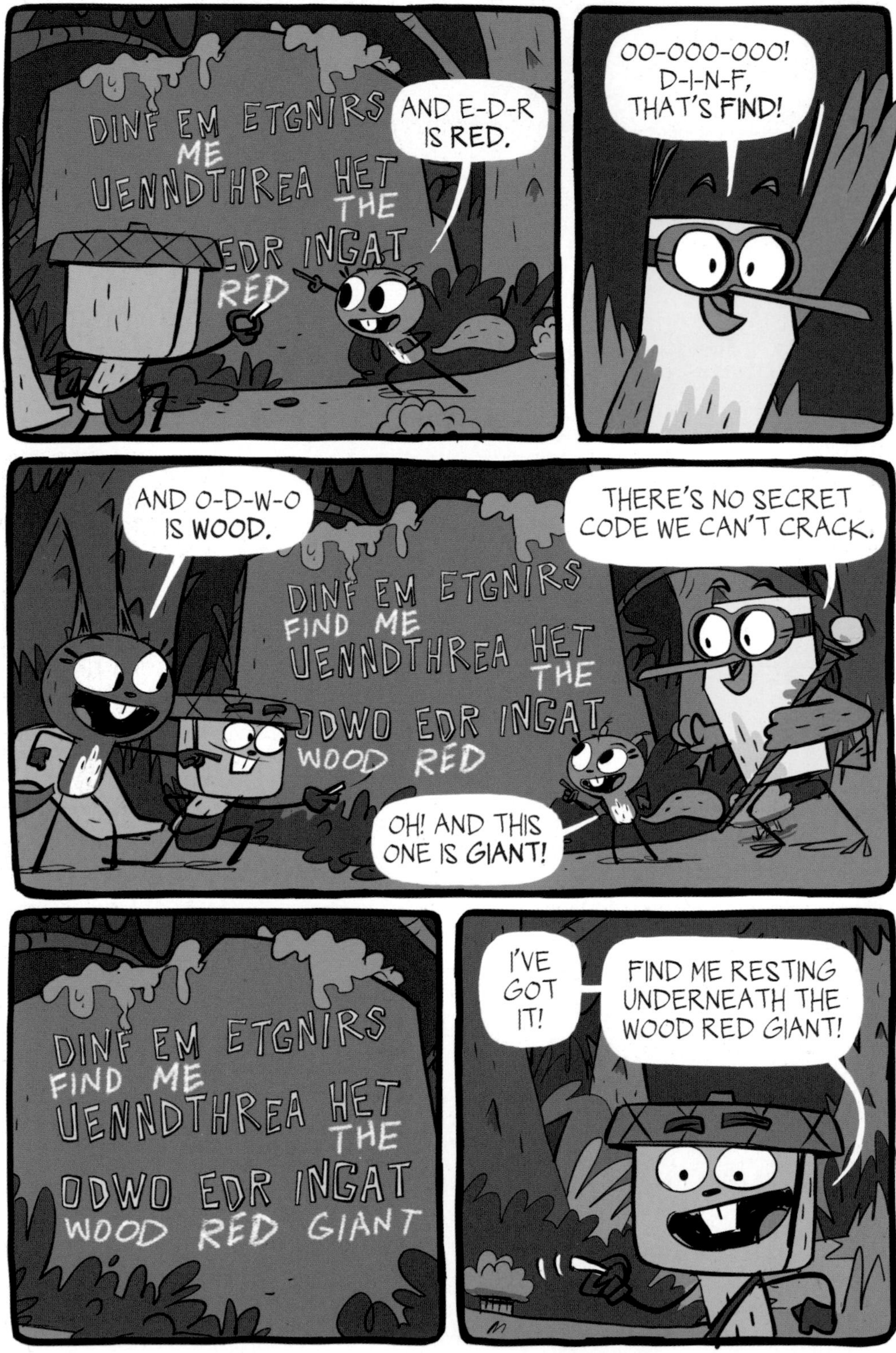
DINF EM ETGNIRS
ME
UENNDTHREA HET
THE
EDR INGAT
RED
AND E-D-R IS RED.
OO-OOO-OOO! D-I-N-F, THAT'S FIND!
AND O-D-W-O IS WOOD.
THERE'S NO SECRET CODE WE CAN'T CRACK.
DINF EM ETGNIRS
FIND ME
UENNDTHREA HET
THE
ODWO EDR INGAT
WOOD RED
OH! AND THIS ONE IS GIANT!
DINF EM ETGNIRS
FIND ME
UENNDTHREA HET
THE
ODWO EDR INGAT
WOOD RED GIANT
I'VE GOT IT!
FIND ME RESTING UNDERNEATH THE WOOD RED GIANT!

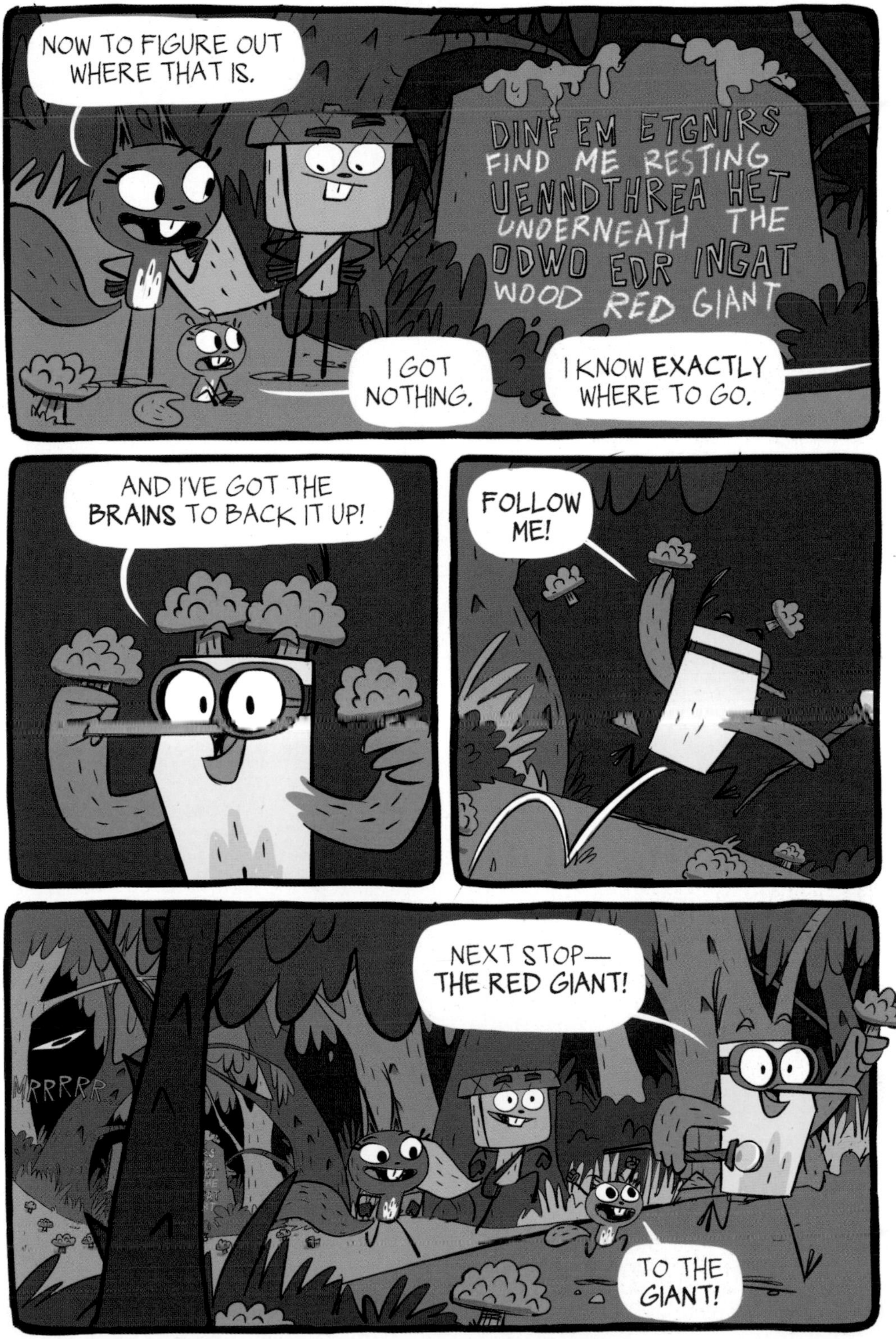
NOW TO FIGURE OUT WHERE THAT IS.
DINF EM ETGNIRS
FIND ME RESTING
UENNDTHREA HET
UNDERNEATH THE
ODWO EDR INGAT
WOOD RED GIANT
I GOT NOTHING.
I KNOW EXACTLY WHERE TO GO.
AND I'VE GOT THE BRAINS TO BACK IT UP!
FOLLOW ME!
MRRRRR
NEXT STOP— THE RED GIANT!
TO THE GIANT!

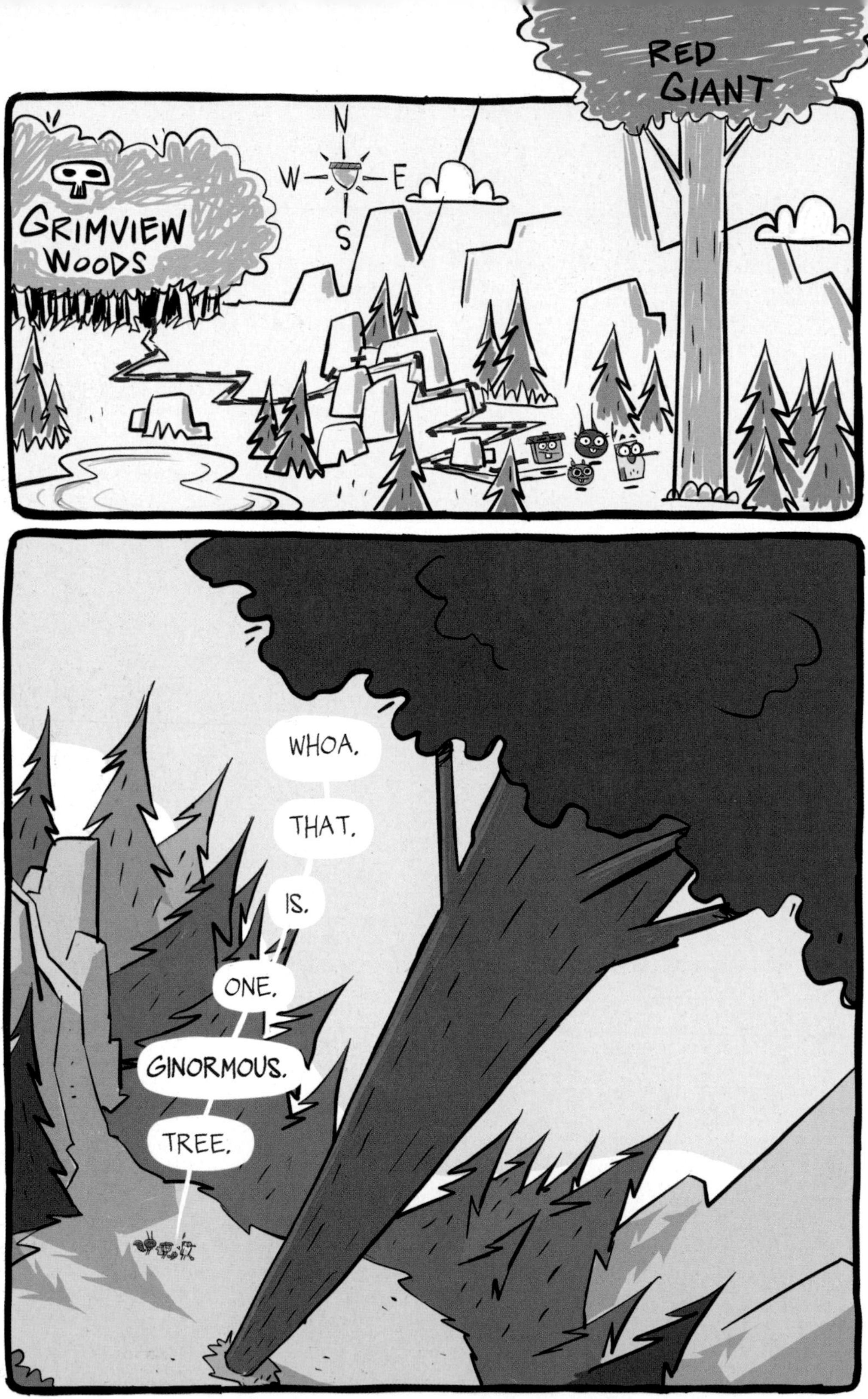
RED GIANT
N
W
E
S
GRIMVIEW WOODS
WHOA.
THAT.
IS.
ONE.
GINORMOUS.
TREE.

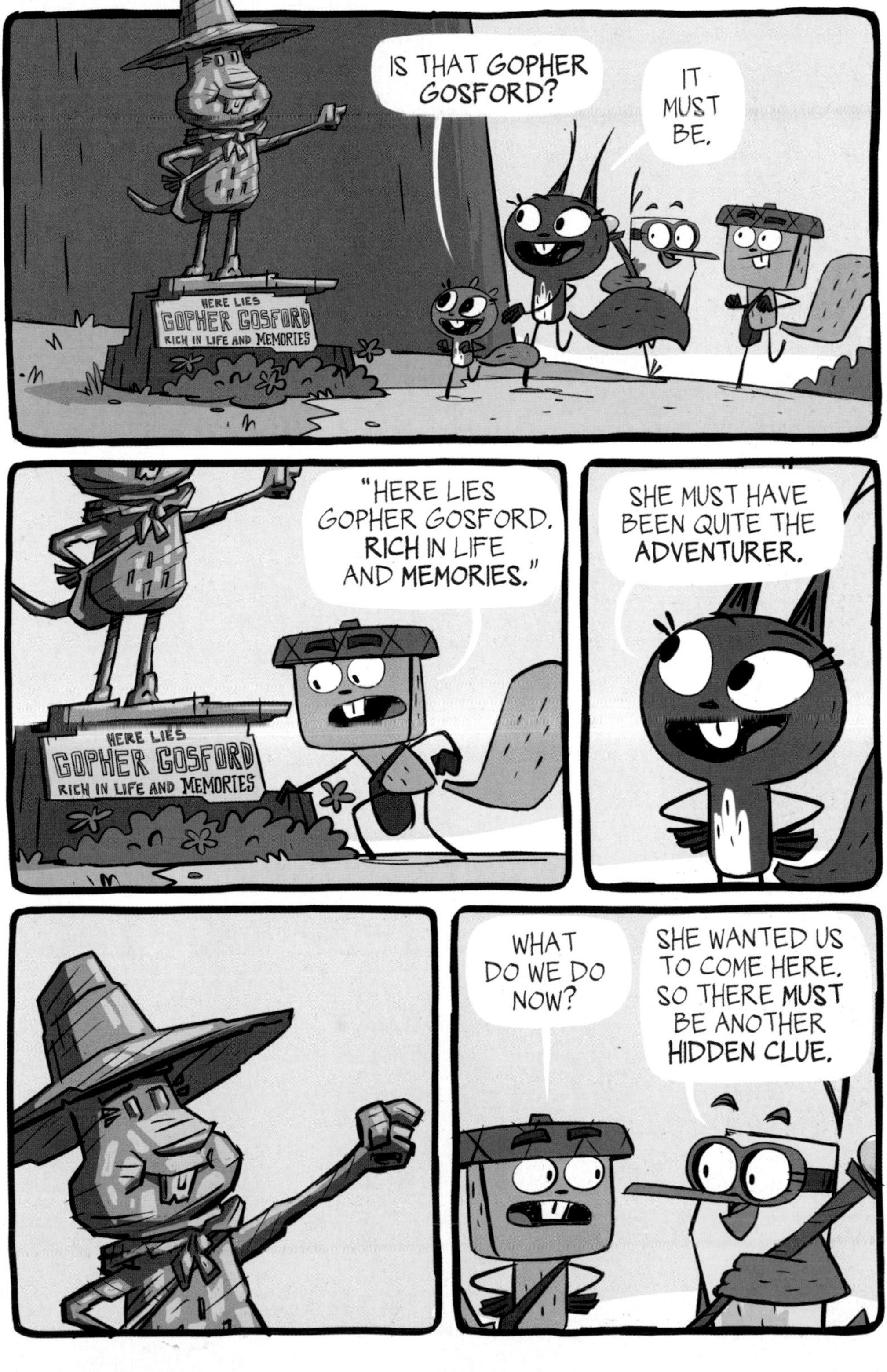
HERE LIES
GOPHER GOSFORD
RICH IN LIFE AND MEMORIES
IS THAT GOPHER GOSFORD?
IT MUST BE.
"HERE LIES GOPHER GOSFORD. RICH IN LIFE AND MEMORIES."
HERE LIES
GOPHER GOSFORD
RICH IN LIFE AND MEMORIES
SHE MUST HAVE BEEN QUITE THE ADVENTURER.
WHAT DO WE DO NOW?
SHE WANTED US TO COME HERE, SO THERE MUST BE ANOTHER HIDDEN CLUE.

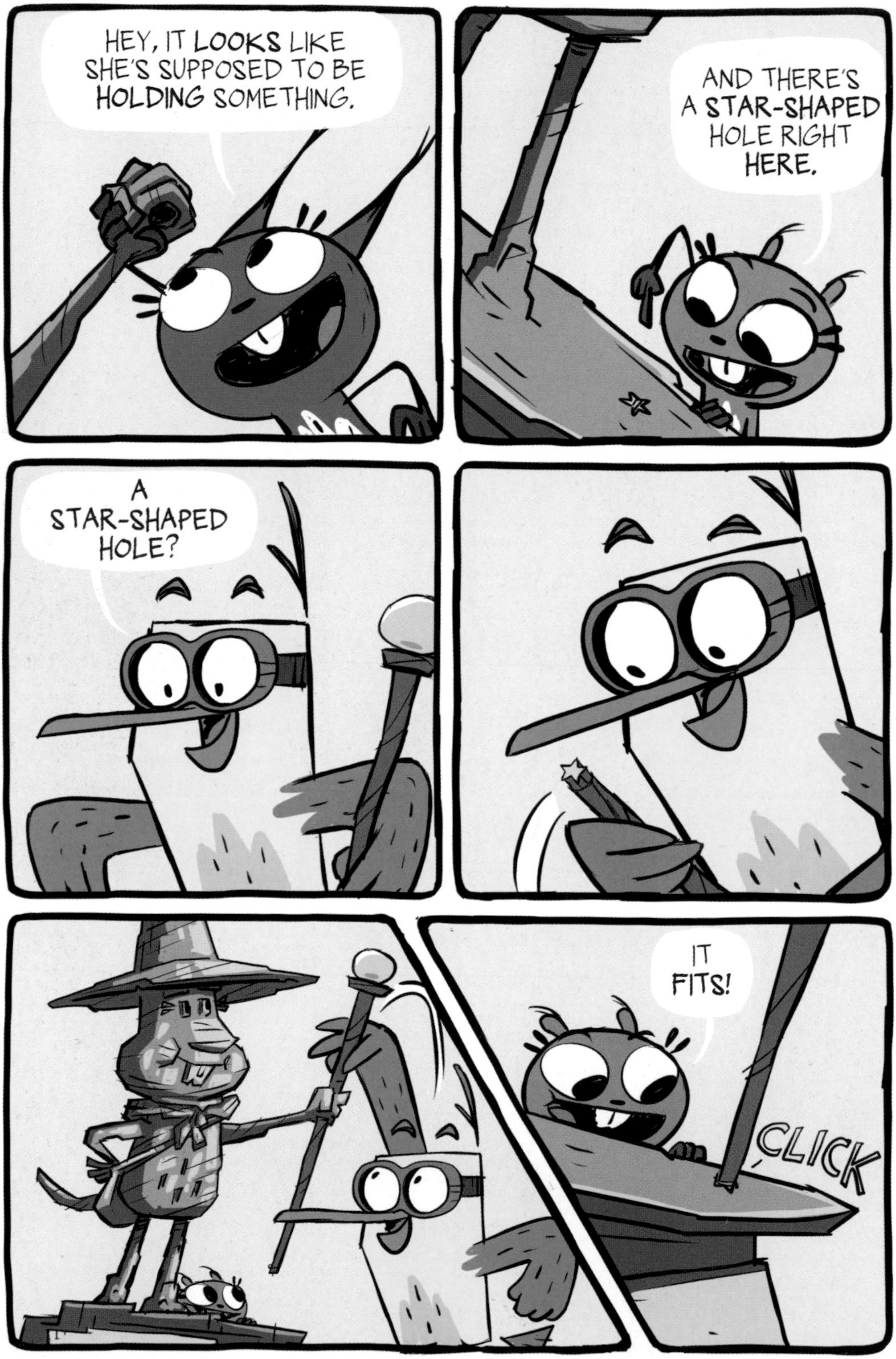
HEY, IT LOOKS LIKE SHE'S SUPPOSED TO BE HOLDING SOMETHING.
AND THERE'S A STAR-SHAPED HOLE RIGHT HERE.
A STAR-SHAPED HOLE?
IT FITS!
CLICK

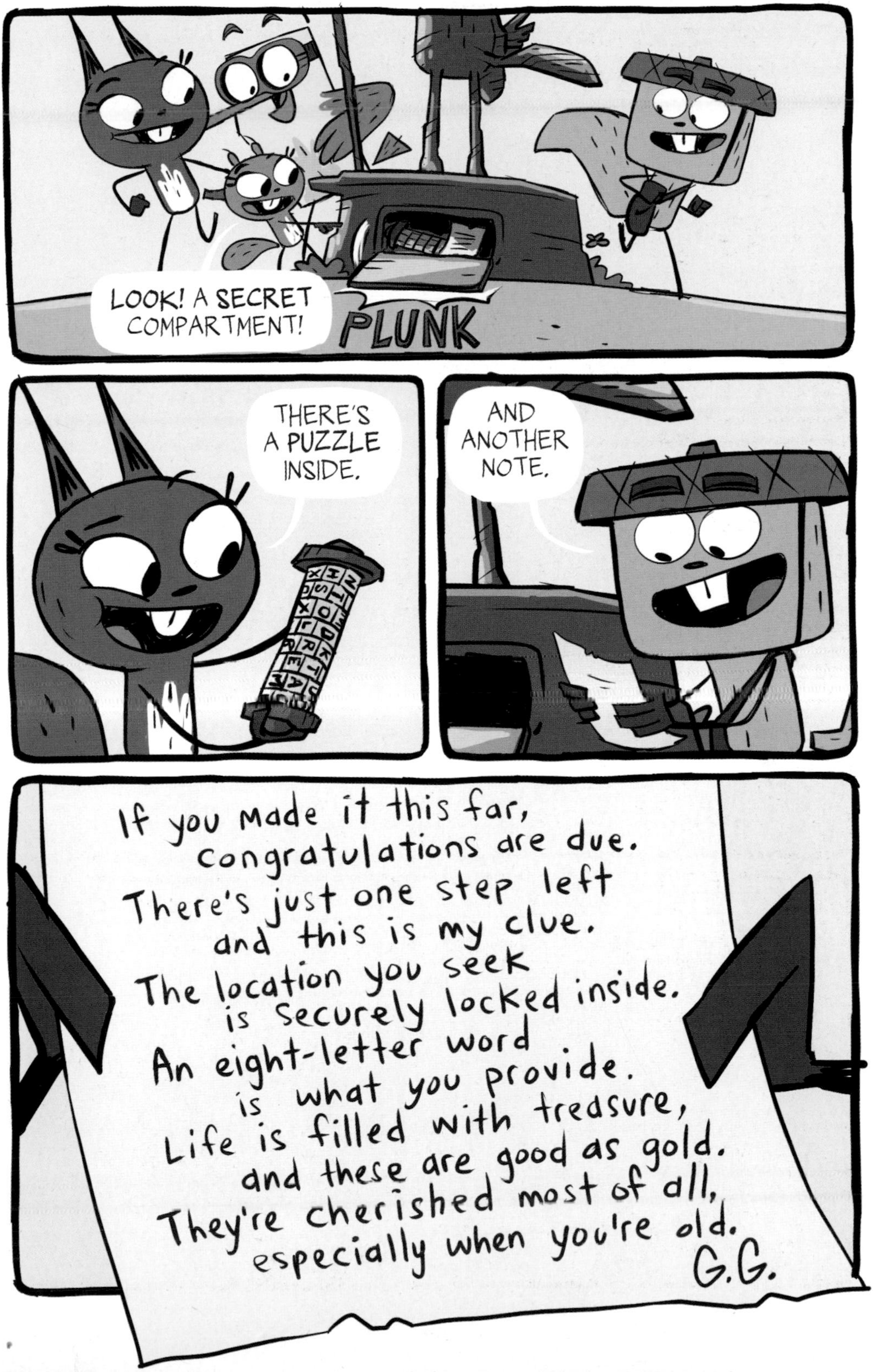
LOOK! A SECRET COMPARTMENT!
PLUNK
THERE'S A PUZZLE INSIDE.
AND ANOTHER NOTE.
If you made it this far,
congratulations are due.
There's just one step left
and this is my clue.
The location you seek
is securely locked inside.
An eight-letter word
is what you provide.
Life is filled with treasure,
and these are good as gold.
They're cherished most of all,
especially when you're old.
G.G.

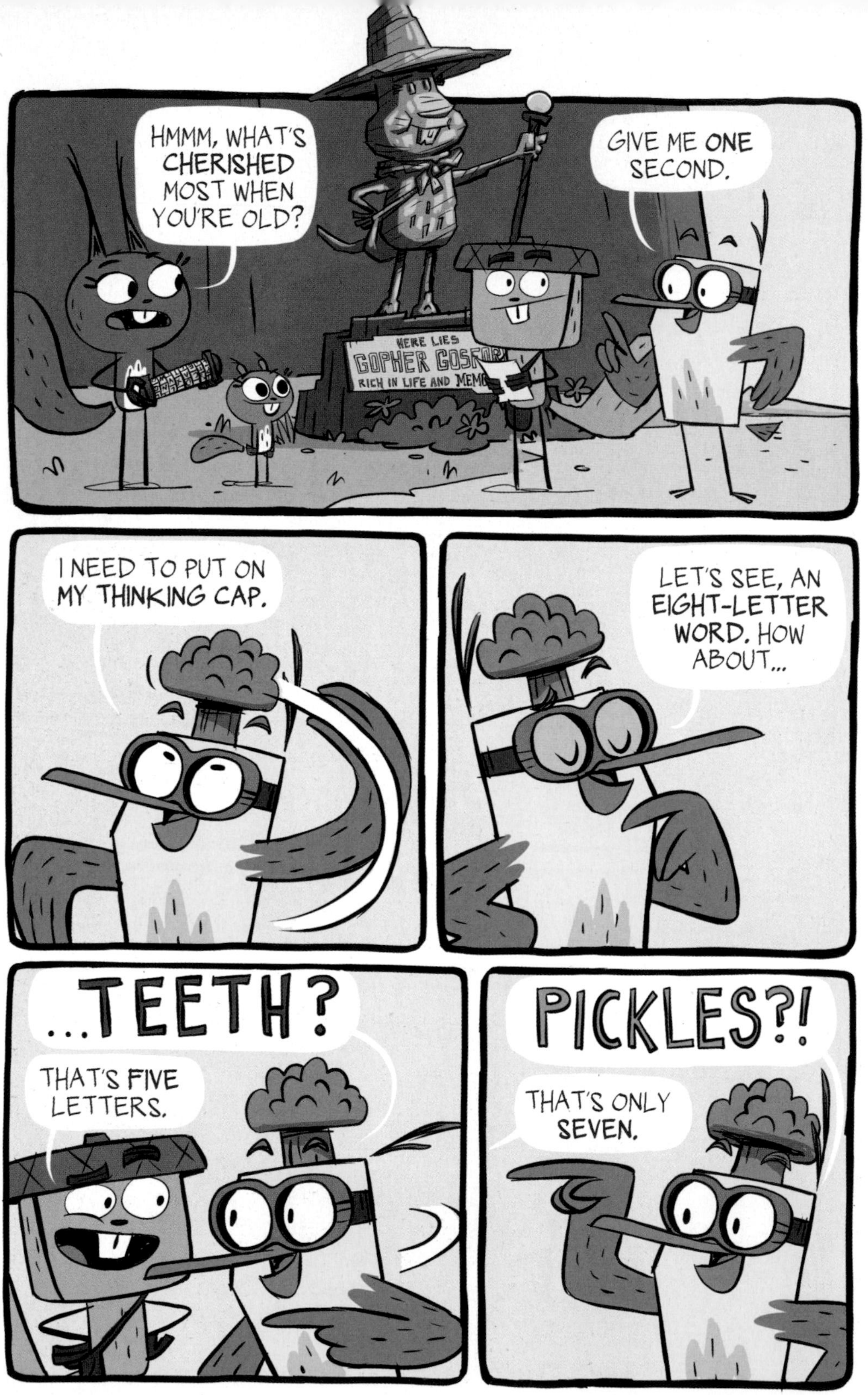
HMMM, WHAT'S CHERISHED MOST WHEN YOU'RE OLD?
GIVE ME ONE SECOND.
HERE LIES
GOPHER GOSF
RICH IN LIFE AND MEM
I NEED TO PUT ON MY THINKING CAP.
LET'S SEE, AN EIGHT-LETTER WORD. HOW ABOUT...
...TEETH?
THAT'S FIVE LETTERS.
PICKLES?!
THAT'S ONLY SEVEN.

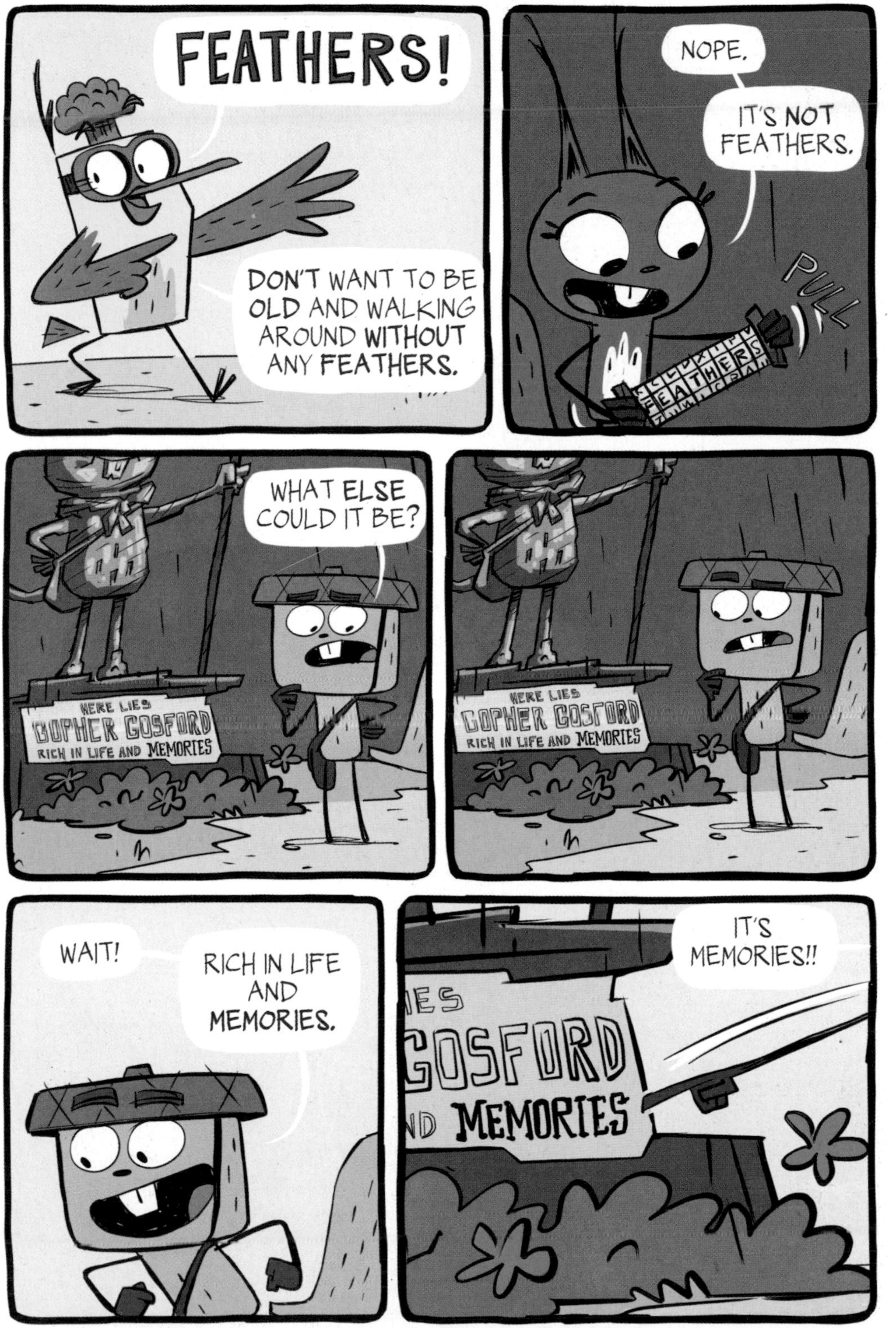

FEATHERS!
DON'T WANT TO BE OLD AND WALKING AROUND WITHOUT ANY FEATHERS.
NOPE.
IT'S NOT FEATHERS.
PULL
FEATHERS
WHAT ELSE COULD IT BE?
HERE LIES
GOPHER GOSFORD
RICH IN LIFE AND MEMORIES
HERE LIES
GOPHER GOSFORD
RICH IN LIFE AND MEMORIES
WAIT!
RICH IN LIFE AND MEMORIES.
IT'S MEMORIES!!
IES
GOSFORD
ND MEMORIES

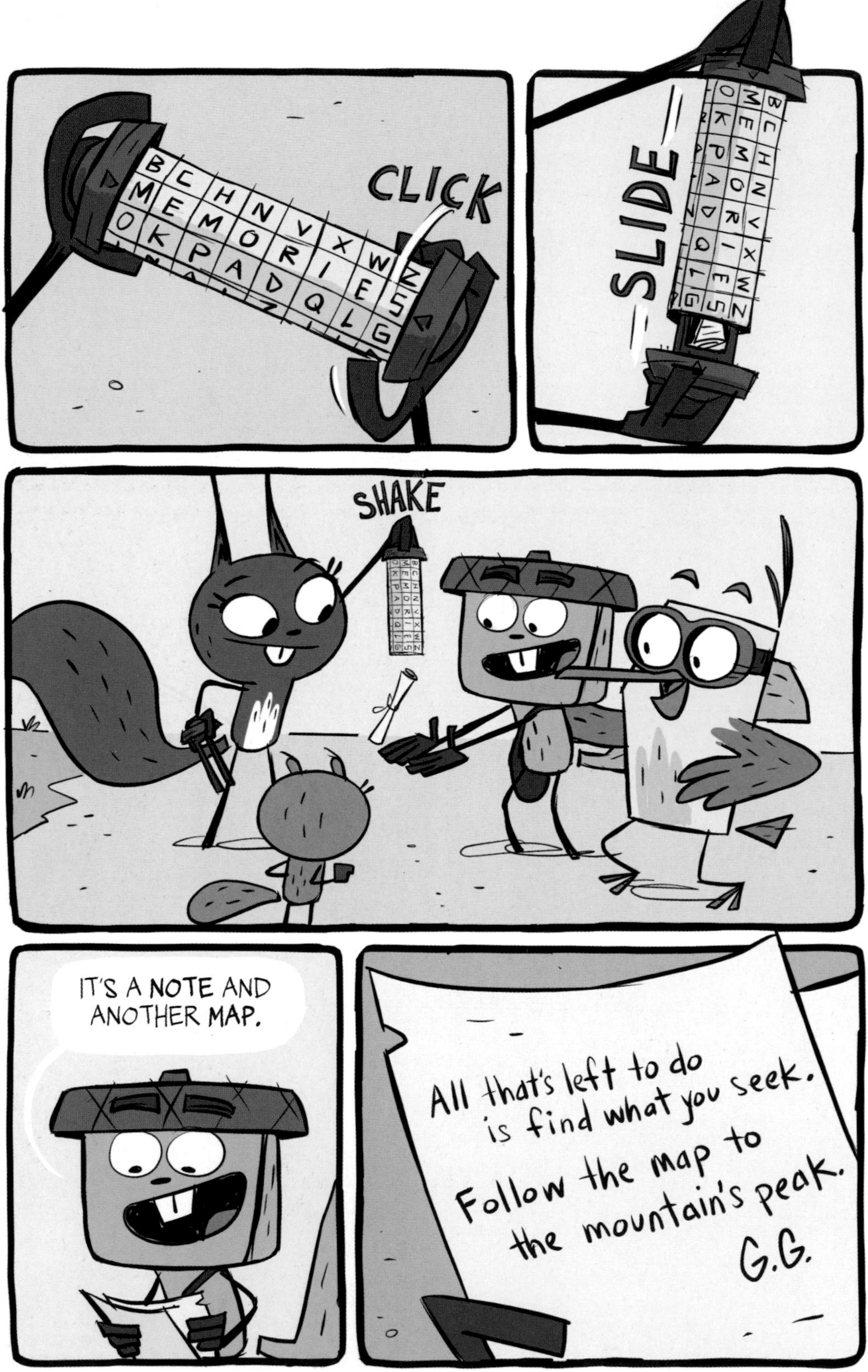
CLICK
SLIDE
SHAKE
IT'S A NOTE AND ANOTHER MAP.
All that's left to do
is find what you seek.
Follow the map to
the mountain's peak.
G.G.

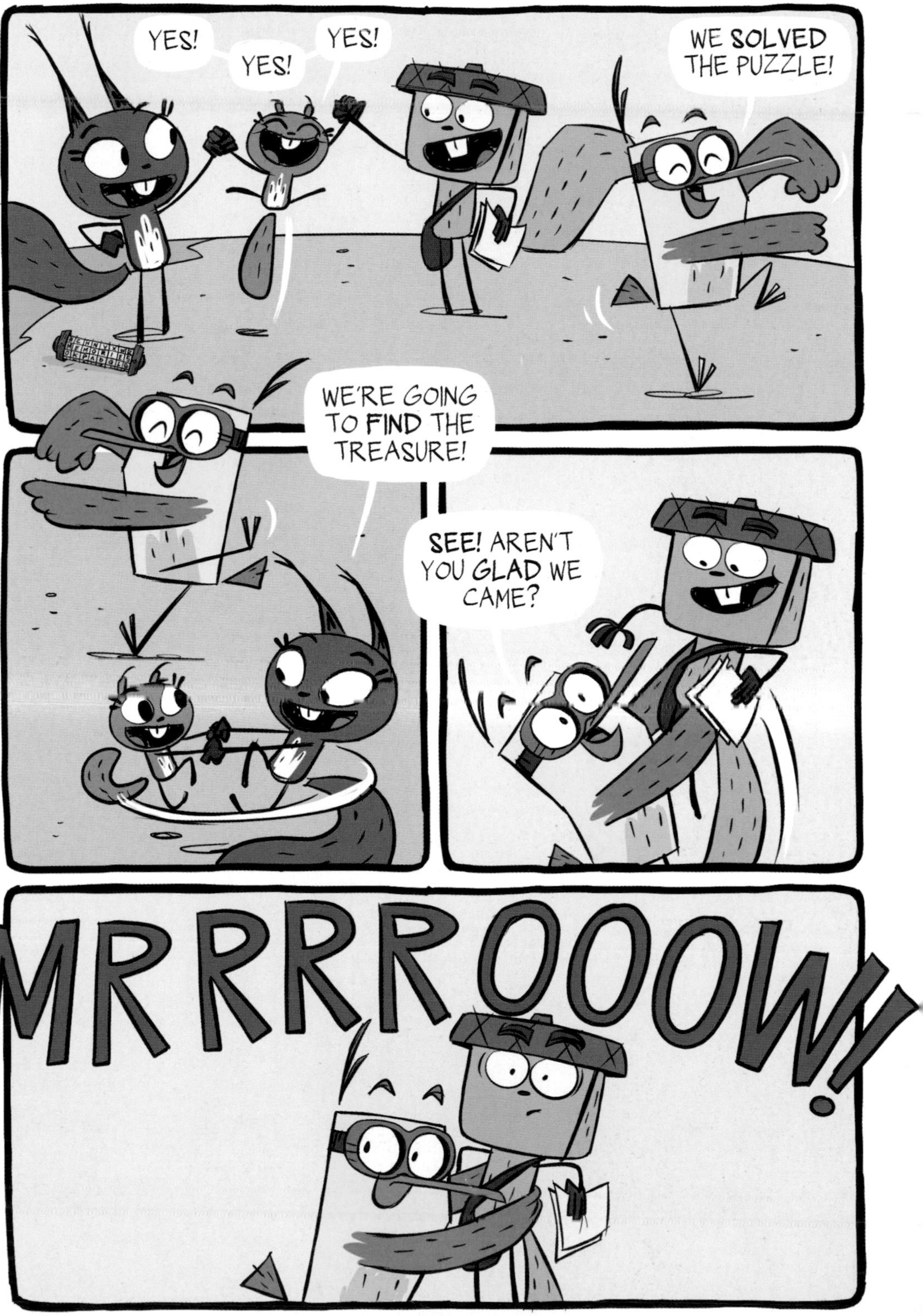
YES!
YES!
YES!
WE SOLVED THE PUZZLE!
WE'RE GOING TO FIND THE TREASURE!
SEE! AREN'T YOU GLAD WE CAME?
MRRRROOOW!!

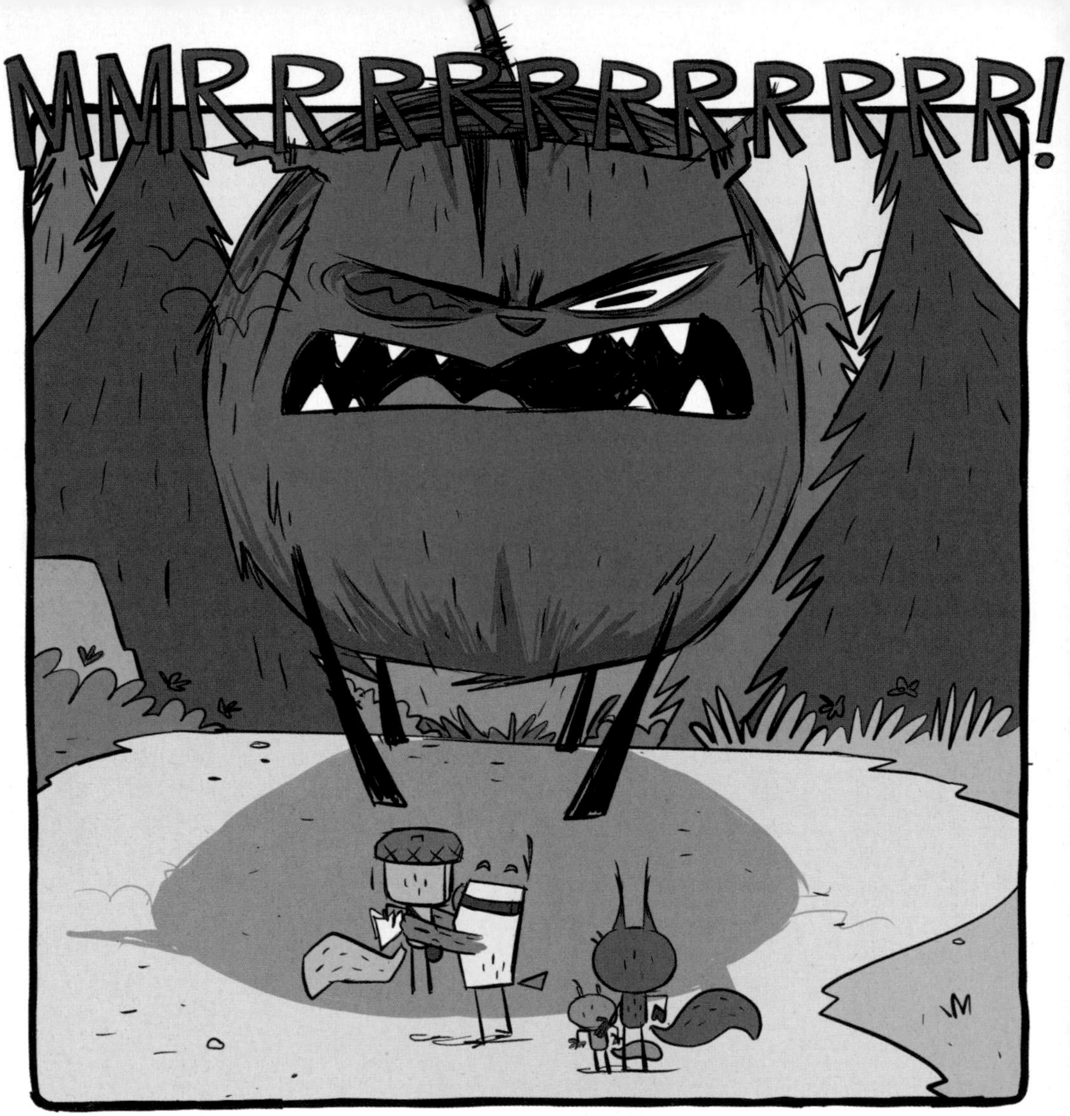
MMRRRRRRRRRRRRR!

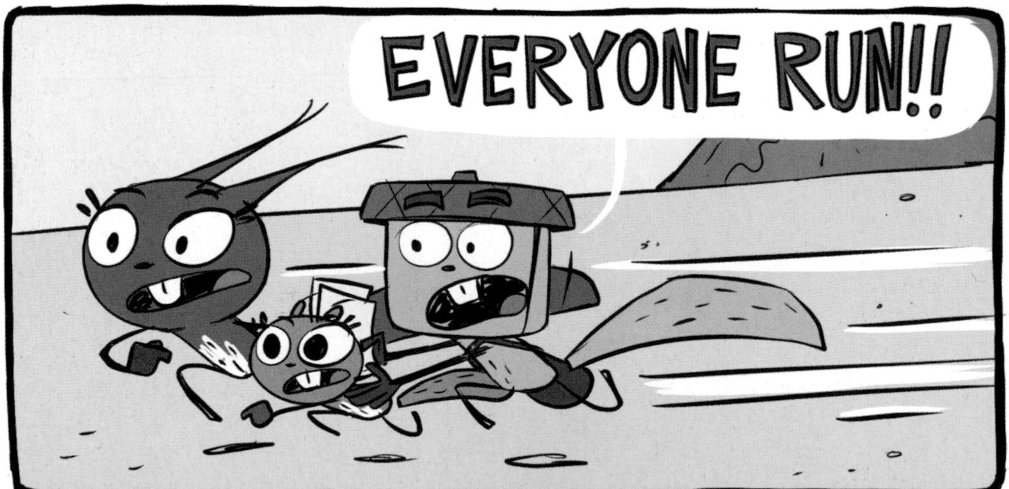
EVERYONE RUN!!

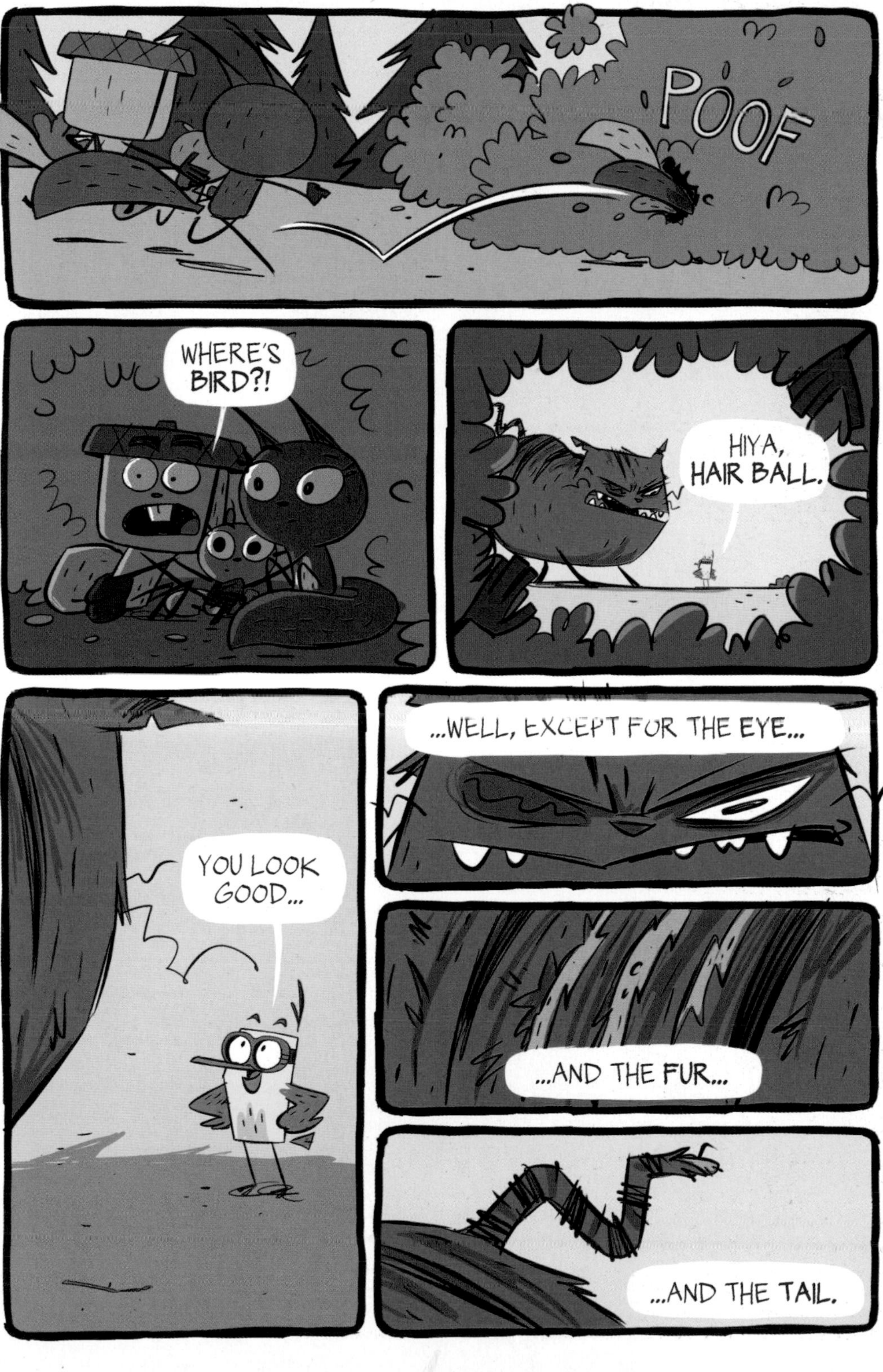
POOF
WHERE'S BIRD?!
HIYA, HAIR BALL.
YOU LOOK GOOD...
...WELL, EXCEPT FOR THE EYE...
...AND THE FUR...
...AND THE TAIL.

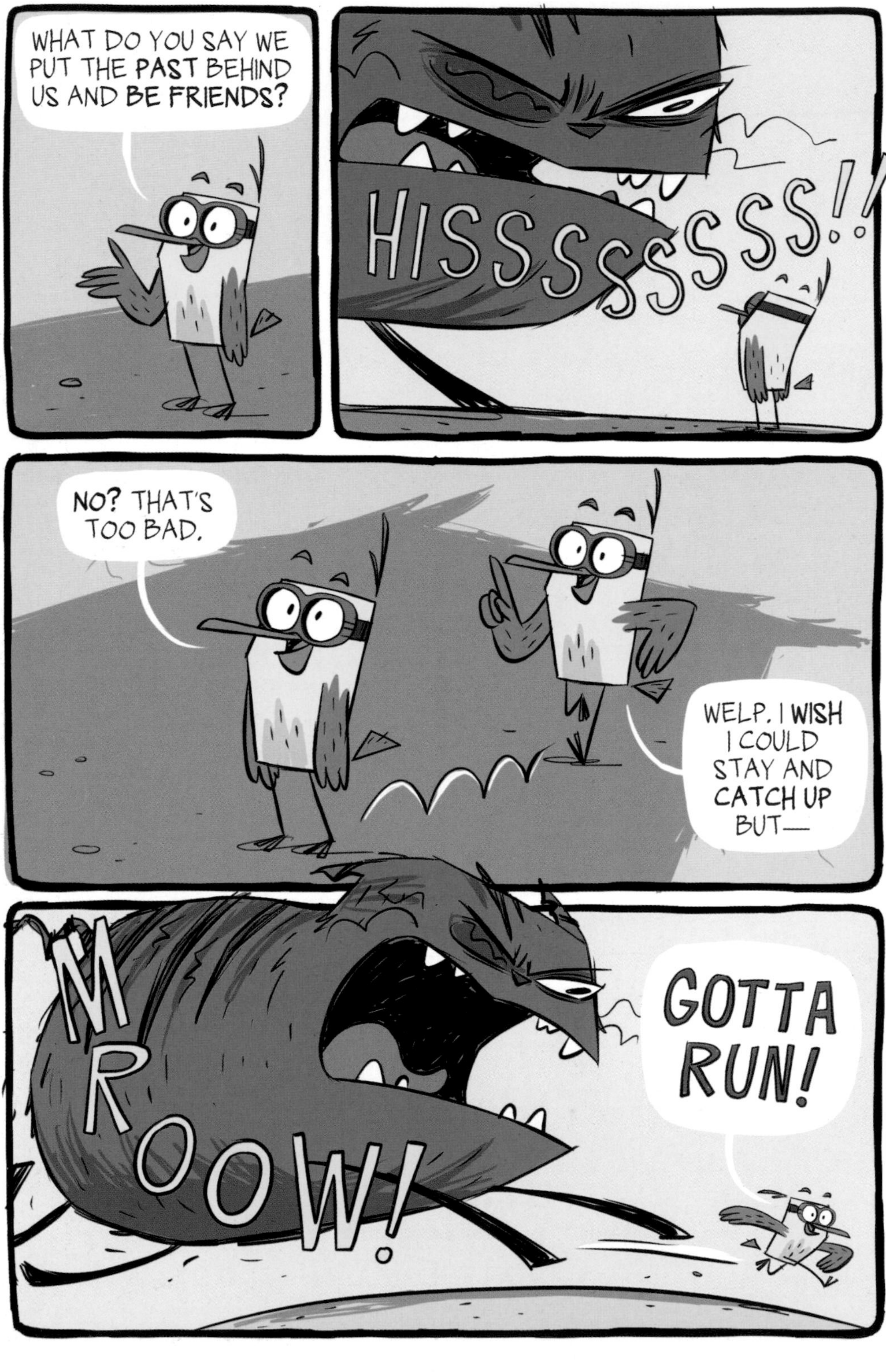
WHAT DO YOU SAY WE PUT THE PAST BEHIND US AND BE FRIENDS?
HISSSSSSSSS!!
NO? THAT'S TOO BAD.
WELP. I WISH I COULD STAY AND CATCH UP BUT—
MROOOW!
GOTTA RUN!

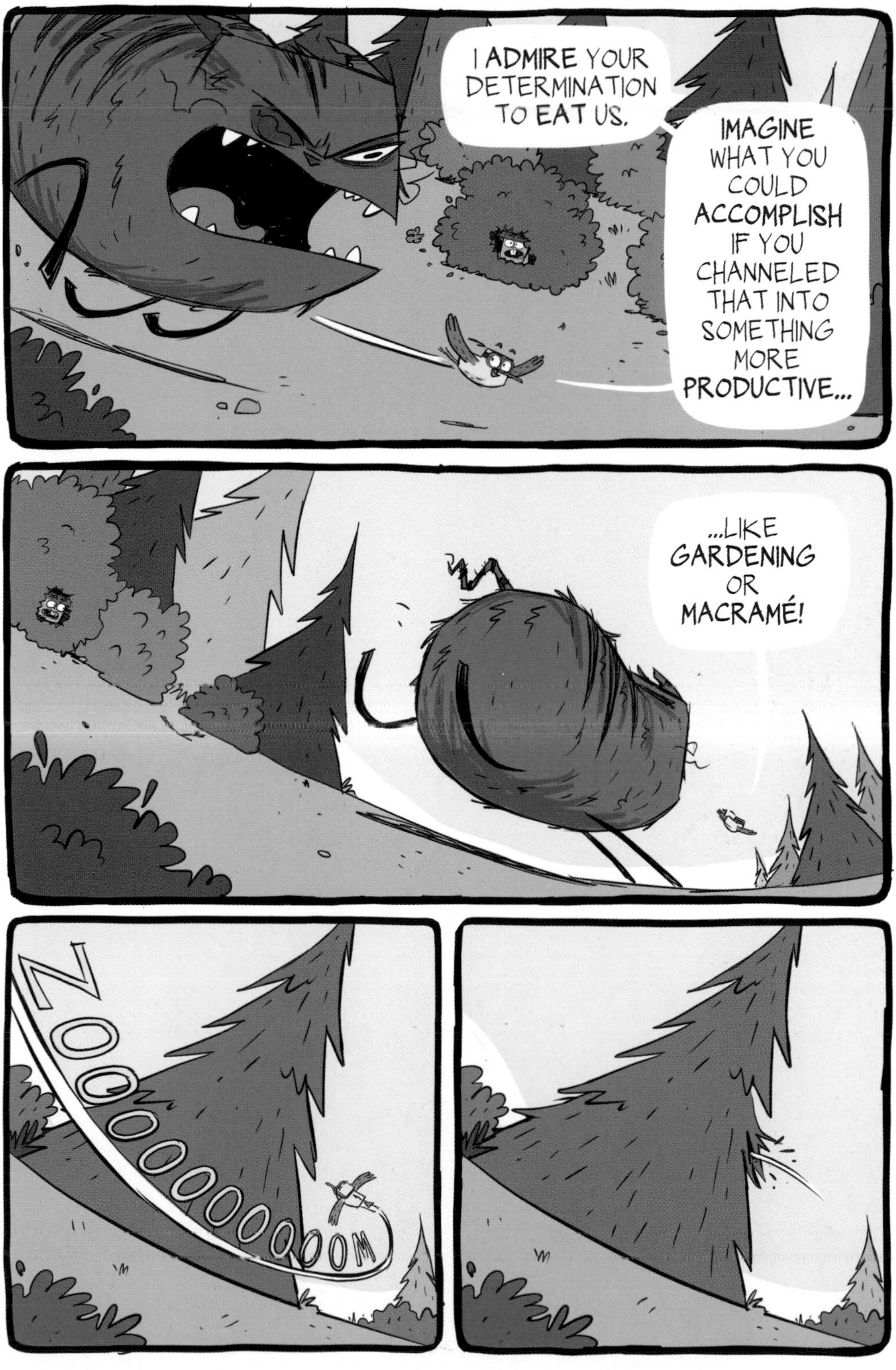
I ADMIRE YOUR DETERMINATION TO EAT US.
IMAGINE WHAT YOU COULD ACCOMPLISH IF YOU CHANNELED THAT INTO SOMETHING MORE PRODUCTIVE...
...LIKE GARDENING OR MACRAMÉ!
ZOOOOOOOOOOOOOM

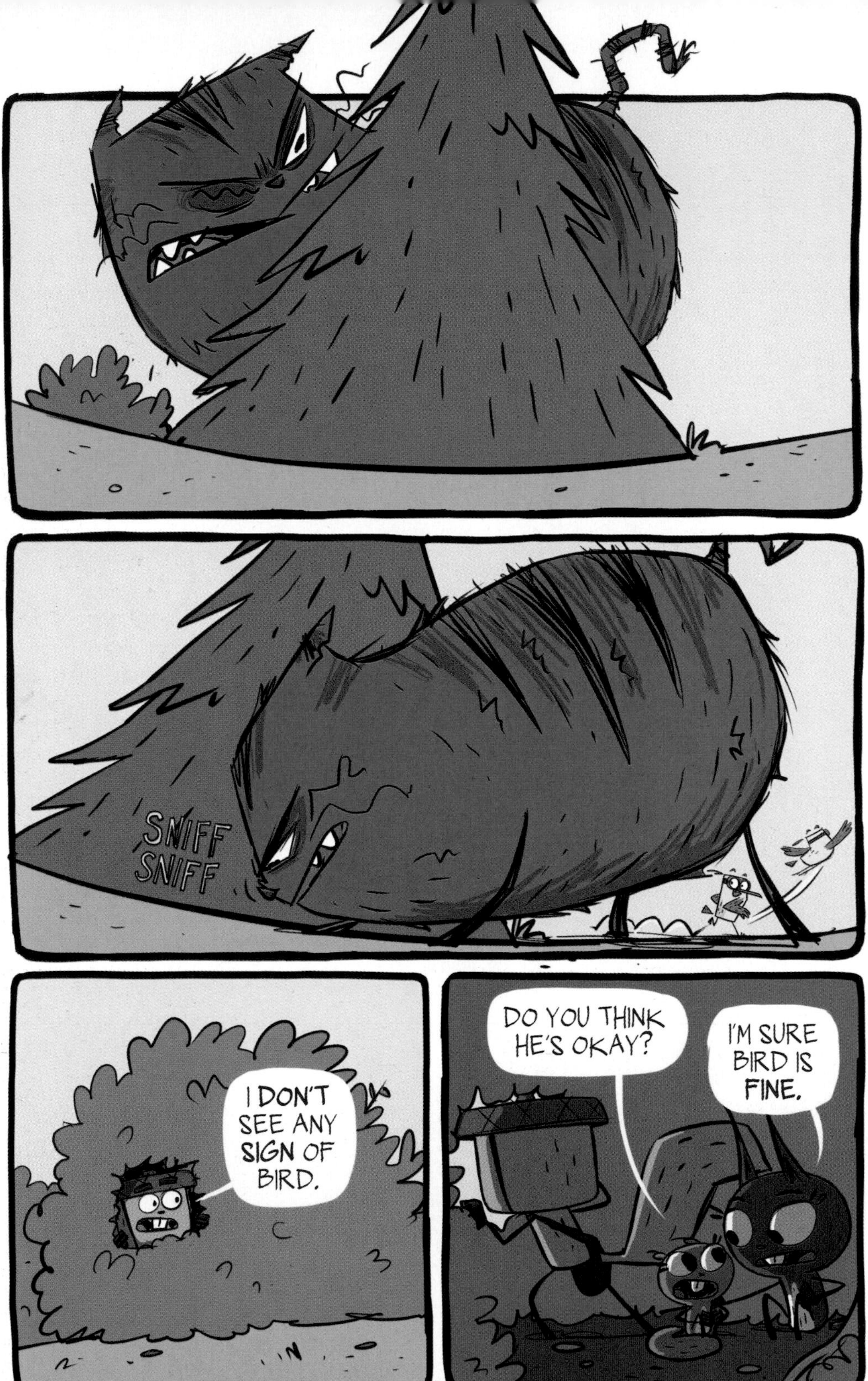
SNIFF
SNIFF
I DON'T SEE ANY SIGN OF BIRD.
DO YOU THINK HE'S OKAY?
I'M SURE BIRD IS FINE.

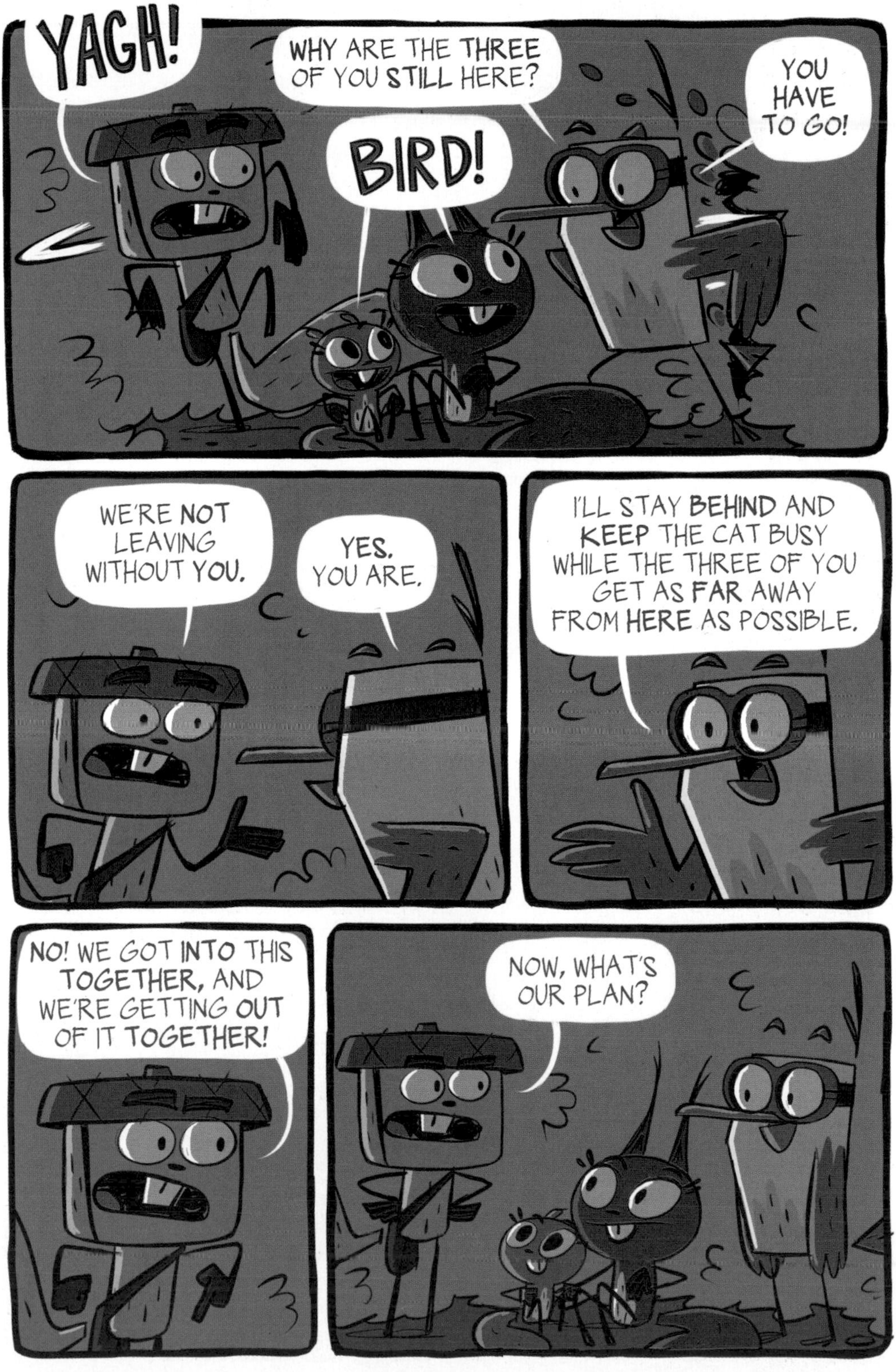
YAGH!
WHY ARE THE THREE OF YOU STILL HERE?
BIRD!
YOU HAVE TO GO!
WE'RE NOT LEAVING WITHOUT YOU.
YES. YOU ARE.
I'LL STAY BEHIND AND KEEP THE CAT BUSY WHILE THE THREE OF YOU GET AS FAR AWAY FROM HERE AS POSSIBLE.
NO! WE GOT INTO THIS TOGETHER, AND WE'RE GETTING OUT OF IT TOGETHER!
NOW, WHAT'S OUR PLAN?

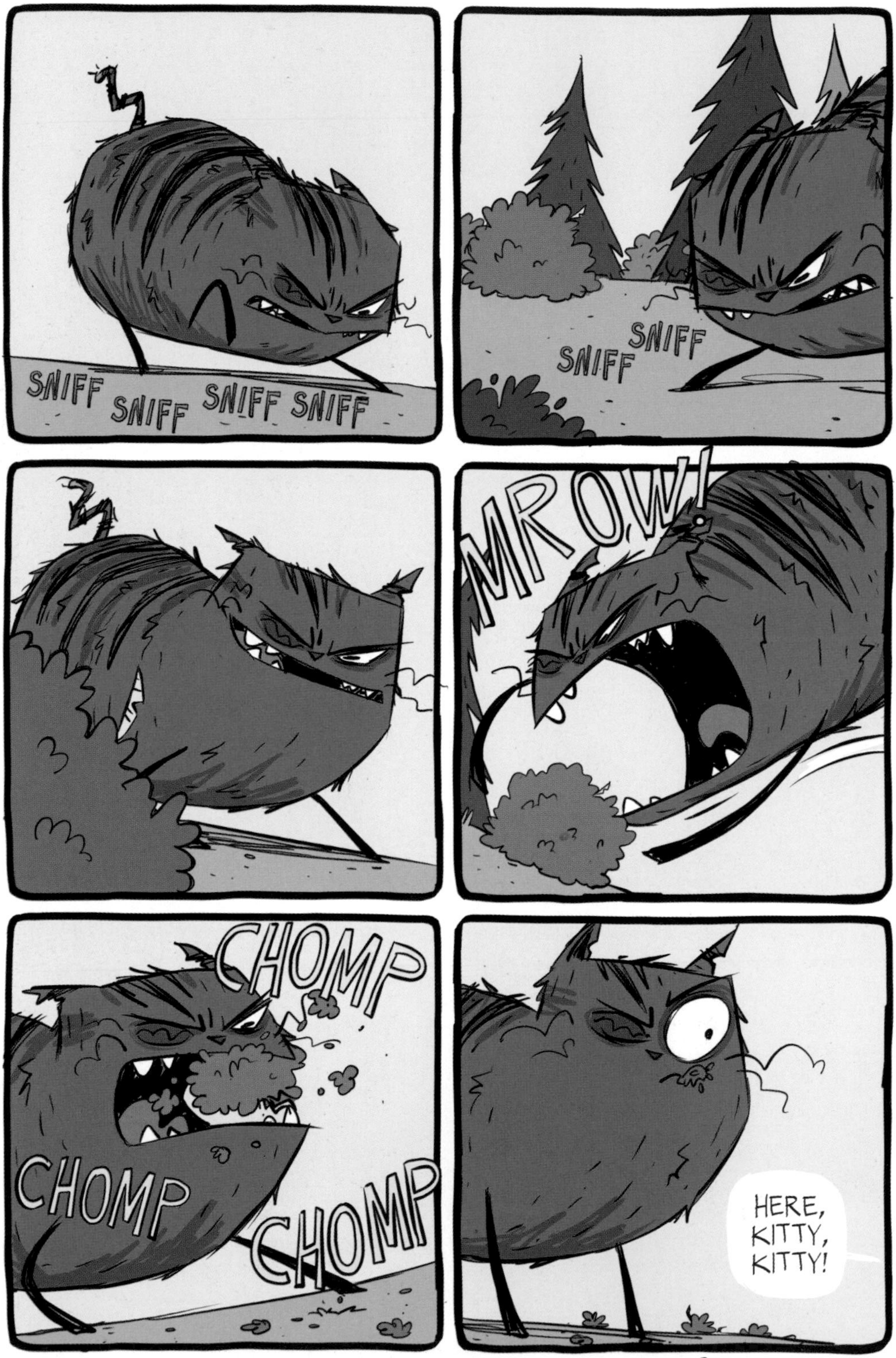
SNIFF SNIFF SNIFF SNIFF
SNIFF SNIFF
MROW!
CHOMP
CHOMP
CHOMP
HERE, KITTY, KITTY!

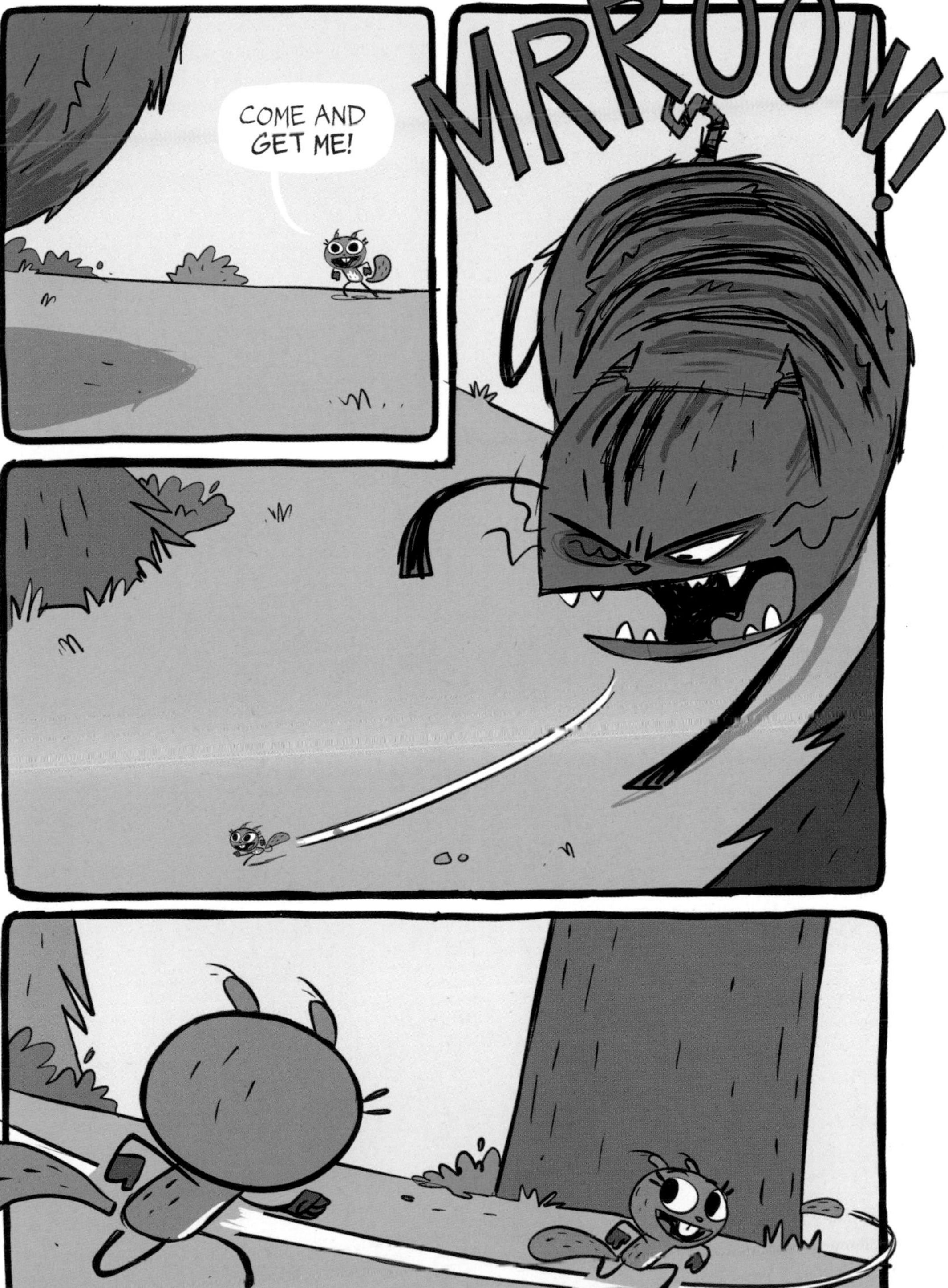
COME AND GET ME!
MRROOW!!

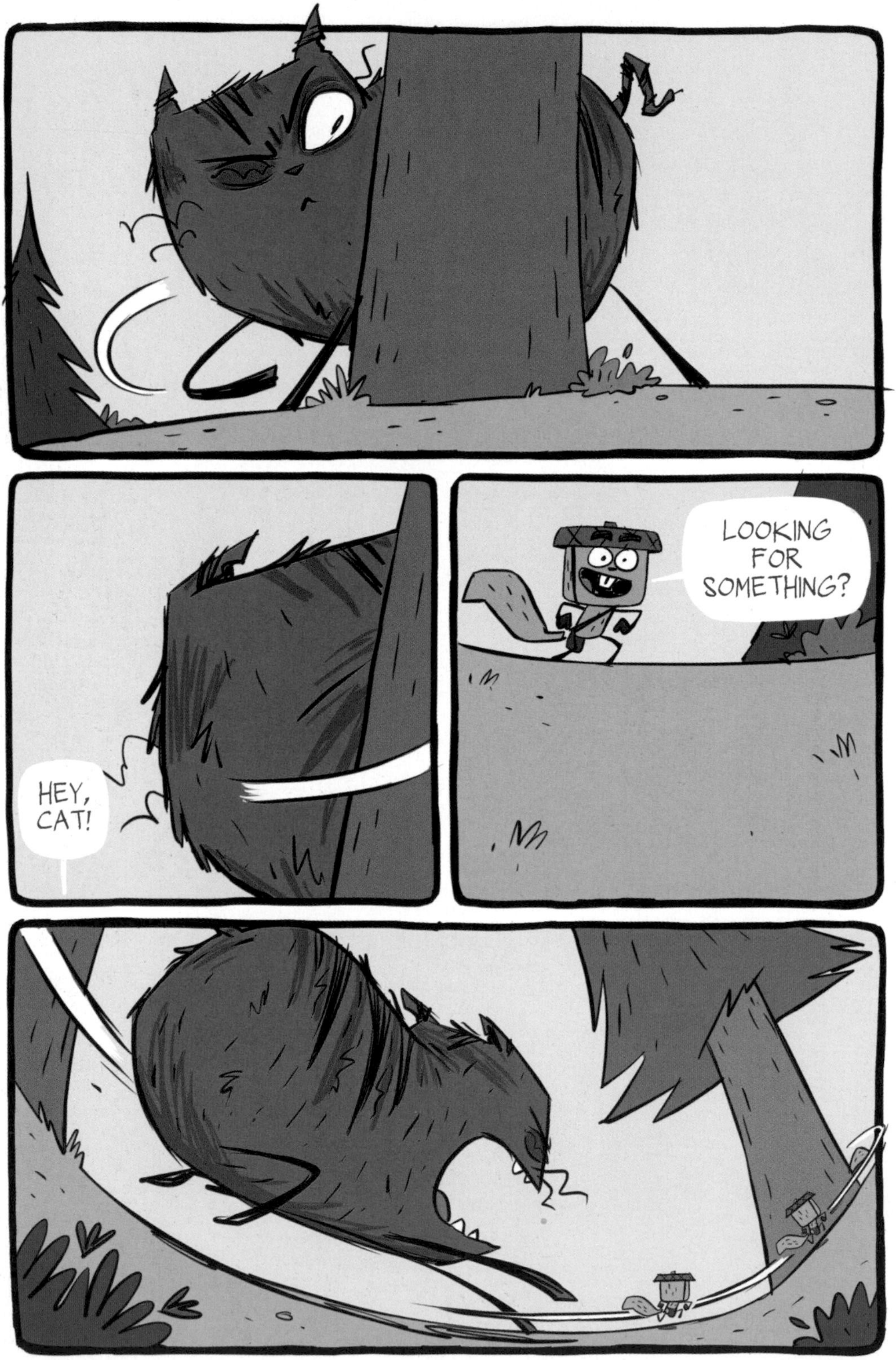
HEY, CAT!
LOOKING FOR SOMETHING?

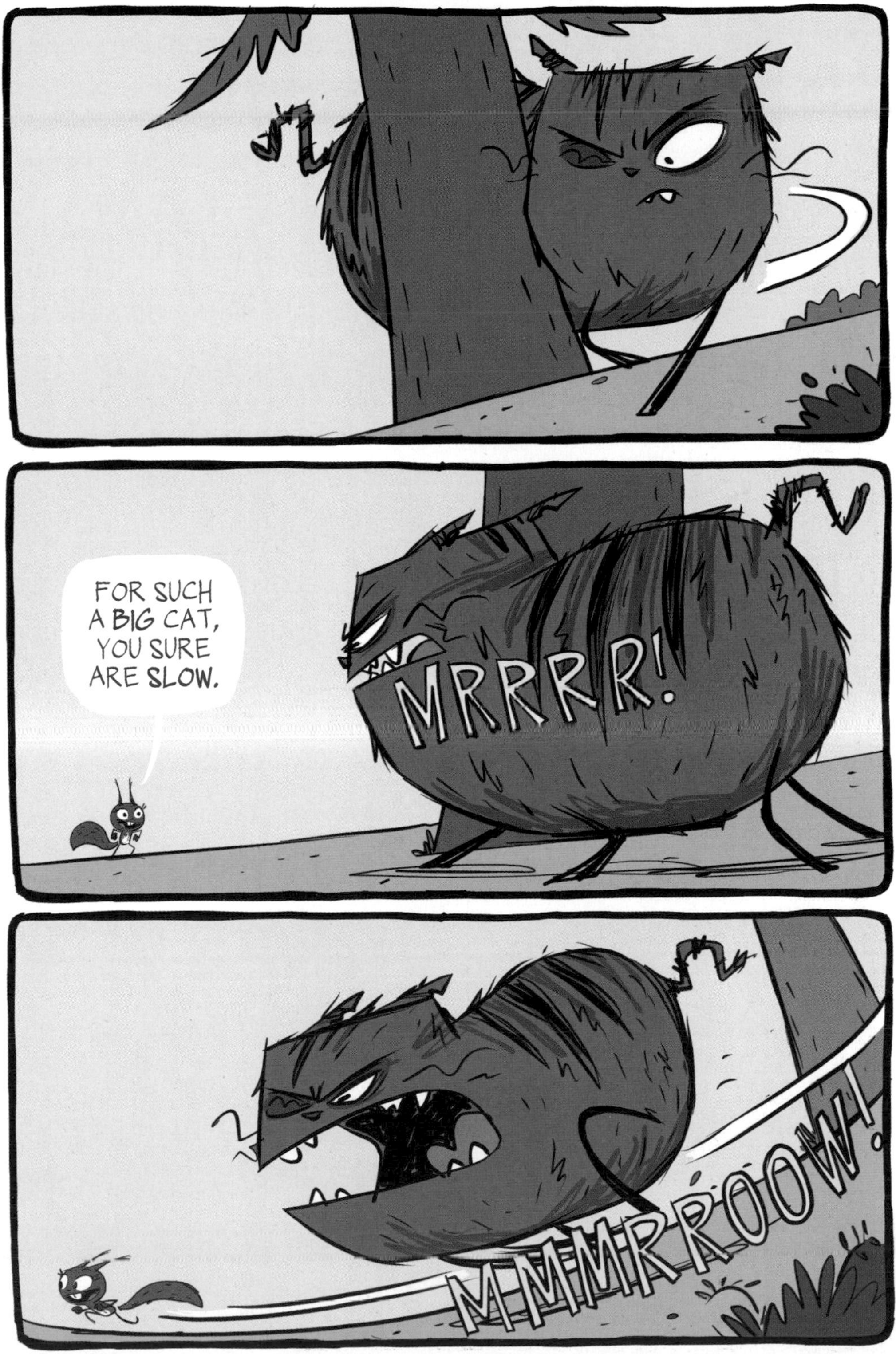
FOR SUCH A BIG CAT, YOU SURE ARE SLOW.
MRRRR!
MMMMRROOOW!

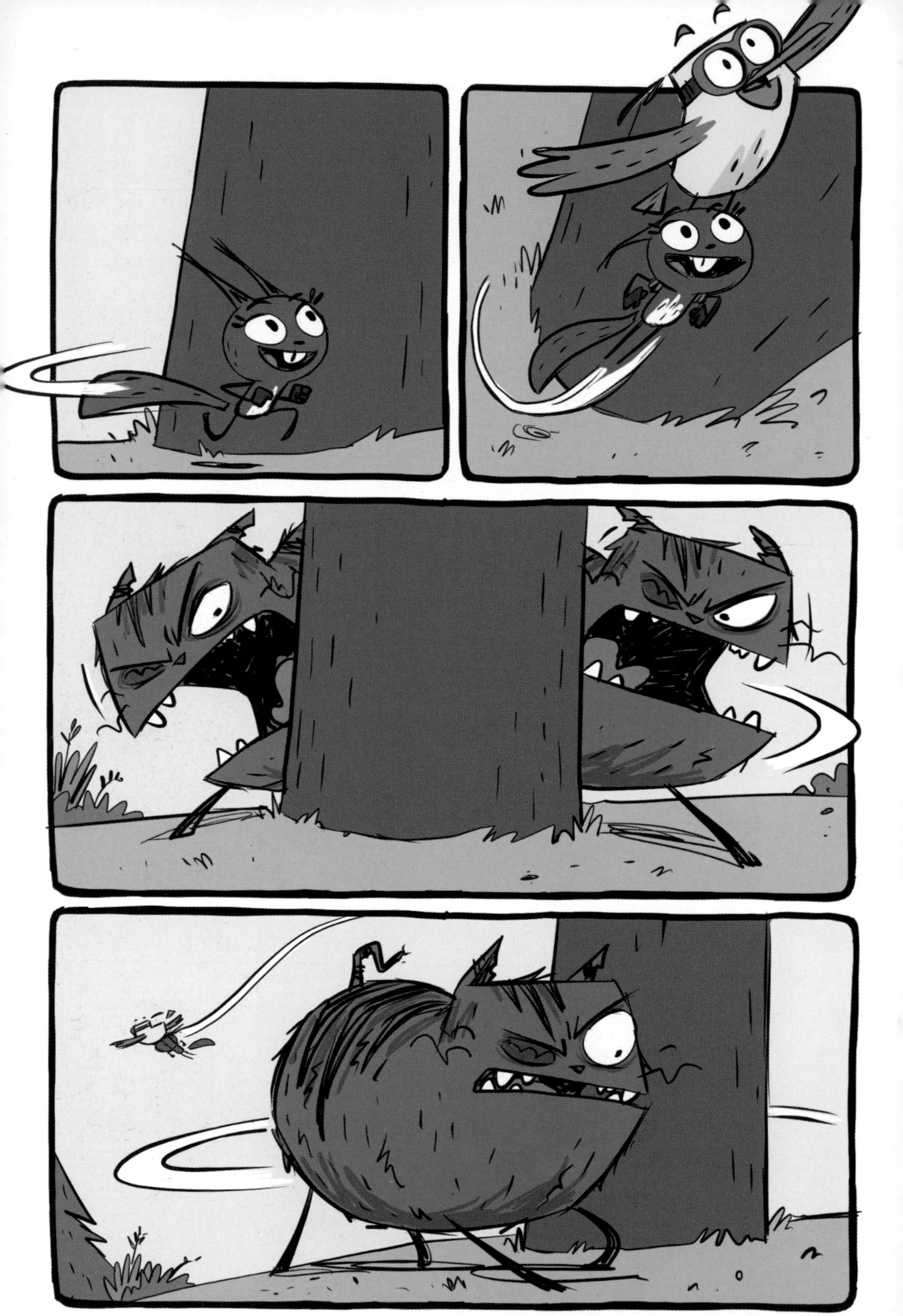

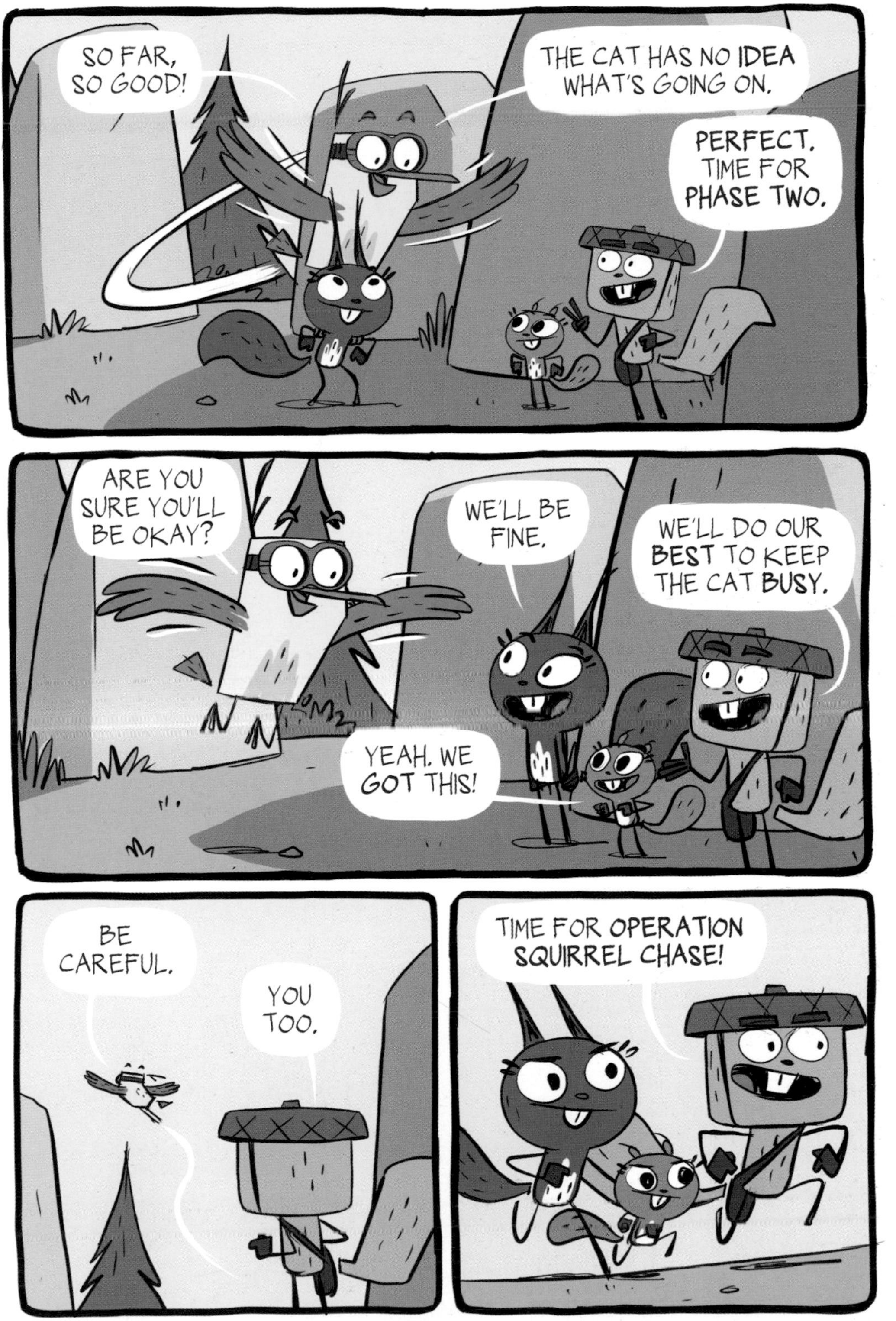
SO FAR, SO GOOD!
THE CAT HAS NO IDEA WHAT'S GOING ON.
PERFECT. TIME FOR PHASE TWO.
ARE YOU SURE YOU'LL BE OKAY?
WE'LL BE FINE.
WE'LL DO OUR BEST TO KEEP THE CAT BUSY.
YEAH. WE GOT THIS!
BE CAREFUL.
YOU TOO.
TIME FOR OPERATION SQUIRREL CHASE!

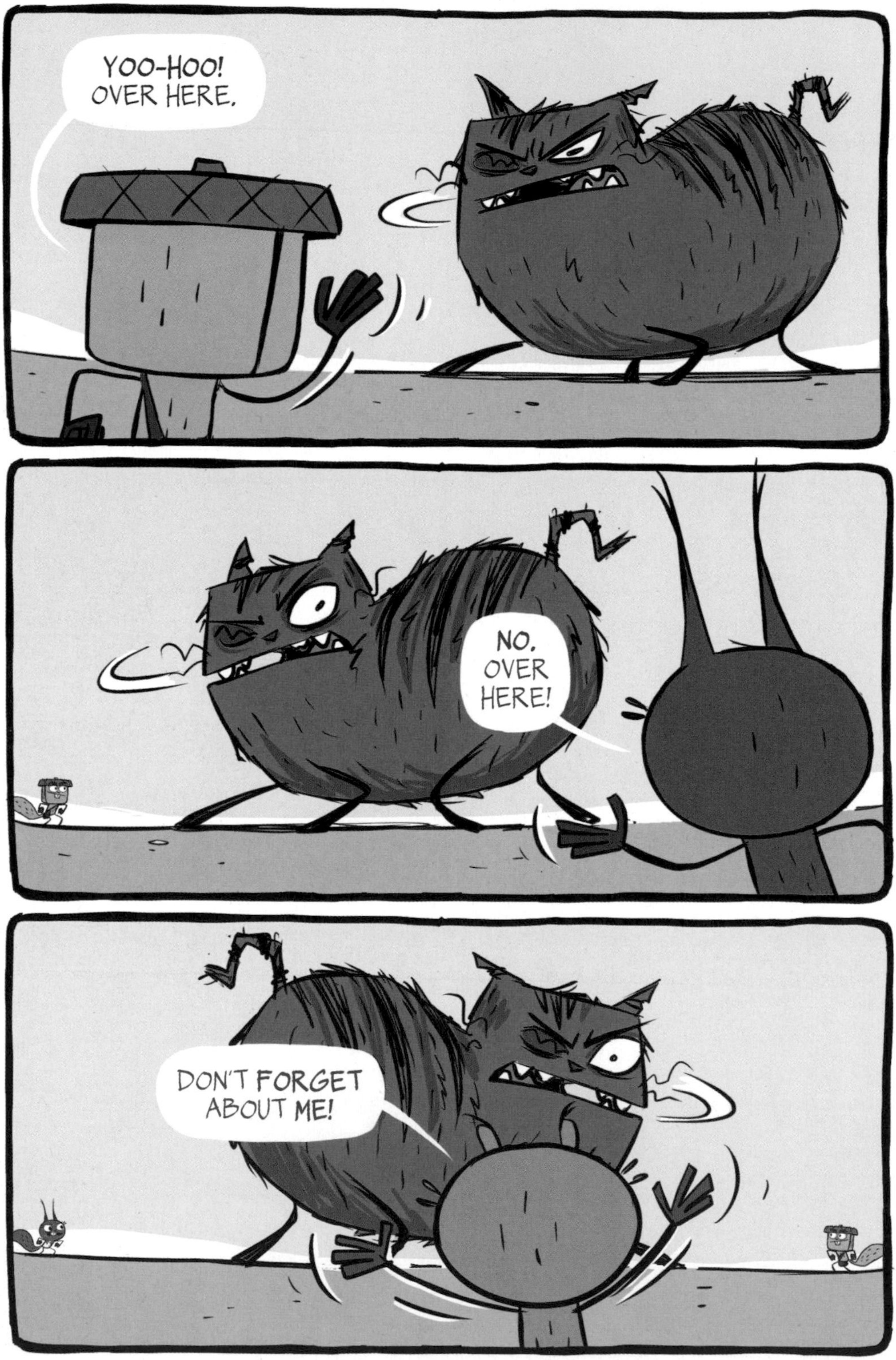
YOO-HOO! OVER HERE.
NO. OVER HERE!
DON'T FORGET ABOUT ME!

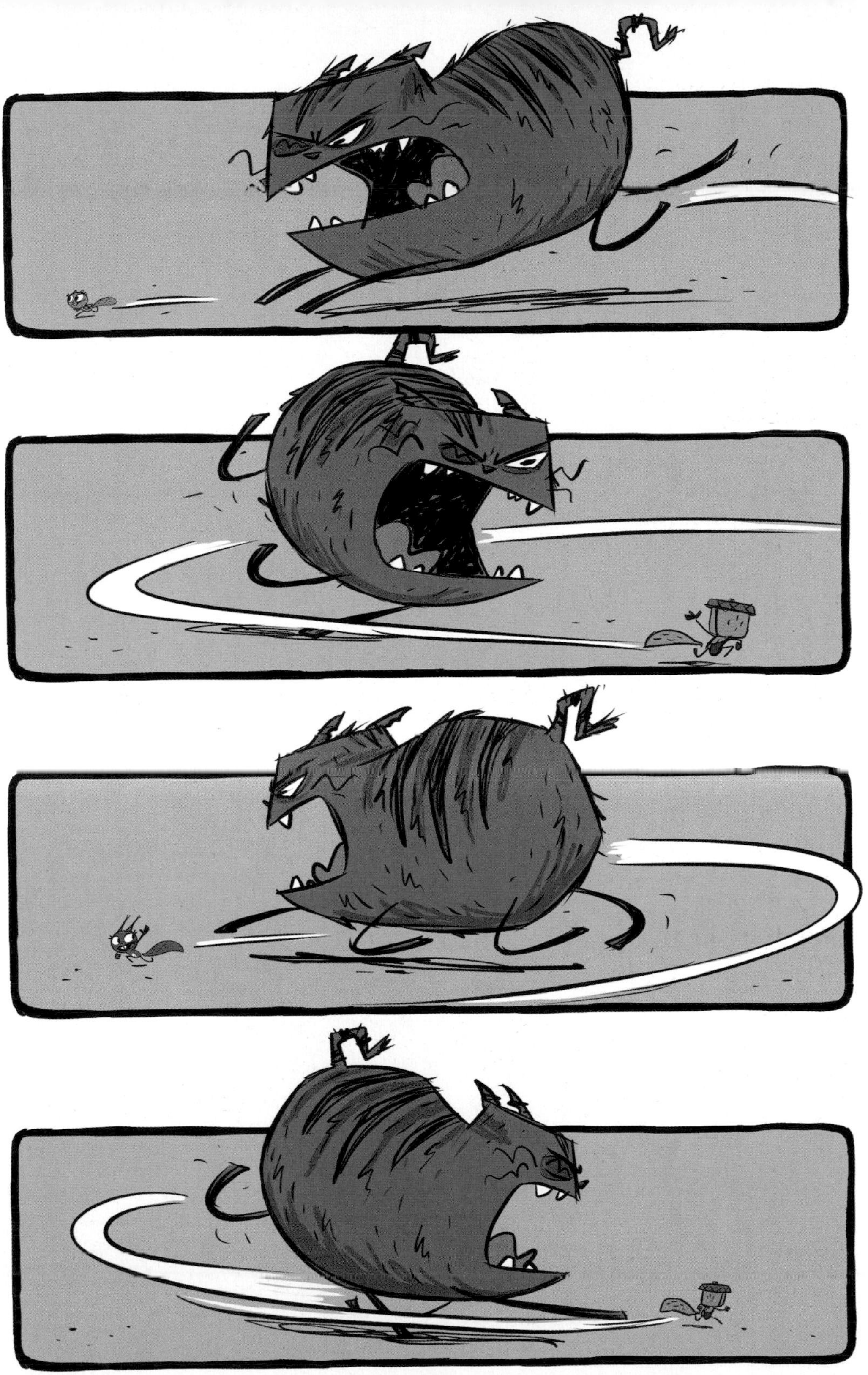

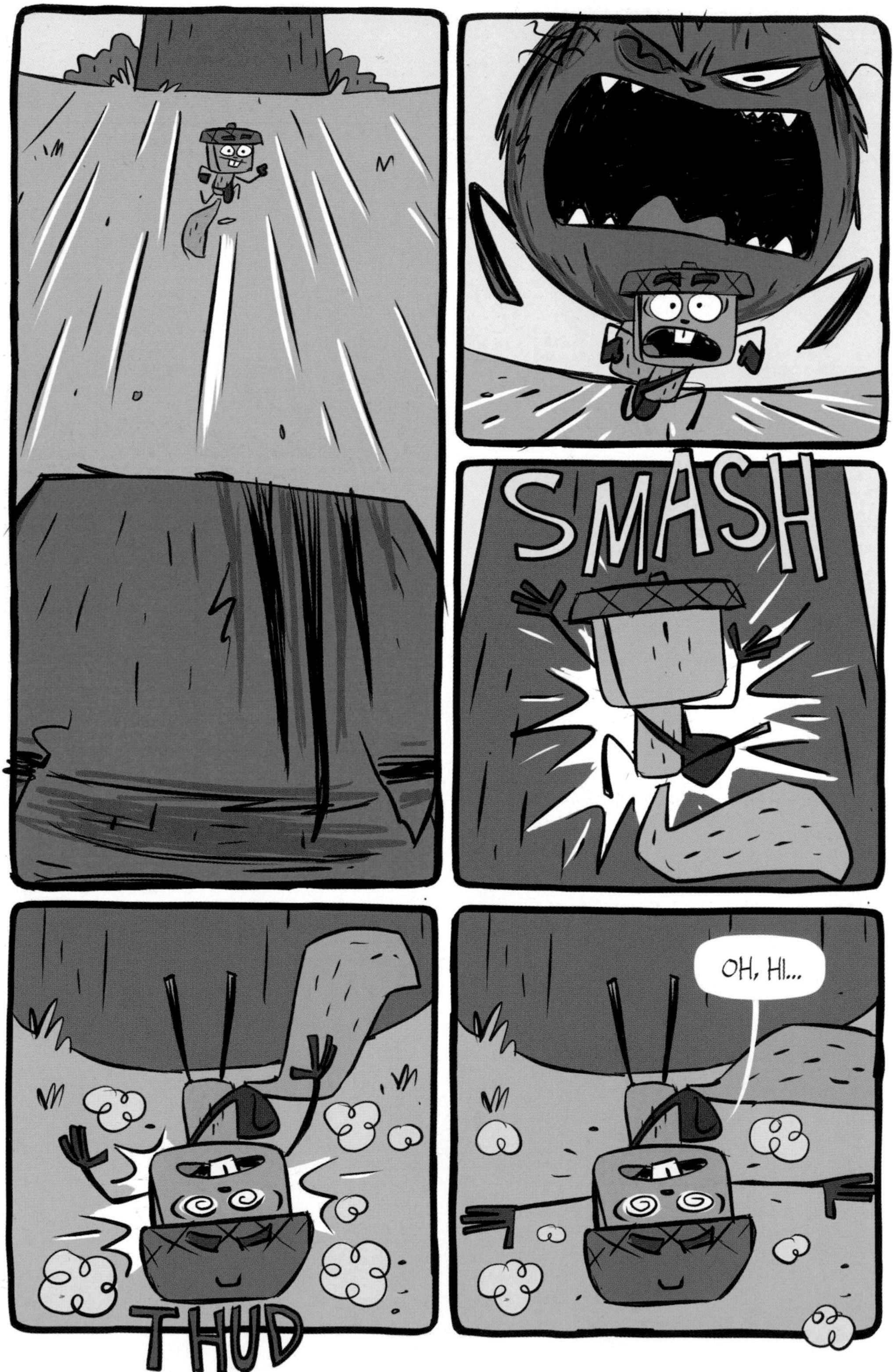
SMASH
THUD
OH, HI...

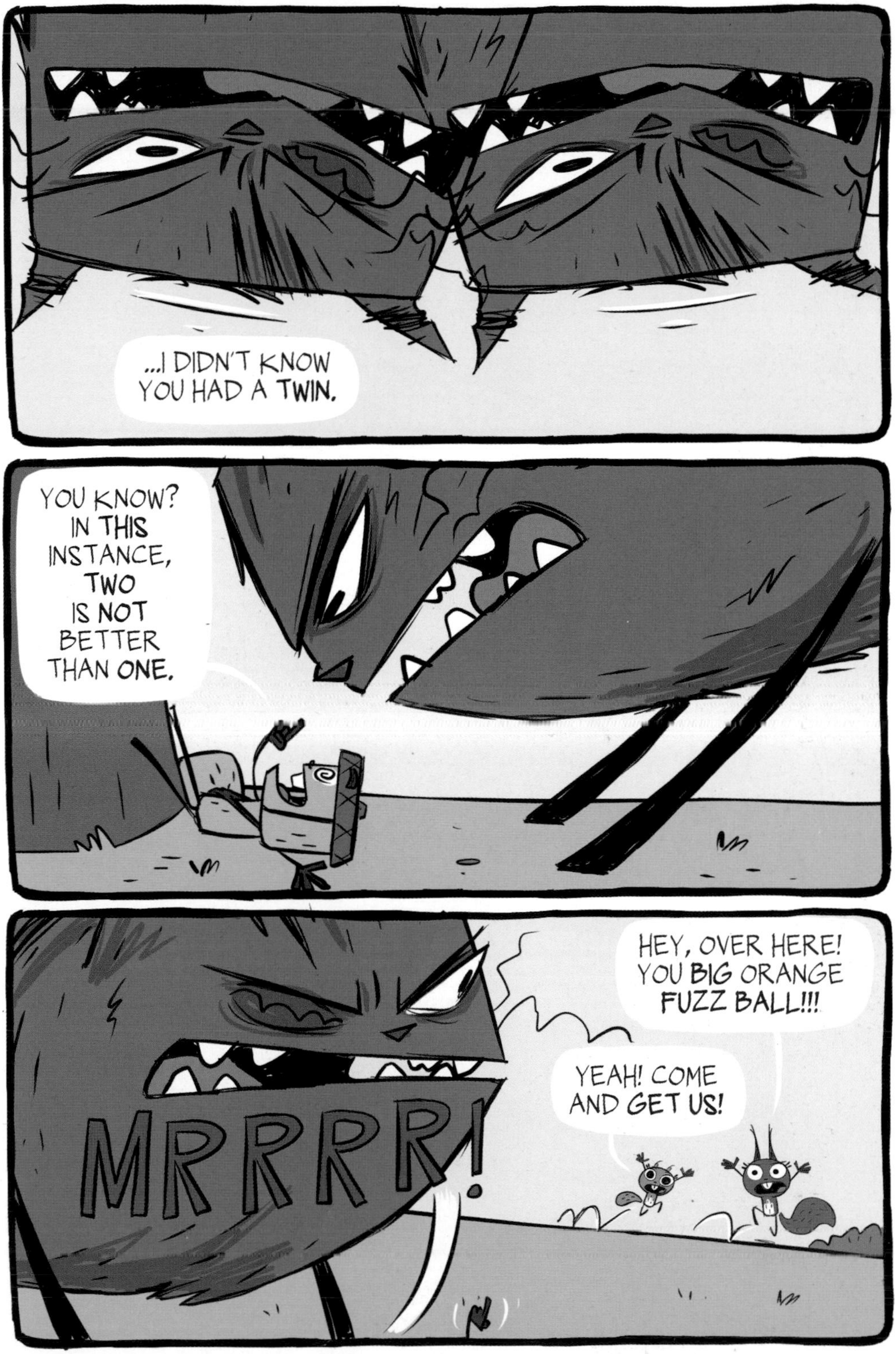
...I DIDN'T KNOW YOU HAD A TWIN.
YOU KNOW? IN THIS INSTANCE, TWO IS NOT BETTER THAN ONE.
HEY, OVER HERE! YOU BIG ORANGE FUZZ BALL!!!
YEAH! COME AND GET US!
MRRRR!

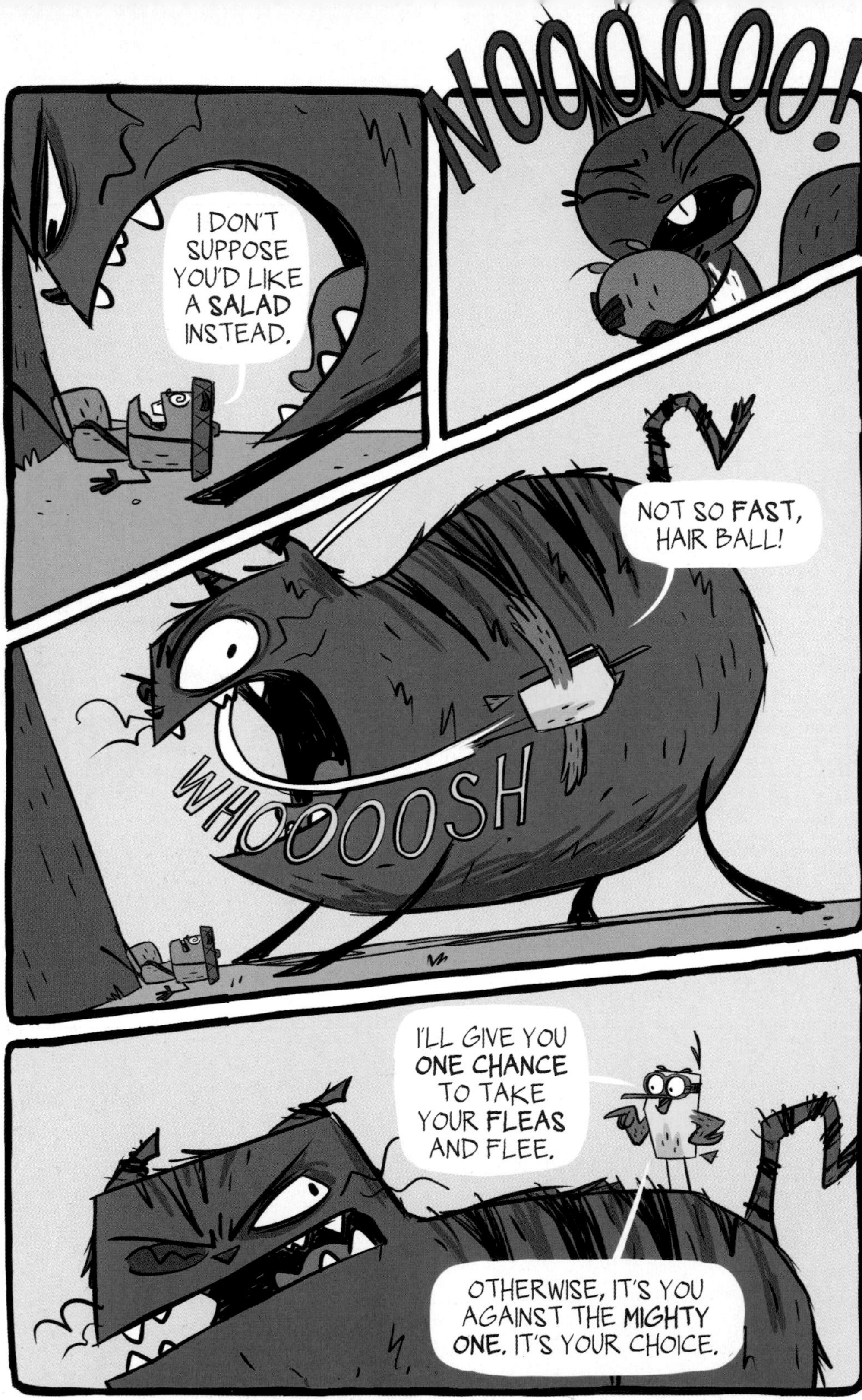
I DON'T SUPPOSE YOU'D LIKE A SALAD INSTEAD.
NOOOOOO!
NOT SO FAST, HAIR BALL!
WHOOOOSH
I'LL GIVE YOU ONE CHANCE TO TAKE YOUR FLEAS AND FLEE.
OTHERWISE, IT'S YOU AGAINST THE MIGHTY ONE. IT'S YOUR CHOICE.

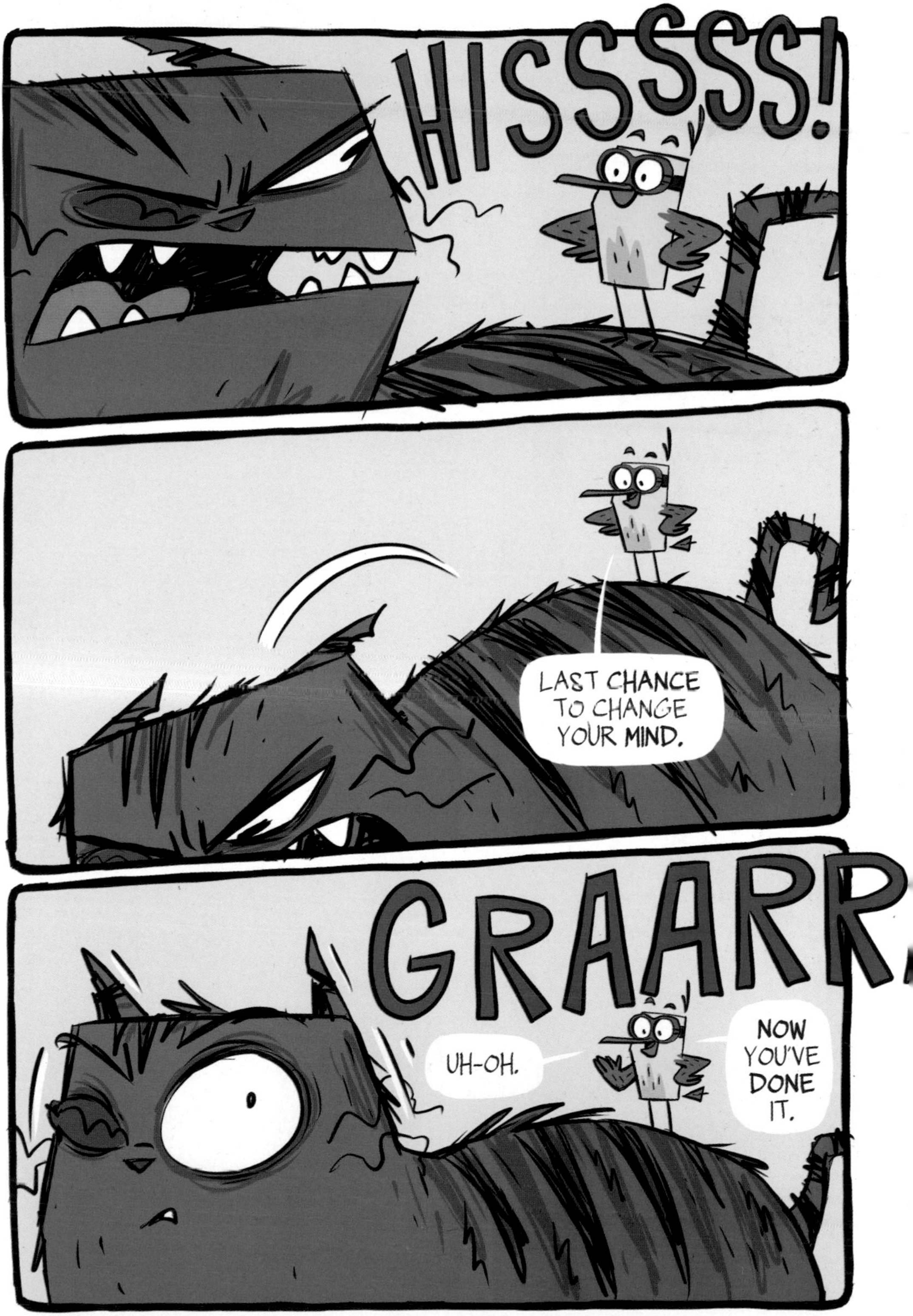
HISSSSS!
LAST CHANCE TO CHANGE YOUR MIND.
GRAARR
UH-OH.
NOW YOU'VE DONE IT.

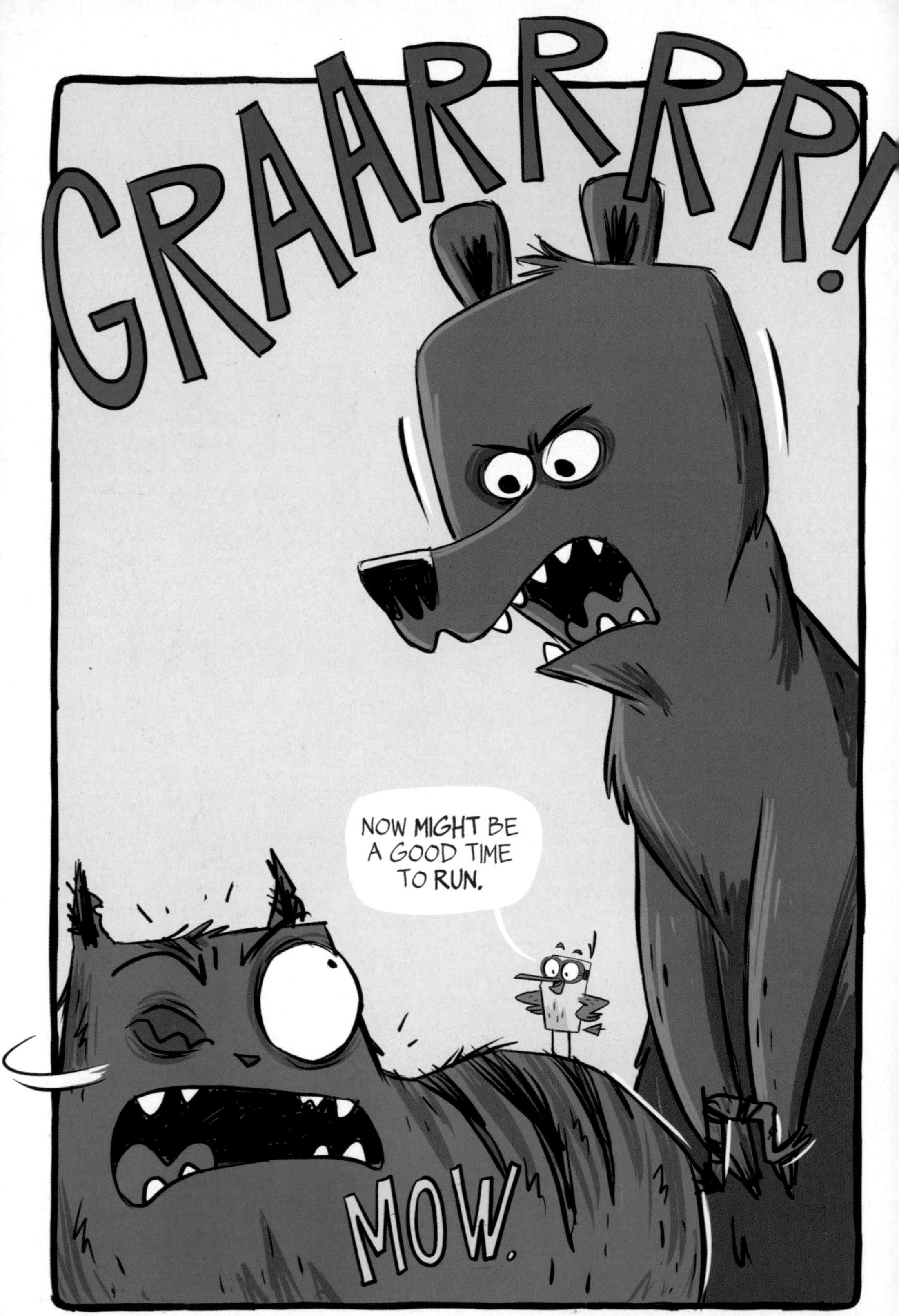
GRAARRRRR!
NOW MIGHT BE A GOOD TIME TO RUN.
MOW.

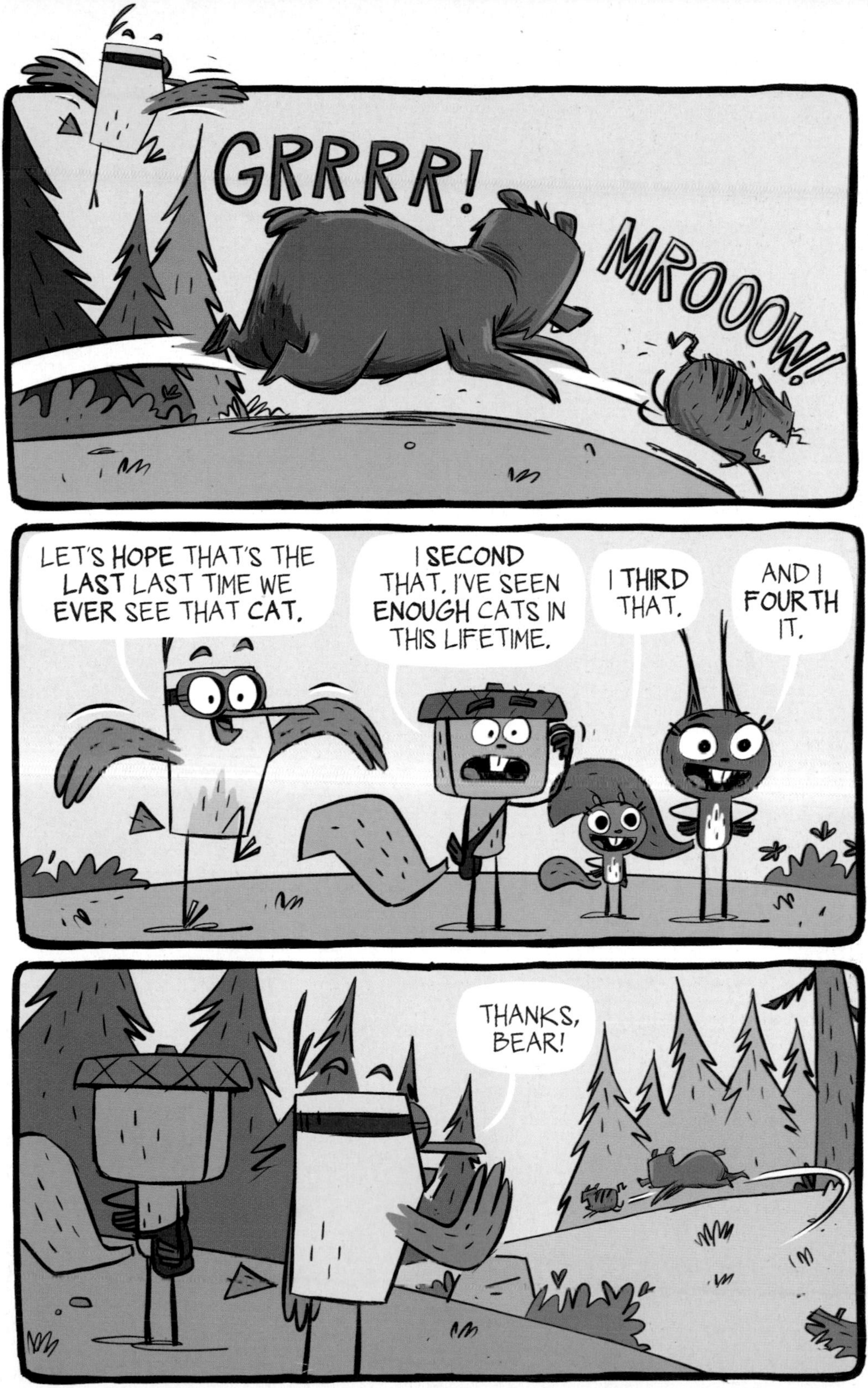
GRRRR!
MROOOW!!
LET'S HOPE THAT'S THE LAST LAST TIME WE EVER SEE THAT CAT.
I SECOND THAT. I'VE SEEN ENOUGH CATS IN THIS LIFETIME.
I THIRD THAT.
AND I FOURTH IT.
THANKS, BEAR!

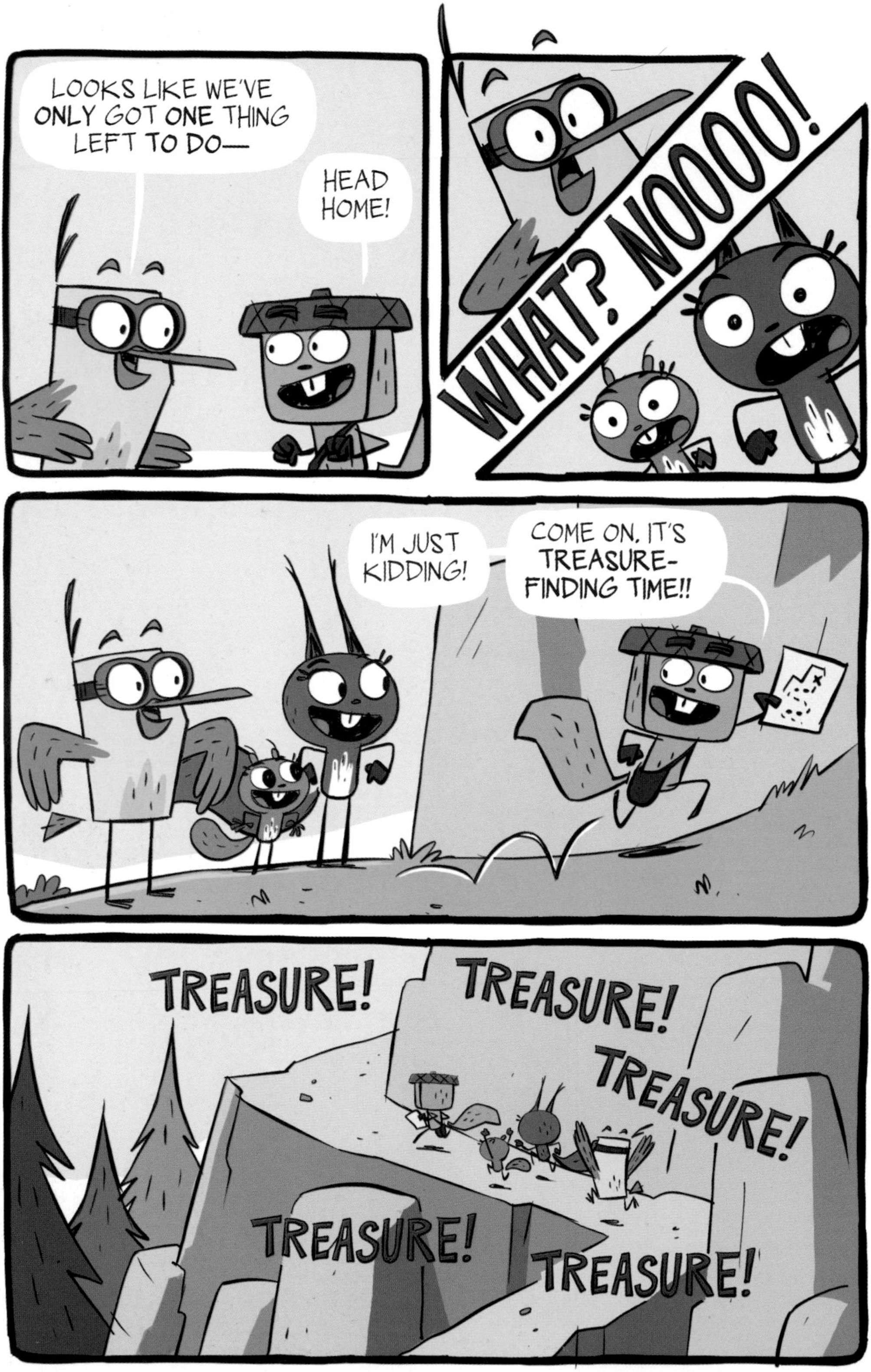

LOOKS LIKE WE'VE ONLY GOT ONE THING LEFT TO DO—
HEAD HOME!
WHAT? NOOOO!
I'M JUST KIDDING!
COME ON, IT'S TREASURE-FINDING TIME!!
TREASURE!
TREASURE!
TREASURE!
TREASURE!
TREASURE!

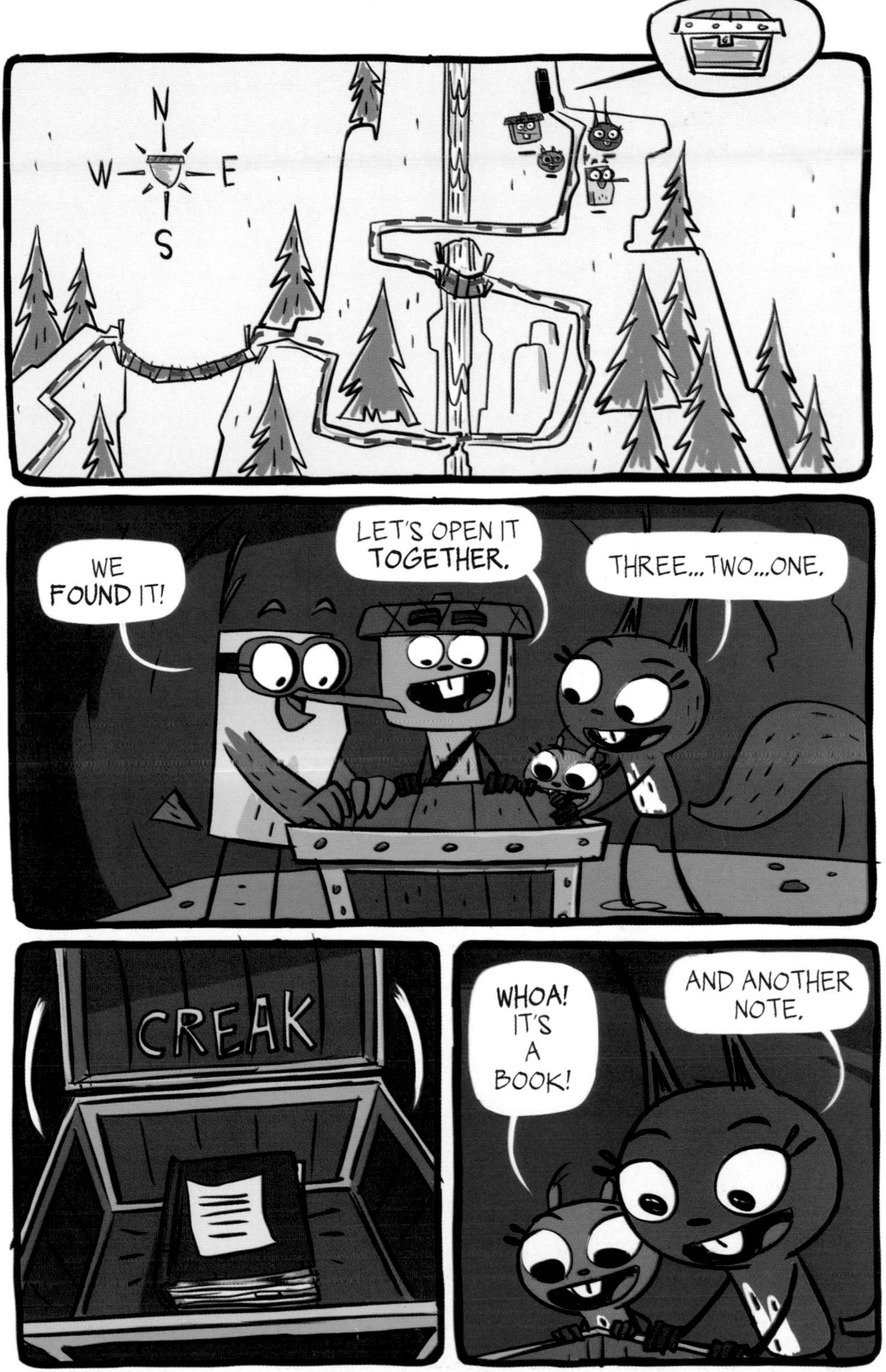
N
W
E
S
WE FOUND IT!
LET'S OPEN IT TOGETHER.
THREE... TWO... ONE.
CREAK
WHOA! IT'S A BOOK!
AND ANOTHER NOTE.

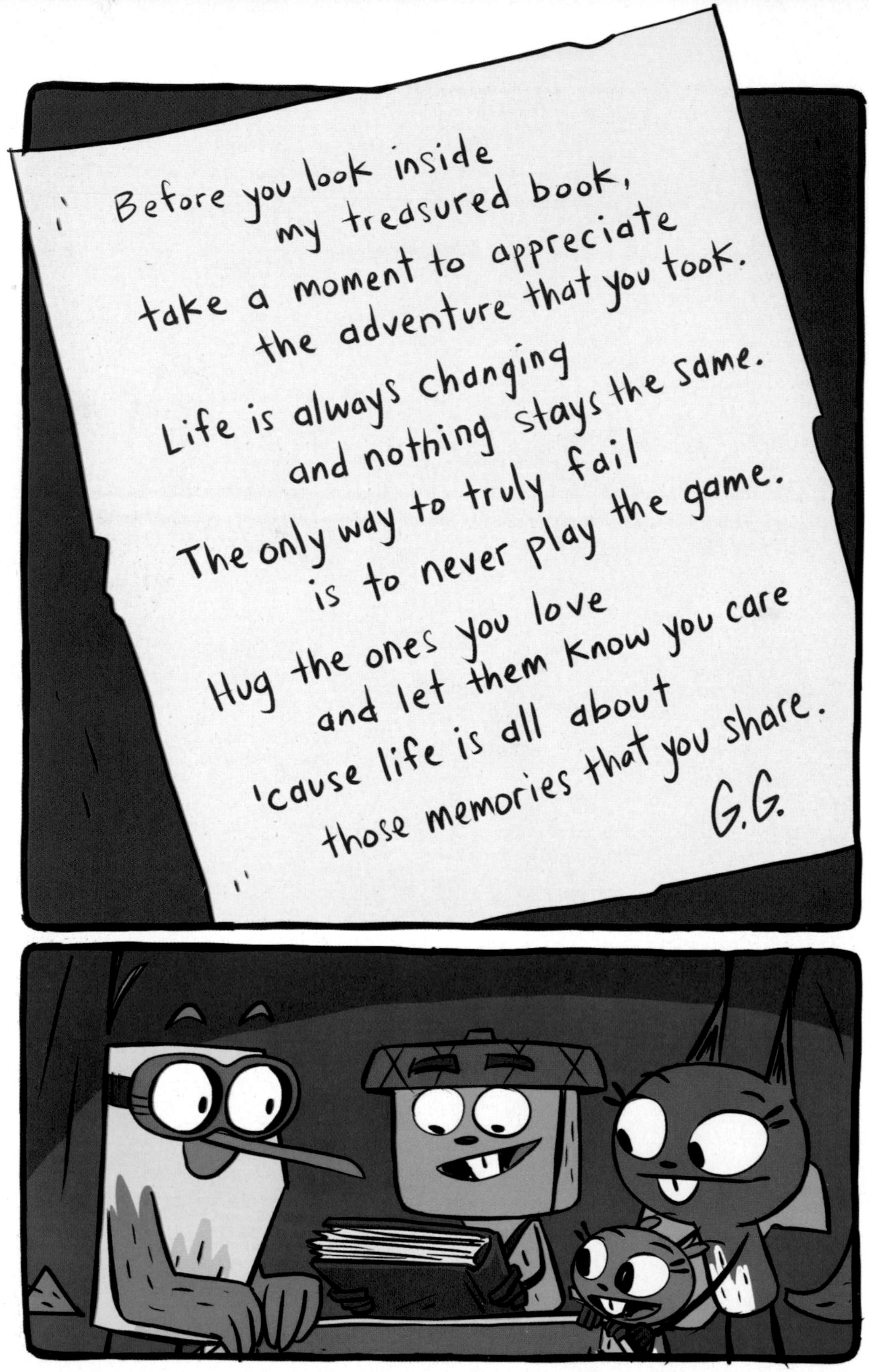
Before you look inside
my treasured book,
take a moment to appreciate
the adventure that you took.
Life is always changing
and nothing stays the same.
The only way to truly fail
is to never play the game.
Hug the ones you love
and let them know you care
'cause life is all about
those memories that you share.
G.G.

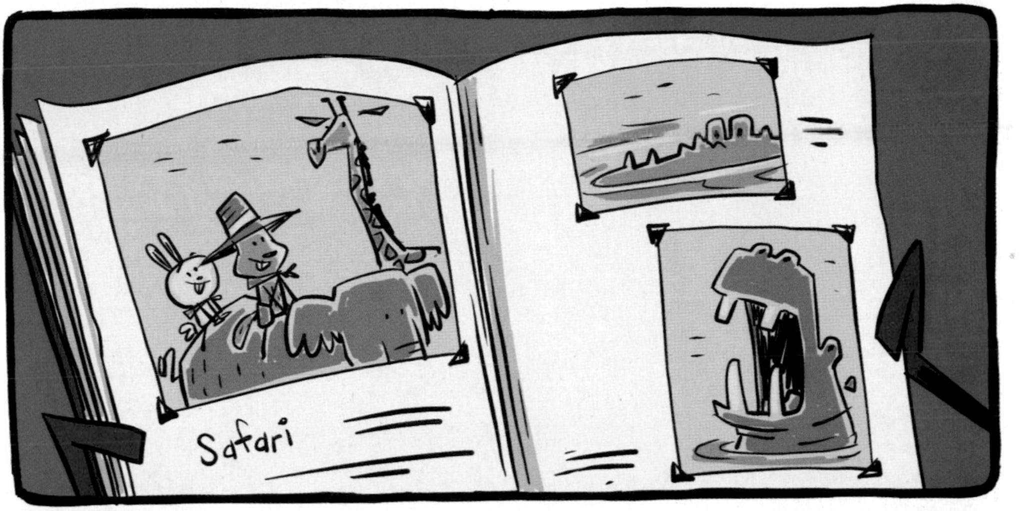
Safari

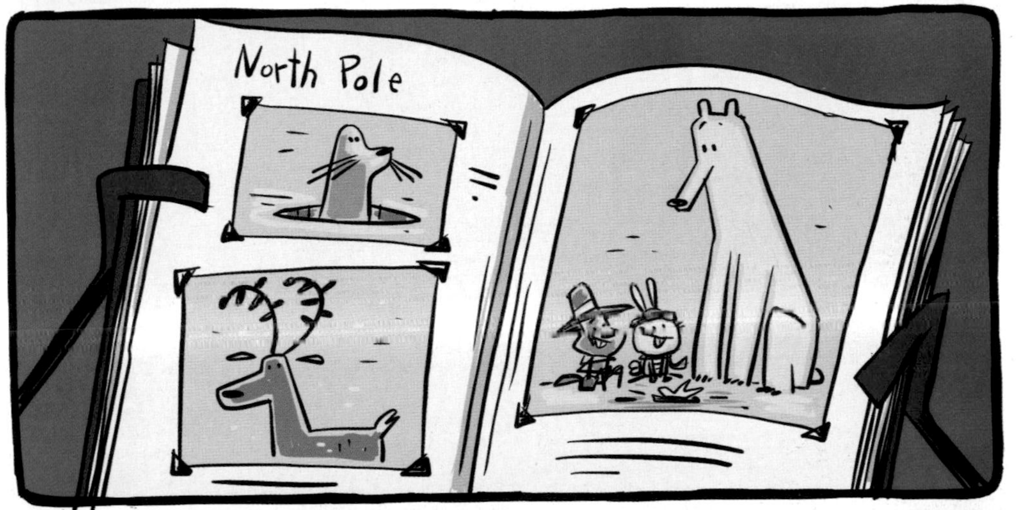
North Pole

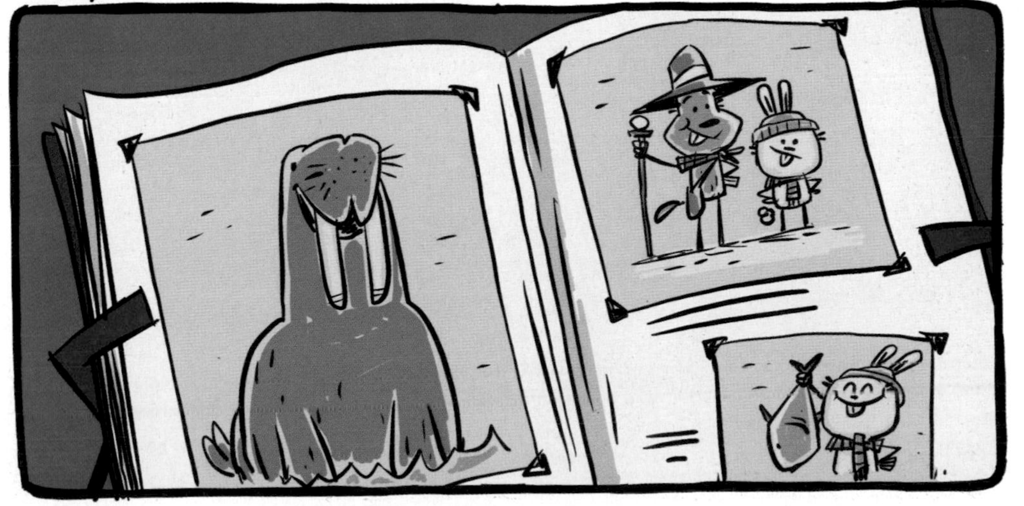

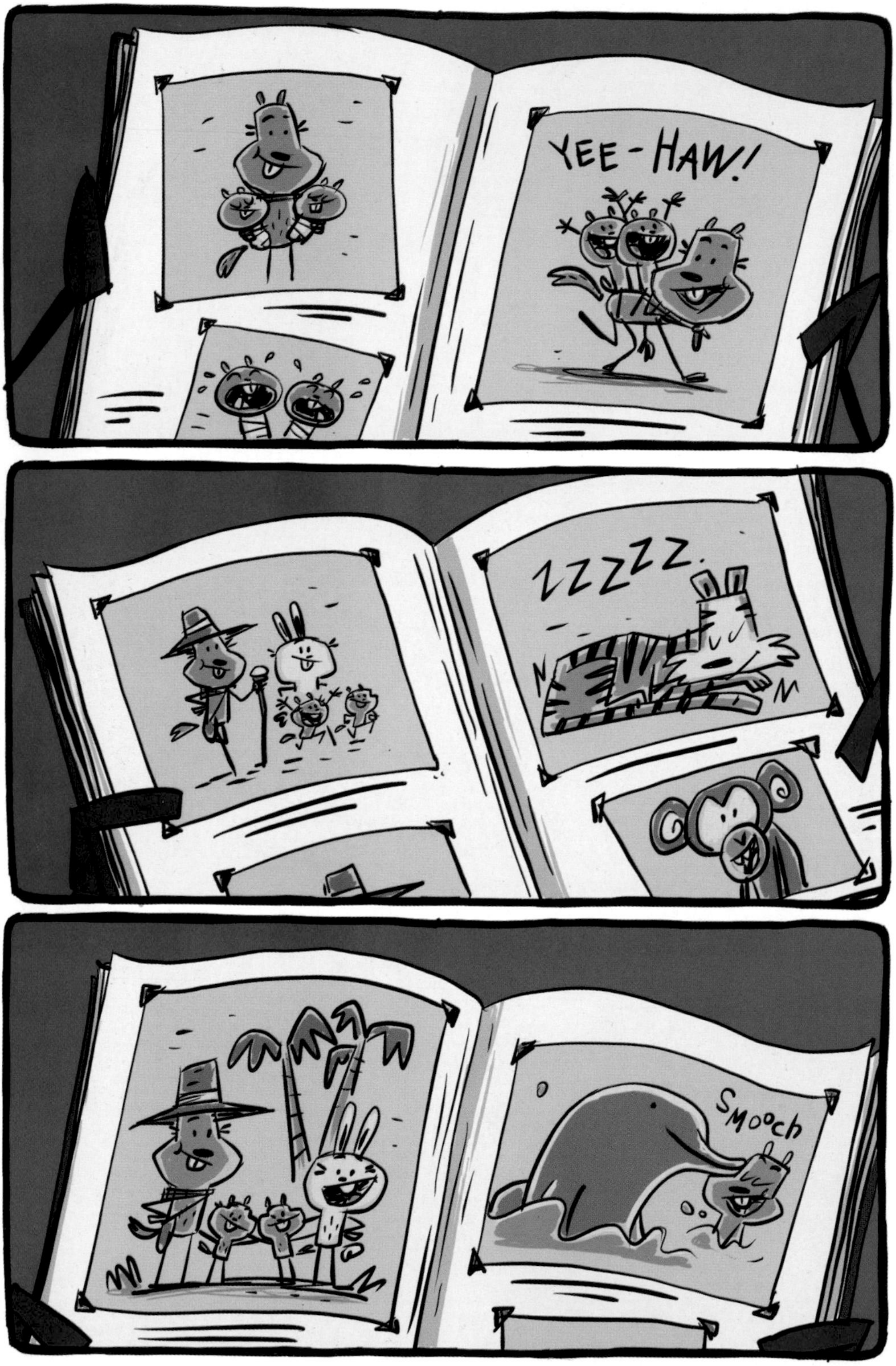
YEE-HAW!
ZZZZZ.
SMooch

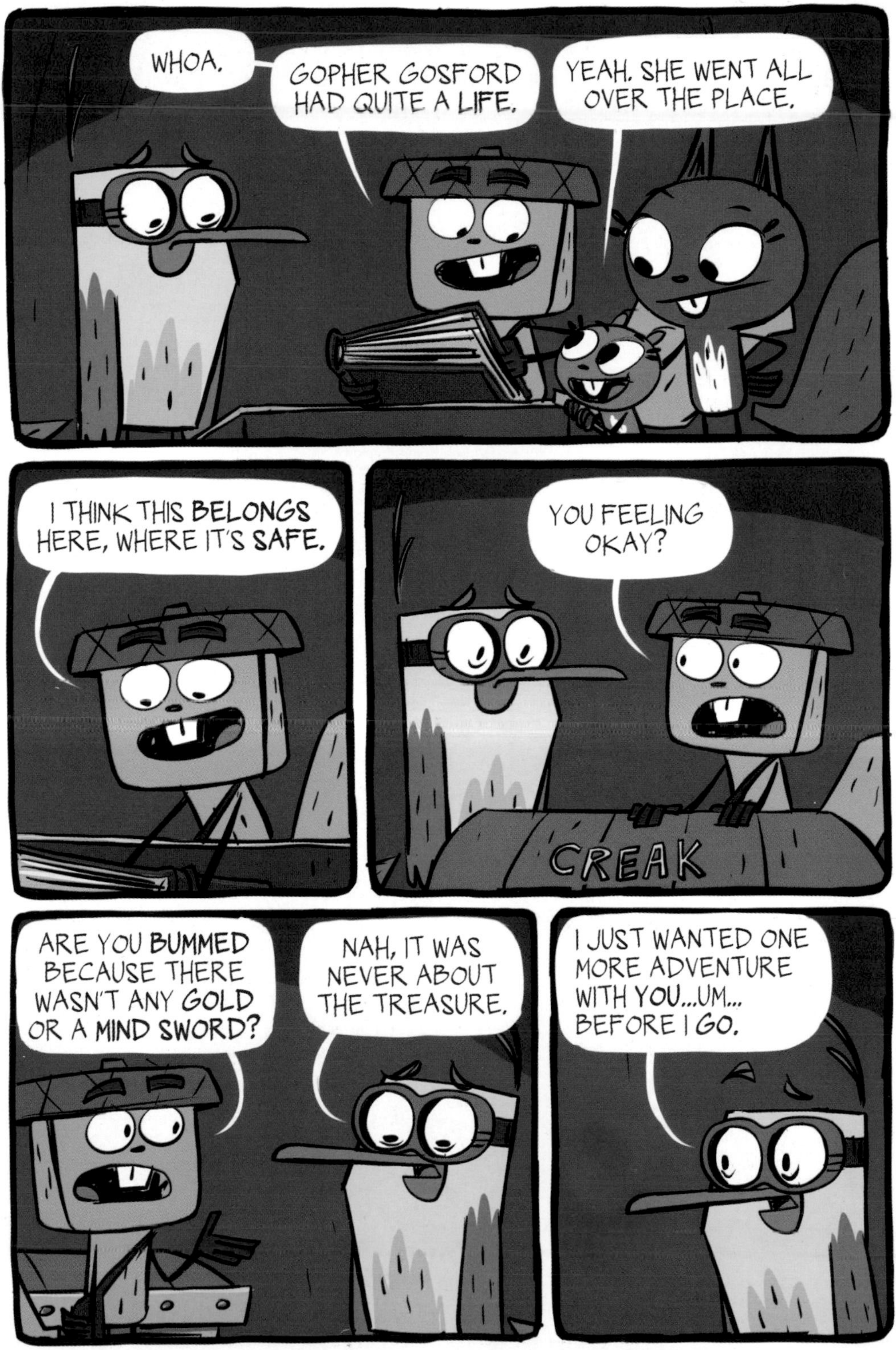
WHOA.
GOPHER GOSFORD HAD QUITE A LIFE.
YEAH. SHE WENT ALL OVER THE PLACE.
I THINK THIS BELONGS HERE, WHERE IT'S SAFE.
YOU FEELING OKAY?
CREAK
ARE YOU BUMMED BECAUSE THERE WASN'T ANY GOLD OR A MIND SWORD?
NAH, IT WAS NEVER ABOUT THE TREASURE.
I JUST WANTED ONE MORE ADVENTURE WITH YOU...UM... BEFORE I GO.

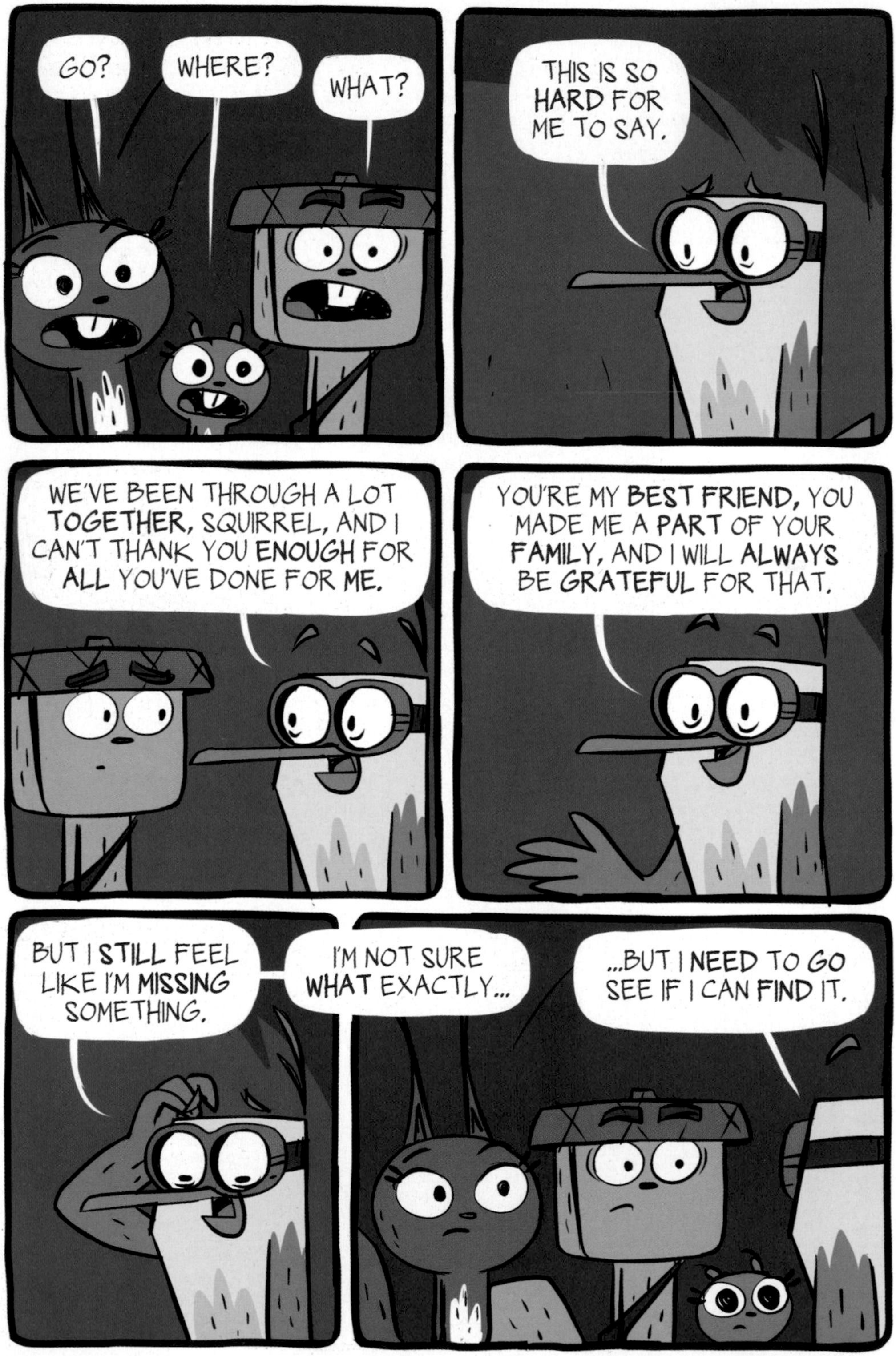
GO?
WHERE?
WHAT?
THIS IS SO HARD FOR ME TO SAY.
WE'VE BEEN THROUGH A LOT TOGETHER, SQUIRREL, AND I CAN'T THANK YOU ENOUGH FOR ALL YOU'VE DONE FOR ME.
YOU'RE MY BEST FRIEND, YOU MADE ME A PART OF YOUR FAMILY, AND I WILL ALWAYS BE GRATEFUL FOR THAT.
BUT I STILL FEEL LIKE I'M MISSING SOMETHING.
I'M NOT SURE WHAT EXACTLY...
...BUT I NEED TO GO SEE IF I CAN FIND IT.

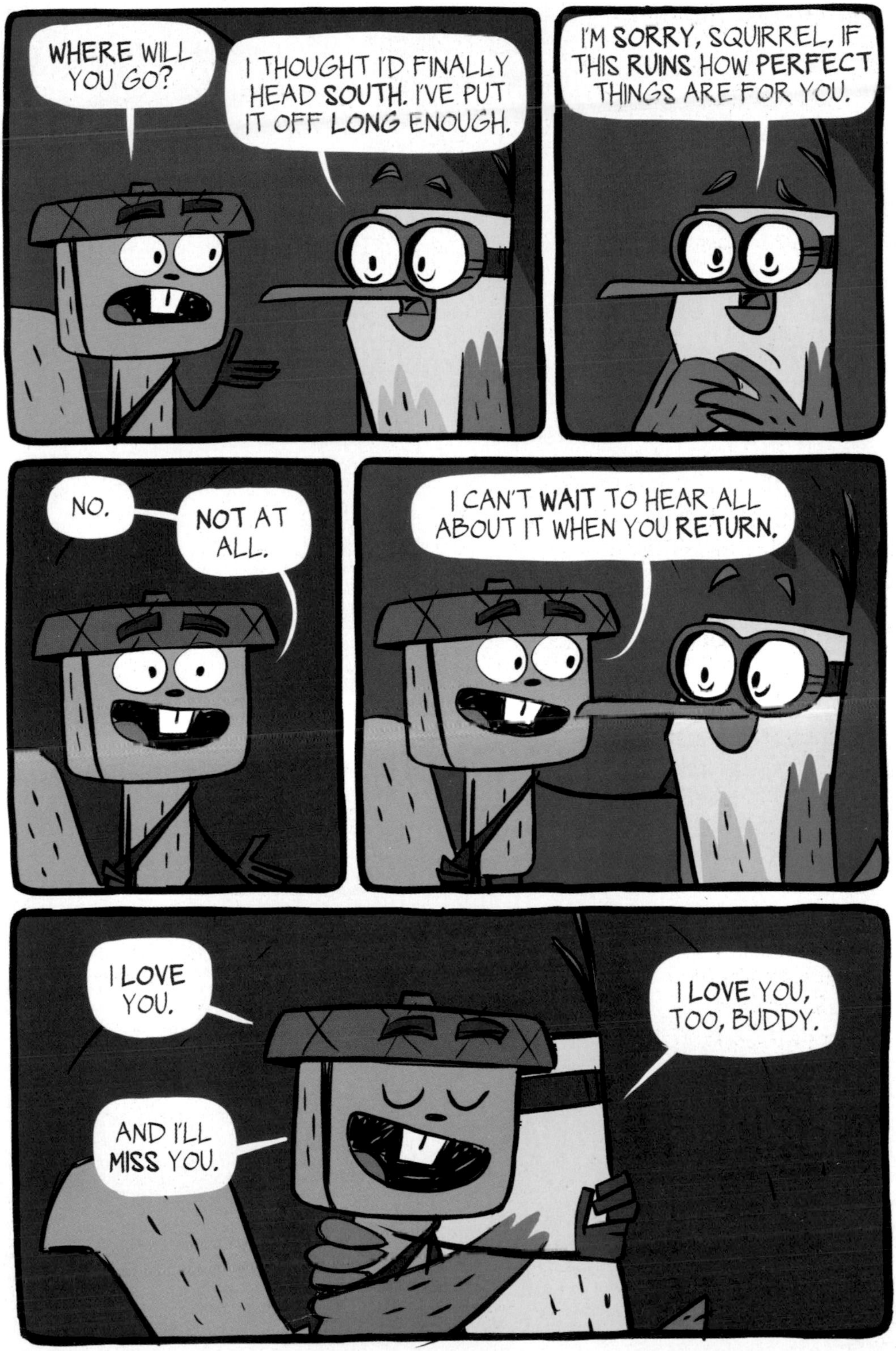
WHERE WILL YOU GO?
I THOUGHT I'D FINALLY HEAD SOUTH. I'VE PUT IT OFF LONG ENOUGH.
I'M SORRY, SQUIRREL, IF THIS RUINS HOW PERFECT THINGS ARE FOR YOU.
NO.
NOT AT ALL.
I CAN'T WAIT TO HEAR ALL ABOUT IT WHEN YOU RETURN.
I LOVE YOU.
AND I'LL MISS YOU.
I LOVE YOU, TOO, BUDDY.

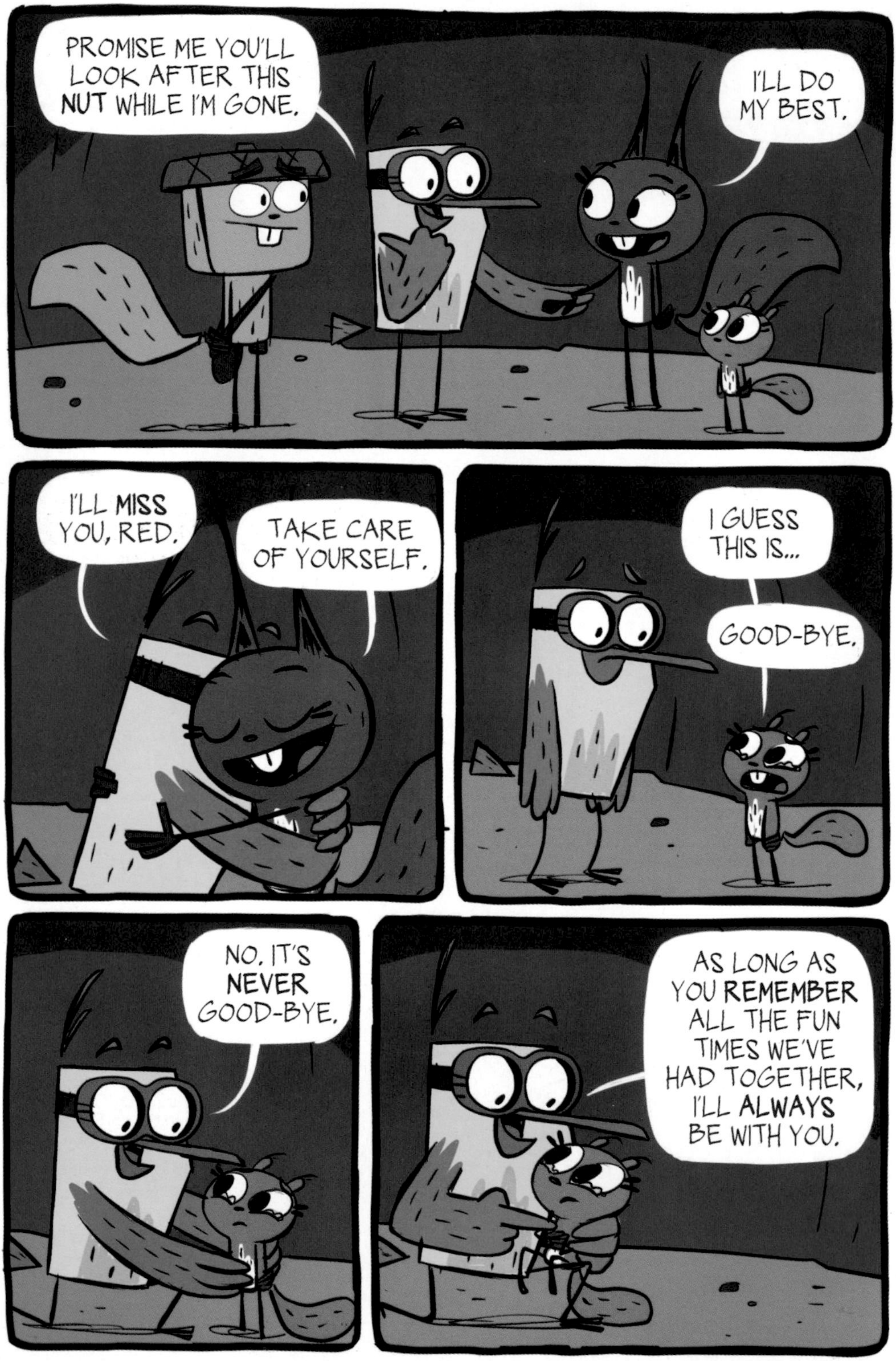

PROMISE ME YOU'LL LOOK AFTER THIS NUT WHILE I'M GONE.
I'LL DO MY BEST.
I'LL MISS YOU, RED.
TAKE CARE OF YOURSELF.
I GUESS THIS IS...
GOOD-BYE.
NO, IT'S NEVER GOOD-BYE.
AS LONG AS YOU REMEMBER ALL THE FUN TIMES WE'VE HAD TOGETHER, I'LL ALWAYS BE WITH YOU.

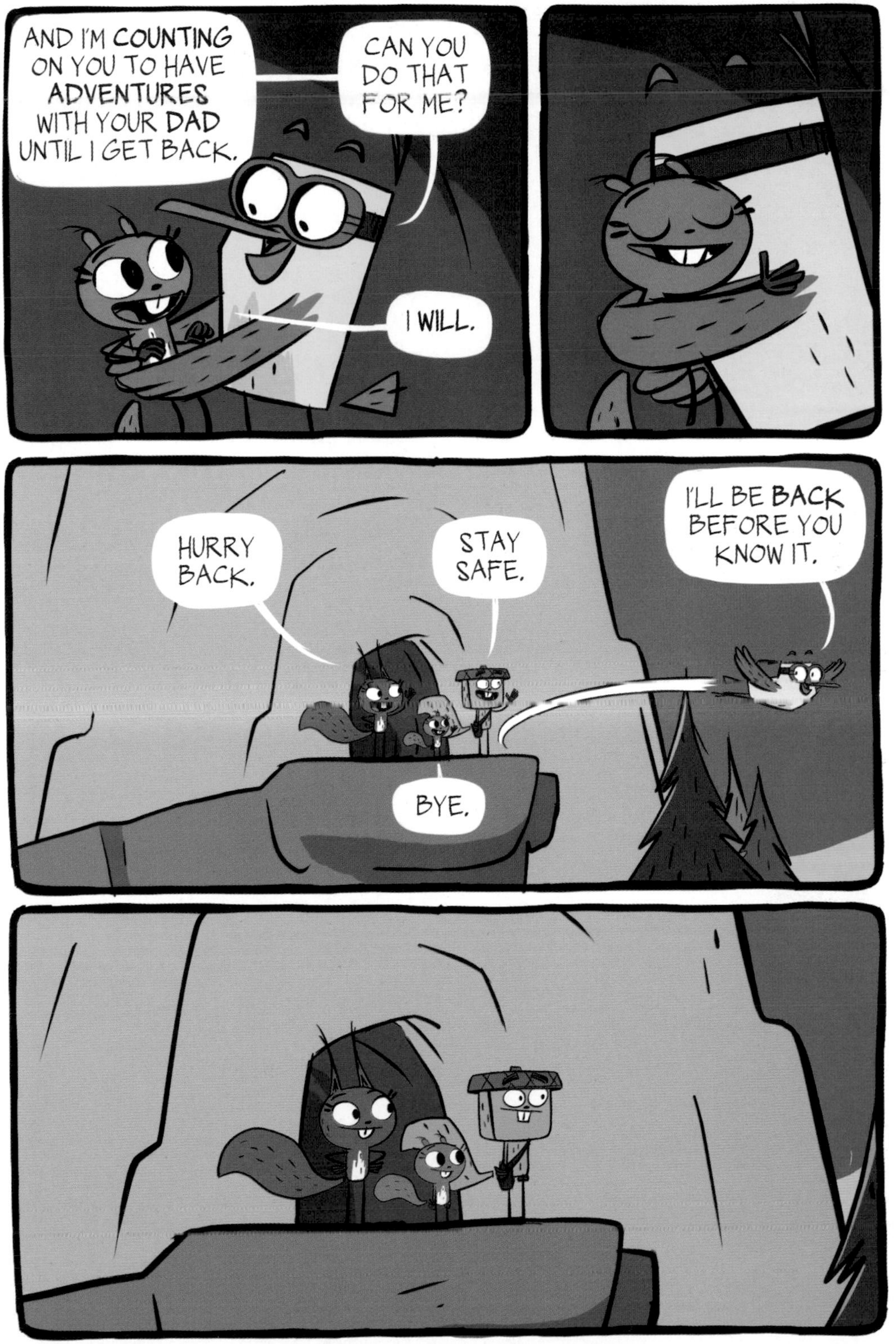
AND I'M COUNTING ON YOU TO HAVE ADVENTURES WITH YOUR DAD UNTIL I GET BACK.
CAN YOU DO THAT FOR ME?
I WILL.
HURRY BACK.
STAY SAFE.
I'LL BE BACK BEFORE YOU KNOW IT.
BYE.

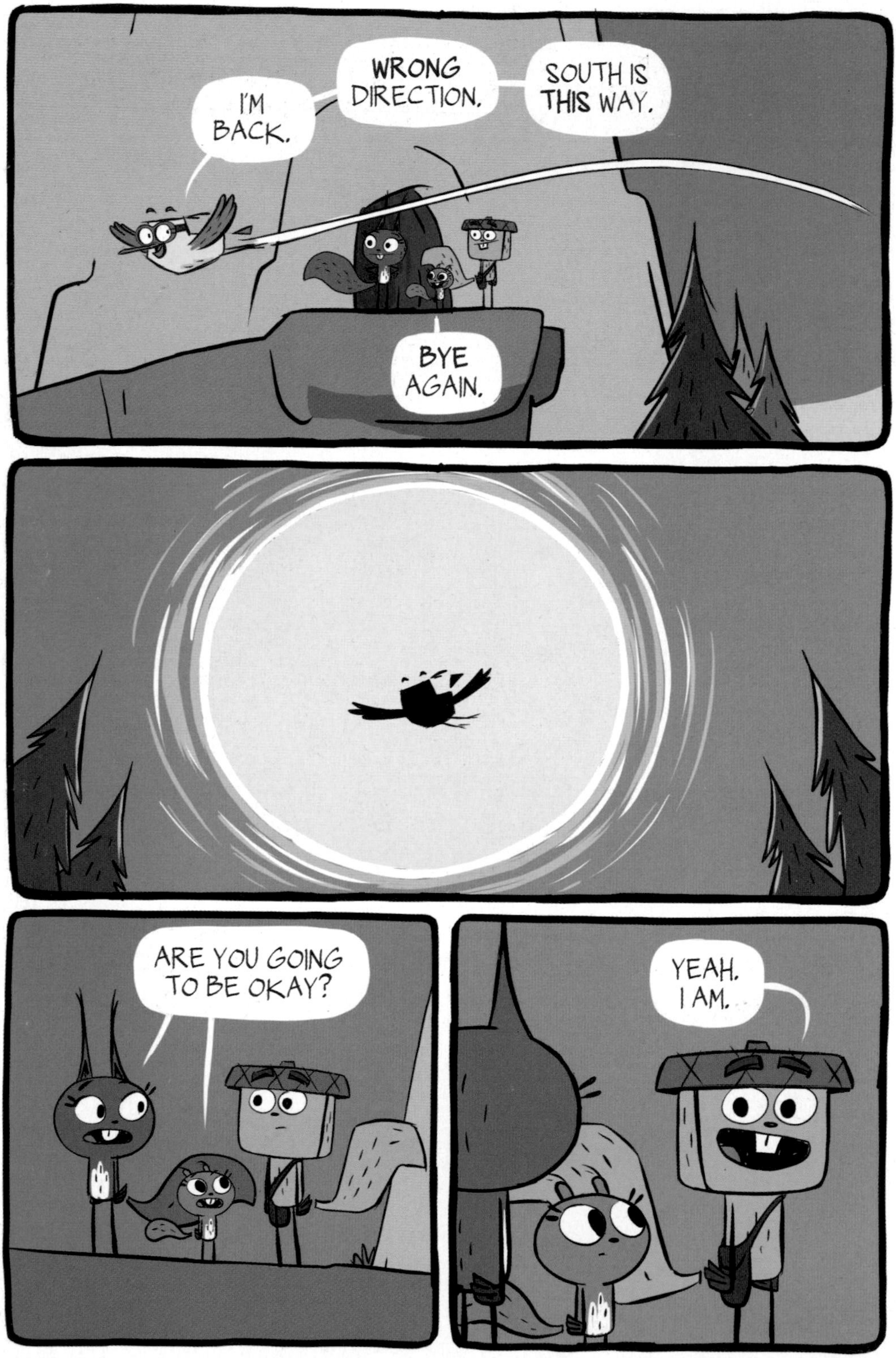
I'M BACK.
WRONG DIRECTION.
SOUTH IS THIS WAY.
BYE AGAIN.
ARE YOU GOING TO BE OKAY?
YEAH. I AM.

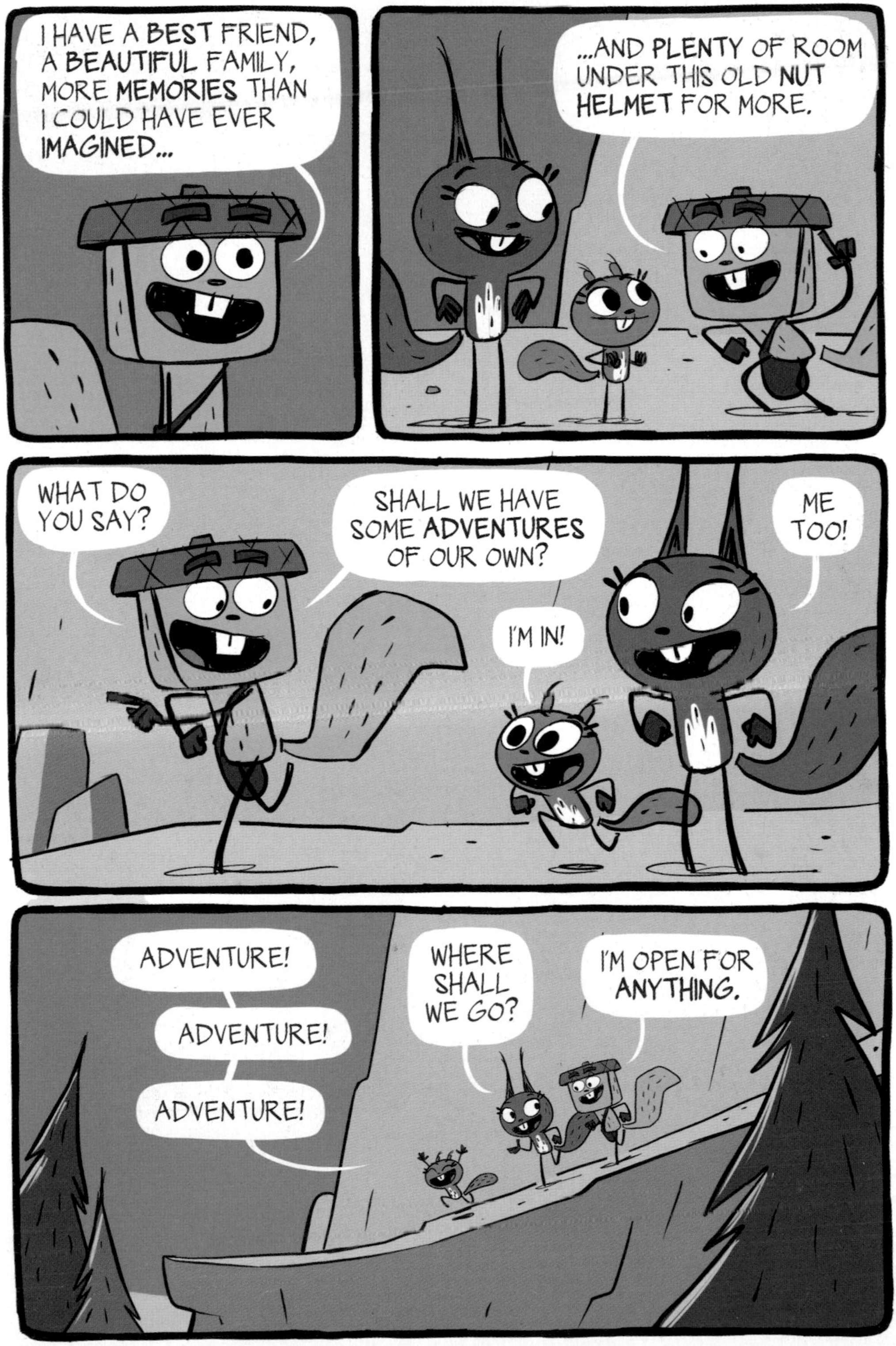
I HAVE A BEST FRIEND, A BEAUTIFUL FAMILY, MORE MEMORIES THAN I COULD HAVE EVER IMAGINED...
...AND PLENTY OF ROOM UNDER THIS OLD NUT HELMET FOR MORE.
WHAT DO YOU SAY?
SHALL WE HAVE SOME ADVENTURES OF OUR OWN?
I'M IN!
ME TOO!
ADVENTURE!
ADVENTURE!
ADVENTURE!
WHERE SHALL WE GO?
I'M OPEN FOR ANYTHING.

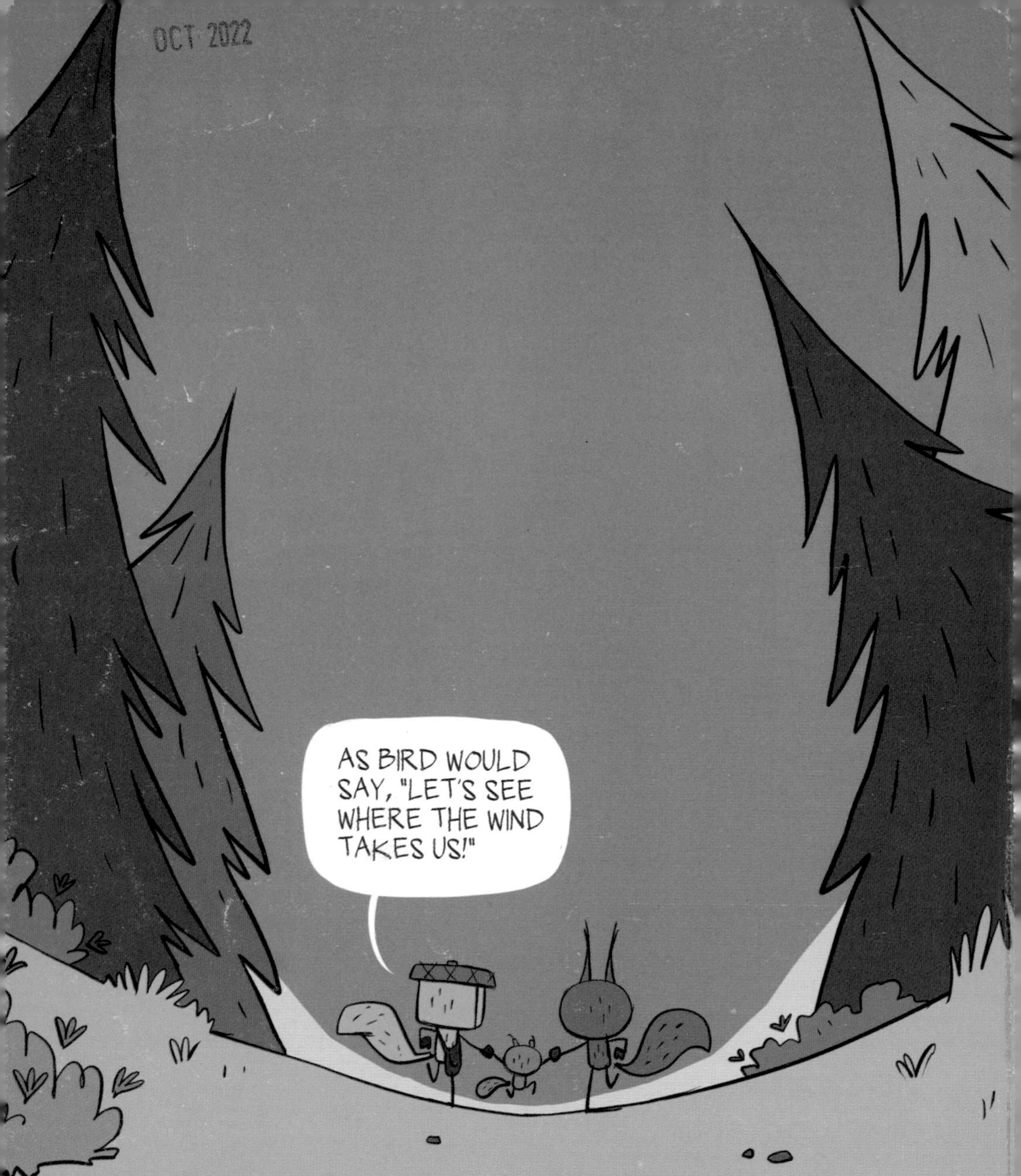
AS BIRD WOULD SAY, "LET'S SEE WHERE THE WIND TAKES US!"

THE PURPOSE OF LIFE IS TO LIVE IT,
TO TASTE EXPERIENCE TO THE UTMOST,
TO REACH OUT EAGERLY AND WITHOUT FEAR
FOR NEWER AND RICHER EXPERIENCE.

— ELEANOR ROOSEVELT